And Ordered Their Estate

A FICTIONAL ACCOUNT OF THE
TOLPUDDLE MARTYRS

SHEELAGH GREEN

◆ FriesenPress

Suite 300 - 990 Fort St
Victoria, BC, V8V 3K2
Canada

www.friesenpress.com

Copyright © 2017 by Sheelagh Green

First Edition — 2017

All rights reserved.

No part of this publication may be reproduced in any form, or by any means, electronic or mechanical, including photocopying, recording, or any information browsing, storage, or retrieval system, without permission in writing from FriesenPress.

ISBN
978-1-5255-0446-4 (Hardcover)
978-1-5255-0447-1 (Paperback)
978-1-5255-0448-8 (eBook)

1. FICTION

Distributed to the trade by The Ingram Book Company

For my children
Jeremy, Stephen, Timothy, and Vanessa

DIALECT

BY THE NINETEEN CENTURY THE FORMAL *THEE* OR *THOU* was mainly used when addressing the Deity in places of worship. However, *thee* lingered on in rural dialect and became abridged to *'ee*, frequently replacing the word *you*.. Thus *have 'ee* for *have you*.

Tenses were often jumbled. For example: *he were* for *he was*; *she be* for *she is*; *it were* for *it was*; *it weren't* for *it wasn't*; *be I* for *am I*.

GLOSSARY

Afore	Before
Argufying	Arguing
'Cos	Because
Cooties	Lice
'Ee	Thee
'Em	Them
Ent	Is not, Isn't, Aint
Frazzled	Exhausted
Flummoxed	Bewildered, Disconcerted
Girt	Great
Hisself	Himself
Little'un	Little one
Mazed	Dazed
'Minding	Reminding
Murmet	Scarecrow
Partial	Having a liking for
Summat	Something
Terr'ble	Terrible
'Tis	It is
'Twas	It was
'Twere	It were (It was)
'Twixt	Between
'Un	One
Wonnerful	Wonderful
You'm	You are (You am)

"..The rich man in his castle,
The poor man at his gate,
God made them high or lowly,
And ordered their estate.."

> All things bright and beautiful.
> Cecil Frances Alexander,
> 1818-1895

BOOK ONE

Chapter One
Workhouse 1842

'TIS ONLY A MATTER OF DAYS NOW AND I'M ACCEPTIN' OF the fact. What be there that'd make I want to linger? There's nothin' left for me nor mine. Mary be only allowed to visit me once a week. She come yesterday. Or was it today? I be so burnin' up with the fever, hours and days is all the same. I keeps seein' this mug of ale, seein' and smellin' it. I reaches out for it and 'tis gone. In periods when I be more lucid I knows there's no ale. In the workhouse infirmary!

Where's that gin-soaked bundle of rags that's meant to care for us that be sick?

"Water! For God's sake bring I some water."

Didn't do no good, callin' for her. Just brung on another bout o' coughin, and then choking on bloody mucus. No doubt her be in the store room with the overseer. What her won't do for a sip o' gin, though I'd 'a thought the overseer could find himself a juicier piece to put his leg over.

God, but 'tis cold in here. That old stove ent giving out nought but smoke which worries at my throat e'en more. And this pallet - so thin the cold seeps up'ards from the stone floor. How I hankers for that feather mattress us had. Kep' me and Mary cozy even on the coldest night. But that was afore us had to come here. Now the chill eats into my bones; I can't stop shakin' even though I be burnin' up with fever.

Regrets! Aye, I've plenty of regrets. That Mary be in this situation too, and all our children exceptin' Tabitha taken from us by some disease or another. Mary had our first-born awhile after Squire's wife at The Hall had hers. They sent for my Mary: Said as how they'd pay her two shillin' a week and a jug o' milk daily if she went as wet-nurse. There was to be no contact between Mary and I, mind, for fear of sickness, and there were plenty of sickness around that summer. Mary's sister took in our little 'un. Her says as how cow's milk didn't suit him, but I wondered at the time if the milk intended for our babe she fed to her own young 'uns. Not that I ever voiced such ideas to Mary, mind you. He were dead within six weeks. After that I tried not to feel any warmth for any that followed until there were a likelihood of us being able to rear 'em. At least that were my intent but it only took that first smile for any of 'em to clutch at my heart.

I never thought us would be spendin' our last days in this miserable place. But with this new Poor Law the whole family must be admitted, not just the one as can't fend for hisself. 'Twas lucky us found a position for Tabitha afore we was turned out of the cottage.

And yes, I be filled with hate too. 'Tis hate as much as fever as burns within me. Hate for Master Wainwright and Parson Warren and Squire. Makin' me betray friends. Tellin' I to trust 'em and then not givin' me the five pounds they promised. One thousand pounds were offered later by the Crown for information to be used at the trial but none came forward to give evidence. One thousand pounds and Squire give me only thirty shillin' of the promised five pounds. Told I, "Seth Fielding get you the balance from Master Wainwright and Parson."

But is it hate I has for Squire? Now there's a question I've thought on often as I lies here. Some days I'm certain sure on the answer. Others my mind ent so definite. Did Squire regret what he made I do? 'Tis a rare old puzzle.

I were forced into my part in it all, and I only done it for Samuel's sake, for a little comfort for him. And assurances that Master would keep I on, and us would have a roof over our heads. But they'd of convicted 'em regardless.

My Mary came this evenin'. Brung me an apple. She knows how powerful fond I am of apples. Where her got it from I knows not, for apples be no part of inmates' fare.

'Tis a poor 'un, bruised on the one side but I minds not. Should I try to eat 'un I know it wouldn't pass down my gullet, but make I choke. I has it here under the coverlet, cupped in one hand while I stroke the smooth skin of it with the other. Or hold it to my nose and draw in the smell of it.

Apples ... Apples ... What memories the smell do bring back...

'Tis Harvest Home Supper and us all be at the tables set out on the grass.

The tables be just rough plankin' set up on saw-horses and barrels and covered with old sheeting and livened with jars of wild flowers some of the young girls picked earlier. The sky has darkened to a dusky mauve lightened by a moon just gainin' strength. Preston's fiddle screeches a lively tune accompanied by the stable-boy's whistle pipe. Farmer Wainwright's wife and the women have done well by us, but little now remains of the hams and pies, the cheeses and fresh baked bread. The cider barrel is nigh empty and two men are rolling out a second.

Mary takes my mug from my hand and sets it on the table. "Dance with me," she says, pulling me to my feet. I takes her in my arms and join the other couples weaving around in the light of the lanterns, moths dancing against the lantern sides as we dance on the grass. Gradually I moves us away from the others until us be on our own, away from the lights and the music. I leans her back against a tree and kisses her hard and she slides her arms around my neck and returns my kisses. I tries to pull her down onto the grass.

"No, Seth," says she, resistin' with a laugh. "The dew! It'll soak through my dress and spoil my new petticoat. I knows where us can go." And she takes my hand and pulls me after her, shooshing me with a finger to her lips. Up the steep steps that run behind the dairy up to the apple loft, the both of us stumblin' and gigglin' in the dark.

"You'm like Master's bull, Seth Fielding. Hold off a minute afore you rips my bodice." There in the narrow shaft of moonlight let in through the skylight, Mary strips off her dress and the precious petticoat and stands before me, her breasts firm and round, minding me of the apples in my granny's tree just afore they be ready for pickin'.

On the wooden floor, amidst the powerful smell of the fruit, I has my Mary, and after we be done we share an apple and I gently licks at the juice that runs down Mary's chin.

Parson married us early that December. Gentry puts great stock in keeping their daughters virgins afore they go to their marriage beds. To we poor folk 'tis all a part of life and many a young woman weds with a babe already in her belly. A man needs know his bride be a breeder, for what children they manage to raise be help and a source of income and later, hopefully, provide shelter in a couple's old age. The shame be when a girl gives herself unwisely and her be left with a babe in her arms, no weddin' band and no husband for support.

It was April when Wainwright's bull gored John Preston. Master offered me and Mary Preston's cottage, for Preston's widow and young'uns had to leave once he were buried.

Seemed at the time that we were blessed, for it was terr'ble crowded living with Mary's family. Aye, blessed we thought ourselves, there being no rent to pay, the cottage being tied to the land. Us were young. We did'st not see that us had doubley chained ourselves to Master, for job and cottage were his to give or take back at will.

Chapter Two

Tolpuddle 1833

THE WIND HAD STACKED THE PEWTER CLOUDS AGAINST the hills. It tore at the branches of the beech and oak that arched across the narrow track, as if determined to have them leafless by morning. Although the torrential rain had eased to fitful flurries, the wind drove it like needles into the faces of the three figures trudging along the lane, their bodies bent into the forceful gusts.

The two men, the brims of their round felt hats bent to channel the raindrops down over the back of their up-turned jacket collars, kept up a steady pace. Deep in conversation with Seth Fielding, George Loveless was unaware at first of eight year old Samuel's faltering steps even though George and Seth had waited several times when Samuel, racked with another bout of coughing, had spat globs of phlegm onto the grassy verge. His flushed cheeks contrasted sharply with the grey pallor of his skin.

Seth and George stopped yet again for Samuel to catch up with them. When, with dragging footsteps, he reached his father, Seth placed an arm round his son's shoulder. "Nearly home," he encouraged, "It ent much further."

"I'm too tired, Father. M'legs is givin' way." Samuel sank against the bank of the steep, tree-lined ridges that bordered both sides of the stoney track.

"Climb on my back, lad. I'll carry 'ee awhile."

"I'll carry him to the turning," said George. "You can take him on from there." George bent down in front of the boy and Seth helped his son up onto George's back. Over Samuel's shoulders, Seth replaced the piece of sacking Samuel had been using as protection against the rain.

"He shouldn't be working, Seth. It's wrong. The boy's sick. Working all day for a couple of pennies in wages."

"Yer think I wouldn't keep him home if I could," said Seth bitterly. "But with Master yesterday sayin' to bring 'un for there'd be stone-pickin' work for 'un, and not listenin' when I says the lad be sick. That man don't never listen to what others be sayin.'" He kicked angrily at a large pebble. "You knows my wages be lower than what you makes, us bein' in a tied cottage, an' Sam seemed livelier this mornin.'"

Most of the day had been spent ploughing Ten Acre Upland with Samuel following behind, stone-gathering. It was the heavy rain turning the soil to water-logged clay that fought the plough's blade, that sucked at their boots as if to wrest them from their feet, that had caused Farmer Wainwright to dismiss them an hour early.

"Ent nothin' us can do," Seth muttered bitterly, more to himself than George. "What choice do the likes of us have?"

"Have you not heard a word of what I'm saying? We must band together, all of us that work the farms. It's the only way, Seth, that we'll get a fair wage. Will you at least come to a meeting and listen to what's said?"

"And run the risk of Master turning me off if 'e finds out. Me, with young 'uns to feed? Where would us live? No, 'tis a chance I ent free to take." He raised a threadbare jacket sleeve and wiped the rain from his face. "Look what happened three years back. So many imprisoned and transported, nine of 'em even hung."

"But *we're* not advocating violence like those others. A Friendly Society, call it a Trade Union if you like, is for peaceful means only." George's voice rose forcefully: "We're not for the burning of ricks and intimidation like Captain Swing's followers used back then." Samuel's grip tightened round his neck as George abruptly turned towards Seth. "We've no other way of getting a fair wage. A man can no more keep himself on seven shillings a week, much less a family."

"I ent argufying with you on that score." Seth wiped again at his face.

"And now there's talk of them lowering it to six. Six! Where will it stop? We have no power *unless we band together.*"

They had reached a bend in the track where a narrow lane meandered downwards.

"I'll tek 'im now, thank 'ee, George." Seth helped his son down from George's back and up onto his own. "Us'll soon have 'ee warm and dry, Sam." Although delivered in a soothing tone, a hint of his earlier anger at Wainwright underlined his words.

George, continuing along the wider track, called back, "Give it thought, Seth. Forming a Friendly Society is our only hope."

Seth gave a nod of his head, whether in agreement or not George could not tell. The image of Samuel's small head, laid against his father's shoulder, moving slightly with each step Seth took, stayed with George as he strode on.

The track joined a wider road that led to the village of Tolpuddle. Approaching a row of stone cottages with steps leading to each doorway, he glimpsed a face watching for him through the window of the end one and raised a hand in acknowledgement. As George bent to scrape his mud-caked boots with an old knife kept on the step, the sound of a latch being lifted and someone tugging at the handle reminded him the door needed attention. Too wet tonight, he told himself as with a rasping noise the door swung open.

"I guessed you'd be earlier than usual," Sarah said, smiling a welcome. The red shawl wrapped around nine-year-old Sarah's shoulders and tied at her back lent colour to her dark features. With her deep set eyes, eyebrows so thick and straight they acted as a demarcation line between nose and high forehead, no one would have mistaken her for anyone but George's daughter.

Not demonstrative by nature, the hand George brushed briefly across Sarah's head was received as a token of his affection. Even in the bedroom, between husband and wife passion played little part; their coming together in union was more a deep appreciation of the support and steadfastness one received from the other.

At the clack of his boots on the flagstone floor Elizabeth turned and her face broke into a brief smile for her husband." Wind's in wrong direction," she greeted him as a billow of smoke was blown back down the chimney. Each spring Elizabeth waged war, applying a fresh coat of white-wash to walls and ceiling turned a pale sienna by vapours from the oil lamp and smoke from the hearth; a battle lost again within a matter of months.

She turned back to the three-legged pot suspended over the fire by a hook and chain that hung from the wide recessed fireplace, while simultaneously hitching the wailing infant she held higher against her shoulder. "Tis his teeth. They're comin' through early," she said. Her rounded body contrasted with her usual facial expression. Even at rest her mouth was firm, curving into a gentler expression only for members of her family. She bent to poke the fire. "I feared Wainwright would keep you working in spite of the weather."

"No, he gave us leave to finish early, but Seth's lad was exhausted. Couldn't finish the walk home. He's in a bad way."

"Their cottage is very damp his wife was tellin' me. Like as not 'tis lung-rot. It runs in his family I've heard said."

"I fear you're right. It shouldn't be allowed, a child that sick having to work. Seth should have stood firm with Wainwright. Said no."

He unbuttoned his jacket and removed his neckchief. "You'd think Wainwright would see to the upkeep of his property. Letting Seth's cottage fall into disrepair like that is bad husbandry. It'll be the day though when Wainwright spends money looking after his workers. Harvest Supper is the only time he shows some generosity."

"It is more thanks to Mistress Wainwright. She insists on it, not wanting to be shamed by the spread other farmers put on for their workers," responded Elizabeth.

George handed his sodden clothing to Sarah who hung them on a nail near the fire. "Seth has a cough too I noticed. When I spoke of it, he said 'twas nothing, just a nuisance that aggravated him at times."

Sinking into a high-backed chair he stretched out his legs to the warmth which soon drew a pungent odour from his wet trousers. Idly he ran his hands along the arms of the chair, stroking the curves, taking in the dark patina the wood had acquired over time. An image of his father sitting in this same chair, nodding approval as a then seven year old George recited a passage from the Bible, slipped into his mind. To the child George, his father had resembled the black and white lithograph in his father's Bible of Elijah sternly confronting the prophets of Baal. Would this union they were proposing have received his father's blessing? Stand upright, bow to none but God he'd always instructed, but George had a feeling he'd see their ideas as going against God's order of things.

Sarah had dropped to her knees on the old rag rug in front of her father and taken his boot onto her lap. George drew his foot back from her administrations. "No, leave them, daughter, I must visit with your uncle after we've eaten. Let me just sit a minute. Give me the child, wife, while you finish the meal." Cradling his son in the crook of his arm, he ran a callused finger along the chair's armrest.

"This chair brings back memories of my father, your grandfather," he said as Sarah seated herself on the floor beside her father, retrieving from her apron pocket a half-kitted sock. "A strong voice your grandfather had. Chapel, field, market square: his preaching could be heard a great distance." The clicking of Sarah's knitting needles added to the muted background sounds of the spluttering fire and her mother's busy movements.

"Your preaching draws crowds too," replied Sarah, oblivious to her mother trying to get near the fire to once more stir the pot's contents. Elizabeth's foot caught against Sarah's thigh. With an irritable gesture of her head she indicated that Sarah should get up and set the table. Rising quickly, Sarah stowed her work back in her pocket and took four bowls from the oak dresser. The floral pattern round the edge of each bowl was almost worn away, the cream glaze spidered with minute fissures. She placed them on the equally well-worn table together with some chipped mugs, spoons and a knife, pausing for a moment to draw a face on the steamed-up window.

Stooping to poke at the fire yet again, Elizabeth said, "Your sister's fretting on you meeting there tonight. She's fearful the neighbours may notice." She placed more wood on the embers. "There's little can be kept secret in this village for long. She's a feared Thomas and John could be stood off should Thornton hear talk of starting a union. You know what a hard man Thornton is."

"Dinniah has nothing to worry on. There will likely be only the five of us."

"Well, at least inside you'll not attract as much attention as if it were summer and you were meeting on the green."

"We're doing nothing illegal. It takes little to make Dinniah fret. I thank the Lord, wife, for your sense and fortitude."

""It never ceases to amaze me that you and Dinniah are brother and sister." Elizabeth straightened up, and stood for a moment, hands on hips, regarding her husband.

"Takes after my mother, it would seem. Here now, Sarah, take your little brother while I wash myself."

Cuddling Daniel close, Sarah began to blow softly into his face. Waving his fists, he crowed his pleasure, his smiling eyes encouraging her to blow again. George paused for a moment, his face softening a little at the picture they made. Turning, he went to a recess at the back of the room where a bowl of water stood on a wooden bench.

A stocky man of thirty-seven with dark, swarthy features, his sturdy frame was shorter than average. Like his wife, George wasn't given to laughter. His deep set eyes looked severely at a world he found full of sin and injustice. There was no humour to be found in the constant struggle of the labouring man to support his family. Government corruption stirred him to write letters of condemnation to the press; the great divide between rich and poor, an obstacle that unionization might help to lessen. No, life was a hard and serious business and not to be taken lightly.

He bent to remove the twine that gathered his trousers in below the knees, carefully placing the pieces in his pocket. Pushing up the sleeves of his coarsely woven shirt, he dipped his hands into the bowl and scooped water up to his face. He rolled the bar of brown soap round and round in his hands, and then attacked his face with the lather.

Drying himself on a piece of cloth that hung from a nail, he glanced up at the shelf above the bench to his precious collection of theological books; he had inherited three from his father, the others he had purchased over time with a penny put aside now and again towards their acquisition. But there had been no additions for some years. Once again he thought of his father, this time with gratitude, for instilling a love of learning in him, the skills of reading and writing that he and his brother-in-law Thomas Standfield attempted to pass on to any adult or child after the chapel prayer meetings in the winter. Many came, he knew, for the chance of a little education as much as to worship.

"Knowledge and learning are our only hope for bettering ourselves," a mantra he repeated often to Mathew in just the same way as his father had to him. But how much further had he progressed, bettered himself? Like his father he was still a farm labourer working for a pittance.

Oh, the hopes he'd had for Mathew when he was born. Attending school, that had been his vision for him. The grammar school in Dorchester, not the charity school in the next village run by an old dame whose learning was limited to a smattering of reading, writing and figuring. A chance for Mathew to get his feet on the first rung of the ladder to advancement. But the small sums they'd struggled to set aside in the little tin box on the mantelpiece towards such a dream had dissipated: keeping a family fed on a few shillings a week, burying the son and daughter they'd lost to illness, the doctor who'd had to be called in for the birthing of their youngest child, on mundane items such as new work boots for himself.

Were girls admitted to the grammar school, he recognized that it was Sarah, though, who'd make the better scholar, not that he'd ever voiced such an opinion. Her brain grasped concepts and ideas immediately. How quickly she could read a page, memorize a biblical passage, remember the proper usage when he corrected her grammar. Instructing her was a pleasure he looked forward to of an evening. But it didn't sit well with Elizabeth to see Sarah with her head bent over a book. "Now she can read and write, she's no need of more learning. It'd be more to the point her applying herself to what I have to teach her of household duties." In many ways Elizabeth was right, George knew. More advanced studying would be of little use to Sarah except for her own pleasure. "And no man wants a wife cleverer than himself," Elizabeth would argue. "Far better she learn to turn the heel of a sock, hem a shirt."

Now, with talk of wages being cut again, keeping his family fed and housed would be almost impossible, let alone finding money for school fees for Mathew. Anger and frustration welled inside him. "Education should be the right of all who desire it, not just gentry folk," George addressed the row of books as he angrily flung the drying-cloth towards its hook. He watched it miss and fall to the floor. Sarah, judging her father's mood, silently stooped and retrieved the cloth and restored it to its proper place.

A passage from Spence's dissertation on the biblical rich man being unable to enter heaven had been running through his head all morning while ploughing. What was it Spence had penned? Not that he agreed with the Spencean Society's extreme ideology. It had been too radical and had even espoused violence. But that particular phrase, how did it go now? He reached upwards and took hold of a volume of collected sermons to refresh his memory but, resisting the temptation, he let his hand caress the spine of the book for a brief moment. There wasn't time now for after they'd eaten he must hear the children's lessons before going round to see Thomas.

Walking back towards the fire, he asked, "Where's Mathew? He's not after firewood in this weather?"

"Master Kenton sent for him. Wanted him at the mill, sweepin'. He should be in shortly."

At that moment a small body thrust hard against the door and eight year old Mathew entered. He headed towards the fire and held his hands to the heat. His hair, like the pin feathers of a fledgling rook, was plastered to his scalp. Rain droplets had rivered down his forehead, streaking the white dust that filmed his face. Looking up at Mathew's arrival, George mentally contrasted his son's sturdier frame to that of Wainwright's son, a weak-looking, pale lad always in fear of his father's wrath.

"You're like a ghost," said Sarah, grinning.

"Don't stand there mocking your brother. Take his jacket and give it a good shake outside like you should have your father's, then hang it near the fire to dry." Elizabeth's tone was sharp. "Put the babe down first, girl. In his cradle. Think before you set about a task."

"I trust you worked well for Mr. Kenton, son."

"Yes, Father. Like you always tell us, a *good* labourer is worthy of his hire."

"Did he pay you in cash or kind, lad?" asked Elizabeth.

"Two pennies, Mother, and a small bag of sweepings. The sweepings be fairly clean. I raddled 'em m'self afore I left. Used the finest sieve."

"Put the coins in the money pot and wash th'self quickly. The meal's ready," said Elizabeth, the look of pride she gave her son contrasting with the timbre of her voice as Mathew hurried to carry out her instructions.

Sarah brought the bowls one by one over to her mother who ladled into each a rabbit broth thickened with barley. Holding them with great care she set them on the table, anxious for her mother's approval. The baby started fretting again as Elizabeth placed his cradle near her chair. Her mother's dexterity as she cut slices from a coarse rye loaf held firmly against her aproned chest always fascinated Sarah. Spearing the large heel of the bread on the knife blade, Elizabeth passed it to George, and then a slice to Mathew and Sarah before she took a seat next to her husband and bowed her head.

A flame-licked piece of damp wood hissed on the fire. Daniel beat at the side of his cradle with his teething ring. George gave thanks for their food, asked for God's blessing on his family, his voice deep and firm. At his father's "amen", Mathew's foot nudged Sarah's. She nodded her head at her brother, an acknowledgment that she too had noticed the briefness of her father's prayer and was equally appreciative. When George was praying, preaching, or holding meetings his oration was flowing, erudite and frequently lengthy.

Parents and children ate in silence. The oil lamp and the flickering firelight threw elongated shadows on the walls, while the wind sighed down the chimney.

Chapter Three

Workhouse 1842

ENT NO ONE AS CAN DO A JOB QUIET LIKE AROUND THIS place. Always summat bein' banged or knocked. Someone shoutin'. Boots clatterin' against the flagstones. Every sound jars through my skull an' scatters my thoughts.

Towards the end ... now why be I thinkin' in words like that? My end ent come yet... Mind you, I owns that there were often days I couldn't drag myself to work. Mary would beg Master to bear with me; that all I needed were a couple of days in bed. But I were gettin' weaker, and, if I be honest, Master weren't gettin' a fair day's work out of me. Then come the time when us were thrashin', the chaff and dust thick in the air. 'Twas like my chest were filled with the stuff. As if banded with iron like a brewer's barrel, my lungs were held tight, and I were taken with a fit of coughin'. Racked with the coughin' while strugglin' for air, blood ran from my mouth and I fell to the ground.

That were when Master said as how he'd have to lay me off. And, o'course, that meant us had to move out of the cottage seein' as how it went with the job. Five soddin' days he give us to get out.

Oh, us had see it comin', those last few months; knew it were likely us would end up here in the workhouse as us had no money put by. That were why Mary an' her sister Martha enquired everywhere for work for Tabitha. Not that Tabby didn't help at home as well as her goin' with Mary to help with washdays at the farm. An' she kep an eye on a neighbour's

And Ordered Their Estate

children when needed. But us didn't want her endin' up in the workhouse too. And she'd have had to come if she'd still been livin' with us.

Tramped to Piddlehinton, even as far as Piddletrenthide, Mary an' Martha did. Wherever they heard there might be a position. Mary's sister would've taken Tabby in, but her has a clutch of children herself and Mary's mother livin' there since Mary's father died. It just weren't possible. They had scarce more money comin' in than us.

"Go see Squire," I says to 'em. You get to speak to him an he'll give her work." But he were away travellin'. Then they got to see the Ponsonby's housekeeper, over in Bere. Mary tells her as how they needs a position for Tabby. Looked like Tabby would be taken on, but when Ponsonby's wife hears from the housekeeper that I be sick, she demands to know what I were sick of. Then her said, no. Said as how she were sorry but she weren't prepared to run the risk of Tabby carryin' the lung-rot into their house. Didn't matter as how Mary swore as how Tabby ent never been sick in her life.

Mary's sister, it were, as heard how Kenton at the mill, were lookin' for someone to watch out for his small son, him as weren't born right. Seems the woman as had looked after the child since birth, had swigged gin once too often and neglected the child. Mary didn't think as how he'd take on someone as young as Tabby. Tabitha were well favoured enough – her with rosy cheeks an' a good coverin' of flesh on her bones an' big for her age. But nothin' were asked and nothin' said about my bein' poorly. I think he took her on mindin' what I'd done for him. Cried, poor Tabby did, at havin' to leave home, her not really graspin' why us was doin' this, for I was still managin' to get to work most days then. And you can be certain sure Mary an' I were terr'ble upset at her leavin'. Mary points out to her that most girls her age were out working away from home long afore they'd reached Tabby's age. It weren't as if she were miles away, and us had no choice if she were to be saved from the workhouse.

Cor, what a stench! Be there foxes around?

Damn! It've happened again. When I has a fit of coughin', sometimes my bowels let go at the same time. I've little enough to pass, but it smells foul. But why do it make I think on foxes?

Aah ... now thought be joinin' with memory! Back when us were first livin' in the cottage and I were emptyin' the tub from the privy, that's right.

A strong wind blowin', an' I'd just dragged out the tub, an old wooden thing with rope handles. Filled to almost overflowin' it were, for 'tis a job I'd always put off doin'. You'd think I'd give no attention to odours, my life havin' been spent workin' with cattle. But human stench be far worse than that of animals.

A sound of horns and the bayin' of dogs makes I pause to listen. I be stood there, graspin' the two handles, thinkin' on huntin'. How it don't seem fair on the poor old fox bein' chased by all them hounds an' men on horseback, and yet, at the same time, feelin' a sort of stirrin in my bein', if you gets my meanin'. The sound of a huntin' horn do call to summat ancient and deep inside a man, an urge to join the pursuit.

Like I says, there I be standin' when a streak of red flashes between my legs and into the privy. At that same moment, the wind catches the privy door and slams it shut. Next thing I knows, I be surrounded by dogs, yelpin' and sniffin', Squire and Parson and the others millin' round astride their horses, and it unsteadies me. One handle slips from my grasp, and there be them dogs all covered in shit. It put them dogs off the fox's scent for sure!

Well, Squire's concerned for his dogs and is flickin' at 'em with his whip and yellin' at the pack leader to get them out of the mess, while Parson be demandin', "The fox! Which way, man?" Me, I canst do nothin' but roar with laughter. I points past the privy, as if it had gone to the left. The pack leader be blowin' on his horn fit to bust his lungs; the dogs be covered in all that foulness, while, with tub still drippin' muck hanging from one hand, I be laughin' like a lunatic.

Weren't till much later that I lets the fox out, cursin' at the way all them horses 'ave churned up the garden in front of the privy into a mud bath. Lucky as how we'd done the tattie-diggin' and there weren't nothin' that'd got spoiled. Not that us could of stopped 'em anyways. Was Wainwright as owned the land and even he ent got no power to stop the gentry huntin' over his property.

Every time us thought on it, for days after, Mary an' me would have a chuckle together.

Mary has such a laugh. It starts as a warm chuckle, bubblin' up from deep inside her, burstin' to a laugh that at times would set her whole body shakin'. But her weren't laughin' just after our first 'un were born, when she says as how she's been asked to go as wet-nurse up at Squire's.

"It ent necessary for you to go. Let 'em find someone else," I says to Mary. "Us can manage."

"You think I wants to leave my baby?" Mary be pacing back an' forth, not knowin' what to do.

"Why've they got rid of the wet-nurse them already has?" I asks. "Seems mighty strange when in a couple of months theirs'll be ready for weanin'."

"Stealin', 'tis rumoured."

"Don't go," I says again. "Our littl'un needs you. An' what about me? Who'll see to my needs?"

"You'll survive," she says. A smile in her voice, and comes and stands behind me. Puts her arms around my neck, strokes the top of my head. "I don't know what to do. Will be like cuttin' off a part of me, leaving him, but Martha says as how she'll suckle him along with her own and share the farm milk between 'em too."

"But her has such a brood to look after of her own. I doubts our littl'un 'll get a fair suck."

"Seth Fielding, I knows you have little love for my sister, but you think I'd consider leaving Little Tom with her if I didn't think she'd see to him right?"

"It ent that. I just feels she be pushin' you into this. Her always has to manage things."

Mary gives my head a gentle slap and walks over to the window where her stands, hands cuppin' breasts heavy with milk, head pressed against the window pane.

Turnin' to face me, her says, "Think what us could do with the money. There's so much us needs."

I looks around the room, sees what little we have through new eyes. I own that everything be well-used, pass-ons from her family and relatives. I feels anger and shame that I can't do better by her.

17

"A feather mattress. Couldn't us snuggle in warm of a winter's night," says Mary, her voice filled with longing. "Much warmer than that old straw 'un."

"I'm against your goin'," says I, "but 'tis up to you."

I should've done things otherwise, stayed firm, for then our baby might've lived.

Sometimes, Mary'd creep out from the big house and us'd meet in the copse of an evenin'. Not often, mind you, for Mary'd have difficulty slippin' away. Always askin' how Tom was, and I has to tell her he weren't thrivin'. Then comes the night I walks up to the big house, thumps on the kitchen door, demands to see Mary. Caused quite a fuss, but when they hears as how our babe had died, they let me in. She starts a sobbin', and I leads her outside, round the corner so as I can hold her and try an' give her comfort. She keeps a'crying and says as how she were comin' back with me there and then, and sod Mistress Finchbury's littl'un.

"Well, you knows I can't wait to have you home again," says I, holdin' her tight. "It'd be a comfort to us both. "I wipes at her tears with the back of my hand, gentle like. "Though it'll gain you little leavin' now, and there be the funeral to pay for. But you do whatever you feels like, my sweetin'."

She sees my reasonin', and, when the housekeeper agrees to her bein' allowed to have time off for the funeral provided Mary scrubbed up real well on her return, Mary says she'll stay on a while longer, seein' as how Squire's child be takin' to solids well, and it would only be a few more weeks afore she'd no longer be needed.

They be tryin' to spoon some gruel down me. My Mary'd do it gentler than this old biddy be doin', scrapin' the spoon against my lips as if she'd have the skin off 'em. Most of the slop ends up on my nightshirt, for I has difficulty swallowin'. "Water," I manages to get out. "Just a drink of water is all I fancies."

My mind be leapin' about again. How come 'tis now fixed on chestnuts? An autumn afternoon, walkin' along our lane. The earthy smell from leaves thick on the ground, and Mary stoopin' to pry a gleamin' chestnut from its prickly casing. Caught me fair an' square on the back of the head with it, an' soon us were having a rare old battle, throwin' leaves an' chestnuts at each other, like a couple of young'uns. That image of Mary, hands full of yellowing leaves, standin' in a shaft of late sunlight, laughin', have always stayed with me. How her could laugh.

Hard as life were, us had some happy moments those early years when us were young and lusty.

Chapter Four
Tolpuddle 1834

THE HUGE SYCAMORE STOOD AT THE EDGE OF THE GREEN. Under the shelter of its widespread branches, from the first warm days of spring, the old men would gather. Gnarled hands resting on a sturdy stick, chin supported on hands, they would sit contemplating the scene before them. In its shade, screened from the summer sun, aged grandmothers would rest and gossip, each anxious to speak their piece of news while keeping a watchful eye on infant grandchildren left in their care. As the days lengthened, George and others would meet in the evenings and talk. Summer Sundays when not preaching in other villages, George used the bench beneath the tree as his pulpit. His strong voice and his oratory drew a congregation of labourers and their wives and families.

This was the only feature, this great tree, that distinguished Tolpuddle from the other small hamlets and villages that nestled in the curves of the Dorset hills. Surrounded by arable fields, steep elevations and wooded areas, Tolpuddle encompassed in its straggling boundaries a population of less than two hundred.

The notice, nailed to the sycamore tree, was surrounded by villagers. Mathew had met his father on his way home from work, bursting with news of men posting printed sheets around the village. As George approached the tree he saw his brother-in-law Thomas Standfield already studying the proclamation. Older by several years and fairer skinned than George, Thomas was the more cautious of the two. He turned at George's approach.

"You've heard then. I was just coming to get you."

"Mathew here came to tell me. What's it all about?"

Earlier grey skies had shed intermittent rain during the dreary February day. Now, as George stood with Thomas under the tree's dripping branches contemplating the notice, one of several villagers drawn by the unusualness of such an event called, "Tell us what it says, Loveless."

Hat held in one hand, massaging the back of his neck with the other, George started reading aloud. In large black letters was the heading, CAUTION. He read slowly, pausing now and again to assimilate the information.

> "Whereas it has been represented to us from several quarters, that mischievous and designing Persons have been for some time past, endeavouring to induce, and have induced, many Labourers in various Parishes in this County, to attend Meetings, and to enter into Illegal Societies or Unions, to which they bind themselves by unlawful oaths, administered secretly by Persons concealed, who artfully deceive the ignorant and unwary, we, the undersigned Justices think it our duty to give this Public Notice and Caution, that all Persons may know the danger they incur by entering into such Societies...."

George's voice deepened, became harsh, when he reached '**Guilty Of Felony, and be liable to be Transported for Seven Years**', printed in letters of great size. George cleared his throat, took a step nearer to better see the smaller print, and continued reading to the end.

"I read it through before you came," said Thomas, his taller frame stooped to study the notice. "I've been pondering on that phrase 'unlawful oaths'. What is meant by unlawful oaths?"

"Its meaning is beyond me," replied George. "I see it as intimidation. They think by threatening us with transportation, we will be silenced. But we both know we've done nothing wrong. Nothing illegal. Turning to the others gathered on the green he asked, "Are there any more of these displayed elsewhere?"

"Aye," came the reply. "Several. In Tolpuddle and beyond."

George, with Mathew trotting at his heels, turned and walked away followed by Thomas. "Does it mean you, Father? Will you be transported?" questioned Mathew, grabbing onto his father's coat.

As they passed another warning, George reached up and removed it in order to study it further on reaching home.

"Should you be doing that," asked Thomas with a look of concern, "removing an official notice?"

"I want to think on the wording at home. They're trying to frighten us, Thomas. You notice these are posted today, Saturday. No doubt Parson will be making it part of his sermon tomorrow."

"They know a warning that size'll get peoples' attention on their way to church or chapel tomorrow, I agree." As if to give his total attention to the matter Thomas paused, removed his hat and ran his hand through his greying hair. "Forming a Friendly Society is not breaking the law, therefore the intent of the notice must be to make those workers who know no better fearful of joining us." Replacing his hat firmly, he added, "Or is there more to this than we realize, think you?"

Thomas was a quiet-spoken man of deep convictions. Many were the debates he'd had with George on how to improve the lot of labourers such as themselves. It was Thomas who, after much reading and research, had put forward the idea of a Friendly Society, a proposal grasped by the more forceful George and brought to fruition.

Realizing George was several yards ahead of him, he hurried to catch up. Dinniah would be in a rare tizzy if she'd heard about the notices. She was so unlike her brother George, emotional and fretting over the smallest thing. It would be difficult convincing her there was nothing to worry about, especially as he was filled with unease himself.

Seated at the table that evening, George found his thoughts straying from the Bible open in front of him. He pulled the proclamation from his pocket, laid it on the table, brushing it with the edge of his hand to smooth out the folds. He felt confident they had done nothing that could be considered breaking the law. They had met in secret, certainly, but they had not concealed themselves when initiating new members. His mind ranged over all that had taken place over the past few months organizing the union.

~~~

The four men, George Loveless and his brother James, Thomas Standfield and James Brine took up positions round the table in Standfield's cottage. The flickering fire danced shadows on the walls.

"Is John not coming, Thomas?" enquired George.

In answer to George's question, the door opened and John Standfield, ducking his head to miss the door lintel, entered with a lurcher at his heels. "Sit!" he commanded, and the coarse-coated animal dropped to the floor in front of the fire.

"Evening all," John greeted the others. "Wind's powerful strong tonight."

As the other men responded to John's greeting, George urged "Come sit, John. We've a reply from Robert Owen," his voice and body emanating an intense enthusiasm.

"Robert Owen of the Grand National?"

"Aye. Our cousin in London made contact with him."

"What does he have to say?" asked John, nudging the scratching dog to stillness with the toe of his boot.

Sounds of footsteps and soft words could be heard overhead, and then the feet, skirt and finally the head of Dinniah Standfield appeared down the steep, narrow-treaded stairs.

"Evening, Dinniah."

"The young 'uns settled?"

"How be things with you, Dinniah?" the others addressed her, while John rose and bent to greet his mother with a kiss on the forehead. Dinniah raised a hand and gently patted her first-born on the cheek.

"Did'st get here with none seeing you?" she questioned nervously as she took a seat on a stool near the fire and picked up some sewing that lay on the floor beside her.

"Wife, I've told you repeatedly not to fret," said Thomas gently. "Surely a son can visit his mother without causing comment. We're cautious in our movements, though our meeting together breaks no law."

"Cautious you may be, but there's little goes unmarked in this village. I know I've said it many times afore, but 'tis true. What if you'm seen and word gets back to Wainwright or Thornton, even Squire. They'll have 'ee stood off long afore your union be organized. Then where'll us be?"

Dinniah, having voiced her concerns once again, bent over her sewing.

"Mother's right in that someone's bound to notice our comings and goings. Is there nowhere else that we could meet that will not draw as much attention?" asked John.

"You know well we've discussed this matter often, John. Were it summer we could meet outdoors, away from all eyes, but..."

"Come, we're wasting time."

George read aloud the letter from Robert Owen, making comments occasionally.

"It'll be a wondrous help to have the two delegates from the Grand National Consolidated come and advise us on how to go about this matter," said George. "I had not expected such an offer."

"Their coming will cause more comment in the village, especially if they are to stay overnight," said John, concerned at seeing his mother so worried.

Brine nodded his head in agreement, his bright eyes shifting from George to John. "Maybe us can find them lodgings away from here."

"Where could we meet? Thomas, you prefer us not to meet here?" queried George.

"It will be terrible crowded, but the long room above is the only place unless we use the chapel, and I'm against that," said Thomas. "It would sit badly with me to use the chapel for anything but the worship of God."

"I'm of like mind. It'd not be right to use the chapel."

Dinniah's face showed her worry but she made no comment.

The dog at John's feet stirred, passed wind and scratched vigorously. "What about the old barn out Tarnsley way? We would be less conspicuous there," John attempted again.

"And should word get out, we could be charged with trespassing. Leave it, John. Let the matter rest."

"But it's getting late. We must be on our way. The morning and another day's work will be here before we know it. Our thanks, Thomas, for having us here. As soon as I have news I'll let you know. All of you do what you can to encourage others to join us." George rose to his feet and the others, bidding good night to Thomas and Dinniah, stepped out into the night.

~~~

John Standfield stood in the lane quietly directing the men as they arrived to the back door of his father's cottage. Many were from Affpuddle and Bere Regis and as far away as Hinton. Most of the Tolpuddle labourers were already gathered in the long loft-room. Thomas and John had hung blankets over the two small windows so that the numbers gathered there could not be seen from outside. The last arrivals, greeted by a low rumble of conversation and coughing, pressed against the walls, as those already there, wedged tightly against each other, tried to make room. All strained to catch a glimpse of the strangers from London. The smell of tallow wax and lantern oil mingled with that of sweat and unwashed bodies. On a small bench at the front sat the two representatives of the Grand National. George and James stood on either side. As the last arrival fought for space, Thomas closed the door and pushed his way to the front to stand beside George and James.

George rose and stood on the bench so that all might see him more clearly. Hats were hastily removed, shuffling feet stilled, coughs silenced as he prayed for guidance.

"We had hoped that twenty might come, to have nearer thirty present makes our visitors' journey worthy of the effort. Now let us listen to what they have to say."

With great solemnity, firmly pressing his bowler-shaped hat to his head, the first London representative mounted the bench. His black cloth coat cut away in the front exposed a waistcoat of dark grey. Carefully trimmed sideburns extended well below his cheek bones. "Looks like a soddin' toff," came a whispered comment from the crowd.

"My colleague and I appreciate that it is easier for those dwelling in cities, living in close proximity to each other such as workers in factories, to meet and organize than it is for you farm labourers carrying out your individual jobs on many separate farms. It is easier for them to gather in some degree of anonymity, but if you are to better your wages and conditions, forming a Friendly Society is the only way open to you." He spoke further of the necessity to unionize and the rules of the society.

The second representative, attired more like the listening labourers, with his short, broadcloth jacket and a scarf tied at his neck, drew more response from those present.

"What my friend here says is only too true. You will have many difficulties to overcome, but, I stress, *it is the only way you will improve conditions for yourselves.*" He discussed the practicalities of how to organize workers scattered over such a wide area, repeatedly mopping at his forehead with a handkerchief, for the heat generated by the tightly packed bodies was oppressive.

"What chance do we stand with so many unemployed men ready to take over our jobs should we be forced to withdraw our labour to support our demands?" asked a voice from the back of the room.

"Aye. What chance do we have?" chorused several others.

"What chance do you have to be paid a decent wage without banding together?" responded George. "There is no other way. It has been proved that we cannot put our trust in the landowners' word alone."

"To what use will the shilling we have to pay to join be put?" queried another.

"If a master attempts to reduce wages or stand-off a man solely for belonging to a union, then those stood-off members would be supported by other members and the general funds. This general fund will be built up from the shilling and the penny a week a member pays thereafter. Should a member be sick or unemployed then he does not have to pay during that period."

Heads were nodded at this, and comments passed quietly between some of the men. A strident voice asked, "But what if our masters gets to hear us is planning a union and sets us off afore there be enough of us to stand against them?" A chorus of voices took up the refrain. "How do we know the masters will listen to us even when we be unionized?" "How dare us take such a risk?"

Not all were convinced they would benefit George realized, as the Grand National speakers did their best to answer questions and allay the fears expressed. But it has gone well he told himself, confident that many had been persuaded of the advantages of forming a Friendly Society. Yes, it had gone well.

It was past ten o'clock before the meeting was brought to a close. Descending the steep stairs the villagers emerged one by one, joining up later in groups to trudge homewards, still debating the risks involved.

~~~

The December night was raw with a touch of frost in the air as selected men gathered at the Standfield cottage for the initiation ceremony. There had been much discussion between the Standfields, the Loveless brothers, and Brine about how the ceremony should be conducted.

"We must conduct the ceremony so that any man will be awed by the solemnity of the occasion. It must be firmly fixed in their minds the importance of the promise they are making," Thomas had said.

It was James Loveless who had suggested the picture and arranged to have it painted, while George was for stressing a religious aspect to the occasion.

"Nigh all the men are believing Christians, be they Church or Chapel, and swearing on the Bible will impress on them that what they are promising is binding."

James Hammett conducted the first man, George Romaine, up the narrow stairway, bidding him blindfold himself with his handkerchief. "Kneel," he was instructed once inside, while George Loveless dressed in a long, white surplice-like smock, his head bare and his face uncovered, read a passage from the bible. "Uncover your eyes."

Romaine found himself in front of a large painting. In a black, flowing robe, stark eyes staring from a hooded, skeleton face, 'Death the Reaper' stood with a scythe in his hand. The dim, flickering light from two candles placed on either side of the picture gave an appearance of movement to the crudely painted canvas. As Romaine knelt, mesmerized by the picture, James Loveless, also dressed in a white surplice, pointed to the painting and intoned "Remember thine end." Romaine dragged his gaze from the picture and fixed it on George.

The strangeness of the setting, the shadows cast by the candles, made Romaine's voice quaver as, repeating the words after George Loveless, he promised not to reveal the members or the activities of the Society. Extending a bible, James instructed, "Kiss the Good Book." Visibly overcome by the eeriness of the proceedings, Romaine did as instructed, anxious to have the ordeal over. As he descended, another man waited at the foot of the stairs to be conducted up.

~~~

George read the notice through yet again. A feeling of unease would not be calmed. The words 'illegal oath' beat rhythmically in his head while his fingers tapped an accompaniment on the table. He was missing something, something important. Unions were no longer illegal and yet the wording implied that they were, and 'unlawful oaths secretly administered'. Each man had been required to swear not to devulge what had taken place but was such a promise an oath in the eyes of the law and what made an oath unlawful? Surely all oaths did not have to be submitted to a government committee to be declared legal or otherwise?

"Tis getting late, husband, and our stock of candles is running low," called Elizabeth from the bedroom above.

"I'll be with you in a few more minutes." George carefully folded the notice, rose from his seat and crossed over to his shelf of books. Selecting one, he inserted the paper in between the pages. Elizabeth had been full of anxious questions all evening; best not leave it around. It would only cause her to fret. Then he changed his mind again and slipped the paper into his pocket. When the opportunity arose, he'd go over the wording again with Thomas. There must be some way of finding out what was meant by an unlawful oath.

He lay awake long after Elizabeth started gently snoring, unable to quieten his thoughts. He turned over yet again. Elizabeth stirred in her sleep and muttered that he'd pulled the coverlet off her. He must get some sleep, he was preaching in Hinton in the morning which meant an early start to be there by ten. He tried reciting a psalm but the words 'unlawful oaths' kept insinuating their way into the verses. Those in authority were devious in their dealings. He must put his trust in the Lord for his untrained mind was not equal to their crafty twisting of the laws.

At last he he crept from the bed. Standing by the window with his head bowed, oblivious to the cold, he prayed long and earnestly, asking his God for guidance and protection for his family.

Chapter Five

Workhouse 1842

I COULDN'T MAKE IT TO THE SLOP BUCKET. I WAS TOO weak to get m'self off the bed. Lay in my own foulings all night till the doctor come this morning, him as is contracted to attend the workhouse sick.

"Get this man clean bedding and night shirt," he berated the overseer. "If I find any patient laying in his own filth again, I'll have you dismissed."

And, o'course, the overseer raged at the dame who is meant to take care of our needs. 'Twas good to hear someone speakin' up for us poor sods. And Doctor has the power to have his orders carried out. 'Tis no good speakin' out if you've no power.

I be wanderin' in my mind a lot. Things gets all mixed up. Everything dark and then in dim light I sees this picture of Death with a scythe, and Death keeps beckoning with a crooked finger. Then, like a puff of wind sendin' dandelion seeds flyin', my earlier thoughts be scattered and others have taken their place.

Next moment I be back on the farm. Mistress Wainwright had the chimney sweep come. He come in his cart with this poor scrap of a lad sitting in the back. The lad's coat sleeves be worn out at the elbows and the knees gone from his trousers, showing the flesh beneath. Crusted with soot-blackened scabs they was, where the skin had been scraped away and never given the chance to heal proper. Raw places oozing blood and yellow pus. The young 'un were weepin' and wouldn't leave the cart,

And Ordered Their Estate

beggin' not to be sent up the chimney. His master takes him by the collar and drags him out, beatin' him about with a stick.

Mistress Wainwright appears at the door to see what were the delay. Calls to Sweep to get a move on for she would have much cleanin' to do once Sweep was finished. 'Tis likely she'd not seen what went on, for boy and man were hid by the cart.

I be hankerin' to grab the stick from Sweep's hand and lay into him m'self, but there were nought I could've done or said as would've affected the outcome. They'd have stood me off and the boy would still've been send up the chimney. To ease my feelin' of helplessness, I takes my pitchfork when there be none about to see, and gives a jab to Sweep's sorry excuse for a horse. Poor thing rears and rolls back its eyes with fear. I be that ashamed of my actions I filches some oats from Wainwright's stable and feeds 'em to the dumb beast. No, the likes of I be powerless.

I once were moved to piss down Wainwright's well when things went badly at work. A feeble gesture. Like the stabbin' of Sweep's horse. It achieved nought and I be just filled with regrets later. That feeling of helplessness that oft times fills me, that on occasion be so strong it forces I to take a tankard of ale. But it takes more than the one tankard afore the seethin' be stilled, and 'tis my young 'uns that be worse off for I have drunk their food.

Not long after Mary and I was married there were much discontent, for landowners in Tolpuddle were paying less than workers was gettin' in villages such as Tarnsley and Bere. George Loveless called a meetin' of Tolpuddle men on the village green. Master Wainwright, Thornton, and other farmers were gathered there to hear what were said. Even Parson Warren come. And the masters agreed to match the wages as were being paid elsewhere. Parson Warren stood up and swore afore us all. Says he, "If you will go quietly to your work, you shall receive as much for your labour as any men in the district." Then he adds somethin' like, "If your masters should attempt to run from their word, I will undertake to see you righted, so help me God."

We was soon back working, for the whole affair took less than two hours. But the masters never kept their word. Another meeting were called and we all - aye, I was amongst them for I was braver then - marched

31

to the nearest magistrate's house out Dorchester way. Loveless and others were of the opinion the magistrates had the power to see the agreement be kept. Loveless told Magistrate Frampton, "We are not trying to impose new terms but endeavouring to uphold an agreement already made."

But Magistrate said, "Where's your agreement? Show me the signatures. Labourers must work for whatever wages their masters chose to pay."

It were passed around the village that later Frampton makes contact with Parson Warren and rumour has it that Parson denies that any such promise were made. 'Cos, it were only rumour, mind. For it weren't likely that Parson would stand up and admit to bein' a liar, were it?

Y'see, us hadn't any power.

That finger keeps beckonin' I, and that gapin' mouth spews words: "Prepare to meet thy God." Light strikes the metal of the scythe, dazzles me. Leave I be, damn you, leave I be.

This time of year I wouldst be set to hedgin' and ditchin'. Ditchin' be rotten work for no matter how much grease I rubs into my boots, it don't keep out the water long, they bein' oft-times in need of repair. By day's end my feet would be so cold as to have no feelin'.

Some folks have skills of one kind, others another. George Loveless, his skill be ploughing. Mine be hedging. A pretty sight, a well-layered hedge.

Y'see, yer takes a sturdy piece of last year's growth and cuts into it low down with a hedging knife. Only a little ways, mind, for if yer cuts too deep the shoot will wither. Then yer bends and weaves it, careful like, into the hedgerow. Bein' as I favours my right hand, I layers mine to the left, but them as is left-handed layers to the right. Come spring, the hedge grows thick from base to top, and be filled with birdsong. Many's the time when walking round the village, I nods approval to myself at my handiwork.

Now George, he could plough a furrow straight as an arrow. I minds early one spring a ploughing contest were arranged. Landowners, farmers, all sent their best men. Held it in Ten Acre Upland where there be plenty of room for all ploughmen to take part. I knows Master had laid wagers with the other landowners. Parson were a great bettin' man, too. So I says to George, sly like, "I be surprised that you be taking part, you being

Methody and against gamblin' and games of chance." George looks at I straight on and says, "There is no *chance* to it, for I'm the best ploughman in these parts." He were not braggin', mind. Said it like I wouldst say 'I be called Seth Fielding' or 'My eyes be blue.'

'Twas a fair day, the clouds scuddin' across a sky pale blue and sunlit. The trees still leafless and the elms hung with the twigged nests of rooks. Many had turned out to watch, their hollerin' out support joined with the jingling of the horses' harnesses. Black rooks and grey-white gulls swoopin' down into the furrows of fresh-turned sod. An earthy tang to the air an' the breeze strong enough to lift coat tails and stir what dried leaves still lay around .

When all were finished and George declared the winner and money had changed hands, Master comes up to George. 'Well done," says he, clappin' George on the shoulder, and tried to press some coins into George's hand. It were obvious Master had been drinkin' heavy. In the normal course of a day he were tight-fisted with his money.

But George would have none of it. Says he, "Wagerin' and gamblin' are sinful, and I cannot accept money made thus."

Master shoves the money back in his pocket quick enough. Parson, standin' alongside him, demands, "Do you dare to criticize your betters?" Parson's face be red with anger, his neck bulging over the white stock at his neck.

It were common knowledge that Parson had no likin' for George, what with George bein' Methody, an' all. Village gossip tells as how Parson turned off the fellow as tended his garden when Parson learned he were attendin' chapel. Mistress Greenaway reported that Parson yelled at him as how it were a personal affront that the gardener should eschew his church for some upstart Methodist preacher. Although I ent familiar with the words she said Parson used, the meanin' were clear enough.

I believes the gentry was against George for his cleverness at readin' and writin' and for voicin' his opinions. Saw it as aping his betters, and poor folk weren't meant to behave thus. So, in spite of his hard working ways, they were opposed to him long afore the union be started.

Chapter Six
Tolpuddle 1833

HENRY FINCHBURY, SQUIRE OF TOLPUDDLE HALL, MUTtered a reply to the woman seated on his right and raised another forkful of food to his mouth. Maria Ponsonby was a twittering fool. If only she would address herself to the meal in front of her, fill her mouth, silence herself. He turned his attention to the conversation taking place between William Ponsonby and Parson Warren further down the table. Agnes, his wife, seated at the other end, appeared to have lost the battle to keep the conversation on general matters.

"Henry, please, for the ladies' sake, try and keep the conversation off politics. At least until we've left you men to your port and tobacco," she had requested before their guests had arrived. Deeply fond of his wife, he had done his best to do as she wished, but as the meal progressed and general topics had been well discussed, labour unrest was becoming the subject of deliberation. And surely, felt Finchbury, all present would prefer politics to Maria Ponsonby's shrill prattle.

"My gamekeeper reports there are an unusual number of foxes around this year. Should mean a good hunting season," Henry offered in a final attempt to steer the conversation in accordance with his wife's wishes. "Hear you've got a new hunter, Warren."

Before Parson Warren could reply, Ponsonby voiced the opinion that if matters weren't dealt with soon, the country would be brought to its knees and there'd be no gentlemen left that could afford to hunt. Henry shrugged his shoulders in a gesture of helplessness to his wife. She smiled gently and shook her head.

"Something has to be done, goddammit!" Ponsonby was expressing heatedly. "No disrespect meant to your cloth, Warren, but the situation is likely to get out of hand." His heron-like frame, all long limbs and awkward joints, was topped by a balding head flushed red with indignation. The length of his neck was emphasized by a fashionable, tall cravat.

"You're right. This talk of the workers forming unions is very distressing," said Parson Warren.

"Distressing! It's sedition, pure and simple. Mark my words, they'll be following the Frenchies' example if something isn't done soon and we'll have a revolution on our hands." Ponsonby stabbed at the air with his fork for emphasis.

"I agree with you whole-heartedly. Only yesterday I was reading something Edmund Burke wrote, 'Good order is the foundation of all good things. The people, without being servile, must be tractable and obedient.' Yes, good order, the maintenance of the status quo, is essential, for the other road leads to ruin."

"What's your opinion, Finchbury?" asked Ponsonby.

Henry Finchbury, surveyed his guests, avoiding his wife's look of disapproval. "I fear there's much truth to the rumours that are circulating. And if it be so, the forming of trade unions strikes at the very foundation of our society."

Ralph Tremain, who had contributed little to the conversation until now, asked, "But are their demands so unreasonable? A couple of shillings more a week? A small price to pay to put an end to this unrest."

The three older men turned on Tremain as one.

"A small price, Sir! And how long will it be before they make further demands?" Ponsonby demanded. "*I've* not forgotten the Swing Riots, burning ricks, our womenfolk too terrified of the threat of mobs attacking to sleep at night. Let this union thing spread and we'll have a repetition of such goings on, you mark my words."

"They should be paid what employers can afford and not what they may dictate," said Parson Warren.

"I can tell you this, Tremain. Your father would turn in his grave to hear you voice such radical views, and I can assure you, you'll have exhausted your inheritance within five years should you put your ideas into practice," said Ponsonby.

"But they are not threatening to riot. I understand they are for peaceful means," replied Tremain, a quiet, thoughtful man whose pale blue eyes blinked constantly behind eye-glasses perched on the end of his nose.

"You've been away from the area for some years, Tremain. Take advice from men who are older and more knowledgeable on such matters. At day's end your labourers will not thank you. They will expect more and more and make our men further dissatisfied. It won't work, Tremain. We must stick together on this." Ponsonby wielded his eating utensil as if it were a pitch-fork, nearly catching it in the floral arrangement in front of him.

Parson Warren moved his chair back a little. The edge of the table was pressing uncomfortably against his full stomach, and he fought with a desire to reach beneath the table and ease the pinch of his gaiters around his plump calves. He raised his wine glass to his lips, touched his lips with his napkin, then dabbed at a splash of wine on one of the tabs of his clerical collar. "I hear that it's one of Wainwright's labourers who's at the root of the problem."

"Well, I for one am determined to see a stop put to the matter before it gets out of hand, said Ponsonby. "Lord Melbourne, the Home Secretary, is a distant connection of mine, and I wrote him a strongly worded letter about the situation."

"The relationship is on my mother's side," Maria Ponsonby imposed. "Her mother and Lord Melbourne's were cousins." Unlike the vigorous gestures her husband used when expressing an opinion, her hands continuously fluttered. Poised for a moment on her generous breasts, then toying with a laced handkerchief in her lap, briefly lifting a mouthful of food from plate to mouth, they moved constantly to an accompaniment of jangling bracelets.

" How interesting," said Agnes Finchbury. In an attempt to once again direct the conversation to less controversial matters she asked, "Do you

And Ordered Their Estate

visit with them at all in London, Ma'm? We go far less frequently to London of late. Is that not so, Henry? And, for myself, I much prefer Bath."

"No, Ma'm," responded Ponsonby before his wife could reply. "Very infrequently, and with the situation as it is now, it would be most unwise to leave ones property unattended."

"You're that concerned about the situation?" questioned one of the other guests, a landowner from Piddlehinton.

"I am, Sir, and so should you all be."

Agnes Finchbury, noting that everyone had finished eating, stood up. "Gentlemen, I'm sure you wish to discuss this matter amongst yourselves, so if you'll excuse us, we ladies will withdraw." Henry deflected her accusatory glance with a smile. Agnes paused as she came to where he sat, placed a hand on his shoulder. "Don't be too long before you join us." He looked up at her, his face, guilty as a school-boy caught out in some infraction. "You did your best," she acknowledged softly.

"We'll be with you shortly, m'dear," he said, giving the hand on his shoulder a gentle pat.

The five men stood as the ladies left the room. Henry Finchbury nodded to the butler who, placing decanters of port and brandy on the table, signaled to the rest of the servants to leave the room and withdrew himself.

"Melbourne, has he replied?" asked Henry, passing the decanters down the table and with a gesture indicating to his guests to help themselves from his ornate tobacco tin.

"He has. Says he can do nothing unless we have firm evidence that the law is being broken. Forming a union is not unlawful. But," stressed Ponsonby using a finger now for emphasis instead of a fork, "he mentions an obscure law about the swearing of unlawful oaths. Something to do with naval law, mutinies, and all that."

"I still question the need for such drastic measures," said Tremain, retrieving a delicately carved pipe from an inner pocket and filling it from the proffered tin of tobacco. "If wages are dropped by another shilling and the price of bread so high, how is a poor labourer to feed his family?"

"Tremain, wishing no offense, you're down here what, two, three months a year at most? What knowledge do you really have of the

37

situation? " asked Ponsonby. "Should workers get an indication that we are not united on this issue, all is lost."

Ponsonby declined the offer of tobacco but reached for the brandy and refilled his glass. "We have to get irrefutable confirmation of what is actually taking place. You say you know who's fomenting all this unrest, Warren?

"Loveless," snapped Parson Warren. "He's a born trouble-maker." He removed a snuff box from his pocket, placed some snuff on the back of his hand and sniffed noisily.

"Aye, Loveless is at the bottom of it all, I fear," said Henry as he thumbed tobacco into the bowl of his long-stemmed pipe.

"And who employs this Loveless?"

"Wainwright. Farms about three hundred acres. His land adjoins mine."

"Then I suggest that you have words with Wainwright. Find out what you can. Talk to his workmen. There's sure to be one that can be persuaded to give us information." Ponsonby emptied his glass and set it back on the table.

"You're right, Ponsonby, We cannot let matters continue as they are. We must make a stand. I'll speak with Wainwright tomorrow."

The brandy and port circulated the table again. The talk moved to the heavy duty on tobacco and the effect the repeal of the Corn Laws was having on the price of corn and gradually worked its way back to the consequences for them all if the business of unions was not halted. Ponsonby mopped his head with a silk handkerchief, reached for the decanter yet again. Tremain said little until the talk turned to hunting. Glad the conversation had become less controversial, he found Parson Warren shared his interest in horses. "You must come and see my new mare, Tremain. A truly beautiful creature. Yes, when next you are in Tolpuddle, call on me at the parsonage. I shall be delighted to show you my stables."

Eventually Henry rose to his feet. "Gentlemen, I think we should rejoin the ladies, before they descend on us and drag us out."

As the men entered the drawing room, Maria Ponsonby was still in full spate.

"...one of the cottagers' wives. I make a point of trying to visit any who are sick on the estate. The wife had recently been brought to bed with twins – a difficult birth and the mother still very weak. I instructed the old woman who was caring for her, her mother I believe, on how to make beef-tea. There's nothing so recuperative as beef-tea. Do you not agree?"

The other women murmured agreement.

Maria fingered her elaborate hair arrangement then gestured with open palms. "Both mother and grandmother were respectful and thanked me for the gift of clothing – garments our Sewing Circle make for the poor of the parish – but I sensed a ..." Maria paused a second to find the word she needed. "I sensed a surliness in the attitude of the grandmother, especially when I repeated the instructions for the making of beef-tea. She dipped a curtsey as I left, but as the door closed I heard her say to her daughter, 'Beef-tea! How does she think the likes of us can afford to buy beef.' I am of the opinion the poor have no initiative to help themselves." The ladies sighed and assured each other that things were not as they had been in the past.

Agnes Finchbury looked up as the men joined them, smiled at her husband and before Maria could launch herself into another long-winded spiel, said "I hear you play remarkably well, Mrs. Tremain. Please play something for us." Encouraged by her husband and the others, Abigail Tremain seated herself at the piano.

Chapter Seven

Workhouse 1833

A HEAVINESS IN MY GUT TOLD I IT BODE NO GOOD. A message to present myself at Park House that evening at six. Squire had an arrangement with Master and sometimes, when things was slow, he'd send for my services. For hedgin' and the like. But usually 'twas Master would say that I'd be workin' at Park House for a while. I didst try and convince myself that that be what I were summonsed for, but I couldst not shake the feelin' of unease. Why only that day I'd seen two magpies a sittin' on a fence, and not the once but twice. My Mary would say 'twas a sign of bad luck and most times I would laugh at her, tell her it was just an old wives' superstition. But 'tis three magpies together that tells of good fortune.

So I smartens m'self - clean neckchief an' my moleskin jacket, albeit thirdhand by the time 'twas passed to me an' the nap have mostly worn off so it be threadbare in places – and sets off. 'Tis a goodly walk to Squire's. Just from park gates to the house itself must be half a mile, and a fair old drizzle comin' down. When I gets to the back entrance, I be shown to the kitchen and told to wait.

A girt, big room that kitchen. Two separate, big wooden tables scrubbed white were in the centre. A large black stove and oven on the one wall: an equally large fireplace against another. Further along a dark oak dresser with shelves of plates and dishes; pots of every size hanging from big hooks. Maid-servants scurryin' around as the cook shouted instructions. The boot-boy, arms filled with boots gleaming polish, passed through. The smells! It did make my mouth water. But nought was offered nor a chair to sit on.

Then a footman come and told I to follow him. I kept him close in sight for fear of losing m'self. Turn again into a wider passage, across a hall and then stoppin' at this big carved door whilst the footman knocks and ushers me in.

Squire stands with his legs straddled in front of the fire, his hands tucked under the tails of his coat which be cut away in the front showin' off his high-waisted trousers. Two great hounds lie at his feet. Parson and Master Wainwright be sittin' in high-backed chairs on either side. Comes as a surprise to see Master there for apart from things like a ploughin' match Squire and Wainwright don't mix, Master not belongin' to the same social class as Squire. And what's Parson doing here I asks m'self? My stomach knots and I clutches my hat tight in my hands as I takes some steps towards them.

"Evening, Fielding. I trust you are in good health," says Squire, while Master and Parson just acknowledges me with a nod.

"Evenin' Squire," I replies, takin' in the solemn faces of the three of 'em. I feels even more disquieted and my guts churn.

"Now Fielding," says Squire, "we wish to speak with you. What have you heard about a union being formed by the farm labourers? We've heard rumours of it, so I'm sure you must."

"I've had nought to do with such matters, Sir. I wants no trouble," says I.

"You are saying you've not joined?"

"No, Sir. As I says, I turns away when there be such talk. I just does the task I'm set to and leaves those things to others."

"What talk? What others? That is what we must know before such things get out of hand. Believe us, unionization will bring no good to anyone and must be stamped out."

Master joins in now, askin' for names of those takin' part, and I keeps repeatin' that I knows nothing, but under their questionin' I has to admit that I knows there've been meetings, not during work but in the evenings.

"Aha," says Parson, fixin' I with a look as if he could see into my very soul. "I knew it! Now, speak up man and give us details." It comes to me then. O'course, with Parson's living comes Glebe Farm. Village gossip has it that Farmer Carson, his tenant, be always at odds about how much is due to Parson each year as glebe rights.

Squire glances Parson's way, who silences hisself, though I sees from Parson's face there's much he wishes to say. But Squire be Parson's master so to speak, for 'tis Squire that holds Parson's living.

"We have given this matter much thought, and wish you to join the union, Seth."

"Why wouldst you want that, Sir? I told 'ee I've no wish to join."

"We wish you to join and all that that may mean and report on everything that occurs. We want details of all that takes place."

"But Master will turn I off, " says I, lookin' at Wainwright who's said nothin' for a while.

"That I will not," says Wainwright, "but if you wish to remain in my employ then you will do as we request."

Standin' a feared, I looks at the floor. My hands tear at the brim of my hat. My mind be so tangled with thoughts I feel fair mazed. These be my workmates and friends they wants I to betray.

"You do this, Fielding, and I assure you that not only will you not be dismissed but we will pay you five pounds as a reward." The others nod in agreement, though Master pulls a face at the mention of five pounds.

"Sirs," I says, "Find you someone else to do this, I begs you. You be askin' for somethin' I be feared to do."

"Feared? Of what are you afraid? Your master has assured you, you will not be let go," says Parson, sharp like.

"But you be askin' me to be false to those I lives and works with. They will know 'twas I informed against them."

But they kept pressing. Said I had nothin' to fear. I suggests a couple of other men for 'em to ask, but they insists it be me as joins. What real choice do I have? I knew Master would find reason to turn me off if I refused, and work be hard to find with so many unemployed. No home and Mary due to give birth to another baby shortly. The money would mean we wouldst not have to set Samuel to work. Even, maybe, buy him some milk to strengthen him.

How canst I tell on Loveless and the rest and still live alongside 'em? Why be Master and the others wantin' *me* to do this? I tries again.

"Sirs," I says. "I wants no part of this. I've told 'em no to takin' part an' they'll wonder why I've changed my mind. I be no good at lyin'."

But they keeps badgerin' I, and won't take no for an answer. Feelin' powerless, I finally submits to their demands.

"Good man," says Squire when I agrees. "You'll not regret this, Fielding." He puts his hand in the pocket of his fancy waistcoat and pulls out some coins. "Here now, here's five shillin' as an assurance of our good will. Once we have information from you and can put a stop to this matter, then we shall see you are recompensed for your troubles." He pulls on a fancy bell-rope and a footman comes in. "Take this man to the kitchen," Squire commands, "and see he's given a basket of food to take back to his family. Good night to you, Fielding. You are doing a service to us and your countrymen."

Aye, I be helpin' Squire and the rest, but doing a service to my countrymen? That I knows be not true.

I takes a different path home, slippin' into a coppice of trees out of sight of Park House. In Squire's woods, I takes a couple of snares from m'pocket and sets 'em where I knows game be plentiful. 'Tis not likely the game-keeper will be out, a night like this and this time of the season. Then I shelters neath a sturdy beech and waits.

Crouched with my back to the tree, collar turned up and hat pulled down against the rain, I turns things over in my head. Curses Master and Squire and Parson. I must have stayed there an hour, two maybe.

The rabbit screams as the wire tightens round its neck, its back feet frenziedly scrabblin' in the earth. 'Tis a chillin' sound, the high pitch of a rabbit's scream. I bangs him on the head to put 'un out of his misery, and wishes someone would do the same to I.

Samuel and Tabitha be overjoyed with the fare I brings home from Squire's kitchen, but not a morsel could I force down. My Mary senses my lowness of spirit and does her best to ease the blackness of my mood. But 'tis not until the mornin's small hours, the both of us laying sleepless, that I canst bring m'self to tell her what I be forced to do.

Chapter Eight
Tolpuddle 1834

THE ICE IN THE CART TRACKS CRACKED UNDER HIS BOOTS as he stepped briskly along the rutted lane, sending opaque bubbles of air flitting across the puddles. The temperature had dropped suddenly after Saturday's rain, and now, as Brine, the local constable for the area, entered Tolpuddle village his breath curled out before him. Hoar frost outlined each blade of grass, each twig. It was scarcely daylight. He glanced back at a second constable, a few steps behind him.

"Look sharp, Harding. We needs be there afore they leave for work."

"Who'd a thought we'd have it this cold so late in February," said Harding, banging his hands against his side to warm them making the length of chain he carried on his shoulder jangle. "You think us'll be able to handle six of 'em? That there won't be no trouble?"

"I hear they're all Methodists. Law abidin', Methodies be. 'Tis unlikely they'll be violent."

"If they be so law abidin', how come we be arrestin' 'em?"

"Because we've been ordered to do so, and that's all as concerns us. Now Loveless lives down here. We were told to take him first."

"I'd a thought people would be up and movin' by now, but there's no sign, no smoke from out the chimneys."

"Oh, they'll be up all right. People here abouts burns wood, coal bein' too expensive for 'em, most of 'em bein' employed on the land. They be saving their fuel for later, when they wants to get the evenin' meal ready."

"Aah! I gets your point." Harding ran his tongue round a tooth that was giving him trouble, making a sucking noise. "You said as how there's a James Brine to be picked up today. Be he a relative of yours?"

"None of my kin. 'Tis a common Dorset name as well you know."

Approaching the huddle of cottages, Constable Brine stepped up to the door of the first in the row and rapped on it with his truncheon and then, anxious to get his authority recognized, rapped again. The door was pulled open by Elizabeth Loveless, clutching a shawl around her; her hair uncombed, her feet hastily thrust into a pair of old shoes. She looked at the two uniformed constables with dismay.

"Husband," she called. "George, come quick!"

Elizabeth stepped back as George came to the doorway, one arm inserted in his jacket, still chewing on the last mouthful of bread. He allowed no emotion to show on his face as he viewed Brine and Harding. My unease was justified then he told himself.

"Constable. What is it you want?" He extended his shirt-sleeved arm across the doorway to block their entry.

"I have a warrant for you, from the magistrates."

"What is its contents, sir?"

"Take it yourself, you can read it as well as I can," replied Brine, unwilling to show his lack of scholarship before Harding.

George studied the document with care in order to gain time, his mind racing to grasp its implications. A muffled cry escaped from Elizabeth as George then read out loud the charge of administrating an unlawful oath, while Sarah, clutching the baby, tugged at her mother's arm. "What is it, Mother? What's happening?

George put an arm around Elizabeth's shoulders. "Tis all right, wife. I've told you many times we have been doing nothing wrong." He turned to Brine. "This is a grave mistake you're making, Constable."

"Mistake or no, I have orders for your arrest. Will you come quietly to the magistrates with me?"

"To any place wherever you wish me that we may get this matter put right. Don't fret, Elizabeth. All will be straightened out shortly. Give me a moment, Constable, for I have not yet readied myself for work."

And Ordered Their Estate

Brine nodded his head, relieved that there was to be no argument. George walked over to the fireplace, retrieved his hat and a thick knitted scarf that Elizabeth, with shaking hands, took from her husband and placed around his neck.

"You'd best send Mathew along to Wainwrights to say I'll be delayed awhile. I'm sure this matter can soon be sorted out, though it means a day's lost wages," George said with more assurance than he felt. The warning notices had been posted on Saturday, and here was Constable Brine with a warrant this early on Monday. It was likely signed by the magistrate on Friday. Why then put up the posters? And this mention of *unlawful oaths* again. If only he had more knowledge of what the wording meant.

"Where're you taking my man? Is he the only one you're taking?" Elizabeth asked of Brine, inserting her body between that of her husband's and the constable's.

"There are others." Brine turned to Harding. "Now let's be moving on. The Standfields live in this row of cottages too."

Dinniah Standfield's screams rang sharply in the cold air. She clutched wildly at Thomas' coat as he was led away, causing Harding to grab her arm and push her off roughly. She collapsed on her knees sobbing. The sound of her cries, strange voices and unusual activity at such an early hour brought the rest of the cottagers and their children to their doors. Ignoring the fact that she was not yet properly dressed, Elizabeth ran to help Dinniah up and, circled in each other's arms, they wept together - Elizabeth, quietly, for her husband, Dinniah, with noisy, gasping sobs, for a husband and brother and, she feared, a son. Circled by her crying children, Elizabeth gently guided Dinniah back into her home, while the village folk stood in doorways or in the lane watching and muttering, sullen and helpless as George and Thomas were led away.

A stream of curious children followed, cautiously distancing themselves slightly from the men. The constables made their rounds of the village, arresting James Loveless, John Standfield, James Hammett and finally James Brine. Urged on by Constable Brine, Harding had each man remove their left arm from their jacket while he slid a length of strong chain down the empty sleeve before the prisoners inserted their arms once again. Linked to each other by the chain, the eight men led

47

by Constable Brine and with Harding at the rear set off on the long trek to Dorchester.

Several times George tried to get the constable to discuss the charges against them, demanding to know what was meant by the wording on the arrest warrant. Finally, his voice charged with anger, Constable Brine ordered George to hold his breath. "Save your questions for the magistrate once we get you to Dorchester."

"Can'st us pause for a moment, I need to relieve myself?" called out John Standfield to Constable Brine at the head of the line. They had been walking steadily without stopping since leaving Tolpuddle. Apart from an occasional muttered comment from one to the other, each was locked in his own turmoiled thoughts. Little had passed between the men lest either of the constables overheard.

"Ay, I reckon we all needs a piss," responded Constable Brine. Although he doubted that any of his prisoners would try to escape, still he was reluctant to take a chance. "You can manage as you are. There's no point wasting time undoing your chains." The eight men faced the hedgerow and the hiss of urine spraying the frozen grass accompanied the clink of chains as each fumbled with his clothing.

Reaching Dorchester, they turned in a direction opposite to that which George had anticipated. "The gaol lies to the right of us, not left," he whispered to Thomas. To Constable Brine he called, "Where're you taking us?"

The constable didn't respond for a moment. The confidence of George's bearing, his learning, had an intimidating effect on him. To impress Harding as much as his prisoners, he put all the authority he could into his reply. "Where I was instructed, to Mr. Wollaston, the Recorder for Dorchester."

Jostling on each other's heels as they were crowded into the library, they were not only confronted by Wollaston, but also by Magistrate Frampton. The severity of Charles Wollaston's expression was outdone by the angry loathing on Frampton's. A silence, broken by the men's shuffling feet as they ringed themselves behind George, continued for several minutes while Frampton and George stared each other down.

And Ordered Their Estate

Finally Frampton spoke, his voice harsh. "The Constable will have read the charge to you when you were taken, is that not so?" Allowing no time for response, he barked, Well, what've you to say for yourselves."

"We are unaware that we have broken any law, " replied George on behalf of them all.

"But we have witnesses that you administered an illegal oath," said Frampton.

"We are all law-abiding citizens and know nothing of oaths, legal or illegal. I would further question how one differentiates between the two?"

"I ask the questions not you," thundered Frampton. "Law-abiding. Bah! Bring in the witness," ordered Frampton nodding to Wollaston who left the room and returned with Seth Fielding.

Head bowed, refusing to look at anyone, although George kept his eyes steadily on him, Seth reluctantly and with much hesitation responded to the questions put to him. Frampton's bullying tones finally forced from Seth's lips an acknowledgement that George, Thomas and the others had been present when he was inducted into the union.

"And you were forced to swear an oath. Correct?"

"The only forcing' come from Squire, Parson and my master."

"But you were made to swear an oath?"

"An oath, Sir? I just had to kiss the Bible and repeat some words after 'em."

"An oath, man."

"I knows not what an oath be, Sir. I knows I ent done nothing but what Squire and the others told I to do."

"But you have just testified that you swore on the Bible."

"But that were to seal a promise I made. It weren't no swearin' an oath, whatever that be."

Eventually Seth was let go and the two constables instructed to take the tired and hungry prisoners on to Dorchester Gaol.

Chapter Nine

Workhouse 1842

THE DOCTOR COME AGAIN THIS MORNIN'. STOOD BESIDE my bed and took my wrist in his hand. Even openin' my eyes were too much effort so I didn't see the expression on his face as he says to the overseer, "This man will be dead before the day's out. I'll sign the certificate now and you can fill in the time as appropriate. It's not worth my making a second visit today for that."

Sometimes I can be a stubborn old sod, and I says to m'self, "You hang in there, Seth. You show 'un. I'll prove 'ee wrong."

They lets my Mary visit more frequent of late. When she last come she could see somethin' were botherin' I. I managed the strength to whisper to her, "They took the apple you give I. They took it from me."

"Don't 'ee fret, Seth, my lovey. I'll find 'ee another," Mary promised, but I've worried since where she'll get one from. I'm a feared for her gettin' into trouble. 'Tis just I likes to linger on the scent, the feel of an apple's smoothness. It brings back powerful memories of when times was happier for her and me.

My mind wanders all over the place, from one thought to another - all disconnected - just flitterin' images. Like when our Samuel took his first steps, and he would totter after me as I went about my business. And my Mary, heavy with the twins, standin' in the doorway laughin' at the pair of us. "Don't 'ee lose 'un in the long grass mind," she would call, for that June the grass among the apple trees reached up over Samuel's head. It were a pretty sight.

The twins were born early - one stillborn and the other dyin' in a matter of days. I be certain sure Mary walkin' to Affpuddle to help with the layin'-out of her father brought on their birthin'. But 'tis not for me to voice such thoughts for Mary be terr'ble cut-up about their loss. Parson Warren wanted money for two burials in spite of the fact there be just the one small coffin. But I refused and when others in the parish voiced complaints, he backed down. It ent often that we be able to stand up to them as be placed in a position above us.

'It ent as if I didn't try to stand up to 'em when Squire and Master and Parson forced I into betrayin' Loveless and Standfield, but they would have none of it. I never done it for the money as some think. There was no way out for I. 'Twas not done willingly. And then they *arrested* 'em. I figured they might get set off from their work and have to seek employment elsewhere. As I saw it, them bein' known for their hard-workin' ways and George for his ploughin', they'd be taken on elsewhere for certain sure. I be fair stunned when word cum they be arrested and taken to Dorchester Gaol.

Spat at me she did, Mistress Loveless. Caught me full face and afore I could raise my sleeve to wipe her gob away she had slammed the door shut. Being so torn up with what had happened to her man, I'd walked over to try and explain that I'd been forced into betrayin' him, and I brung over the last piece of the pig to help her feed her young 'uns - a bit of smoked bacon. But I could scarce blame her for actin' thus.

It seemed a long walk home, and the bacon - it were naught but a small piece that Mary had packaged up - seemed heavier with each step I took. I've not been able to abide the smell o' pork since.

It were just a runty little thing. Master's sow had farrowed late, birthin' fourteen. Master said it were a record, fourteen! One were dead already and this other little 'un Master threw by its hind leg onto the manure I had just shoveled into a pile.

"No point in keepin' it. It won't see the day out," says Master. "She'll have her work cut out feedin' the rest of 'em."

Later that day when I goes to move the pile, there be that piglet still breathin'. The warmth from the dung must've kep' it goin'. Well, says I to m'self, it've put up a good fight. Master's chucked it away. I'll take it back to Little Tabby. It'll pleasure her tryin' to keep it alive. And, bless me, if it didn't live!

Us made it a pen alongside the cottage when it got bigger, and it grew a fair treat on the skimmed milk I sneaked from the farm that were meant to be fed to Master's sow. It would never be more than a runt, mind, and its back leg grew all crooked, but it would mean meat on the table come winter. The end of October, when there were naught else to give it but the acorns the children gathered, us slaughtered it. Joe, my brother-in-law, helped with the butcherin'. Nothin' us could do would console Tabby, but as us told her all along, over and over, that us has to eat, and the pig were a luxury that weren't likely to come our way again.

Now how did my mind get on to pigs? Aah, I was thinkin' of apples and my Mary. The children used to gather the droppers from the tree and those that Mary couldn't even use for cookin', were fed to the pig. My mind do wander so.

My Mary've been a great comfort. Try hard, she did, to ease the situation with the other cottagers. Done her best to try and explain to 'em that Squire, Parson and Master had forced I into it. But none would listen. They'd turn their backs on her and some'd even call out "Judas" when I be passin'.

It were the same day as they were all arrested that I were taken to Dorchester, to Mr. Wollaston's house. When the constable came for I, I were fair terrified. Thought I was being arrested too. I were led into this big room with shelves of books all around it. I ent never seen so much learnin' all in one place. George and the others stood chained together, alongside the two constables. I could'st not look any of 'em in the face, though I felt George's eyes boring through me.

"Can you identify these men as those who carried out the initiation ceremony of the Friendly Society of Agricultural Labourers?"

"I don't understand the question you be askin'," says I, trying to avoid answering. All Squire and Parson asked me to do was tell 'em about the union. They had said nothin' about my havin' to testify against 'em.

"Were these the men that had you swear an oath when joining the union?"

"An oath? There were no foul language used."

"Answer the question, man. Were these the men present?"

"T'were dark in the room. 'Twould be difficult to say who was there. Besides I were blindfolded."

"Then how did you know the room was dark?"

Well, they'd caught I out there. I did my damnedest to not give 'em the answer they was after, but eventually they had I trapped by their clever questions and I had to admit that George and the rest had been there and they had I repeat some words after 'em.

It were a terrible time, and all the while our Samuel were gettin' sicker.

Chapter Ten

Dorchester 1834

"WHAT DAY BE IT? I'VE LOST COUNT." CROUCHED IN A corner, his head pressing on his knees, Hammett's question seemed to be addressed to himself rather than the others in the crowded cell.

It was John who replied. "Must be Saturday. Yes, 'tis Saturday."

Hammett, struggling to his feet, massaged his back with his hands. "You were so sure things would be set right the same day, George. Now near a week's gone by."

"I never contemplated it would come to this." George Loveless stood with his back turned to the other five men. Angled forward, arms outstretched and hands pressed against the wall under the high, barred windows, he gave his head a shake as if to clear his thoughts. "I'm heartily sorry that I've brought you all to such a state." He struck the stone wall with the palm of his hand and turned to face the others. "I still have difficulty believing that Magistrate Frampton did not accept that right was on our side." Incredulity and anger deepened his voice. He moved over to Hammett and placed a hand on his shoulder. "Like you, we are all concerned about how our families will manage."

"'Tis not you I be blamin', George, but worry about Harriet is tearin' at me. I think of naught else. With only her mother for assistance and the babe not two months old."

Returning to his position under the window, George quoted, "Behold I cry out of wrong, but I am not heard. I cry aloud, but there is no judgement..."

Thomas raised his head. "The Book of Job. You think that God is testing us as he tested Job?"

"No, not God. We're the victims of Whiggery. It is the Whig politicians, the landowners who are the authors of our misfortune." The words *whiggery* and *landowners* exploded from George's mouth, the pitch of his voice rose. "It's man's inhumanity to man that's responsible for our being here."

Seated in a corner, his arms folded around raised knees, James Loveless spoke, his deeply timbered voice accentuated by the stone walls. "The responsibility's not yours alone, brother. I ... we all felt our cause was right; were as set as you on starting a Friendly Society."

Suddenly Brine started kicking at the wall again and again. "That soddin' Fielding. If I ever gets my hands on him I'll pull his head off like he were a chicken bein' readied for the pot." Hammet roused from his stupor quickly stood up as Brine leapt and grasped at the bars across the window as if he'd wrench them from the brickwork. Dropping to the floor he turned his fury on the slop bucket, sending it and its contents flying with his boot. "I'll kick his head in, the bloody traitor. I'll ..."

"Steady now, steady," urged John as he and George attempted to grab him.

"Brine, for the love of God, what's got into you?" said George pinning him against the wall. "Easy, man. You'll do yourself harm."

With George and John holding him firmly, Brine's raging gradually subsided. Between gasps for breath he sobbed out, "I could'st kill 'un... that he could betray us, his friends. How could a man... ?" His voice trailed away.

Brine's explosion of rage had taken them all by surprise. The Brine they knew, thoughtful, questing for knowledge, eager to debate an issue, had never shown this side of himself before.

"That he was forced into it there is no question." said Thomas. "Not that I'm excusing Fielding for what he did."

"Dear God, look at the mess, and we've to sleep on that floor tonight," said James Loveless. "You think they'll give us a broom, some water, to clean it up, if us asks?"

"When we've had nothing to wash ourselves with since coming here?" said John looking at the floor fouled with the bucket's contents. "There ent a chance."

During the six days of their imprisonment they had endlessly discussed the situation. As each day passed, anger at the injustice of being arrested had been overcome by apprehension about their fate, and concern for their families. That there might not be an end to this nightmare now ruled their thoughts. George's mind returned again and again to their arrival at Dorchester Gaol.

The weak sunshine could not soften the sight of the high walls of grey granite, topped with metal spikes. Huge metal doors were opened to allow the six men accompanied by two constables through and then swung shut again with an ominous clang.

They were led through a narrow hallway, another iron door was unlocked and re-locked as they passed through. Doors with a narrow slot at eye level lined either side of a corridor that allowed little room for movement, at the end of which was a large room with low, wooden benches set against each wall.

Dressed in black serge uniforms and heavy boots, four warders greeted them, each with a truncheon held in readiness should any prisoner challenge their authority.

"Take off all your clothes," ordered one of the gaolers. "Be quick about it."

"We do not deserve to be treated like common felons. We've broken no law." George Loveless responded in a firm voice. The gaoler made a motion to one of the other warders who stepped closer to George in a threatening attitude. Without further protest George and the others stripped, self-consciously turning their backs on each other, which caused ribald remarks from some of the warders.

The blunt razor ripped at George's scalp. As he flinched, the warder's fingers tightened on the back of George's neck. "Hold hard or you'll lose an ear," he warned. Clumps of dark hair fell to the floor. "That'll do. You,

you're next," he said giving George a shove to indicate he should move so that Thomas could take his seat.

"What have we here?" asked the warder given the task of searching their discarded clothes. He held the warning notice that George had removed, together with the letter from the head of the Friendly Society, and a key.

"What's this key for?"

"Am I not allowed to own a key?" responded George.

"When I asks a question I expects an answer."

"And I will answer no such questions unless they are put to me by a magistrate." His reply brought a rain of heavy blows on his back and shoulders, but George refused to give any information about the key.

"Why would you not say what it was for?" asked Thomas later, when the six of them were locked in a room together.

"It's for the box I keep our subscription records, union rules and so forth. 'Tis to be hoped it does not fall into their hands."

The gaoler's heavy bunch of keys jangled as he unlocked the door and ordered them to make ready and follow him.

"Make ready! We have seen naught of water to cleanse ourselves with since we came."

"You want short rations? " This silenced Thomas, for what food they had been given was of such poor quality, the bread hard, the cheese mouldy, what passed for soup little more than a thin gruel, that risking less could not be contemplated.

"Do you think they be letting us go?" Hammet asked quietly of Thomas.

"Shut your mouths and get a move on," snarled the gaoler, leading them along corridors to another part of the prison.

~~~

A shaft of sunlight danced a pattern on the table, flecked Dinniah's cheek as she sat with her arm propped against the wooden surface, her hand cupping her forehead. As if of its own volition, her other hand traced the table's contours, the nicks and gouges from years of use. Her bout of crying now reduced to hiccups and deep intakes of breath. Elizabeth stood behind her, hands resting gently on Dinniah's shoulders.

"Tis all turning out as I feared," Dinniah snuffled. "Why didn't they heed me? Oh, Thomas, Thomas."

"We've both slept scarce at all since they were took, but carryin' on like this'll get us nowhere, Dinny. We must do somethin'."

"Do! What can us do?"

"I've been thinkin' on it all night long. It's over two weeks now. We knew when we went to Parson for news, there was little chance of him answering our questions, even if he could."

"That man don't know the meanin' of compassion!"

Elizabeth's mouth tightened. "Right unchristian is the term I'd use for him." She pressed more firmly on Dinniah's shoulders. "Dorchester. That's where we're more like to find answers." Stepping back, holding her body more erect, she announced, " It's a fair step, but if I leave now, noon should see me there."

Dinniah, startled by the determination in Elizabeth's voice, swung herself round to face Elizabeth. "Dorchester? She echoed.

As if fearing Dinniah might try to weaken her resolve, Elizabeth moved briskly to where a pair of low-cut black boots stood neatly in the corner of the room beneath a couple of pegs from which hung an assortment of clothing. Over her shoulder, as she picked up the boots, she asked, "You'll watch out for the young 'uns, Dinnie?"

Dinniah's eyes followed Elizabeth's movement, took in Elizabeth's determination as Elizabeth, seating herself on the bench end across from her sister-in-law, began to pull on the well-worn footwear.

"You'm right, Lizzie. That's were us'll get more news." Dinniah pushed herself up from the table. "But you ent goin' alone." She wiped at her eyes with her sleeve. Sniffed hard. "Wait while I gets my things. I'm goin' with you." With an automatic gesture she tucked a strand of graying hair under her white cap. She patted Elizabeth's hand. "Alice'll keep an eye on the young 'uns for us."

~~~

The six men stood arraigned before a bench of magistrates. Frampton they recognized, but the other two were unfamiliar. Seth Fielding was once again brought in to give evidence about the meeting held at Standfield's cottage. His hands clasping the finger-worn brim of his hat were never still.

Seth's reluctant testimony differed from that of five days before. Several times Frampton angrily reminded Seth that he was under oath. To most of the questions put to him he replied, "I ent sure on that point, Sir" or "My memory be bad and I canst not swear that what you say be true," his voice so subdued he was repeatedly instructed to speak more loudly. Not once did he raise his eyes and look at his questioners, nor would he make eye contact with any of the prisoners.

"He's right terrified," whispered John Standfield to his father.

"Silence! This is a court of law," ordered Frampton, glaring in the Standfields' direction.

By the time Seth was dismissed from the stand the wad of black felt in his hands no longer resembled a hat. There was a low, brief conversation between the magistrates, then Frampton, striking the bench with a small gavel, spoke again. "We find sufficient evidence to commit all the prisoners for trial at the next Assizes in March. Take them away!"

"George Loveless, step forward," ordered the gaoler a few days later. George rose to his feet and approached him.

"Follow me."

"Where are you taking me?"

"There's a solicitor to speak with you."

"With me? On whose instructions?"

"Best ask him y'self."

The gaoler led George along a corridor and up some steps. He thrust open a door and stood back so that George could enter. A man dressed all in black except for a white stock at his neck sat at a table. His hands, loosely clasped in front of him, held a lace handkerchief. He turned his head at George's entry and immediately raised the handkerchief to his nose, his facial expression indicating that he found George's odour offensive. He studied George in silence, giving no indication by word or gesture that George should take the seat opposite him. Finally he spoke.

"George Loveless?"

"That's my name."

"I have been instructed to make you the following offer."

"How do you mean, an offer?"

"I have it on the highest authority that if you will give your word to have nothing more to do with unions and will tell the magistrates all that you know of their formation and plans in the area, you will be allowed to return home immediately to your wife and children."

"I don't understand what it is you're saying, Sir."

"It's simple enough, Loveless. If you will turn King's evidence, give full details of all that has transpired regarding the formation of your union, then you will be allowed to go free."

"You mean, betray my companions?"

"Betray! Hardly. You are being asked to tell all you know about what went on in return for your freedom."

"Then Sir, betrayal is the correct term for such a suggestion."

"I am not here to argue terminology, but to lay out before you the offer that is being made."

"It is a monstrous suggestion. We've done nothing illegal, and to suggest that I should be so disloyal to my friends is infamous. I have nothing further to say on the matter."

With a shake of his head the solicitor rose quickly, glad the prisoner's refusal to accept his terms had not protracted the interview and he could escape to fresh air. He banged loudly on the door to attract the guard's attention and George was taken back to his cell.

Would such an offer be made to the others, contemplated George? No one else had been removed from the room they were being held in. He was filled with uncertainty. Were the authorities working on the principle of divide and conquer? If any of the others were approached: would they weaken? He was certain that Thomas and John would stand firm, as would his brother. He felt confident about Brine too. But Hammett? Unable to think on anything but his wife and baby, could Hammett be relied on? Should he talk it over with the others?

"In the name of Heaven, stop pacing like that. It's enough to drive a man crazy," James said, quickly drawing his legs away from George's feet. "It's that solicitor fellow who sent for you, isn't it? Were his views like those of the chaplain?"

They'd had only one visitor since they had been imprisoned, the prison chaplain, who had made it plain that he considered them to be a discontented, idle set of men, set on trying to ruin their masters. "Ruin our masters! All we were doing was striving to live honestly, to improve conditions for ourselves," but the chaplain would not listen to George's response.

"No, the solicitor brought me a different message." George stood still. He massaged his forehead with his fingertips and began to tell of what had passed between him and the solicitor. To George's surprise Hammett spoke up quickly, agreeing with Thomas' comment that George had made the only honourable response possible to the solicitor's offer. "They be testin' us, George, tryin' to break us, and I thank 'ee for standing up to 'em."

~~~

Sunk in despondency Elizabeth and Dinniah were oblivious to the evening's chill. For the last few miles no words had been exchanged between them. Treated with disdain when enquiring at the Magistrate's office, curtly directed by a clerk at County Hall to the prison, begging for information at Dorchester Gaol: all they had learned was their menfolk were awaiting trial, that they wouldn't be allowed to see them but they could leave money for the purchase of food.

"As if we had any to leave! If we had I think it would be more like to end up in the gaoler's pocket," Elizabeth said. "Taking some food, bread, cheese, would seem a better idea."

Dispiritedly, all Dinniah could reply was that with no money coming in, they couldn't even feed themselves.

""We must pray, Dinniah. Pray hard."

Chapter Eleven
Workhouse 1842

I BE THINKING ON HOW MARY HAD TO BEG TO GET US admitted to this place. Yes, beggin' the gate-keeper to let us in, while all I could do was lean against them great gates for support, I were so weak. Them as is on the workhouse Board of Governors make certain sure none but the really destitute be allowed in. See, 'tis landowners and the like as has to pay a sort of tax towards the cost of runnin' the place, though I ent sure of all the details. By keepin' down the number as is admitted, they don't have to put their hands in their pockets so deep. But bein' as how I were born in Tolpuddle an' lived there all my life, I couldst claim what were known as *settlement* and so were entitled to admittance. You has to have lived in a parish for more'en a year. Many as is destitute be forced to travel great distances back to where they was born afore they be taken in, no matter how much they begs.

Beggin'. It were Mary as well as I the villagers shunned. No longer did they give a call of welcome, but, as her be passin' by, they'd turn their backs and talk louder between themselves. About things like Elizabeth Loveless and Dinniah Standfield havin' to walk to Dorchester to beg for news of their husbands. Or as how Elizabeth and Dinniah would soon be forced to beg for charity. Poor Mary. Cut her to the quick, it did, for she be such a friendly being and loves to stop an' chat with the other women.

Them as worked alongside me at Wainwright's turned their backs on I as well and did all they could to make things difficult. Took to hiding the tools so as I couldn't find 'em. I'd go to muck out the cowshed and the pitchfork be missin' or the wheelbarrer's wheel be loose. 'Cos when Wainwright comes yellin' at me for bein' behindhand with my work and I tries to explain, there be the pitchfork propped against the wall. The wheel of the barrer be suddenly back in its socket. And I saw Jim Coldmar strike the young lad as helps with the horses across the ear for saying 'good mornin'' to I. I dreaded goin' to work of a mornin' but, o'course, I had to go.

'Tis only us as be in the hospital ward as gets night-shirts, but they be of such coarse cloth 'tis as if they be made out of sackin'. I ent never been of any size even afore I were took so sick and this night-shirt be far too big. 'Tis always slipping off one of my shoulders and gets all rucked up under me. Chafes on my hip bone. When I can't stand the rubbin' no more, I tries to pull it up away from the sore spot forming there. Then my feet be froze, for any warmth the one blanket us be given may have had be long worn away. Icy feet or hip chafed raw – 'tis a choice I be too weak to make.

Raw ... Carrots ... Raw carrots, them small new 'uns you pull to thin out the row in early summer. Rub 'em against yer sleeve to get off the loose soil, and then that first crunch! 'Tis like bitin' into heaven. Mary allus tried to keep a pot simmerin' over the fire in the cold months, addin' this and that, whatever be to hand – carrots, taters. But often times, come the winter months, there were nothin' but turnips and a handful of oats to thicken the gruel a little, not even a scrawny squab to give a little flavour. Samuel were a dab hand at climbing up to pigeons' nests and takin' their young. I recalls how once us teased him when he come home with his shirt so stuffed with young squabs, he looked like a woman with tits full o'milk.

'Cos it were some years after the government changed the Poor Law that Mary and me come here to the Workhouse. Though us as lives round abouts still calls 'em workhouses, them changes government folks made, orderin' parishes and townships to unite and do away with the parish workhouses as had existed for years and build big new 'uns that took in the poor for miles around, they named 'em Union-houses. Same time as they done this, they stops payin' what were known as outdoor relief, like what Loveless's wife and Standfield's wife went askin' for and were denied when their husbands were first took.

It were Martha's husband hearin' as how Wainwright were evictin' Mary an' me, whispered to Mary that his employer were sendin' him out Dorchester way with the cart to fetch some machinery for the mill, and he'd give us a lift to the workhouse. It were a kindly gesture on his part, for I were scarce able to stand on my own by then, and could never have walked the distance, that's for certain sure. We give what little us had to Martha, knowin' us couldn't take it with us. So when, true to his word, he come by early on the Thursday mornin', Mary and me were waitin' with just a small bundle of things that meant a lot to Mary, like the red vase I give her some time back, tied up in an old shirt. He'd even spread some hay in the cart for I to lie on. He dropped us off some ways from the workhouse, for to gain admittance it were a rule that a person had to make his own way there. Them in charge, you see, had visions of authorities from other places roundin' up all them as they considered destitute and dumpin' 'em on the doorstep of another parish. Took us hours to walk that last mile for I couldst only walk a few yards afore I had to rest. Almost carry me, Mary had to, at the end. When us were at last admitted, them buggers took Mary's few keepsakes. Wouldn't let her keep nothin'.

When I thinks back to the miles I've walked since I took my first staggerin' steps as a babe … Why, I were only five when I were hired out to walk after the plough stone-pickin'. Walkin' the furrows, draggin' a sack. Mid-day, while the men ate the food their wives had packed for 'em, I were curled up under the hedgerow sleepin', too tired to eat.

All us country folk has good, sturdy legs. Ten mile were nothin' to us. It were the only way us had to get around. That time though, when I has to give evidence at Dorchester, now that were different. Them seven mile to Dorchester and back seemed like every mile were ten times its length, and when I got back home my feet were all swolled up as if it were a hundred miles they'd trod.

That first time I has to go to Mr. Wollaston's house in Dorchester, the worry as to why I be ordered to go there had me gettin' scarce any sleep the night afore and feelin' too sick to eat anything in the mornin'. I couldn't stop shaking. It were fear as much as the bitter cold mornin'. "Where be that, Wollaston's house?" I asks, knowing little about Dorchester but the big market square in the centre.

"Turn to the left off the main road just afore you gets to the town. Keep walkin' a ways and then you'll see some big houses. Look for the one with big, tall chimneys. You can't miss it."

Well he were right about that. Huge chimneys all patterned about with clever brickwork so that it looks as if were brick vines twistin' round the pot. It were right skillful. Any other time I'd 'ave liked to spend time studyin' them pots, but I were too nervous and scared of bein' late to linger.

There, now my mind be set on chimneys again, and when I thinks on chimneys my thoughts always turns to that tale of that little lad lost in flues leadin' from one chimney-breast to another. I tells m'self, as I've done many a time, that it's like to be an old wife's tale. But it do tear at me, the pictures that come into my head of that poor child sobbin' and callin' for help. Tries to give m'self comfort that at least it weren't my Samuel or little Will. No, there can't be truth in it. They'd 'ave sent another lad up there with a rope around his middle to find the first 'un. 'Cos they would. Wouldn't they?

Chapter Twelve
Dorchester 1834

SATURDAY, MARCH 15TH, DAWNED DULL AND OVERCAST. Chained to each other the six men were led from Dorchester Gaol to the County Hall and installed in cells beneath the Crown Court. Smoke from a smouldering fire in the Head Gaoler's room, channelled down a narrow passageway lined with cells on either side, made the prisoners cough. It crept under the locked cell doors, catching at their throats. The cells, only a few feet in depth, the walls running with damp, and with no windows, light or heat, were like black boxes. George had slept little all night. It was not only worry about the outcome of their trial that had robbed him of rest but he, who couldn't recall ever having been sick, had been unable to stop coughing. Now he found his chest hurt and he had difficulty breathing.

The court room hummed with conversation, people jostling for the last few seats. Soon there would only be standing room at the back.

William Ponsonby, stood towering above the crowds, turning his long neck this way and that for signs of his friend. Aah, there he was at last.

"Finchbury," he called, waving his arm, oblivious to the fact that he had narrowly missed knocking off someone's hat. "Finchbury, thought I'd see you here."

"G'day, Ponsonby. Yes, I wished to see this matter through." Henry, in the act of extending his hand to Ponsonby, was forced to step back as people pushed their way past. "The crowds, and on a Monday, too! This court room will never hold such numbers."

"Come," said Ponsonby, laying his hand on Henry's arm. "I was here Saturday, sitting as a member of the grand jury to rule this case go to trial. I had the forethought to speak to a court official and he's holding seats for me. We'll sit together."

"This trial's sparked everyone's interest. I didn't anticipate such numbers."

As the two men moved towards the front, heads were nodded in their direction, hats raised, greetings exchanged. "Good day to you Squire, Mr. Ponsonby."

"Did you read the article in the *Dorset Chronicle*?" asked Henry. "The so called laws of their Friendly Society?"

"Ay, I did. I had to agree with the writer about the twin dangers of revolution and trade unionism. And there was much the same comment in the *Journal*. But the London papers are lax in support of our cause."

Once the last few spaces at the back were taken, the heavy oak doors to the court room were closed. Ponsonby, nodding in the direction of the jury box, said. "I understand there are many land-renters in the jury."

"Well, they'll be as much interested as we land-owners are, in seeing unions don't get a hold."

The court rose as the judge, Mr. Baron Williams, entered, and then the prisoners were led in. Pale and unkempt, James and John looked around them; Loveless and Standfield stared straight ahead while Brine and Hammett kept their heads lowered. Ponsonby removed a handkerchief from his pocket and held it to his nose in an attempt to exclude the strong body odours of the prisoners.

The charge against the six men was read out: "...That they feloniously and unlawfully did administer and cause to be administered unto one Seth Fielding a certain oath, binding said Seth Fielding not to inform or give evidence against any associate or other person..."

Making no attempt to hide his strong bias against the prisoners, Judge Williams addressed the court. "Men joining the union were *compelled* by the force of the oath they were taking to pay *large* subscriptions and contributions from their scanty means." Ponsonby nodded his head in approval.

"That ent true," shouted James Loveless from the prisoner's box.

"Silence," the judge ordered. "Silence!" banging with his gavel for emphasis.

"Can they conduct their own defence?" whispered Henry.

Ponsonby, not bothering to lower his voice answered, "Aye, if they wish to or, for that matter, know how – cross examine witnesses, make speeches on their own behalf. But they mayn't give sworn evidence in their own defence, and as I've said, most have no knowledge how to go about such things."

Henry found the prosecutor's opening remarks long-winded and complex. The heat from so many bodies packed into a courtroom built to hold only a third of the number present was oppressive. He pulled at his cravat and leaned forward, plump chin cupped in his hands, intent on grasping the implications of the prosecutor's argument. The onlookers' noise was distracting. Many were talking to each other, their whispers becoming louder. Others acknowledged friends sitting across from them; some, who had had a long journey beforehand, were eating food they had brought with them. Several times the judge had to call for order.

"Let's get on with things," muttered Ponsonby, more to himself than for Henry's hearing, continuously trying to find ease for his long legs in the cramped space.

Studying Seth's face as he entered the witness box, Henry noted his almost palpable fear. His voice when he took the oath was scarcely audible. Henry whispered his concern to Ponsonby that Seth's testimony was being twisted, that words were being put in his mouth. "As long as he's believed, that's all that matters," was Ponsonby's response.

A Mr. Whetham took the stand. He testified that James Loveless had asked him to make a painting of Death and that he had refused, wanting nothing to do with such a commission.

The final witness for the prosecution was the gaoler who gave evidence that a key and a letter had been found in Loveless's pocket, and that the key was later found to fit a box containing a letter about election of the lodge committee, rules and regulations of the Society and a list of contributions, stored in a cupboard at the cottage.

"Well, that's damning enough," Ponsonby commented to Henry in low tones. "Nothing further needs to be said."

As the trial proceeded, Henry Finchbury felt a profound sense of unease. He told himself that he knew little enough of court proceedings, that he was ignorant in matters of law, but he was unable to rid himself of the idea that what he was witnessing was not justice. All those taking part in the proceedings, particularly Judge Williams, made no attempt to hide the prejudice they bore towards the prisoners.

"I must say that the defence counsel provided for the prisoners seems totally lacking in any legal skills," he commented to Ponsonby, putting some of his concern into words. Ponsonby's response was a dismissive grunt.

Finally Judge Williams asked the prisoners if they had anything they wished to say. George Loveless, prepared for this moment, stood up, saying he had a written statement on behalf of them all.

"Do you wish your remarks to be read to the court?"

"I do, my Lord."

Henry cupped a hand around an ear, for the judge read George's statement in such a low voice, his words were audible only to those sitting close by.

> "My Lord, if we have violated any law, it was not done intentionally; we have injured no man's reputation, character, person or property; we were uniting together to preserve ourselves, our wives and our children, from utter degradation and starvation. We challenge any man, or number of men, to prove we have acted, or intended to act, different from the above statement."

"Dammit, it should at least be read so all can hear," said Henry, by this time thoroughly disquieted.

With a dismissive gesture, Ponsonby responded, "It's of no consequence. All of us present know they're guilty."

Henry turned away from his friend. This was a travesty of justice they were witnessing. He shook his head as if to clear it of the disturbing agitation he felt.

It took but twenty minutes for the jury to find all six guilty as charged.

Chapter Thirteen

Workhouse 1842

WELL, I CAUGHT 'UN! FAIR SURPRISED 'E WAS, THE DOCTOR, to find I still be breathin' when he come next. But as I said, I can be stubborn old bugger at times. Breathin'. That's about all I can manage. M' lungs makin' shallow gasps, with longer and longer periods between each fought-for breath. Only my mind be active now, dartin' from one thing to another and no connection seemingly between each thought. And a terr'ble thirst from the fever that burns within. What I wouldn't give for a tankard of ale.

Or cider. I thinks cider be my favourite – its very smell holds memories of September fruit layin' in the grass, all dew covered. And cobwebs stretched between yellowed stalks.

There were none as would drink with me once Loveless and the others were took.

Three times I had to make that walk to Dorchester, and the courthouse were on the furthest side of the town. So it were more like sixteen miles, there and back. Three times I had to stand afore Standfield, Loveless and the others while I was made to give evidence against 'em.

That last time, when they was on trial before the jury, when they led 'em into the prisoner's box, it was beyond belief how rough they looked. Unwashed, pale, and smellin' somethin' foul. Their hair lookin' as if it'd been hacked at with a hedgin' knife. And George racked with coughin'.

They didn't stand a chance. It were obvious all were against 'em.

Squire were there and that tall, thin friend of his, him as owns a spread of land in Bere. What be 'is name? Ponsonby. Aye, they was all there to see the six of 'em brought down. And all the while I plodded them long miles to Dorchester, I were wishin' myself dead.

Time an' again I gets torn from my sleep by the clankin' of chains. I know 'tis in my dreams, but each time it do leave I in a fair sweat.

Samuel were gettin' thinner an' thinner, and bringin' up great gobs of blood-streaked phlegm each time he coughed. Finally I carried him on my back to the doctor in Bere. Not the one as tends us here in the workhouse.

"What can be done for 'im?" I asked the doctor. "Surely there be summat you can do?"

"I'm afraid there's no hope for your son. Oh, there might be a chance if he could go to a sanitarium in, say, Switzerland, but..." He extended his hands in a gesture of helplessness.

"Where be this Switzerland? How far beyond Dorchester?"

"Dear God! The ignorance!" he said, the scorn in his voice cuttin' into me like a knife.

Rage overcome me, and I flung at him, "What chance 'ave us got of bein' anythin' else?"

His head dropped forward exposin' pink scalp through thinned, silver hair. He pressed the bridge of his nose with his thumb and forefinger, and seconds ticked by afore he said anythin'. Then he raised his head, looked I straight on and said, "I apologize for that remark. It was inexcusable." 'Tis the first and only time I've known someone above our station to apologize to the likes of us.

The only sound in that room were Samuel's coughin', and it come to me that the doctor's remark about ignorance were directed at himself as much as I. Him bein' filled with regret for not bein' able to help Samuel. Finally he asked, "Can you get him fresh milk? Eggs? And send him somewhere where it is cool, dry? Away from any damp. A good diet would give him more strength to fight the disease."

"There's naught we can do about sendin' him elsewhere, but milk, eggs. I'll get 'em. Somehow I'll get 'em."

I"ll tell 'ee what my Mary's real fond of. Beastings. 'Tis an' old country dish made from the first milk from a cow that've just calved. Thick it is.

Thicker than cream. Put it in a dish, then stand that 'un in a bigger dish of water. Set it near the fire where the heat ent too fierce and let it cook real slow. 'Twill set into a rich custard and has a wonnerful flavour. How my Mary would smile if sometimes I were able to get hold of some from the farm.

The evenings being lighter, I sets off after work, over to Squire's, chancin' he'd be in. I waited a full half-hour afore he comes to where I be kept standin'.

"Well, Fielding, I understand you will not leave until I have spoken with you. What is it that you want?"

"Evenin', Squire,' says I, nervous, but determined. "It be about the money you promised. My son be real sick and I must 'ave the money if he is to get the food the doctor says 'e must 'ave. You promised I five pounds, Sir."

"Five pounds, you say," he says, sort a rockin' on his heels. "Yes, I recall the conversation."

"Ay, five pounds, Sir. I done what was asked of me and have suffered much for it ever since. 'Tis for Samuel's sake I come. He be powerful sick. Doctor says 'e must 'ave good food if 'e be goin' to live."

I thought he were goin' to refuse. But no. He stood silent for a moment and then said, "You did what was asked of you and I am a man of my word, Fielding. But the agreement was a joint one between Wainwright, Parson Warren and myself. I will give you thirty shillings, you must get the rest from Warren and Wainwright. Wait here."

And he turned and left the room, and when he come back he placed thirty shillin' in my hand sayin' "I have settled my obligation to you, Fielding." But it was his tone of voice that caught at me. Not havin' any learnin' it be hard for me to explain my meanin' right, and I canst only put it this way. 'Twas as if, inside hisself, he felt the debt could never be settled. A foolish fancy – summat that were in and out my mind like lightning. 'Tis more like that were how *I* felt.

And he reaches for the bell rope, sayin', "Cutter will see you out."

While I was waitin' for him to get the money, I were able to roughly figure out that thirty shillin' be about five pounds split three ways, but there were summat forebodin' about it. 'Tis impossible to say rightly what

I means, but I wished with all my heart that Squire had give me thirty-one or even twenty-nine.

The new babe born to my Mary that February seemed a healthy 'un, but I would not let m'self take an interest in it, which give pain to Mary. I daren't let myself get fond of it. Samuel were a real strong young 'un, and look at him now. No, I could not risk the hurt should he be took later. Too many littl'uns we've buried.

Every time I manages a breath, my chest rattles like dried beans on a vine come autumn. I wonder if they'll allow my Mary to visit today. I needs to feel her hand on mine awhile again. She be a good woman, a lovin' wife. Her've stood by me in my troubles, been by my side since not long after that Harvest Supper. I canst still bring it to mind – the moon low in the sky, cheese yeller, and my Mary worryin' about her new petticoat getting' damp. Would that that 'ad been the only worry in our lives.

"You ent nothin' but skin and bone," says the old hag that tends us sick 'uns. Pulls the coverlet back an' wipes I down with a smelly rag drippin' cold water, then dabs at my body roughly with a coarse cloth. I be shakin' with cold by the time she be finished. Oh, for my Mary's gentler touch.

Parson comes ridin' down the road that leads to the church. The great chestnut trees archin' over, every twig swollen with sticky buds ready to burst. A playful wind smellin' of fresh turned sod and comin' spring danced the branches about, and sent clouds scuddin' across the sky as if blowin' thistledown.

Parson's horse, one I'd not seen him on afore, her black coat gleamin' from curryin', were being skittish too, and he had to rein her in real hard.

"Parson, Parson Warren," I calls. "I needs speak with you."

He looks down at me from where he sits up high, and in an impatient voice asks, "What is it Fielding?"

"That be a beautiful beast, you 'ave there, Sir," I says knowin' his love for horse flesh and thinkin' to get him in a good mood. "Be it new?"

"Yes, she's a recent purchase. Fifty guineas, and worth every penny," he says full of boast. "Now what is it you want, I have an appointment to keep?"

"Tis about the money, Parson."

"The money! What money?"

"The money you and Squire and Master promised I. I've done what were asked of me, and now I needs the money."

"It was Squire Finchbury made you that promise. See him. It has nothing to do with me."

"Beggin' your pardon, Sir, but Squire says you all three made the promise. Squire've paid me his share and says I must get the rest from you and Master."

"If Finchbury has made you a payment, that should suffice. Why should you expect payment for doing your duty. It is a poor state of affairs if men expect to be paid for doing what any good citizen should do. You'll get nothing from me."

"But you all did promise me money, Sir, and my Samuel is terr'ble sick. He needs good food if he's to get well."

"Let's have no more of this, Fielding. You've wasted enough of my time."

The wind had gathered strength as we be talkin', and a gust catches under the brim of Parson's hat, lifts it from his head and sets it dancin' down the lane. I lets it skip along past me, the wind pickin' it up and puttin' it down.

"Fetch it, man. Get hold of it," yells Parson at me. And I looks at him, the black hate that filled me showin' in my face. As his hat dips into a puddle, I says to him, "Tis your hat. You get it." He be beside hisself with fury. And I turned my back and walked away, cursin' him, his church, and his black, black soul.

Later I sees his mare hitched to the railin' near the lych-gate. No sign of Parson. He's like to be inside, I says to myself. With a picture in my mind of Parson on those fat legs of his chasin' after his horse, I loosens her reins and gives her flank a mighty slap, expectin' her to gallop off down the road. But instead of racin' off, her swerves and takes a run at the low wall that runs round the churchyard. Her hoofs trample on graves as she canters to a yew tree standin' in the corner, knockin' over flowerpots and the like in her hurry to get to the tree.

As young 'uns, we liked to suck out the sweet syrup from the yew berries. Only the juice, mind, for the rest be deadly poisonous. Parson's horse be takin' in mouthfuls of the greenery. "No!" I yells and starts scramblin' over the wall to try and stop her. But just then a young couple come walkin' along the path as circles the church just as Parson comes out the vestry door. So I ducks down out of sight for Parson be certain sure to link I to his horse gettin' loose.

It is clear that the couple and Parson had arranged to meet, though I couldst not hear what were said. But they seemed to be argufying, and Parson seems to be angrily dismissin' 'em.

I recognized the young gentleman; two year ago or more his family had moved into the big house as looks over the green. 'Cos, their arrival caused much gossip, newcomers to the village be so unusual. Stirrin' a pot over the fire one evenin', Mary told as how she heard they come from Ireland.

"Cath'lick," said Mary.

"Cath'lick!" I queried. "You mean, them as worships different from us."

"That's right, Cath'licks." Then Mary laughed that wonnerful laugh of hers. "Worships different from us! 'Tis little worshippin' you does, my luv," and Mary, playful like, tapped her finger on my nose and then gave I a quick kiss. Turnin' back to the fire, her was still chucklin'. "My Sethy worshippin'!

"I worships you," said I, and put my arms around her waist.

The wall be of no great height and I be getting' a crick in my back crouched down so low. There be nothin' I can do about the horse now what with Parson still standin' there a'waggin' his finger at the young man so, quiet as I can, I creeps off and head home. But that poor horse, I didst feel badly about 'un. She were a lovely beast. I swear I only meant for it to go runnin' off.

I couldst not bring m'self to face Master's refusal, seeing as he had already denied I payment for the time I had lost from them three days I had to give evidence. Knowing there would be none as would drink with me in Tolpuddle's ale house, I walks to Bere and wasted four pence of Samuel's money in the ale house there.

Chapter Fourteen
Dorchester 1834

"WHAT'LL HAPPEN TO US NOW?" QUESTIONED JOHN Standfield in a whisper as they were led back to their cells.

"I know not. We've not been sentenced yet," replied his father.

The gaoler's "Be silent! No talking!" echoed off the stone walls as they shuffled along the prison corridor.

It seemed an endless two days, waiting to hear their sentence, each man torn with anxiety as he huddled in his cell, cold and despairing. George's rasping cough disturbed what respite could be obtained in sleep. Thomas was deeply concerned. He had never known his friend to be ill before, but when they were given a brief period in the exercise yard, he was shocked at George's condition. Burning with fever, George could scarcely find the strength to walk in circles with the other men.

Wednesday, March 19th saw many property owners and anti-unionists crowding into the courtroom to hear the sentencing, while a strong representation of unionists and radicals as well as reporters from London and local papers also pushed and fought for seats.

Judge Williams adjusted his wig, searched under his robes until he located a handkerchief from a hidden pocket and blew his nose loudly. Finally he directed his gaze to the six men assembled at the bar of the court.

"George Loveless, James Loveless, Thomas Standfield, John Standfield, James Brine, James Hammett, you stand before me having been found guilty of the charges brought against you." Again he made use of his handkerchief. "I have noted your plea that you intended no harm to anybody by your actions. However, what your intentions were can only be known to yourselves. What I must take into consideration is the effect your actions could have had on public security and an example *must* be made. The object of all legal punishment is not altogether with the view of operating on the offenders themselves. It is also for the sake of offering an example and a warning. I therefore sentence each one of you to seven years transportation."

A muffled cry came from James Hammett. Thomas reached out to his son. James Loveless turned an ashen face to his brother. George, looking directly at the judge, icy anger overcoming his fever, struggled to make himself heard above the expressions of approval from the crowd in the courtroom.

"This is British justice?" he rasped. "We've been sentenced not for anything we have done, or that could be proved we intended to do..."

"Silence. Silence. This is a court of..."

"but as an example to others." *I will be heard. They can't do this to us.* "Tis a travesty of justice..." *Damn this cough. I must speak on our behalf.* "We have done nothing..."

His desk reverberating from the pounding of his gavel, Williams demanded that George be silent and ordered the prisoners to be removed. George, racked with a bout of coughing, bent over the dock and wiped at his mouth with the back of his hand. *Get your hands off me, I'll not go silently.* He pushed aside a jailer's hand, tried again to make himself heard and brought on another fit of coughing.

Hammett's cry of "Tis wrong. Harriet! How'll Harriet manage?" was lost in the noise. A jailer brought his stick down hard on James Loveless' hands to loosen their grasp on the dock rail. Thomas staggered and John reached out a hand of support to his father. As the prisoners were led out of the dock reporters scribbled furiously. George reaching into his pocket, removed a sheet of paper and flung it in their direction. Several of them scrabbled for it.

"What is it? What does it say?" the others clammered.

"Looks like a poem," said the reporter who had retrieved it.

"God is our guide, from field, from wave,
From plough, from anvil and from loom;
We come, our country's rights to save,
And speak a tyrant faction's doom,
We raise the watch-word liberty,"

He started reading aloud. "Each verse ends 'We will, we will, we will be free.'"

"I recognize it ," said another. "Tis sung at many radical and union meetings. It's become almost a hymn – a hymn to freedom."

"Where is my brother?" anxiously enquired James Loveless of the gaoler engaged in fettering their hands and feet, then linking them together with a long chain.

"Shut y'mouth," replied the man striking James hard on the shoulder. Then, in a less belligerent tone, added, "They've taken him to the prison 'ospital."

"He'll not be coming with us?"

"I've answered y'question. That's enough!"

"He had a heavy fever yesterday, James, that was obvious," said Thomas. "He was in no state to make a journey such as this."

"There is truth in that," replied James bitterly. "Will they let him join us later, think you? 'Tis double hard to be separated."

A keen wind blowing from the north bit through their clothing as the five men clung to the outside of the coach to which they were chained, "Like a damned load of monkeys," John Standfield muttered.

Conversation was difficult above the noise of the coach rattling over the uneven roads. Hammett moaned a continuous litany of concern as to how his wife and baby would manage. Brine concentrated on controlling his fear of water and the long voyage ahead. The idea terrified him. He had never even seen the sea. Gradually their minds focused only on keeping a grip on the coach with hands and feet that had become frozen as the miles to Portsmouth passed.

~~~

The baby's gums parted. Letting the nipple escape his lips he wailed in frustration and hunger. Rising from her stool by the empty fireplace, Elizabeth held him against her shoulder, pacing back and forth in an effort to sooth him, but Daniel's cries grew louder.

Hearing the door open, Elizabeth clutched at her open bodice. "Oh, 'tis you, Dinny."

"You look fair frazzled. Is the young 'un teething?"

"I've not enough milk to satisfy him. He'll have to be weaned." Elizabeth's voice cracked as she added, "but, I've no money for ..."

"Tis why I came round. To talk about money. Food." Holding out her arms Dinniah took Daniel from Elizabeth and cradled him against her crooning 'Hush now. Shush." She lowered herself onto the stool Elizabeth had vacated, while Elizabeth, crossing over to a pail of water, lifted the wooden dipper and drank deeply. Keeping her back to Dinniah, fighting to control the tremor in her voice, she said, "It don't seem to help, no matter how much I drink."

'Tis the worry. There's nothin' stops the milk comin' in like worry."

"Dinny, I've been thinkin' hard." Elizabeth's tone was stronger now. With head erect she faced her sister-in-law. "I know the Good Books says the Lord will provide, but I figure we must do our bit. My mind's been churnin' and churnin', as yours has to, I've no doubt."

"I can think on nothin' else."

"Well, I've two thoughts on the matter. First we must apply for Parish Relief. No, don't look like that. We've no choice, Dinny."

"You're right, I know. But to go on the parish 'tis..."

"It'll go against the grain for the both of us, but we'll just have to bury our pride. Then second, if we pool what little food we have, both families cookin' and eatin' together..." Elizabeth's voice trailed away.

Daniel's furious sucking on his fist was the only sound for several minutes. Dinniah raised her head. "You know where we'll have to go?"

"Magistrate Frampton. Thursday mornings. And be prepared for a long wait I'm told. There's always many others applying."

~~~

A foul odour arose from the decomposing refuse tangled in lines of kelp left by the tide along the mud-black shore. The raucous cry of gulls swooping down on debris floating on the water made a background accompaniment to the shouts of the warders. The hulks sat low in the water, their rotting timbers stark silhouettes against the darkening sky. The gangplank creaked under the weight of Brine and Hammett and the two Standfields as they were led onto the *York*. A warder placed a hand on James Loveless' shoulder, stopping him from following the others.

"Your name James Loveless?" questioned the warder. "You're to be separated from the others. Take 'im to the *Leviathan*," he ordered another man.

The smell of decay, filth and damp was overpowering as the prisoners were stripped and a bundle of convict clothing thrust at them.

Dressed again in coarse grey jackets, waistcoat and trousers and nailed boots, heavier irons than the fetters they had worn in prison were riveted to their legs.

"For the love of God, they ent takin' us across the sea in these rottin' tubs, be they?" questioned Brine nervously.

"No, no," Thomas assured him. "They're old naval ships, no longer seaworthy. They hold us in them until they've enough prisoners for transportation." He shrank back in disgust as a rat scurried across the berth to which they had been assigned. The two men already occupying the roughly five and a half feet square area cursed the gaolers and the new arrivals as they were forced to move over. The stench was overpowering and Brine began to heave before he had even settled himself.

~~~

Taking George's wrist in his hand, the prison doctor regarded George. "Well, your fever's eased and your lungs less congested." He addressed the gaoler standing at his side. 'This man'll be ready to travel in a couple of days." Pointing to the prisoner lying beside George he added, "That one's dead. I'll arrange for him to be taken to the training hospital. We need more cadavers."

"Does he not even get a decent burial, be it only a pauper's grave?" George cried out, but the doctor refused to acknowledge his question, turning his attention to the next bed. George caught at his arm.

"I hear those sentenced with me have been sent to the hulks today. As you say I am much improved, may I not join them?"

"That's not for me to decide."

It was strange this lying in bed. As a child he may have been sick, but George couldn't remember such an occasion. But as an adult, no, he'd never been ill. With no work to distract his thoughts, concern for his family, the injustice of their sentence, the very fact that they'd been charged seethed like acid inside him. He wished when he'd been brought before that solicitor he'd had the foresight to ask what made an oath legal. Judging from the man's attitude, though, it was doubtful that the man would have answered the question had he raised it.

Restless, George rubbed his shin with the heel of his other foot, eased himself to a sitting position and tried to fix his mind on something other than family and oaths. But the courtroom scene could not be blotted out: Judge Williams' bias against them, the evidence presented, Seth Fielding. To think a fellow worker, a neighbour, someone he'd considered a friend, had behaved so treacherously. There was no denying Fielding had not played his part willingly. At Wollaston's house, when they were first questioned, and again when they were tried, every word of Seth's testimony had been dragged from him. What had they threatened him with? Dismissal? That he'd be charged himself? "Judge not" the Bible said. But to betray ones friends! The Bible was right, George told himself. Until a person was forced into such a position as the one in which Fielding had found himself, how could that person say how he'd react?

George's deliberations were interrupted by the approach of a warder. "Look lively, now, the warder commanded, "You've a visitor." Turning to the well-dressed gentleman standing behind him, he said, "You're lucky. This 'un will be discharged soon. Doctor said he'll be fit to travel shortly."

"Do you recognize me, Loveless?"

George carefully studied the man standing in front of him, taking in the powdered hair, the expensive cut of the man's coat, his cream-coloured breeches and knee-high boots. The mouth, not smiling but curved slightly, eased the severity of the eyes that stared down at him.

"I do, Sir, though I know not your name. You were with Magistrate Frampton when we were first brought before him."

"That is so. I am Magistrate Wollaston. I've come to enquire after your health."

"My health, Sir? As you've just heard the warder say, I'm soon to be discharged from here."

"I must say I'm heartily sorry to see a man of such intelligence and good character as yourself in this situation. A terrible shame."

George pulled himself upright in the bed. "*You* are sorry, Sir? When you had much to do in placing me here."

"You brought it on yourself, Loveless, listening to the words of evil men going round the country deceiving people, and failing to heed the warning of the magistrates."

"You say you've come to enquire after my health and then start lecturing me thus. Telling me I should have heeded the magistrates' warning!" George's voice rang with indignation.

"I can't say I like your tone. I would have expected to see you more contrite."

George could not contain his anger. "Contrite! When we're convicted on a trumped up charge. How *could* we have heeded the warning when it was issued nine weeks after the event for which we were arrested, and when three days after its issuance we found ourselves in gaol? Answer me that."

Wollaston looked flummoxed at George's violent rebuttal. Regaining his composure, in an icy tone he responded, "It appears there's no use talking to you, Loveless."

"No, Sir, 'tis not, unless you talk more reasonably."

"I had hoped to see some remorse for your actions that have brought you and your friends so low."

"Remorse! All we were trying to do was improve conditions for ourselves. How can any man support a family on a mere six shillings a week?"

"Most men would have been thankful to have employment."

"The Bible says 'A labourer is worthy of his hire.' You mention my being of good character. At the trial, when questioned, our employers all had to admit we were good labourers and that they'd never heard any complaints about us. Surely a good labourer is worth more than six shillings!"

Shaking his head, Wollaston turned and started walking away. George shouted to his retreating back, "It is not *justice* but British law, two entirely different things, that has condemned six innocent men. That has ruined six families. Think on that, Sir."

Since Wollaston's departure George's mind could not let go of their conversation. For hours he churned over the question as to why the magistrate had come? I should have harnessed my anger, he told himself. It was impossible to believe a man of Wollaston's standing had concern for him. Why *would* a magistrate who'd played a part in their arrest and sentencing come to see him? Dare he put credence in Wollaston's claim of concern for him, that there might be some hope? Had Wollaston been instructed to visit or had he come of his own volition? Whatever the magistrate's motive, his hasty tongue has not helped matters.

Sleep evading him, George left his bed, crossed to the waste bucket, wincing at the painful, stinging sensation as he relieved himself. This acidity that burned inside him was strong enough to singe the side whiskers from every judicial and parliamentary face that had brought him to this state.

~~~

"Finchbury. Glad you could come. Come in, come in." William Ponsonby ushered Henry Finchbury into his library and indicated a chair beside a glowing fire. "Last week's hint of spring did not last long. Will you take a hot toddy?"

"Thank you, Ponsonby. A toddy would be most acceptable. Yes, the change in temperature from last week is surprising."

Ponsonby issued an order to the man-servant who had answered his summons, and he took a seat opposite Finchbury.

"Well, what d'you make of the news from London? The papers are full of nothing else," said Ponsonby, gesturing to a pile of newspapers on an intricately carved desk.

"The *Times* and the *Globe* are strong in their argument against the severity of the sentence," responded Finchbury "and I must say that I agree with them in part."

"Agree with them! I never expected to hear such a statement from you, Finchbury."

"Had they each been given a year's hard labour, I think it would have acted as deterrent enough to make any man think twice about joining a union. It seems to me now that seven years' transportation is overly harsh."

"Well, you've changed tunes since this whole business started. I cannot disagree with you more. The more severe the sentence, the stronger the message."

Ponsonby rose, crossed the room and returned with a tin of tobacco which he offered Finchbury, who declined with a wave of his hand.

"The *Herald* dares declare that treachery was used to obtain the verdict," continued Ponsonby as he seated himself again. He opened the ornate box, felt around for his pipe but, changing his mind, closed the box noisily. "But it is the *Sun* that has me fuming. Did you read it? Here, I have it on this table." Ponsonby set down his tankard and picked up a paper. He ran his eye over the page until he found the article. "Here, listen to this. '…*Based on this ruling a large number of persons, including the whole of the members of the numerous Trades Unions are liable to the same penalties on the same grounds…*' But this", he tapped the paper with his other hand, "this incenses me most of all. This suggestion that the same law would include members of clubs and lodges." Ponsonby, his body craned forward, shook the paper at Finchbury. "You know who the Grand Master of the Orange Lodge is? The Duke of Cumberland!"

"It had slipped my mind that you're an Orange man. On what grounds would they make such a statement?"

"For swearing an oath, goddammit! I'm a member, yes. To suggest that we should be charged also is not only ridiculous, it's outrageous!" Ponsonby's face purpled with anger.

"I understand that Magistrate Frampton wrote Lord Melborne that farmers should turn off all labourers known to belong to unions," said Finchbury. "But if unions are legal, then surely farmers cannot discharge men for belonging to same?"

"Sounds as if you're arguing *for* unions, Finchbury."

Aware of Ponsonby's growing lack of composure, he replied, "No, no, certainly not. A way must be found to stop their spreading if we landowners are to survive."

"But have you heard of Tremain's actions? The same Tremain that dined at your table less than a year ago. You'll have read that hundreds, some say thousands, of pounds have been raised to assist the wives and children of these men?"

"Yes, but what of Tremain? I heard he'd inherited another estate through an aunt."

"You heard correctly." Ponsonby had risen from his chair and was striding the length of the room in his agitation. "And what's the damned blackguard done? Sold his property in Tarnsley and subscribed a large amount of the money he obtained from the sale to the prisoners' fund. And, goddammit, took great pleasure in telling me so." To emphasize this last piece of news, Ponsonby thumped his tankard down so hard onto a small table that some of its contents slopped over his breeches, infuriating him even further.

"I recall he didn't seem to share our views that night," said Finchbury, "but what you say certainly takes me by surprise." He found Ponsonby's revelation disturbing. That Tremain would not only have turned against them, but had openly acknowledged the extent of his disagreement with their views, views that he himself was beginning to question – no, not question, but feel uneasy about – confused him. Not given to analyzing his reasons for any action he might take or views he might hold, he now felt a strong need to be by himself and rationalize what was causing him such concern.

To steer their talk in a different direction, he said, " What I came to speak with you about was the Dorchester Races."

At the mention of the races, Ponsonby abruptly switched from his diatribe about unions and settled back in his chair. "Dorchester Races. Aah, yes! We must arrange where we're to meet and the time."

Thankful that his change of topic had had a calming effect on his friend, Finchbury gladly acquiesced to Ponsonby's suggestion that they book rooms at the Dorchester Hostelry so that they might make the most of their day at the races.

Chapter Fifteen
Workhouse 1842

'TIS FEAR THAT FORCES MY LUNGS TO FIGHT FOR ANOTHER breath. For I has heard that if there be none to claim the body of some 'un as dies in the workhouse, his body be given to young doctor students to practice their skills on.

But then I argues with myself as how there be a small plot in the churchyard set aside for paupers' burials. And my Mary be alive. She'd see that I be buried proper. But 'tis a fearful thought, bein' all cut about even though I would'st be dead.

There be a big open sore on my hip and backside now where the bone have worn through what be left of my flesh. I's ready to go, but fear holds I back. And fear makes a man stubborn and stick his heels in even if I hast only this straw-filled mattress to dig my heels into, if you gets my meanin'.

Stubborn ... My Mary could be stubborn when she had a mind. There be no talkin' her around once she 'ave set her mind on somethin'.

When us first moved into the cottage, seeing as we were lucky enough to have a fair bit of garden with the cottage, she were determined us should grow as much food as were possible. Not that there were anything unusual in that. Any of us as had a patch of ground, and there was many as hadn't, would have it planted. But Mary, she nagged I into diggin' it over and over. The night-bucket contents must be spaded in and any droppings that horse or cow might leave in the lane, for the soil were poor.

One year she and the young 'uns made a murmet out of crossed poles and a pair of old trousers and a jacket. It were Tabby as found a battered straw hat and placed it on the straggledy-straw head.

The young 'uns, all excited, drags I down the garden to see it when I gets back from the farm.

"Why didn't 'ee use a turnip for a head?" I asks.

"Waste a good turnip! There be only a few left to see us through till the next crop be ready," says Mary. "I know's you don't care much for 'em, Sethy my love, but they's fillin' food."

Then Tabby starts laughin'. Pointin' at the murmet where a crow had perched on its head, her says, "It don't seem to unnerstand what it's job be," and then us all be laughin' along with her.

"Why do 'ee call it a murmet instead of a scarecrow?" questions Sam.

"Aah, that's a bit of yer muther's family comin' out. Us've always called 'em scarecrows. Odd lot, yer muther comes from," I jokingly replies. And Mary gives I a slap across the back of the head, then, slippin' her arm around my shoulders, says laughin' that it were a good Dorset word, one her family've always used.

A happy memory that. Us all merry together, standin' there in the garden enjoyin' the remains of the spring evenin'. One of them moments your memory clutches tight.

Yes, Mary were real set on her garden. She had I luggin' buckets of water from the pump durin' the summer months, and the children pickin' off slugs and such. And some years, when, for all her efforts, there were little to harvest, she kep' on at it.

When I were just a littl'un, I recalls bein' taken to visit my grandad. He were full of times gone by, when there were common land that all could use for small crops and the grazin' of a cow or goat. Said as how 'twere all lost when the Enclosure Act were passed. The landowners' gain were the common-folks' loss. But that were many years afore my time. We has only the village green left now.

I can still picture him in that old flax smock Granny had stitched, all tucks and fancy stitchin' across the chest. His beard and side whiskers, white as white, and a black, tall stove-hat atop it all. Unions! He'd 'ave no idea what such talk were all about.

And Ordered Their Estate

After they was all arrested, Master Wainwright cum to realize he'd lost the best workers he'd ever had with George and James Loveless gone. But it were a long time till Martinmas Fair and contract hirin', so he just took on one temporary chap and had the rest of us carryin' out the work that George and James would've been set to.

And in the village, still none spoke to I.

God's curse on the overseer. Why do 'ee have to shout his orders so. Yellin' as how the floors should be mopped by now. It do shake a fellow from his thoughts.

When Loveless and Standfield and the others were sentenced, there were a rare old outcry. The newspapers wrote of nothin' else. Not that I can read, mind, but it were much discussed by them as could. There be an ale house in Bere where I'd found a quiet nook where I'd bide by m'self. On occasion, a man there would read out what were bein' said. Should anyone start up conversin' with I, I'd say I cum from Tarnsley so as none would link me with Tolpuddle. It were made plain that I weren't welcome at *The Sycamore* in Tolpuddle. Some of 'em drinkin' there cursed I, and even fists were raised.

Magistrate Frampton had refused parish relief to the Standfields and the families of the others that were took. Told Dinniah Standfield, "You shall have no mercy because you should have known better than to have allowed such meetings to be held in your house." Said as how families as could afford to pay a shillin' to join the union and a penny a week thereafter had no need of parish relief.

My Mary's here. I canst smell her. I must find the strength to raise m'self. 'Tis my last chance. "Mary!" I shouts, liftin' my head from the pillow.

"What be it, Seth, my lovey? I canst scarce hear you."

"Don't let 'em cut I up. Don't let 'em give I to them doctors."

"Cut 'ee up? What be you on about, Seth? 'Tis terrible hard to hear what you be whisperin'. Ent nobody goin' to cut 'ee up."

Mary tries to get I to lie back, but I must have her promise afore I can rest again. I clutches at her sleeve. She strains her ear to my mouth.

"See they buries I proper, Mary. Don't let them doctors get I."

"Don't 'ee fret so. This be the first time you've talked for days. What's that? Bury 'ee? 'Cos they will! 'Tis all right. Rest now."

The unions and such held meetings. But it weren't just unionists as gave to the fund they'd started. The papers said as how there were hundreds and hundreds of pounds given to help the families now left fatherless in Tolpuddle.

One evenin' the man read out as how petitions were bein' presented to Parliament. I ent sure what were meant by that havin' no knowledge of what goes on in such places, but it were all to do with askin' for the men to be pardoned. The paper said as how thousands had put their names to the petitions. 'Tolpuddle Martyrs" they be callin' 'em.

Apart from the gentry's visitors there be none as comes to the area that ent noticed, so when a stranger were seen in Tolpuddle askin' questions, news of his comin' were soon all round the village. Wanted to know where Loveless, Standfield and the others lived. 'Twas said he had brought money from London to be given to the families, and left more with a Methodist preacher to distribute later.

It were towards the end of April that I comes across Squire and Parson talkin' by the lych-gate of the churchyard. Squire astride his bay mare, Parson afoot. I were cuttin' through the churchyard and, havin' no wish to acknowledge either as there were a hare I'd poached in my bag, I ducks down behind a large tombstone.

"I hear you lost that new mare you purchased. Did you discover what she died from?" asks Squire.

"A terrible loss. A terrible loss," bemoans Parson. "She got at that yew tree there. It's a mystery how she got free, for I secured her firmly before I entered the church."

"She must have eaten a fair amount to have killed her. I'm sorry for your loss for I hear she was a beautiful animal."

"Fifty guineas I paid for her. *Fifty guineas.*"

There's almost a sob to Parson's voice, and I nearly gives myself away holdin' back my glee.

"Well, I must be on my way," Squire says, raising his riding crop to his hat in a gesture of farewell, but Parson delays his departure with, "You'll have read about the march on Whitehall?"

"Yes, of course. Some papers are reporting that as many as thirty-five thousand protestors took part."

"Rabble-rousers," says Parson. "It should never have been allowed."

"The papers would disagree with you about the term *rabble*. All report upon the decorum of the numbers taking part. They comment on how well organized the whole event was."

"It's to be hoped Lord Melbourne is not swayed by such demonstrations."

"It looks as if the London-Dorchester Committee, as they call themselves, will continue to agitate for a reprieve," says Squire. "It could come about that they reduce the men's sentence."

"You think it will come to that?"

"A year's hard labour would have been a fairer sentence I feel, but there are many that don't espouse that view."

"And I'm one of them," says Parson firmly. "I must say I am surprised to hear you voice such sentiments."

"Well, be that as it may, I must be off. I have visitors awaiting my return. Good day to you Warren."

How much longer before 'er 'ave finished moppin' the damn floor. 'Tis as if she be throwing the bucket at the wall, she do clang it so much. The noise cuts through my head like a billhook.

I made an arrangement with the mistress to take home fresh milk for Samuel each day and an egg or two. She made sure I paid for 'em too. But I has no shame in saying as how I helped myself to what I could for Samuel, figurin' it were no less than what was owed me by Master. I had to be right careful, mind. They could ship I off to Botany Bay, wherever that be, should I be caught. Mary sewed a deep inside pocket to my jacket, and be it only a swede, that pocket oft-times had summat in it.

And Samuel seemed to put some flesh on his bones for a while, and I told myself 'e weren't coughin' as much. But the improvement were short-lived. Tempt him as we tried, he began to lose interest in whatever were offered. What little he swallowed 'e had trouble keepin' down. Mary would sit up with him at night, offerin' him water to ease his cough, wipin' his forehead with a cool cloth.

One evenin' he begged I to carry him outside to sit under the apple tree, Said as how he wanted to smell the apple blossom. And with the breeze sendin' petals driftin' down, twas there our Samuel died. So quiet, he were gone afore us realized.

Chapter Sixteen

The Surrey 1834

THE THICK, FETID AIR OF THE HOLD HUNG LIKE A DAMP sheet over them, cloying with the stench of vomit and the odour of the many who suffered from dysentery. Weakened by months spent in prison or held on prison hulks, most of the convicts were in poor health. Since they had left England on the *Surrey* the wretched conditions, rotten food, the crowding, had reduced many of the prisoners to little more than animals who would snatch a crust from a weaker man, steal clothing, bedding, a coin. The Standfields, Brine and Hammet were overwhelmed by the viciousness to which they were exposed.

Scurvy had reduced Thomas' gums to a swollen, purple-coloured mess and loosened several of his teeth. As he sat alongside Brine, heels against thighs, knees raised, sucking on a corner of the hard-tack until it had softened sufficiently enough to be swallowed, a dried lump of feces struck him in the face. Startled rather than hurt, he dropped the biscuit into the filthy straw on which he sat. From across the narrow gangway, a heavyset convict gestured rudely at Thomas, mimed Thomas' sucking motions. From his mouth almost hidden behind a swathe of facial hair, came a hoarse bray of laughter.

Before Thomas could retrieve the dropped food, Brine's hand had closed over it, raised it to his lips. It was John Standfield's cry of outrage that stayed Brine's hand, held it as if it were welded in ice. Staring at the horror and disbelief on Hammett's face, the enormity of his action registered with Brine. The hard-tack fell from his fingers back into the straw. Turning from the others, he buried his face in his arms moaning, "God forgive me, to think I 've been brought this low." A silence hung between the four as John rescued the biscuit, wiped it clean as best he could on his sleeve and returned it to his father: a silence that extended for minutes, hours it seemed to Brine. It was Thomas who finally spoke. Placing a hand on Brine's turned back, he said quietly, "We must each give strength to the other or we shall surely become like the rest of these sorry creatures."

From then on, should one of them feel a need to vent his anger, despair, the others would try to offer a listening ear or reach out in the night to press a hand encouragingly. But as the weeks passed there were days when none had a word of solace to offer.

The *Surrey* weathered two storms, both of which had lasted for several days. The small vessel was pounded by huge waves as it plunged into deep troughs. Down in the hold it was not only Brine who was terrified by the deafening roar of screaming winds tearing at the sails and the groaning complaint of the ship's timbers. On deck, casks not securely fastened were flung from side to side while down below the contents of slop buckets mingled with vomit and sea water that had seeped through loosened caulking, sloshing around the prisoners feet as the ship lurched from side to side. Only the periodic shrill sound of the bosun's whistle marking a change of watch gave indication that captain and crew were still at their posts. Fervently Thomas and John, Brine and Hammett prayed that the *Surrey* would not founder.

For an hour morning and afternoon when calmer weather prevailed, the prisoners were brought up top for exercise where they shuffled about on a confined area of the deck with six Redcoats' guns trained on them. It was this opportunity of taking in deep lungfuls of fresh air after the atmosphere of the holds was all the four Tolpuddle men looked forward to as they lay huddled against one another in the hold.

Shivering in sodden clothing on deck after the weekly hosing down of all the prisoners, Thomas said, "Terrible as conditions are, at least us can be thankful we share the same berth," a view he expressed on more than one occasion. It was a sentiment to which the others agreed with either a nod or a muttered "that be true."

It was on Hammett Thomas and the others focused much of their attention. At first Hammett, normally a monosyllabic man, was constantly voicing concern about how his wife and baby son would survive with none to provide for them. Knowing the sickly, helpless nature of his wife, made it difficult for them to form words of encouragement, but now he seemed to have withdrawn deep into himself.

"You must eat, Hammett. Look, there ent too much mold on the bread today," urged Brine. Thomas joined his voice to Brine's. "Starving yourself won't help Harriet, lad."

Hammett showed no repose to their pleas but stared blankly at the bulkhead. Thomas held a slab of grey-green coloured bread to Hammett's lips. "Eat!" he commanded. The forcefulness of his father's tone made John look up sharply. Even when Thomas had rebuked or chastised them as children, his voice had been moderate but firm. Like an automaton, Hammett opened his mouth and accepted the food, grinding away at the hard lump, masticating it slowly. Thomas pushed the rest of the food into Hammett's hand. "Eat!" he ordered again, With eyes closed, Hammet obeyed.

Thin legs drawn up to his chest, a thirteen year-old boy in the berth across from Thomas and the others, called for his mother in a monotonous whimper until the huge, coarse-bearded man chained to him threatened to kill him if he didn't quiet himself. Thomas tried to call out comforting words but the shouted obscenities of the man-made Thomas desist. Back propped against a bulkhead, Thomas was the only one to note the boy's passing a few days later, and prayed quietly for the lad. The boy's companion didn't report the death for several days, but snatched up the rations intended for the lad, daring anyone else to lay claim to them.

Thomas startled up from sleep. It had been a fearful dream, a dream of when they were first imprisoned. He tried to dislodge remnants of the nightmare from his mind: George appearing to him as Satan, tempting him as Satan had tempted Job, while John and the others had listened, mouths agape. Fully awake Thomas tried to pray, overwhelmed with a feeling of guilt that his mind should portray his friend and companion as Satan. It was he who had initiated the idea of forming a Friendly Society, not George, but it was George's leadership that had brought the idea to fruition. But he had whole-heartedly supported him, worked with him in their group's formation.

In the days and nights that followed, Thomas found himself reduced to tears, tears he struggled to conceal from the others, as he fought to retain his faith in a God it would seem Satan was determined to persuade him to deny.

A sharp blow from the officer's billy club sent a convict sprawling to the deck. "You want trouble? I'll give you trouble," he said raising his stick again in a threatening gesture. The falling convict, raising his arms to protect his head, dragged Thomas down with him. Fearing his father would be trampled as men brought up on deck for exercise pushed and shoved for a coveted spot near the ship's railings, John struggled to assist Thomas to his feet. John's protectiveness of his father caught at an officer's attention. Solicitude towards another was rare amongst the prisoners. He took note of John, studied Thomas' quiet, thoughtful nature. As the weeks passed, the officer occasionally would exchange a few words with him. At first just a glance of recognition, but later Thomas was able to glean snippets of information from him to pass on to the others.

"How many of us be on board? Prisoners, I mean," Brine had questioned.

"Well, from the daily count, there's seventy-six of us on this deck. Three decks. I reckon about two hundred and thirty," replied Thomas.

"Tis hoped the crew be better fed than us, if they're to get us to Botany Bay."

"I overheard the food is shared six-to-four. What would feed four sailors must do for six of us prisoners and, while there was some supplies, the crew got vegetables and fruit."

"An' theirs'll be better than what is fed to us poor sods, I'll swear. An' when we gets there, what happens to us then? Do they have prisons large enough to take us all?"

"From what I've learned from the officer, they only hold us for a while seemingly. The Governor of Botany Bay is in charge of everything. 'Tis he who decides where we'll be sent. Settlers, top officers, magistrates buy our services from him, and we have to work for whatever master we're assigned to."

"So we'll not be kept in prison then. What sorta work will us be set to I wonders. Be there farms out there? 'Tis to be hoped they be good masters." Brine became silent as he pondered on their future prospects.

~~~

Harriet Hammett had to get away from the sound of crying. She gave a final thrust to the cradle, setting it rocking rapidly. The baby's wails reached crescendo pitch. Hastily she stepped through the doorway, and stood under the pear tree, her hands pressed over her ears.

Three months he'd been gone. Three months, and now he was somewhere on a ship to Botany Bay. What was to become of them. If he'd listened to her, to her mother, stayed at home of a night as they'd begged him, none of this would have come about. Did he ever give a thought to how she and the babe were faring? At least she was with her mother.

But she was left with a baby that always needed feeding, cleaning. From his birth, Edward had latched onto her breast, his gums gripping her nipple so tightly the whole of her body tensed as soon as his lips started their search. Sucked so hard as if he'd drain her of every drop of blood as well as milk

A hand on her shoulder made her turn. Her mother stood beside her holding a screaming Edward. "You knows Mistress Marsh wants her gown by tomorrow. I can't sew *and* tend your child. He needs feedin', Harriet."

"But he never stops crying," Harriet's thin voice whined. "He just don't stop."

"Well, he's a big 'un. Infants that size gets hungry quicker. Let me bring you out a chair and you sit here and feed him. 'Tis warm enough and right peaceful." Placing the baby in Harriet's arms, her mother turned towards the cottage.

Edward, eyes screwed shut, mouth a toothless circle, arms flailing, hiccupped and wailed.

"Hush, for God's sake hush," Harriet hissed at him. Overcome with guilt, she brushed his forehead with her lips, dripping tears on his upturned face. Clutching him awkwardly, she followed her mother inside. Feed him outside, indeed! With only a hedge to shield her from the view of any who might pass! I were a fool, James Hammet, to listen to 'ee. Taken in by the smell of honeysuckle. What didst I know of marriage?

~~~

As Thomas emerged from the hold of the *Surrey*, chained to the other prisoners he lifted an arm to shield his eyes from the sun. This was an unfamiliar sun. Not the sun that had shone in Tolpuddle, whose heat even at the height of summer was pleasurable, but one that radiated such an intense heat it seared the skin. Why, 'tis hotter than the baker's oven in Bere - hotter than ten ovens" he thought to himself. The light breeze that fanned his face offered a little relief.

Three weeks the vessel had been docked in Sydney but still the prisoners were kept below in the stifling, fetid holds. Only when, for a brief period, each convict had been taken up on deck for a cursory examination by a doctor and their physical and criminal details recorded was there any relief.

As they'd neared their destination Hammett became more animated, while Brine repeated over and over how good it would feel to place his feet on firm ground once again, to be free of the claustrophobic confines of the ship. Now the interminable waiting ate at their last residue of resilience. Finally came the news they were to be transferred to the prison barracks.

Dazzled by the brilliance of the sun's rays lancing the curled Pacific surf, Thomas raised a hand to shield his eyes from the glare. He stumbled as his foot caught against a coil of rope. His head dizzied for a moment with pure air, Thomas steadied himself against the ship's side watching as in groups of ten the prisoners were herded over the side of the ship and down rope ladders into boats waiting to take them ashore. Harsh voices shouted orders; two redcoats roared with laughter as a prisoner lost his grip on the ropes and fell, screaming, into the water dragging another prisoner with him. Noise and confusion was everywhere. Always bellowed instructions, cursing, fighting. It seemed to Thomas that he'd not known a moment of quiet stillness since they'd been arrested. Even at night, sleep had been disturbed with the clanking of chains as men tossed and turned, cursed yet again, or called out in their sleep.

Silently he sent up a prayer of gratitude that they'd not been separated as John, below him, guided his fumbling movements down the ladder and helped him into the small boat. Then several of the stronger convicts were ordered to help with the rowing.

Uniformed soldiers marched them four abreast through Sydney. Several times John had to steady his father. Thomas gazed around him. The streets were wide, lined with buildings of brick and sandstone, while up on the hills ornate houses of the wealthy overlooked the harbour.

"Tis not as I'd expected, but what picture was in my mind 'tis difficult to say," he remarked to his son.

"Look at the size of the houses up there on the hills. Why, some of them are the size of Parson's rectory," replied John. The houses hugged the base of cliffs that rose steeply, their stratification clearly marked in varying shades of brown and yellow. Above the cliffs grey-green shrubs were interspersed with splashes of yellow mimosa and, far away, the blue of distant mountains.

"This heat, though. I've never known such heat. My scalp feels as if it's on fire."

There was a bustling energy all around them. Roughly constructed carts pulled loads of building materials; men moved briskly about their business, others gathered to talk on the steps of a building. A woman, almost buried under a bundle of washing, with a child clinging to her skirts, turned down a side street. John, noting no one turned a head to watch as they were marched past, concluded it must be a common enough sight for the inhabitants of Sydney.

At last Hyde Park Barracks came into sight. The red, white and blue flag, with no breeze to stir it, hung limply from its pole. A soldier, his once bright red jacket reduced by the sun to a faded pink, opened iron gates and closed them shut behind them.

Chapter Seventeen
The Workhouse 1842

'TIS ONLY A SMALL MOUND, RIGHT BY THE HAWTHORN bush. I'd sit there awhile on my way home from work if the weather weren't too bad. You just has to cross the ford and pass through the back opening in the churchyard wall.

Sit and think on Samuel. And on my Mary. Us used to be able to talk on most things, but after Samuel's death, words, comfortin' words, neither of us seemed able to voice to the other. Us could only share our sorrow by touch or doin' summat for the other. Me drawin' her close when I'd come on her sobbin' into a sock she'd once knitted for him, or clutchin' that old coat of his. Once I were starin' out the winder at the apple tree but not really seein' it, if you follows my meaning, and it weren't till I felt her arms slip over my shoulders that I knew she'd come into the room. But I hoped her knew what I were meanin' when I'd put a bunch of kingcups gleamin' gold, I'd plucked from the water's edge by the ford, into her hand.

And Mary'd on occasion would make my favourite. Herb dumplings. She'd place 'em on the table in front of I, then stand by my shoulder, hands rolled up in that old sackin' apron she wore, waitin' 'til I'd tasted 'em and grunted my approval. How she managed to get the fixings for 'em I can't say. And Tabby. Holdin' her baby brother, she'd stand at the other end of the table watchin'. Not askin', mind, but with her eyes fixed on my plate, until it were impossible to lift the fork to my mouth afore I holds it out, laden with dumplin', for her to sample.

And Ordered Their Estate

Oh, ay! We both done some weepin', but in a quiet corner on our own. Mine were done by that mound near the hawthorn bush. There were a sparrar buildin' its nest there in the bush, an I likes to think that Samuel can hear its song along with I.

Sparrers ... Busy little things, sparrars. Sparrars'll be around, still busy buildin' away, hundreds of years from now, while me an' mine... Fielding... Ent as if there'll be any more Fieldings once I be gone. But you take them sparrars. Build a nest anywheres, be it in a bush, a flower pot, down a hole. Use anything they canst find to build it.

But lyin' here, I canst but be thankful in some ways that Samuel were took. An' Willie. At least they be spared the workhouse. Oft times, long afore little 'uns reach the age of seven, say, or eight, the workhouse overseer'll apprentice 'em out. What if my Samuel had been let go to a chimney-sweep like that little lad the sweep brung to clean Mistress Wainwright's chimney? They has to use small boys 'cos men be too big to climb into the narrow flues. I heard tell once of a boy as got lost in the maze of chimneys in one of them big old houses. Couldn't find his way out no how. It were said his cries could be heard for a day or more, but yell as they might to signal to him which way to come down, the lad were never found. I thought on that tale a lot, wonderin' on the truth of it and how long it took for the little chap to die, and what the owners of the house done later. Them fires would've had to be lit again sometime, so there would've been a powerful stink.

Or what if Little Will were sent to them new mills? 'Tis said cartloads of little 'uns be sent up north, their fingers bein' smaller and more nimble for much of the work. It don't bear thinkin' about. And what'll become of my Mary when I be gone?

And, o'course, there were another debt to pay off for Samuel's funeral. Parson were pressin' for his money before the sod had settled.

Mary's sister, who does rough work at the Parsonage, tells Mary as how tradesmen from Bere an' Blackthrope be askin' that Parson pay 'em some of the money they be owed. She says as how the little kitchen skivvy have been let go, and how her heard Parson tellin' Mistress Warren she must handle her spendin' with more care. Mistress Warren, her tongue as sharp as that pointy nose of hers, replies that it were his spendin' on his horses and such as got them into such straits. That it were no good him tryin' to ape Squire, for without the yearly hundred pounds dowry her father give her they'd be hard pushed to live on his stipend.

Did surprise I to learn that folk such as Parson has money problems. Why, on the sort of money he's like to have, I'd think I were a king. But seemingly we all has a struggle to exist, though I'll swear for us poor sods the struggle be a hundred, no, a thousand times harder.

"Tis quieter in here today. The old chap, whose foot had turned black and were rottin' on the end of his leg, he be gone. It be a blessin' not to hear his groanin', though he couldst not help it. His pain were somethin' chronic. But the quiet be restful. Doctor nor I knows why my lungs still fight for air.

Mary were wonnerful patient about my takin' a drop now and again after Samuel's death. And, if I be honest, it were oft times more than just a drop. It weren't just Samuel's passin'. There were much that weighed heavy on me.

And drink did also quiet my cock.

Oh, I wanted my Mary. Longed to bury my face between her big, round tits. Those breasts of hers, once firm as summer apples. Have her hold me close. She'd beg to know why I'd push her away, turn my back on her when she'd put out her hand and begin to fondle I. But see, I feared plantin' more babes in her. Feared seein' her carry 'em, birth 'em and watch 'em die. For die they were all like to in the end.

A good farmer culls out stock that be diseased. Puts down the abortin' sow. The hen as'll not lay. Gelds the stallion with staggers. And I must keep my seed from Mary.

The cough I dismissed as summat one expects in winter, lingered on past spring and into summer. 'Twas in me, the lung-rot. Just coughin' I was now, not spittin' yet. But it would come. Shouldst Mary catch I in a fit of coughin', our eyes would slide away from each other, neither of us darin' to put in words what were wrong.

Since Samuel's death a few folks started talking to I again. First just to express sympathy and then, I figure, they felt it daft to stop talking once they'd started. And others had cum to accept that I were forced into betrayin' Loveless and the others, that it weren't done willingly. A few, as I say, but others weren't ever goin' to let I forget what I had done. Said Samuel's death were just retribution.

But Squire now. It seemed that he be goin' out of his way to speak. I says to Mary, "There's somethin' worryin' at that man."

"Tis to be hoped 'tis conscience eatin' him," says Mary. "Twas him as led Master and Parson into makin' you go against yours, and don't you tell me different."

So one day when Squire says good day to I from his horse, and I raises my hand to my hat to acknowledge his greetin', I musters up nerve to ask a question of him.

"Squire," says I, "be there any news as to how Loveless and the others be fairin'?"

Well, there were silence for a moment. Then he says, "I hear they've sailed for Australia, but I know nothing more."

"Will they ever be allowed back here, Sir?" I questions further.

And he looked terr'ble discomforted. His mouth seemed as if it were formin' a reply, but he left my query unanswered. Just says, "I must be on my way, Fielding," and kicks his horse into a trot.

Oh, so many things keep coursin' through my mind as I lays here waitin'. Time and again, they comes, ready to strip down my pallet, thinkin' I be gone, only to see my chest strugglin' for one more gasp of air.

Times there were at night when sleep kep her distance from me, and others when frightenin' dreams would plague I. A dream of that paintin' Loveless had done, that hung on the wall when us had to swear that oath. That picture of Death. Many's the time I'd feel that bony hand reachin' out for my shoulder, and I'd leap up in bed shoutin' "Don't 'ee touch me." And Mary'd shush me quiet, sayin' as how I'd wake the young 'uns.

The fellow in the ale house in Bere that 'ud sometimes read from the news sheets said as how there had been no more protestors marchin' or petitions to Parliament.

Round July time he read as how some men tryin' to form a union in Oxford were charged with swearin' illegal oaths but were discharged, and the papers were askin' why the Tolpuddle Martyrs were not brought home. Then at the end of the year there were more in Exeter charged and again dismissed. Anyways you looks at it, it were not fair.

That winter they lowered our wages again another sixpence.

Chapter Eighteen

Sydney, 1834

JAMES BRINE WAS THE FIRST TO LEAVE.

"You're assigned to Gliddon, to a farm there." The sweating officer looked up at Brine. "Here's a blanket, some more clothin' and a shilling. A steamboat will take you to Newcastle and you'll make your own way from there."

"Is the farm near this Newcastle, then?" questioned Brine.

"Not far. About a thirty mile walk. No loiterin', mind. You gets there as quick as you can. Is that understood? An' make sure you've got your travel document with you at all times. Lose it, an' you can be charged with tryin' to escape."

"But, Sir, I knows not the way. Be there roads to follow?"

"You got a tongue in yer 'ead, use it. Ask! And you'd best not get lost."

Brine looked anxiously this way and that. People intent on their own business jostled against him. Who should he approach for directions? Putting down his bundle and giving his hands, sweaty from nervousness, a rub against his trousers, he walked towards a man lolling against a stack of barrels, smoking a pipe – the only person who seemed oblivious to the bustle going on around him.

It was the thought of having to find his own way in this vast stretch of land, he, who before being convicted, had never journeyed further than ten miles from Tolpuddle, that gave rise to Brine's feeling of panic. If only Thomas was with him. On the journey out from England, he had recognized that Thomas had replaced the father he could scarcely remember.

Still leaning against the barrels, the man said, "Glindon, aah! You needs to follow this here road." Brine struggled to follow the man's garrulous instructions which were accompanied by much spitting and hawking and pointing with the stem of his pipe.

Turning to retrieve his pack, Brine found his possessions had been stolen. He cursed himself for his stupidity. Hadn't he learned anything on the voyage? Now all he had was the clothes he was wearing. His boots – well used and of poor quality when they were first issued to him in England – were already separating uppers from sole. Securing them as best he could with some twine he found, he set off on the trek to Gliddon.

He avoided the coarse, yellowed grass that bordered the rough track as he trudged along, fearful of what insects might be concealed in the tangled growth. Convicts who had been returned to the prison to await assignment to another location would recount with relish stories of prisoners dying in agony from stings from spiders or snake bites. Gradually, overcoming his fear of what might lurk in the grass, he focused on the scenery around him. Eucalyptus trees with bark hanging in tattered strips from their smooth limbs; a variety of shrubs all a subdued grey-green; dragonflies with iridescent wings, much larger than the pond varieties of home, flashed their amazing beauty. His presence startled into flight rainbow-hued birds. Later, propped against the trunk of a tree in a clearing, the night seemed to come alive. Continuous strange rustlings in the undergrowth kept him from sleep.

Only twice did he come across another traveler. On the first occasion the marked reticence of a wagon driver to be drawn into conversation took Brine by surprise. The heavy-set man had pulled on the reins to slow the pace of the horse slightly, but didn't bring the cart to a halt. "Yeh, you're on the right road for Gliddon" was all he volunteered. Unfriendly lot thought Brine. He could've offered me a lift. Guess he recognized me for what I am, a convict! Did he think I'd attack him, rob him? Why he was twice my size. It was the first time Brine had applied the label of convict to himself. He'd accepted the fact he'd been convicted, transported, but until now had refused to see himself as others saw him. A convict. A felon.

"Stolen! Sold more likely." His new master, Mr. Scott, spoke brusquely. "You're one of them Dorchester men. Trouble makers!" Stabbing at Brine's chest with his finger, Scott continued. "I only have to give you new clothing, boots, bedding, twice a year. In six month's time you'll get further supplies. 'Till then, make do!"

Set to digging postholes, it didn't take much more than a week for his disintegrating boots to fall apart. Unwinding the strips of sacking he'd wrapped round his feet, Brine studied his blistered, bleeding soles. It was impossible to put pressure on the spade. He'd be on a charge when the overseer saw how little he'd accomplished. Recalling a pile of debris he'd seen dumped behind a shed, he limped over to see if there was anything he could use to protect them. Scrabbling amongst the rubbish, Brine pulled out a piece of iron hoop. With a heavy rock he managed to shape the hoop to go around his foot. Padding the band with rags, he went back to his digging.

With clothes in tatters from constant sweat and exposure to the sun, no bedding, Brine waited for the six months to pass.

~~~

Sarah hesitated in the doorway at the sound of a male voice conversing with her mother. She grabbed at Mathew's coat to stop him from rushing into the cottage. Crouching, they both peered in the open doorway. "Who be it, Sarah?" asked Mathew in a whisper. She gestured to Mathew to be quiet, but Elizabeth, hearing them, turned in her chair and beckoned them to come in.

"These are my two eldest, Mr. Brown. Sarah and Mathew. Two pairs of eyes fastened on the plump gentleman sitting in their father's chair. Their gaze travelled up from the once-shiny, now mud-splattered, boots, tan breeches, a riding coat of dark brown worsted to a round face framed by bushy grey sideboards. He turned in their direction with a smile. Sensing her mother's unvoiced instructions, Sarah hastily dipped a curtsey. Mathew followed his sister's example and made a clumsy bow.

"They're a credit to you, M'am." He studied Mathew carefully. "Are you a good boy, a comfort to your mother?"

Overcome by shyness, Mathew hesitated before replying. "I try to be, Sir."

"Have you learned your letters? Can you read, son?"

"We did lessons with Father every night." Mathew's voice quivered when he mentioned his father. "With Father not here to teach us of an evening, Sarah tries to help me with my studies, and I read the Scriptures to Mother after supper."

"Mr. Brown's come from Dorchester to talk with your Aunt Dinny and me. Sarah, take the baby and the pair of you find something to do outside. The vegetable patch needs weeding."

It was only then that the children withdrew their eyes from Mr. Brown and took in the fact that Dinniah was standing in the shadowed recess of the room. Flashing a quick smile in the direction of her aunt, Sarah hastily lifted her whimpering baby brother from the cradle and followed Mathew outside.

"What's that man doin' here, Sarah? He ent goin' to take Mother away too, be 'ee?" asked Mathew, for Mr. Brown's presence filled him with anxiety.

"No, Silly. He's the man from Dorchester. Brought Mother and Aunt Dinny money."

"Money?"

"From the union people in London. You should listen more and you'd know about these things."

Holding a finger to her lips, Sarah stooped near the window, straining to hear what was being said.

"...prayers have been answered. Dinniah and me were near destitute again, Sir. I can't thank 'ee enough."

"A miracle, you arrivin' just as things were getting' desperate," added Dinniah. "I be lost for words, but thank 'ee." Tears of gratitude began to trickle down Dinniah's cheeks. Dabbing at them with the edge of her shawl, she asked, "Have you any news of our men, Mr. Brown? Any news at all?"

~~~

"See you've worked as a farm labourer in the Old Country so I'm placing you on a spread up near Maitland. Make sure you abide by the rules and cause no trouble." The assigning officer turned from Thomas and addressed three other convicts. "You'll all travel up-river. You lot are destined for Pickford." He turned again to Thomas. "You, Standfield, are further up Hunter River." As the last of the four prisoners stepped forward to receive his travel documents, the officer added, "And don't be thinking of escape! You'll be hunted down, flogged till there's no flesh left on yer backs and then, should you live, sent to the chain gang for the rest of yer term." He made a gesture towards the window. "Out there, you scum of the earth, you won't find a replica of England. You wouldn't survive a week on yer own."

Thomas squatted in the stern of the small steamboat, his back against a tarpaulin-covered pile of cargo. He'd stood for a long time at the start of the journey studying the scenery, the other boats they passed, the great stretches of river bank with not a sign of habitation. Now, hunched into his thin jacket, he watched the dawn breaking. Passengers walked the deck or leaned over the side conversing.

When they finally docked he was not sorry to part company from the other three prisoners' coarse behavior and foul language. He'd had to be constantly vigilant to safeguard his few possessions from them. In the early morning light there was a bustling of figures at the dockside unloading and loading cargo. A man on horseback pointed out the way to Maitland.

"Seven miles at most. You can make it by noon."

Forced to rest frequently by the exhausting heat and his weakened state, it was midafternoon before he arrived.

"You can ride pillion b'hind me," said Nolan's overseer. "It's a fairish distance." Unused to riding a horse, Thomas' attention was focused on keeping his balance and holding onto the bag of supplies the overseer had given him. Finally the overseer halted the horse. "This is it," he said, dismounting. "Now, see that trail. Follow it and you'll come to a creek. Water's clear and fit for drinking. That hut over there'll do you for sleeping."

Thomas looked at the rough wooden structure. "Will nobody work alongside me?"

"No, you're on your own, mate, You keep a good eye on them sheep, now. Just 'cos I'm not breathing down your neck all day, don't mean you can slack off."

"I've always been known as reliable and a hard worker."

The overseer studied Thomas carefully. "It's to be hoped so. We've had some bad 'uns in the past, but you do yer work and there'll be no trouble between us." He took a swig of water from flask and held it out to Thomas. "Come by the house once a week for more supplies," he instructed.

Thomas gazed about him. Rough pasture, sectioned by wire-strung posts, stretched as far as he could see, interspersed with thickets of low-growing bushes, and large wooded areas. From a gum tree came a curious cackle. The overseer caught Thomas' startled look.

"Kookaburra!" said the overseer. "Noisy birds, but, myself, I likes their laugh. Good for keepin' snakes down, too."

Something scuttled up the bark of another tree. "Squirrel?" questioned Thomas, noting the overseer's willingness to talk.

"Nah! Tree kangaroo. Pesky little buggers. 'Tis the big 'uns though that are a plague. Two roos can eat as much grass as three sheep, so we tries to keep 'em down." He tipped his hat forward and scratched at the back of his head. "Mind you, they're not bad eatin'. But keep away from their hind legs. They can do some fearful damage with their nails. Like bloody knives." He started to walk back to where he'd tethered his horse. "You wanna watch out for dingoes. Often run in packs. You'll likely hear 'em at night. Horrible howlin' noise. They usually stays clear of humans, but they'll take down a sheep an' rip it to pieces.

"Well, I must head back. Don't forget to keep a check on the fences. There's wire and tools for repairs in the hut."

He slung his leg over his horse, turned her nose around and started back along the track, callin' over his shoulder, "I'll be checkin' in on yer every once in a while. Make sure you does a good job. Yer should have about a week's grub there. Best come for more after the sheep are penned at night."

~~~

Having heard seasoned convicts' tales of the brutal treatment many suffered at the hands of their masters, John Standfield realized he was fortunate with his assignment. Life at the farm at Balwarra was hard, but his master, Richard Jones, and the overseer both treated him fairly.

"You're a good worker, I'll say that for you," commented Jones one day. "What they ship you out for?"

"We committed no crime, Sir."

"We?"

"My father an' four friends. We were just trying to better our lot, and were unjustly convicted."

"Yeh! 'Tis a claim most of you felons make!"

"It's true, Sir. I swear before God."

"So yer one of those Pollies, are yer?"

"Pollies?" queried John.

"Politicals, from Ireland mostly. You don't sound Irish, though. You one of the Scottish Polys?"

"No. Dorset. England."

"Yer father was shipped out with yer, eh? Where's he bin sent?"

"I'm tryin' to locate him. I've heard he was sent to Maitland."

"Maitland! That's only three mile further up. There's only a couple of spreads, big 'uns, up there. You know which one?"

"I know nothin' more than that, Sir. But he's getting on in years and I'm concerned for him."

"If I gets the opportunity I'll make some enquiries for yer. Can't promise anything, mind."

Dare he put any hope in Jones' words? What likelihood was there of him even remembering the conversation that had passed between them? After weeks went by he began to despair of meeting his father again.

~~~

Kathrine Standfield pulled the door of her cottage shut and set off down the lane to her mother-in-law, Dinniah's, house. David, tied with a shawl

111

to his mother's back, acted as a counter-balance to the bulge of her belly. She reached a hand back to free a strand of her hair from David's grasp. "You'll have to start usin' them legs of yours soon, young man," she said wearily, as once more she paused, hands to the small of her back.

Reaching Dinniah's cottage, she pushed open the door, calling out, "Mother Dinniah, you home?"

At the sound of Kathrine's voice, Dinniah hurried forward, arms outstretched to take David from his mother. "Here, let me have him. Sit down, Kat dear, and rest yourself. Will you take a drink of water?" Setting David down on the floor, Dinniah bustled about, pouring water from a stoneware jug, removing a cut loaf from under a cloth. "A little bit of bread an' cheese? You needs to keep your strength up. "

Declining the proffered food, knowing Dinniah had little enough to feed her own family, Kathrine said, "I've only come for a little company, Mother Dinniah. Found m'self talking nonsense to Davy again, I be so starved for someone to chat to."

"I was thinkin' on you only a few minutes back, Kat. Wonderin' if it wouldn't be better if you moved in with us, seein' as your time's comin' on."

"Tis kind of you, very kind. But you ent got the room, and 'twas but two days back my mother made the same offer. It'll mean help once the babe's born. "Struggling against tears, head leaning against the arm Dinniah had put around her shoulders, Kathrine added. "Oh, I misses John so."

"Of course you do, m' dear. 'Tis only natural."

A gurgle from behind them made the two women turn as one to see David taking staggering steps towards them. "He's walking! Mother Dinniah, he's walking."

"There's a clever lad. Done it all by yourself," said Dinniah. "It's a wicked shame his father not here to see it, nor aware that there's another on the way."

~~~

Under the shade of a jacaranda tree, its heliotrope bells a vivid splash of colour against the bleached grey of the house walls, John stood with the water dipper to his lips.

Jones examined John's work repairing a stone wall and nodded his approval.

"Yer father. I hear he's on Nowlan's spread."

"Praise the Lord! Did you learn how he was, Sir?"

"I can tell yer nothin' more than that. But come Christmas, if you continues to behave yerself an' don't try slippin' off to see him, I'll see if I can arrange a visit. It will need Nowlan's permission as well as mine."

"Sir, it'd be wondrous kind if you'd do so. I knows not how to express my gratitude."

It was a week after Christmas when Jones handed John a letter establishing John Standfield had his permission to leave his property to travel to Maitland and was to return by sundown the same day.

Nowlan's overseer studied John's travel document, folded it carefully and returned it to him. "He's in the pasture over there," he said, pointing out directions. "Check in with me again when you leave."

John found Thomas resting against the trunk of a half-dead gum tree. He was distressed at his father's appearance, how he had aged. The hot climate had leathered the skin on Thomas' gaunt frame. His face was lined. His thinning hair almost white. When John clasped him in his arms, Thomas winced. He seemed exhausted.

"Dear God," said John in low tones. "Look at you! There's sores all over you."

"'Tis the climate and the rations."

"Don't they give you enough to eat?"

"Food enough, but this coarse-ground bread gets hard mighty quick and within a few days I must soak it along with the dried roo meat overnight before I can manage it. The scurvy I got on the ship has loosened what teeth I have left."

"Don't yer get nothin' fresh? No fruit?"

"Oh, on occasion and there be berries around that I canst eat, but they go right through me and I end up with running bowels. "

John sank down on the grass beside his father. Thomas took John's hand in his. "My, but it is good to see you, son. The Lord be thanked for his mercies."

113

Chewing on a strip of dried roo meat, waving away flies with his hand, John asked, "What are your duties? Is there none to help you?"

"No, I'm on my own. Overseer drops by now and then to check on me. I have to keep the sheep in fresh pasture. Oft times it means walkin' many miles for once they've cleared the grass, there's so little moisture it takes a long time to grow back in. Should any of them stray, 'tis up to me to find 'em. I've six hundred in my care."

"Where do you sleep?'

"In that hut, over there, when I'm nearby. If I'm further afield I sleep rough. But there's fresh water in the creek. At least I can wash and keep myself clean. After all those months on board in that filth, 'tis a blessing from God. Though some evenings I canst scarce raise the energy. But tell as how things are with you."

Before he left John made two trips across the rough grassland and down a trail to the river to refill Thomas' water drum, wishing there was more he could do.

"I hate to leave you like this, Father. There must be summat that can be done."

Gently John held his father, kissed his cheek before starting on his journey back.

As he passed the ranch house a man on horseback called sternly, "Hey, you! What yer doin' on my property?"

Quickly producing Jones' journey warrant John explained who he was, taking in the farmer's sturdy frame, a certain kindness in his eyes.

"Your father, you say? You located him okay?"

Dare he risk mentioning his father's condition? He glanced up again at the man. "I be much concerned about him, Sir. 'Tis his age. He's not a young man anymore."

Nowlan 's reception of his comment was hard to gauge.

Hastily John added, "He speaks well of the treatment he has received here, Sir, but.."

"But?"

"My father is a conscientious man, Sir, and gives his all to his duties. Has always done so. But the workload's takin' a toll on him, Sir. I mean no offense."

Nowlan made no comment except to say, "You'd best get a move on if you're to make your curfew."

Striding along, anxious to arrive before sunset and keep his master's trust, John turned the conversation he had had with Nowlan over in his mind. Had he caused trouble for his father by mentioning his concern? And the overseer. If Nowlan spoke to him, would he not be inclined to consider it criticism and take it out on his father? Maybe he would not be allowed to visit again. He plodded on, tired and worried.

Three months later, when John was again given permission to visit, he found his father's health had improved considerably. Thomas had been transferred to lighter duties on a smaller farm owned by Nowlan, and had only good words for his employer.

This time it was the overseer who checked John's journey warrant.

"I'd like to thank 'ee, Sir."

"How's that?"

"For makin' things easier for my father, Sir. I can't tell 'ee how grateful we both be."

"As long as your father puts in a good day's work and causes no trouble, then there'll be no problem."

"And Sir, if you'd be kind enough to pass on my gratitude to Mr. Nowlan and give him this, I'd be much obliged." John extended a clumsily wrapped package.

"What's this?"

"Tis a pipe-rack I carved of an evening; a token of my appreciation."

Holding the parcel, the overseer stood and watched as John closed the high, barred gate, then strode off in the direction of the house.

Chapter Nineteen

Workhouse 1842

STRANGE HOW MY MIND DO DRIFT BACK TO CHILDHOOD so often. Ent as if it were a happy 'un. How my father could wield that belt of his. When I thinks on him, which be rarely, I still hears the slap of his belt on bare flesh. And my stepmother would land a thump across my ear every time she set eyes on me, but I got skilled at bobbin' and duckin' out of her arm's reach. Seemed every time my father laid into her, she'd take it out on me later. Lucky for me my granny, my mother's mother, lived nearby and I was allus sure of a welcome there, and oft-times she'd let I stay overnight.

Now that be a *comfortin'* memory, my old granny. Sitting beside her hearth, Granny'd rake a potato from the embers and, brushin' the ashes from its blackened skin, she'd hand it to me wrapped in an old piece of cloth and tell I to get it down me 'cos I were nothin' but bones draped in skin.

Sittin' in the glow of the firelight, for candles must be saved till it got real dark, Granny would reminisce on how things were when she were a young 'un. Oh, Gran were full of stories, often about the Little People as she called 'em, for her had a strong belief in fairies and witches. Yes, her were certain sure about such things. Planted a rowan tree near the door of their cottage, her did, for protection against witches. Sometimes she'd break into song, her voice all quavery but sweet. Mostly songs about shepherds, 'cos her father were a shepherd also years back. One I recalls her singin', "Shepherds I've lost my love." Now I thinks on it, I ent heard for years.

And, if I pleaded long enough and Grandad hadn't nodded off on the wooden settle, he'd tell I tales of highwaymen and footpads as would hold up coaches on the highway out from London. His voice'd go all deep and gravelly. Shiverin' with fear I'd press up close to Gran, all of a tremble, but not wantin' Grandad to stop.

Always the smell of wool everywhere in that cottage of theirs. Grandad being a shepherd, he brought the smell home with him. Clung to everything, it did, but it weren't unpleasant. There's many as don't like the smell of wet wool, but I'd like to bury my nose in the hanks Granny'd hung up to dry after she'd combed and spun and washed it. Sit for hours, her would, spin-spinnin' away. And when her weren't spinnin', those fingers of hers, all twisted with rheumatics, would have those needles clickin' faster than a cricket in summer.

There were this apple tree as grew by their cottage. The air around it moved with the hum of bees in spring. Come mid-September when the lower branches were all propped up, so bent they were under the weight of the fruit, Granny 'ud get me to help her pick 'em. Her were only a little thing, my granny, but she'd stoop by that tree, fingers linked tight as tight, and she'd say to I, "Put yer foot in my hands, Sethie, and I'll boost 'ee up." Up into the boughs I'd scramble, and her 'd pass me up a bag. "Pick careful now, Seth. Just the high 'uns as I can't reach. Don't bruise none." Leaves turning colour, and oh, the smell of them apples.

There ent nothin' as can measure up to the smell of apples exceptin' new-mown hay to my way of thinkin'. Damn me, us had to work come hayin' and harvest. By the time the skies were purpled with night, a man were left doubtin' he could swing an arm one more time.

Always racin' against the weather it seemed. Us men keepin' a steady stride, scythes movin' together as if to a drummer-boy's beat, and the rows of fallen hay markin' our progress. Later, most of the men's wives would be out in the medder turnin' the swathes. 'Tis heavy work, turnin' the dryin' hay with wooden rakes, but the women was glad of the opportunity to earn a little extra money. My Mary, if her weren't with child, would be there all tanned in spite of her sun bonnet, jokin' alongside the others, and the sound of her laughter would make I glance up and smile her way. There were some women, real rough 'uns, as would go from farm to farm, and when us broke work at noon for a bite to eat they'd disappear behind a haycock with any man as asked 'em. Never saw Elizabeth Loveless hay-turnin' though. Not that I's sayin' as George's wife were afraid of hard work.

Now why be my mind fixin' on Elizabeth Loveless when just a thought ago, I was thinkin' on Granny Havelock? They didn't look a bit alike, but summat about my Granny minds me of Mistress Loveless though what it be 'tis hard to say. Strong face Elizabeth has, not given much to smilin'. Forbidding were the word my Mary used. But I come on her one day standin' on the bridge down near the mill, and she were *laughin'*. Watchin' and laughin' at her young'un throwin' twigs into the water, and then him rushin' across to see them come out the other side. Samuel, when he were a little'un, were always beggin' I to take him to the bridge, he loved that game so.

Us were layin' in bed when I tells Mary about Elizabeth's young'un and how it minded me of Samuel. Us would often chat about our day afore us went to sleep.

"Well," her says, "I can tell 'ee why her spirits be brighter. That Dorchester man brought 'em more money. Oh, I feels for them poor women."

"You think I don't fret my mind on how they be getting' by?" I says all angry like, for Mary be the last person I expects to be blamin' me for what I done.

"I knows you do, Seth. 'Cos I knows. I weren't getting' at you. Just sayin' as 'tis good to know there be some as is makin' their lives a little easier. I often asks m'self what I'd 'ave done if you'd been took along with 'em."

She lies quiet for a bit, just runnin' her hand over my chest. Then up on one elbow and gives me a real smackin' kiss and starts a-playin' with me. My Mary didst certain sure know how to lift my spirits. Her could make I feel like a king.

Chapter Twenty
Australia 1834

WRAPPED IN HIS THIN BLANKET AGAINST THE NIGHT'S chill, his head resting on his pack, Hammett, fixed his eyes on a star that stood out from the others, its light brilliant and cold. The vast expanse of sky seemed to emphasize his isolation.

He pulled the blanket up higher, exposing his boots. Earlier, sitting beside a small creek where he'd been soaking his sore feet, boots laying on their sides where he had tossed them, he'd watched in horror as a small snake had slithered towards one of them. His body rigid with fear, for they'd been warned how deadly the vermin of certain varieties could be, Hammet carefully stepped back into the water, reached down and picked up a handful of pebbles. His first shot missed; the second and third pebble struck the boot's sole, moving the boot across the sandy ground. Stoning crows as a youngster had made his aim true. As the fourth stone hit home, the snake, forked tongue lashing, slid out and disappeared into the tufts of yellow grass that edged the roadway. Hammet threw more stones at the clumps of grass in case the snake should be still lurking there. He moved his feet on the creek bed in an attempt to find a less stony footing. The water, which had at first seemed wonderfully cool, was now numbing cold. It was sometime before he could overcome his fear enough to step out onto the bank again. His boots would remain on his feet from now on.

He moved his head against the unyielding pack. The star, caught in a sky of black velvet folds, shone with dazzling brightness. It would take only a breath of wind to send that particular one spinning down onto his chest. His hands, involuntarily, reached up as it to catch it; just as quickly he dropped them again. *Stupid tricks a man's mind can play on him. I'm as alone and separated from all else as that star be from the others. If I'm to survive this, then I must think of none but me. All else must be set aside.* With this concept fixed firmly in his mind, Hammett drifted into sleep.

Daily, with each step he took towards his posting, he felt the distance separating him from his wife and child increasing, mentally as well as geographically.

~~~

As if to match the biting winds that seemed to have been blowing since the turn of the year, neighbourliness, so much a part of village life, had blown cold. Whispered gossip grew to outright plain speaking.

"Ent right, their husbands convicted and now they's bein' given money, while us law-abidin' folks struggle to make do."

"You'm bein' right un-Christian.. You think life be easy for 'em? Their men taken off on a trumped up charge, and them not knowin' if they'll see 'em again."

"Twas Standfield and Loveless as went against the law, startin' up a union. Notices were put about that what they be doing was wrong. Callin' 'em martyrs, indeed!"

"It ent as if they're bein' given bags of gold. I hears 'tis only a pittance. They can scarce get by on it."

"And do us fare any better?"

The village was divided.

Back home with her mother, Harriet Hammett, rarely ventured out. Avoiding contact with the Loveless and Standfield women, she leeched strength from her mother. Elizabeth and Dinniah, Alice and Kathrine, aware of the village rift, kept to themselves, doing what they could to comfort and support each other.

~~~

The coach jolted over the uneven road with George fastened by the chains from his leg to the outside. Water glistening in the early April sunlight arced from the wheels as they churned through rain-filled potholes and sprayed his legs. Oblivious to his wet trouser bottoms, George gazed at the spring's new greenery, drinking in the fresh air and the change from grey prison walls. Glinister, the officer assigned to accompany George on his journey to Portsmouth, had spoken little. Now he broke his silence. "We're nigh to Salisbury where we'll have to walk a stretch."

"I'll be glad of the opportunity to give my hands a rest from clinging to the grips. The horses were changed just a while back, though. What's the reason for us having to walk?"

"Some of the streets are so narrow the coaches have difficulty passing through and with us hanging from the side 'tis nigh impossible. I'll remove the irons off your legs when we stop."

"It'll make walking easier."

"It's the rattling of your chains. Draws people's attention and there's some find them disturbing."

"But you mean to replace them once we're through Salisbury?"

"Regulations."

"So the removal of the irons is for their benefit, not mine."

"Aye, but you seems a decent enough fellow, I was considering your feelings as well."

"Leave them on, then. I'm conscious that I've done no wrong, so have no shame in wearing them. Would that I had a notice hung round my neck saying 'See here an innocent man in chains'. Might make people think about the many injustices inflicted on the poor of this country."

Glinister looked at George's determined face. "As you will," he grunted.

Both men retreated into their thoughts again. The coach slowed, came to a halt. The house roofs on either side of the mean street almost touched. Glinister quickly detached George's chains from the coach. People pushed and jostled, trying to avoid the stream of filth that ran down the centre of the road. Glinister became separated from George, who paused for him to catch up.

"I'll not be trying to escape, if that's on your mind," said George. "I was thinking on what you said awhile back, that I seemed a decent fellow."

"You're unlike most prisoners I've had dealings with."

"What think you of this then? When we were charged, those that wanted us brought down did all they could to make out we were rioters. Yet some time back, when there was so much incendiarism prevailing through the countryside, I and my brother, among others, were chosen to stand night-watch to see no damage was done to property in our parish. If we were for rioting, does it seem likely we would have been so chosen?"

Glinister shook his head. "You make a sound argument, but I know little about such matters. I'm just doing my job." He pointed ahead. "The coach'll turn to the left up here, and wait for us at the King William hostelry."

~~~

As the assigning officer on the *William Metcalf* destined for Botany Bay checked each prisoner's name against a list, he paused on seeing the notation against the name George Loveless. Raising his head and looking carefully at George, he said, "Seems the governor of Dorchester Gaol's sent a letter ahead attesting to your good character. You're for an upper berth."

Upper berth conditions, although slightly better than those below, still meant stench and filth, overcrowding, days and nights passed to the accompaniment of continual shouts and curses, the rattle of chains each time a prisoner moved. George calculated the size of the berth to which he and five others were confined: five and a half feet square he reckoned. If only he could spread out the pillow and blanket in the space he'd been allocated. Half sitting, half lying, he longed to stretch out fully, but it was too crowded for any of them to lie flat.

His mind caught on the words *if only*. *If only* justice prevailed. *If only* the magistrates had recognized they'd used legitimate means to try and better themselves. *If only* those in authority could see themselves as they truly were, oppressors of the poor. The inability to oppose such oppression in any way, that was what so enraged him. He scratched at his armpit. Reduced to this – a lice-ridden convict when he'd committed no crime. He couldn't smell worse if he'd been buried in a rotting midden.

He shook his head as if to free it from such thoughts. *Pull yourself together, man. Thinking thus isn't going to help you.* Whatever the future held he would continue his fight against injustice but he must trust in his Maker to give him strength. Over and over he repeated to himself the text, 'He is my refuge and my fortress. In him will I trust.'

What George was to witness now, was worse than anything he'd experienced so far. Summoned up on deck with the rest of the convicts, he found himself in the front of the lines watching as a young man was dragged up from the hold, his face under a coat of grime was blanched with terror. Can't be more than twenty, George noted. From the brig the captain read out the charge: breaking into the stores and stealing victuals. All knew the seriousness of the crime. Rations had been severely cut since several barrels of provisions were found to be so rotten they couldn't even be fed to the prisoners and had to be flung overboard. A strong breeze teased at the strips of cloth as the prisoner's shirt was ripped from his back exposing skin an unhealthy white from lack of sun. Two members of the crew fastened the man's limbs to the mast, sniggering as urine stained the man's trousers and pooled at his feet.

The whip, wielded with a steady even swing, cracked, cut into flesh, cracked again. George watched the bosun's muscular arm rise and fall as he counted off each stripe. *Dear God, was there no limit to man's inhumanity to man? The effort he puts into it, as if he enjoys his task.* George clenched his teeth at the sound of the man's cries. He tore his eyes away from the scene and fixed them on the wind-filled sails that tugged at the ropes making them shriek through the pulley blocks. Trails of clouds straggled across the sky resembling the shredded shirt of the prisoner.

Long before the hundredth stroke had been administered, the man's cries had ceased, his slumped body suspended by the ropes that held him to the mast. Lowering the man to the deck, a bucket of salt water was hurled over the unconscious body.

Returning his gaze once more to the scene before him, his eyes met briefly with those of the bosun. "You there!" he bellowed, indicating George. "Take him down to your berth. You can see to his needs."

For three days George gently trickled brackish water over the young man's head, kept his face and lips moistened, tried to ward off the flies that buzzed busily from over-flowing slop buckets to putrefying flesh. Crouched beside him, scratching at flea bites, periodically cracking a louse between his finger nails, George sponged and prayed – prayed that if the man was to die that he be released from his torment soon. On the fourth day his patient gradually regained consciousness. As George carefully picked maggots from festering flesh, the man cursed George. "You should've let me die," he sobbed. "What's there to live for?"

"You'd not have stolen food if you really had no wish to live," was George's response.

~~~

It was late September when the *William Metcalf* docked in Van Dieman's Land. Wind hurled waves against cliffs of black rock barely visible through the mist and churned the water into a hissing froth.

News of George's union activities had proceeded him. Three times the Governor, fearing George would prove a trouble-maker, had him interrogated before he was assigned to a chain-gang.

In groups of ten, with chains threaded through leg irons that chaffed against ankle bones, George and the others clanked their way at daybreak to work on the construction of a new road. Carrying picks and shovels, under the eye of a corporal and six privates armed with muskets and bayonets, they hacked and dug at the bush and sandstone. In the distance ranged a series of hills and beyond them rose mountains dense with eucalypt forest and jungled with vines and fern.

In response to George's comments on the grimness of the conditions they worked under, the prisoner who slept next to him said, "Macquarie Harbour was a worse assignment than this. We were chained together standing waist-deep in water all day long building a great dyke. There were none without foot-rot and sores all over their legs. A man had to force himself just to walk into the sea each morning, the salt was agony on our open wounds."

George looked at the steep cliffs, the gullies, the harsh metallic green of the shrubs and trees as he paused and, using the sleeve of his jacket, mopped at the blood that trickled from his nose. Always, it seemed, a wind: a wind that flicked grit at skin, into an open mouth, grated against eyelids and irritated George's sinuses. His cuffs were stiff with blackened blood.

"Worse than this? Then it truly must have been a hell on earth."

"You, there! I sees you slackin' again and I'll have yer flogged." The guard struck at the ganger in front of George with a wooden billy. The man stumbled, blood flowing from his head, making the chain tug painfully on the shackle round George's leg. George reached out a hand to break the man's fall and received a blow on his arm. Muttering curses at the guard, George, and Van Dieman's Land, the convict made a show of putting effort into his work. Once the guard's attention was turned elsewhere he dug in a dilatory manner, often using his shovel for support.

"You sick?" queried George rubbing his throbbing arm.

"What d'yer think," was the snarled reply. Then a more conciliatory voice, "Don't know as how to stay on my feet."

The prisoners worked hour upon hour. Dust filled their mouths and nostrils; sweat cemented it to their bodies. The rough fabric of George's shirt rubbed where the sun had burned his neck. Long before it was time to return to barracks, the sick ganger had collapsed. Hauled off and dumped near a pile of broken rocks, he was left to lie in the sun with no attention.

It was some weeks later as they were lined up for work that George's name was called out.

"Loveless? Which one of you bastards is Loveless?" shouted a corporal.

Dropping the length of chain that connected him to the convict in front of him, George raised his hand. "I'm Loveless."

"Sir!. You call me 'Sir' when you speak." The corporal struck George a blow across the ear. "Seems you're off chain-gang duties. You're for the government farm." Turning to a soldier at his side, the corporal ordered, "Unchain him then. Look sharp!"

The soldier knelt to unfasten the chain, roughly jerking the links through the ring on George's fettered ankle.

"Take him to get his things," ordered the corporal, "and be quick about it. Cart's near ready. He's to go with it."

Lolling in the doorway, lazily picking at his nose, the soldier watched as George, adjusting his vision to the building's gloom, hastily rolled his few possessions in his blanket. With a laconic, "This way," the soldier led him over to a group of prisoners loading sacks onto a cart.

Walking behind the supply cart to which he was chained, George tried to shield his eyes and throat from the dust thrown up by the wheels. The sky was leaden, the air thick. A couple of times George attempted to converse with the man driving the cart. Completely ignoring George, the driver sat hunched forward, keeping the horse on a steady course, never stopping. At last, straggling farm buildings, their wood bleached to a silver-grey, came into sight.

Assigned to shepherding and stock-keeping duties, George frequently laboured twelve or fourteen hours a day. "But it's a thousand times better than on the chain gang, and it's work I've done all my life," expressed George to a fellow prisoner.

"Ay, if you're one o' the ones lucky enough to get a bed at night," he responded. "Eight men in a hut for five, when we're all wacked out by the time we finishes. Leastways *you* can sleep with the stock."

A grimness had taken hold of George's features giving them the appearance of being chiseled from stone. His deep-set eyes seemed to have slipped back further into their sockets. Lying on his bed of mounded straw, the soft snorting of the cows and the occasional stomping of their feet a backdrop to his thoughts, George pondered on how he could acquire some writing materials. Maybe by mixing soot with a little water or some juice from those dark blue berries he'd seen growing on some low bushes, he could concoct a type of ink. The crumpled piece of paper dropped by the office clerk and surreptitiously picked up by George, had made George heady with the hope of writing another letter to Elizabeth. He'd managed to smuggle one out to her while held on the prison hulk at Portsmouth but had had neither the materials nor the opportunity since. First he must find something to write with: how he could possibly get it delivered he would overcome later.

The fate of his family was a constant concern. A resourceful woman, Elizabeth, a good, conscientious wife, but his mind churned on how she could feed the children, keep them from being evicted, avoid being sent to the workhouse? He and Elizabeth had grown up in the same village, attended the same chapel. Their coming together had been less of a courtship than an appreciation of each other's qualities – he of Elizabeth's dependability, she of his resoluteness of purpose. Harnessed in marriage they pulled together well. But resourceful as she was, without his wages how were she and the children managing? Were there any in the village who would aid them? With him gone and Thomas and John, who could she call on for help? Thank God she and Dinniah had each other for comfort. Mathew, being so young, could bring in very little, and who'd give him regular work? No chance of schooling for him now. It was only sleep brought on by exhaustion that silenced his thoughts.

Chapter Twenty-One

MARY DONE HER BEST TO MAKE OUR LITTLE COTTAGE cosy. Even on the dreariest day, comin' inside were like havin' a comfortin' blanket thrown around my shoulders. On the battered table her mother give us, Mary'd have a bunch of flowers in a chipped white jug. Whatever were in season: bluebells, ox-eye daisies, late summer fire-weed. Come autumn her'd pick leaves of red and yeller mixed in with a spray of berries. She'd always find summat to add a bit of brightness. On the deep-set window-sill a geranium her managed to keep flowerin' summer and winter alike. And rare were the days when she'd not greet me with a smile full of lovin'.

She weren't smilin' that day though when the young uns were playin' foolish and the white jug got broke. Her sat at the table tryin' to put the broken pieces together again but it were beyond repair. It weren't of any great value but it'd belonged to her granny and so were a fair old age. She had a rare old cry over that smashed piece of pottery, like as not because it were the only ornament her had. Women seems to set great store on things like that.

I be thinkin' on primroses but my mind's eye keeps seein' 'em as blue, not pale yeller. Now why be that? Must be the sickness. It just ent possible to think straight since I been in here.

When the carrier man next come through the village with his wares, Mary's eye were taken with a vase he had. She kep' on about the colour. Blue. Blue like a July sky were the way she put it. Two shillin' and sixpence he wanted for 'un. Near half a week's wages. There weren't no way us could afford such an amount, 'specially as it weren't summat as could be eaten, worn or be of real use. I thought hard and long on how I could earn some extra money, I longed so to get it for her.

Able Smithson, the sexton, would sometimes get I to dig a grave for 'un, him gettin' on in years and sufferin' from the rheumatics. With the weather bein' right unseasonable for September, the rain never seemed to give over and the wind were rippin' the leaves off the trees long before it were time for them to be shed, he paid I to dig the one needed for old Mistress Blackstone. So, there be I early one evenin', standin' ankle-deep in water yellowed by the soil, wonderin' whether I'd call it a day and finish the job tomorrow seein' as how sexton said the funeral weren't till the Thursday, when my bladder let it be known it needed emptyin'. With that much water in the pit already, there didn't seem much point in haulin' m'self out and goin' behind a bush. In the midst of relievin' m'self in the half-dug hole, who should come headin' my way but Parson. In a flash I grabs off my hat and holds it in front of my unfastened trousers.

The wind tugs at Parson's umbrella as he demands, "Haven't you finished yet, Fielding? The funeral's early tomorrow so the job must be completed this evening." Cor, I were lucky he hadn't come along a second earlier. It would've been the last bit of grave-diggin' as would've come my way, that's for sure.

"Sexton said the funeral be on Thursday," says I.

"Wednesday morning, man. Tomorrow!"

So I struggled on and finished the job, concentrating my thoughts on the sixpence sexton had promised which I be determined to save towards the vase Mary wanted so much. Turns out sexton were right. Later the thought come to me that maybe Parson were just sayin' the burial were Wednesday to get back at I. He ent never forgot I defied him that spring day, refusin' to fetch his hat.

Parson and that black hat of his with the rounded crown. In my mind's eye I can still see it rollin' along on its brim, headin' for a puddle. Furious he were. He can surely work hisself into a real lather. Like when there be talk of parliament bein' petitioned to bring Loveless and the others back home. Such talk gets him right agitated. Accordin' to what were read out in the tavern, people was still argufyin' on the matter up there in London.

Although one shillin' and nine pence half-penny were all that I managed to scrape together over the months in spite of stayin' away from the ale house, when I hears the carrier man be in the village I heads off to his cart hopin' I can bargain him down on the price of that blue vase.

If there be a god, a matter about which I've many doubts, 'tis certain sure he ent rainin' down blessings on I, Seth Fielding. Carrier man said as how he'd sold the vase long since.

"A white jug, then?" I asks.

"Yes, yes. I have such a ting," says he in that funny accent he have, and hunts through all his wares. When he finds it, under some boxes of pans, the handle be broke off.

How couldst I give my Mary a jug without a handle when her longs for a July-blue vase?

"You got *anything* for puttin' flowers in?"

"Yes," says he. "In a minute I find."

I has to wait while he cuts a length from a bolt of fabric for Betsy Selkirk, while her and her friend sniggers to each other about what the world's comin' to? Men askin' for such fripperies as vases.

Then he climbs back into his cart and opens a wooden box at the back. The sun catches on a glass vase he holds in his hand and sends out rainbows of redness, the colour of them little wild strawberries as grows along the banks come high summer. Two shillings he wanted for un. He could see how much I were taken with it, and us haggled back and forth. Finally he says, "I can tell she means much to you, dis voman of yours," and he agrees to accept what money I have. "A gift for someone so much loved should alvays be wrapped," says he, and he finds a piece of soft red paper to put around it.

Mary's face were such a picture of surprise and happiness when I gives the vase to her. I apologizes for it not being the blue 'un she'd hankered after, but her flings her arms around my neck and says 'Tis the most beautiful thing there ever were."

It ent often I were able to make Mary as happy as I did that day.

Chapter Twenty-Two

HE MUST NOT LET THEM SEE HOW FEARFUL HE WAS. Charged with neglect of duty, George's stomach churned at the thought of the flogging he would receive. Although there was no truth in the allegation, he knew magistrates gave more credence to an employer's or overseer's word than that of the prisoner standing before him. The magistrate had dealt summarily with the previous three cases so he had little hope of receiving a fair hearing.

"In what manner has this man neglected his duties?" The magistrate scarcely raised his eyes from the papers in front of him as he asked the question.

"Nine of the wild cattle in his charge were taken to the public pound yesterday and he didn't miss them until this morning."

The magistrate looked up sharply. "Cattle in your care were impounded! I've not heard a clearer charge of neglect of duty. What do you have to say in answer?"

Look at him full face George told himself. As if addressing a crowd of a Sunday, George spoke forcefully and clearly.

"It is true I have charge of all the cattle and am expected to see the wild cattle in the bush once every twenty-four hours. However, my duties are thus: I rise at sunrise and take the sheep to the bush to feed. I then return to the farm and milk nine cows and suckle as many calves. I am required to follow the sheep and not lose sight of them and I am to search for the wild cattle to see that none are missing." George took a deep breath. "The reason I did not miss the cattle is that I'd just been weaning the lambs, and the ewes being very restless I was afraid of leaving them. This, Sir, is why the cattle strayed and were taken to the pound."

The magistrate, his attention held by George's strong response and his gaze which had been fixed on the magistrate, turned abruptly to the overseer. "Is all this true, what this man has told me?"

"It is, Sir."

"And has this man neglected his duties before?"

"No, Sir, not in the nine months he's been assigned to the farm. But that don't excuse the fact the cattle strayed while under his care."

"But it would appear this man has more duties than he can perform? Why is my time being wasted on such matters? I have more important matters to deal with than this. It's a pity you brought him here."

George wondered if he was hearing correctly: a magistrate speaking on behalf of a prisoner! The magistrate turned to George., "I'm returning you to your duties, my man."

No fifty lashes! A magistrate whose rulings were just!

On the journey back to the government farm, the overseer cursed the magistrate and berated George. "Think you've outwitted me? Believe me, my eyes'll not be off you from now on."

~~~

"I saw Elias Trimble comin' from your place, so I had to come an' see if all were well." Elizabeth stood in Dinniah's doorway, holding Daniel in her arms.

"Kathrine's mother asked him to drop by as he was comin' out this way." Stepping back from the entrance, Dinniah beckoned Elizabeth to come in. "I didn't like to question Elias at length. You knows how men be about talking of women's matters. Another boy."

"God be praised! He's healthy?"

"Smallish, but then I don't think Kathrine were feedin' right towards the end. Givin' what food she had to the young 'un."

"I'll not be keepin' you as I can see you're settin' off out." Elizabeth with Daniel astride her hip, turned towards the door. "But Kathrine, how's she?"

"Poorly, I understands. Thought as how I'd walk over and see how she's farin.'"

"If you care to take a jug with 'ee an' stop by a farm on the way, I can manage a farthing for a little milk for her."

"A grand idea, Lizzie. I was churnin' my mind around, tryin' to think of summat to take over. I'll make it up to a halfpence, then there'll be some for her and Davey."

Hand raised to shield her eyes from the morning sun, Elizabeth stood and watched Dinniah's bonneted head bob-bobbing as with long strides she set off for Affpuddle.

~~~

It took James Loveless fourteen days to walk to his assigned workplace. "Here's your supplies, Loveless. The quicker you walk, the longer they'll last," were his instructions.

Plodding along through a growth of gum trees late one morning, James was startled at the sight of a black man rapidly climbing down from one of the trees. James marvelled at the dexterity of the man, for in one hand he held a dripping section of honey comb. He seemed oblivious to the bees that buzzed angrily around his head.

James had seen some of these blacks before, but only at a distance. Fearful, unsure whether to run deeper into the bush, James hesitated a moment. In those few seconds the black man reached the ground, and with a grin showing dazzling white teeth, held out a piece of comb. He grunted something and again gestured to James to take the honey he was offering. Cautiously James reached out, grabbed at the gift, and stepped back several paces. The man was much taller than James, his body patterned with slashed scars, his face painted with white stripes. It was only his grin that softened the fearsome features, that kept James from running off in terror.

Then he was gone. It happened so swiftly, so silently, that James questioned whether his mind was playing tricks. Only James' sticky fingers were proof that the man had not been an illusion.

Pondering on his experiences, at last James reached his destination. Listening to tales of other convicts experiences, he soon appreciated he'd a fair master, and in some ways conditions were better than he'd known in England. It was the continual worry about Alice, how she and the two young ones were faring, that was hard to bear. She was always forefront in his mind. What did she do for food, with no money coming in? At least she was strong, not a milksop like Hammet's wife, but without him to work and support her, might she be reduced to begging or the workhouse? And George and the others, what sort of treatment were they getting from their masters? At night, sleep often eluded him as his mind raced with such questions, and when sleep came it was tortured with dreams of a skeleton-thin children, wailing with hunger.

Chapter Twenty-Three
Workhouse 1842

THERE WERE A FEELIN' OF FEAR IN THE VILLAGE. MAYBE that be too strong a word; suspicion be more like it. Everyone were careful in what they said to another. Before all this union business come about, us paid little attention to the goings on of the wider world beyond Tolpuddle an' the other villages. Now folks strained their ears for any news but watched when they spoke in case it should be misjudged.

Mary come back from the village one day, sayin' as how she'd heard Parson talkin' to some gentleman, and they were sayin' the unions were fairly at an end. Not accordin' to Master, says I to her, for only that day I'd heard him on about the papers sayin' another demonstration in support of the Tolpuddle men was bein' organized in London. Master were in a foul mood, mutterin' curses. Said as how the arrest and transportation of Loveless and the others had all been for naught; all he'd got out of it was a lazy sod of a labourer in place of Loveless. Yellin' at the man he'd hired a while back, he were, shoutin' that come Hirin' Day he'd find someone a darn sight more useful.

I saw him headin' my way, and fearin' he were goin' to pick on me next, I gets into the pig pen an' starts shovellin' their muck out of the pen in a wide arc so as Master wouldn't want to come close.

Things in the village were different, that's for certain sure.

One as didn't mix were Harriet Hammett. You'd a thought her'd of kept close to the other women whose husbands were took. Katherine

Standfield and her be much the same age, but Mary says she don't seem to venture far from her mother's cottage. Seems strange, cuttin' herself off from everyone like that.

I knows how much I wishes things were like they used to be. When my Mary would like as not be part of a claver of wives exchanging gossip, and others would give I a warm greeting an' stop to chat. 'Tis an awful feelin' this being shunned. There be times when I wants to stand on that bench under the sycamore tree and shout for all to hear, "It weren't done for the money. I were forced into it." But if I were to stand there, yellin' out the truth of the matter, would any've listened? Would any've believed what I were sayin'? No. Their minds were made up, closed.

So I kept company with myself. Many an evenin' I spent in Squire's woods and sometimes further afield doing a bit of poachin'. I recalls one night I near got caught.

I ent got much taste for fish but Mary be right fond of 'em. The season bein' right, there were I one night busy helpin' myself to Squire's trout. Where the bank've been undercut by the flow of water, I slowly puts my hand in, for I know 'tis where trout hide theirselves. I'd already landed one good sized 'un and were so caught up in gently wrappin' my fingers around another, I didn't hear the soddin' gamekeeper 'til he were right behind me. It were panic more 'en wits as made me fling the fish at him. Caught him in the face, surprisin' him a moment. He takes a step back'ards and stumbles over a root and I takes to my heels afore he can recover hisself. Cor, I ent never run so fast. Could hear him pantin', his feet thuddin' behind me. Gaspin' for breath, my lungs and throat burnt dry, on and on I ran, twistin' this way, dodgin' and weavin' about, and all the time seein' myself up afront a magistrate, seein' myself sent off like Loveless and the others. But he were a heavyset man whereas there be no spare flesh on I. In the end I manages to give him the slip.

"No trout be worth losing you, Sethie," says Mary all distressed. "You think I want you transported?" So I stays put by the hearth of an evenin' for many a night until the urge comes on me again, and the need for somethin' in the cooking pot other than taters. And it be an *urge*, a feelin' of getting' back at them as forced us all into this situation. Times were, when for all of Mary's pleadin' and enticin' I to cuddle alongside her in bed, that urge won out. It were hard, mind, for Mary and me were still as taken with each other as when us were first wed. Time and again, in the warmth of our bed, Mary'd make I forget all that were troublin' me.

The woman as washes and changes us ent reached my pallet yet, thank God. Sick as I be just thinkin' on my Mary in bed 'ave got my cock stirrin', summat it ent done for months, just as if Mary were alongside me a'tinkerin' with it.

Tinker … there were a tinker, a travellin' man, as would come round the villages a couple of times a year. Dark and swarthy, real foreign lookin'. Mothers 'd threaten a misbehavin' child with, "The tinkerman'll get yer." I can hear him now callin' out "Mend y'pots, Grind y'knife, Give em all a new life."

Now how come my thoughts have flitted to the tinkerman?

Mary had a pot as needed mendin' once. When she heard the tinkerman were in the village she hurries down the lane with it, Tabby trottin' after her, for it were the only one of any size us owned. As Mary told I later, when the man were finished hammerin' home a plug of metal and Mary asked him how much it'd be, he said as how if she'd come behind the hedge with him, there'd be no charge. "In front of Tabby, too," says Mary all indignant, but I could tell by the flush on her cheeks that she'd seen it as a compliment as well. "And don't 'ee get all worked up like a turkey-cock now, Sethy." So I kisses her hard and tells her as how she's worth a lot more than the mendin' of an old pot. "How much then?" she asks, but there were no way I could put into words what she meant to me.

Chapter Twenty-Four

Tolpuddle 1835

"DAMN IT, WOMAN! A HOUSE-PARTY AT THE PONSONBYS. That twittering idiot, Maria!"

Agnes Finchbury turned towards her husband, with a look of hurt astonishment. She was seated at her writing desk, a letter in her hand. Curled brown hair covered by a starched white morning cap, the strings hanging over each shoulder, framed a gentle, plumpish face.

"Henry! What's come over you? Using such language to me?"

Henry, his back to the room, stared, with unseeing eyes, out of the window. So preoccupied with his thoughts, he was oblivious to the autumn colouring of the rolling countryside, a scene that usually never failed to move him. He was blind to the burnished copper of the beech, the russet of the oaks, the brilliance of rose hips that flamed in a hedgerow. Pharaoh, a large black retriever ambled over to Henry's side and pressed his nose into one of the hands hanging limply at Henry's side.

At last his wife's words penetrated his dark mood. He crossed the room to her side, placed a hand on her shoulder.

"I apologize, my dear. I'm out of sorts."

"You've been out of sorts for some long time, husband. What is it that is troubling you?"

"Nothing, my dear, nothing. Low in spirits."

"But something must be troubling you. I've never known you so irritable."

Henry slumped back onto the settle. Brown-booted legs stretched out straight in front of him, hands tucked under his armpits, he avoided his wife's eyes. "If you really wish to visit with the Ponsonbys, then, of course, we'll go."

"I fear they would be offended should we refuse. But, be that as it may, my concern is with you. Henry, are you having … financial troubles?" Agnes' voice was cautious. She knew Henry considered women to be incapable of understanding money matters.

"I lost a sum on an overseas venture, but it's nothing you need be concerned about."

"But you would rather I declined Maria's invitation?"

Seemingly deep in contemplation of the polish on his boots, he did not answer Agnes' question.

A frown creased Agnes' face. She regarded her husband carefully, studied the way he sat slumped in his chair. When did I last hear him laugh she asked herself? And the way he's ignoring Pharaoh! Normally he's forever fondling the animal. It could be downright irritating at times. Were his losses more serious than he was admitting?

Agnes turned back to her desk saying quietly, "I will use my mother's coming visit as an excuse."

For several minutes there was silence, broken at last by Henry. "That fellow. Fielding. Seems every time I go to the village, he's there. The way he looks at me!"

"Fielding? Is that the labourer that gave evidence at the trial?" Agnes, stroking her cheek with the feathered end of her pen, turned again to Henry. "How do you mean, looks at you? Threateningly?"

"Threatening? What threat could Fielding be to me? No, just his look. It's impossible to explain."

"Then why should it upset your composure so?"

But Henry had turned back again to his thoughts, rubbing the heel of one boot against the toe of the other, hands now resting on his thighs. Pharaoh, flopped to the floor in front of him, soulful brown eyes fixed on his master's face, once again tried to get his master's attention. Agnes, watching Henry intently, saw his fingers curl as if he were going to reach over to scratch the dog's head, but instead he started thrumming on the chair arm. More to the room than Agnes, he said, "He's always there. And something compels me to acknowledge him, to speak to him. Two years back I doubt I'd have done more than nod good-day." He tugged at the dog's ears. "Sits in the graveyard staring at a bush."

And you sit staring at your boots or out of the window thought Agnes. She shook her head as if to clear it of the concern she felt on her husband's behalf. Tearing up the piece of paper on which she had been writing and selecting another sheet, Agnes said, "A change of scene, if only for three days, will do you good. I shall accept Maria's invitation. Once the winter rains set in, traveling anywhere will be difficult."

Agnes came daily to see how her new rock garden was progressing. Shading herself from the late June's heat with a parasol, she watched as two workmen levered a large boulder into place, while another dumped a barrow-load of soil.

"The work's coming along well, Hodgkins. Make sure it curves enough to allow for the fishpond."

"Aye, M'am. It's all been taken into account."

Twelve year old Philip stood impatiently at her side, tapping his riding crop against his boots. "So I have your leave to go then, Mother?"

Turning to face him, Agnes asked, "You are sure you have completed your studies to Mr. Fairfax's satisfaction?"

"Yes, Mother," he replied with an exaggerated sigh. Already taller than his mother, his open face so like his father's, Agnes could not restrain herself from reaching up and gently stroking his cheek.

"A broken leg, you say? Poor Robert. I do so hope for his sake that it has been set well."

"He sounded very low in spirits in the note the groom brought and begs me to visit. I'm old enough to ride to Affpuddle and back on my own, and I promise to return before dinner."

"Of course, you may. Give Robert's parents my kind regards. And Philip, don't ride your horse to death in this heat."

Agnes smiled at her son. He placed a light kiss on her cheek. "I'll be careful. Don't fuss. Oh, I almost forgot. Mr. Ponsonby's with Father. I apologize for not mentioning it sooner."

"Then I must go and greet him." Gathering up the hem of her striped lavender dress, she headed up the grassed slope towards the house. As she drew nearer she gave a flourish of her parasol in acknowledgement of Henry and Ponsonby's presence.

"...found sufficient people to support eight petitions, all requesting a remission of the sentence." Henry turned from Ponsonby to watch his wife's approach.

"This Thomas Wakley is the one stirring up strife again. With the government so newly elected, they should be dealing with more important matters." Ponsonby broke off his diatribe against Wakley and extended his hand to Agnes, bent his long frame in a bow. "Good day to you, M'am. You're well, I trust."

"Very well, Mr. Ponsonby, thank you. And Maria. How is she? It must be October since I saw her last. When we visited with you that weekend."

Having been assured that both he and his wife were in the best of health, Agnes, seeing that the two men's minds were on politics again, said she would go and see about some refreshments for them.

"The papers report Wakley is an excellent orator," said Henry. "And it would seem the new Home Secretary, Russell, feels the men were severely treated." Stooping, he retrieved the ball his dog had deposited at his feet, and throwing it far out over the grass, watched the black form race after it.

"Aah," said Ponsonby, pulling the brim of his hat lower to shade his eyes, "but before Wakley could introduce his bill for remission of their sentence, Russell asked that he postpone it. Said he'd given much thought to the matter and was recommending that all six men be granted pardons on the condition they remain in the colonies."

"I understand that suggestion was poorly received. The paper says Russell then made a further suggestion – the four of them be allowed to return to England when they have completed two years of their sentence, but the two Loveless brothers should not be allowed to return ever."

"The idea that any of them return is preposterous!" Ponsonby mopped at his face and neck with his handkerchief, his volatile nature as much as the sun's temperature causing him to perspire profusely. "They should have considered the consequences before they set about starting a union.

I have no sympathy for any of them. They should be forced to see their sentence out."

"Anyway, reports have it that Wakley stuck to his guns, said unless all were included he would not postpone his motion. He sounds like a man well worth watching."

Ponsonby made a motion with his hand as if to brush away such a statement. "But his motion was defeated." His voice was tinged with glee at having scored a point.

"There were many voted for it." Henry, resting his hands on the stone balustrade and, as staring at a copse of beech trees in the distance, uttered "I wish to God it *had* passed."

Ponsonby, so taken aback at Henry's words, flapped his mouth, fish-like, emitting no sound.

At this moment Agnes reappeared, followed by a servant carrying a tray.

"You will take some lemonade, Mr. Ponsonby? It is freshly made. Our well water is wonderfully cold. Unless, of course, you would prefer something stronger?"

Taking a proffered glass, Ponsonby was forestalled in commenting on Henry's remark by the sight of a group of men coming up the slope of grass bearing something between them. A man at the front was calling something out but his words were indistinct.

"What is it, Henry? What is he saying?" questioned Agnes anxiously.

Henry hurried down the steps towards the group. Four men each supported a corner of a sheep-pen slat, on which lay a body. An arm hanging limply over the side flopped back and forth with the men's movements. Now he could see that it was Seth Fielding who was calling to them.

"…thrown from his horse, Sir. Nothin' us could do." Seth's voice mingled with Agnes' cries as she rushed towards her son. Ponsonby, turned from following Henry and Agnes and hastily reclimbed the steps. Waving his arms, frantically he called for servants to help, for someone to ride to Affpuddle for a doctor.

"I fears a doctor will be of no help. He be dead, Sir."

Henry placed his hands on Agnes' shoulders, but she wrenched herself away, sank to the ground beside her son with cries of "No, no! Not Philip!"

And Ordered Their Estate

as the men lowered the rough bier on the grass. Her cries of grief caused the men to turn their eyes away and draw back. Seth had hastily pulled off his hat and the others followed suit.

Crouched at her son's side, Agnes gathered him in her arms. Clutching him tightly, she rocked back and forth imploring him to speak to her.

Henry knelt beside her, placed his arm around her. "Agnes he's…" His words seemed stuck to the roof of his mouth. Swallowing hard, he tried again. "He's gone, my dear." Agnes thrust Henry away. "No, no. Get a doctor. Doctor Wilborne can save him." she screamed, flailing at Henry with one hand, while clutching Philip tight with the other.

Henry, tears coursing down his cheeks, gently eased the boy from her grasp. Slowly standing upright and holding Agnes firmly in his arms, he helped her to her feet. He drew his wife close, cupping her head against his chest with a hand sticky with his son's blood.

With Agnes's wails muffled against his coat and Henry brokenly imploring of everyone, of no one, "Why? Why Philip?", they stood oblivious to the men, the servants.

A silence enveloped the watchers, broken only by the cawing of rooks and the sound of Ponsonby's boots clattering on the stone steps as he hurried down again to join Henry and Agnes. Some servants who had followed Ponsonby, unsure of what to do, hung back.

Henry, still holding Agnes to him, in a voice cracked with emotion, instructed the servants to carry Philip's body to his room, told the housekeeper to take her mistress back to the house.

Supported by the housekeeper, Agnes allowed herself to be led away, her cries of "Philip, my baby," hanging in the air.

With his back to the men, Henry mopped at his eyes with a handkerchief before turning to face them. With difficulty, he forced his voice to frame some questions. "How … ? Did you see … ?" he eventually asked of Seth.

"I were by the gate. Long Meadow. Sharpenin' my scythe. We be hayin'." Seth shuffled his feet, kept his eyes fixed on the ground. "I hears a horse gallopin' and looks up just as summat, a pheasant I thinks, flew up in front of Young Sir's horse. Startled 'un. Made 'un rear up and the lad were thrown." Hawking noisily to clear his throat, head still bent, Seth

143

continued. "His head struck the big rock us uses to prop the gate open for the haywains." He raised his eyes to meet Henry's. "It happened so quick, Sir. There weren't nothin' us could do."

"We be sorry for your loss, Sir,' said another of the men.

"Aye, that we be," chorused the others.

They stood in an uneasy group. It was Ponsonby, who dismissed the men with a nod and, with a hand on Henry's shoulder, started steering him towards the house. Henry paused, said something in a low voice to Ponsonby. Turning back towards the men, Ponsonby fumbled in his waistcoat pocket and produced some coins. His garrulity for once in check, he extended the coins to Seth, saying gruffly, " For your trouble. Share this between you."

"No Sir. Thank 'ee, but us can't accept it. Not at a time like this," said Seth, shaking his head, while the others murmured their assent. In single file, the men began to make their way back across the park, while Henry, with Ponsonby's hand on his shoulder, slowly climbed the steps to the house.

Chapter Twenty-Five
Workhouse 1842

TABITHA WERE ELEVEN THE SUMMER OF '35, AND WILL comin' on two. He were just a copy of our Samuel at that age. It did cut like a knife to look on 'im. Same as Samuel, he were my shadow and, try hard as I could, there were no shuttin' my heart to him. Such a smile on him and hair that curled about his face. And now a new 'un due.

A man's resolve do weaken on a cold November night.

Be I still here? In the workhouse? It could have come about that I be dead and this be the after-life preachers be always tellin' us to prepare for. How wouldst one know?

I ent never had much truck with religion. I figures there be enough troubles in this world to plague a man, let alone worry on what be comin' in the next.

Come that spring my cough seemed almost to have vanished, though I still suffered from the sweats at night. But I convinced myself the disease be burning itself out. I had pared down some with no flesh to spare, and come the end of day, when it were an effort to unlace m'boots, well I'd tell myself that it had been a hard day and I be older than I were ten year ago.

I still stops in the churchyard when there be a moment. To sit and think. See Squire and his lady there on occasion. That were a terr'ble thing.

My Mary were much distressed about Master Philip's death. He were the one, y'see, that she went as wet-nurse to after she had our first-born. But I were surprised that Mary took it as bad as she did. It were because of him that our first young 'un died, Young Sir havin' Mary's milk instead of our poor babe. Not that I be blamin' him for our littl'un's death, but I thought as Mary might harbour still a trace of bitterness.

In some ways I wondered if Young Sir's death were partly my fault. My dog, y'see, along with others, were drivin' out the rabbits. There were even a fox hid in the long grass. Chances are that it be my terrier as were chasin' that pheasant. You should've seen 'im go after rats! He were like lightnin'!

'Cos I ent sure, but it niggles at my thoughts.

I were sharpenin' my scythe, and runnin' a blade aginst a whetstone don't require a man's full attention. My mind were thinkin' that soon the womenfolk would be bringin' us a bite to eat and I were picturin' Mary comin' across the medder. The same time, my eyes be takin' in a yellerhammer hid in a gorse bush by the gate. His colours blended that well with the yeller of the gorse, you could scarce see 'un exceptin' when he'd start his trillin'. I be very partial to yellerhammers.

So, you couldst say, when it happened, the pheasant, if that be what it were runnin' out between the horse's legs, it were only from the corner of my eye that I saw anything. I just heard this cry followed by a *t-h-w-a-c-k* sorta sound. I kep' hearin' that sound for days after. And there be Young Sir lyin' by the gate. 'Cos, I dropped my tools and ran to 'im, but there weren't nothin' us could do. His body, twisted unnatural like, twitched a bit and then lay still. The side of his head were sorta cupped – aye that be the word – *cupped* aginst that big rock. Like a fist buried deep in dough when bein' kneaded.

I has to yell several times to get others to come and help, for I felt I had to stay by 'im though it be obvious he were dead. When us lifted him onto a pen-slat, me holdin' his head and shoulders, my hands got bloodied. It were the side of his head, all pushed in like, that looked real dreadful. I tried to tear my eyes from it, but it were like they were fixed. Then I staggers to my feet, lurches towards the hedgerow and sicks up all that's in my stomach.

So instead of eatin' with Mary while the young 'uns romped in freshcut hay, us were carryin' that poor lad home to his parents.

Oft times then, there be I sittin' by Samuel's mound, and Squire and his lady placin' flowers on that girt stone monument they put up in Young

And Ordered Their Estate

Sir's memory, and us would nod to each other. Should Squire and I meet when he be on his own, it's as if he be compelled to say somethin', be it only 'good-day.' And I feels a *need* for him to speak. 'Tis odd. Beyond explainin'.

That summer the sun burned down, drying up streams and wells. The cows stood listless in the medders, dogs flopped pantin' anywhere as they could find shade. Come August summer fever were back. We countryfolk call it summer fever, but people with some learnin', like the doctor, give it the name of typhoid. Broke out in Dorchester first, in the poor end of the city, where several families be crammed into one house. Reached Bere next and then found its way to Tolpuddle.

Parson's servant-woman had family in Dorchester and 'tis said she carried it back to Tolpuddle. Be that as it may, she were soon dead along with one of Parson's daughters.

And then my Mary sickened. Terr'ble sick she were and there be little us could do but sponge her down, givin' her sips of water, hopin' her would at least keep some of it in her.

Mary's mother helped with the nursin'. Said as how she'd had the sickness years back and were not likely to catch it a second time. But Mary's sister wouldn't take the young 'uns fearin' the fever might spread to her brood. We lost the infant birthed a few weeks afore, but somehow its death went almost unnoticed. I were fair mazed with fear of losing Mary. Mary be my life.

But she pulled through. Took weeks for her to regain her strength, mind, and we were desperate poor, but unbeknownst to Mary I borrowed money and made sure she had milk and eggs.

I must be dead. I seems to be floatin' in warm water, 'tis carryin' me along like in a stream. It's wonnerful peaceful and not a sound to be heard. Why don't them preachers tell us this be how it is instead of rantin' on about fire and brimstone and the like?

And then there were a flurry in the village. Government folks had come from London to talk with Elizabeth Loveless and the other wives of the men. I only heard the news fourth or fifth-hand through my Mary. Since she spat in my face, George's wife be one of them that have never spoke to me again. Anyways, it seems that two men from Government, in their fancy coats and smart coach, come to tell the wives that they could join their husbands in Botany Bay and Van Diemen's Land.

Village gossip has it that Hammett's wife refused outright. Elizabeth Loveless is said to have told 'em that she would obey her husband's wishes, but not havin' heard from him since his ship sailed she have no knowledge what his wishes be. So she tells those two London gentry that she can't answer their question until her has a letter from her husband tellin' her what to do.

She were clever there, for how could her know whether George be dead or alive even, and it would mean she'd have contact with him at last.

The Government men were took aback, thinkin' as how all the women would've said yes and the matter of the Tolpuddle Martyrs could be put to rest. Now, if they be serious, letters'll have to be sent all that way and then waitin' same time again for a reply to be received.

'Tis puzzlin' how their minds do work in London. Why would 'em think the wives would risk journeyin' all that fearful way, leavin' homes, friends, relations? To what? Would be like steppin' into a darkness you knows nothin' of.

Chapter Twenty-Six
Tolpuddle 1835

ELIZABETH PAUSED FROM STIRRING A POT OF GRUEL OVER the hearth. Taking up a cloth, she lifted the pot from the hook and set it to one side. It would be a tasteless meal without a dash of milk or a little honey for sweetening. She'd save the few potatoes she had left for tomorrow. If only she could offer the children a slice of bread to go with the gruel, but it was weeks since she'd had money for even a small loaf. Until Mister Brown from the Friendly Society called again she had only a couple of pennies left in the tin box on the mantelpiece. Nightly she gave thanks for Mr. Brown but it was now nearly seven weeks since they'd seen him and usually he came near the beginning of each month. What if he didn't come again, if the money the good people of London had donated was all used up? Please God, let him come soon.

Once again she hitched up the waistband of her skirt reminding herself that in the evening she must put another tuck in before it fell around her ankles. Her once firm flesh now hung in pouches and deep creases fenced her mouth. With a sigh, Elizabeth walked over to a shelf and reached up for one of George's books. Maybe if she sold just one … As if her fingers had touched a smouldering coal, she snatched her hand back. How could she think of such a thing? His books! George's treasure! Nothing would countenance such an action. She must wait on Mister Brown's coming.

~~~

William Ponsonby, with no one but his wife Maria as audience, flung down his paper.

"Dear God, will they ever let the matter rest? The end of '35 almost to hand and still it goes on!"

"What is distressing you now, husband?' enquired Maria. Used to her husband's impatient outbursts, her eyes remained on her embroidery.

"How dare they liken the oaths taken by loyal Orangemen to those of unionists. Why they're even pressing for the Duke of Cumberland to be charged!"

"It is certainly a disgrace that the king's brother should be drawn into the matter," agreed Maria in a conciliatory voice.

"And Russell has weakened. He's granting those traitors a free pardon." The words "free pardon" splattered from his lips.

"A free pardon?" echoed Maria, her needle suspended over her tapestry hoop.

"But they've not won yet, thank God. It would appear that such a pardon must be signed by the king, and the king is refusing to sign."

Anxious to calm her husband's mood, for she dearly wished to accompany him on his trip in two week's time, Maria rose and stood behind him, placing a soothing hand on his shoulder. "You'd think more sense would prevail. While we are in London, you'll be able to discuss the matter with your friends. I'm sure they'll be of like mind."

"October is no time to travel. The road will be awash with mud and the toll charges to use the sections that have been repaired are outrageous. And as for talking over such matters, there seem scarcely any that can talk reasonably on the subject. Look at Finchbury! Why, he has long been of the opinion that those traitors should never have been transported."

" But Henry was all for having the forming of unions halted."

"Henry Finchbury is a turncoat. No backbone. All the years I've known him I'd never have thought it of him."

"But packing for our trip is well under way," Maria appealed. "I've written to Cousin Margaret announcing our coming." Maria clutched at his arm. "Husband, you can't change your mind at the last moment like this. I have given orders for this very room to be painted during our absence."

Henry ignoring the agitated pleading in Maria's tone as she added, "You promised I could accompany you this time," strode over to the door. He must get away before she used her most effective weapon, tears. Pausing with his hand on the knob, he announced, "I'm off to the stables. A good gallop may ease my mood, then we shall see."

~~~

The scraggy convict with a movement of his shoulders eased his clothing away from a back still not fully healed from a flogging. With a voiced tinged with malice he said to George, "So they've got yer on a charge at last. They'll 'ave yer married to the three sisters for sure."

"The message was that I am to report to the Police Office in Hobart. There was no mention of any charge," replied George, inwardly wincing at what his fellow convict implied. He'd seen many a man standing in a similar position as the man who now addressed him, the body held stiffly, careful to avoid a sudden movement that might rip open the mending tissue. He had not been reported for any offence, but did that signify anything? He'd witnessed men tied to the triangle known as the 'three sisters' and flogged, often on trumped up charges.

"Don't yer fool yerself. Nobody gets sent nowhere but to be flogged." The malevolence in the convict's voice was not lost on George. What if there was a charge against him? Fortune was unlikely to smile on him a second time, as when he'd been charged with neglect of duty.

Had someone noticed him writing, reported him? Only that morning he'd carefully checked that the precious bits of paper on which he had been recording his experiences were still where he'd secreted them. His views on the injustice of his situation must be well hidden from prying eyes while he was gone. No, there was little likelihood of anyone discovering his hiding place. With his mind churning on the question of why he'd been summonsed, George set off for Hobart.

~~~

Strong November winds hurled icy rain against the window, where the drops raced to join others. Rivulets funnelled down the mullioned panes. Ponsonby, his long frame stooped, contemplated the scene, his mood as sullen as the day.

King Billy had signed the pardon! Pah!

In the past, he had scorned the derogatory shortening of the King's name. On one occasion, when much the worse for drink, he'd challenged the speaker who had referred to the king in such a manner to "pistols at dawn" though, luckily, his friends had quickly removed him from the situation before his challenge was taken up. But now, such was his disgust at the king's weakness, *King Billy* was the only term that came to Ponsonby's mind.

Surely, he thought, others must see where such an action would lead? Workers free to dictate terms to their employers, to *demand* higher wages. Look what happened to the French. Why, it was only twenty years back that the Luddites in Nottinghamshire were smashing up machinery because they deemed it to be responsible for the loss of jobs. There would be no stopping the anarchy that loomed ahead if workers were allowed to have their own way. He could still recall, as a young man, reading Thomas Paine's treatise, *The Rights of Man*. Paine should've been hung, along with any such that shared their ridiculous ideas.

It struck at every conviction he held. Strongly and fiercely, Ponsonby believed that God had ordered man's estate, ordained the distribution of wealth, and that such order must be preserved. But now a signal had been sent, a signal that boded no good, not just for landowners but the whole of society. Disgust at such betrayal dampened his volcanic anger to little more than a smouldering spark.

~~~

Dust motes danced in the January sun streaming through the small window and open door. The magistrate's heavy mahogany desk and high-backed chair seemed to fill the room, as did the Hobart heat. At a small table in the corner, a clerk sat writing in a ledger. Poorly nailed floor boards creaked under foot as George entered and stood before the desk.

Mr. Spode, the Principal Superintendent of Convicts for Van Dieman's Land, chin resting on his hands, studied the convict in front of him, taking in George's stocky build, the thick growth of facial hair, the sun-browned wrists and hands that held a battered hat, the eyes not lowered but returning his gaze with a keen, intelligent look. The prisoner stood silent, unmoving.

Spode's hand reached into his pocket and drew out a gray-looking handerchief. Too fair-skinned for the climate, he dabbed gently at an irritating heat-rash on his neck, wincing imperceptibly as he did so. "Your name's Loveless? George Loveless?"

"It is, Sir,"

"I've summonsed you, Loveless, as the government has asked me to enquire of you whether you wish your wife and family to join you here?" He looked from George to the document that lay on the desk in front of him.

Bewilderment showed in George's expression and tone as he replied, "Join me *here*, Sir?"

"Aye. That's what I said."

There was a long pause while George digested the implications of the magistrate's question. Spode stared at him intently, tapping on his desk with a finger.

"Well, man. What am I to reply?"

"Your question has taken me by surprise, Sir, and before I can answer I must be given leave to ask one of my own."

"What's that?"

"Will I be given my liberty?"

"Liberty! What do you mean?"

"Will the government be granting me a free pardon? If that is not so, I can say nothing further."

Spode's hand rose again as he eased his black stock away from his neck. "How dare you! Insolence like that can get you flogged."

"I meant no insolence, Sir, but what would be gained by my wife and family joining me while I am still a prisoner? What life would it be for her? I could not ask it of her."

Magistrate Spode, leaning on the desk, pushed himself to his feet. "My God! A convict trying to make the rules. Get back to your work place before I change my mind and order fifty lashes." He turned to the clerk who had lifted his head at the magistrate's angry tone. "Make a notation that on January 7th, 1836 I questioned the prisoner and he turned down the government's offer to bring his wife and family out."

~~~

Praise God for the Friendly Society and Mr. Brown. He'd come at last, full of apologies for not having come sooner. He'd been ill.

"Couldn't keep food or liquid down for days. The doctor's draught helped not at all. My wife was much concerned for me."

"But you've fully recovered your health now, Sir, I trust."

"I have, M'am. I have." As he unbuttoned his heavy riding-coat he asked himself yet again how each family managed on the small amount he brought. Lowering himself into George's chair, he declined Elizabeth's offer of refreshment "It's kind of you, but no, nothing, thank 'ee. Just a bucket of water for m'horse, if you'd instruct your lad."

"Mathew's already attending to it, Sir. Mistress Standfield, Dinniah, be visiting her daughter-in-law, so you'll find her there when you call."

"I knew of none willing to ride out this distance who I felt I could trust," Mr. Brown continued. "The responsibility for this money, I take very seriously. It's not mine, you understand. I am just entrusted to see it is delivered to such families as yourself, families of those poor, unfortunate men. A duty, I assure you M'am, I don't take lightly."

"Words can't express our gratitude, Mr. Brown. Without it we would be reduced to begging or applying to the workhouse for admission. With it being some time since you called last, the thought came to mind that the funds were all used up and I was fair beside myself with worry."

"Fret not on that score, Mistress Loveless. I shall be along again in a month's time."

"Think you, Sir, if I were to write to my husband, that there'd be some way of getting a letter to him?"

Mr. Brown paused before answering, fingertips positioned steeple-like to his lips. "That's a question to which I've no answer, M'am, but I'll make enquiries about the matter."

"It would ease my man's mind, I know, if he knew of the wonderful kindness of the London people, and yours for making the journey on our behalf."

"I'll make no promises, but you have a letter written next time I call and I'll see if there's anything can be done." From a deep pocket he withdrew a leather-bound notebook, a small bottle of ink and a quill pen wrapped in a colourful handkerchief. "Now if you'd be good enough once again to sign that you've received the money so that all's recorded correctly." As Elizabeth, lips taut against her teeth in concentration, carefully wrote her name, he said, as always, "Best to have everything done properly, then there's no dispute later."

After Mr. Brown had left to call on the other five families promising to deliver Elizabeth's good wishes to all, she slowly counted the money into the tin box. If only there was enough for clothing for Mathew? He was growing so rapidly. No, the money must be spent on food. It was difficult enough making it stretch from one of Mr. Brown's visits to the next. She'd taken the pair of trousers George kept for Sundays, held them against Mathew, hoping she could cut them down to fit him, but they were just far too big. Maybe she could get a pair the right size from the old Jew in Piddletrenthide, get him to take something in trade. But what? Her shawl! The one gift she'd had from George in all their years of marriage, the one she kept for chapel: soft grey wool with a touch of purple around the edges. Maybe he'd take it in exchange. It was worth a try. Elizabeth closed the tin and returned it to the mantelpiece. Tomorrow, if Dinniah would keep an eye on Daniel, she and Sarah would walk to Piddletrenthide.

~~~

Colonel George Arthur, governor of Van Diemen's Land handed the reins of his horse to his aide with instructions to join him in the office of the Government Farm after he'd found someone to tend to their mounts. Striding into the office Arthur announced, "I sent notice that I would

155

be arriving today to interview the convict George Loveless. Have him brought to me immediately."

The office manager leapt up from his chair and subserviently offered it to Arthur. He barked Arthur's request to a clerk, who in turn stood in the doorway and yelled to a convict trusty to find Loveless and be quick about it. Turning back to Colonel Arthur, the manager enquired, "Will you take something to drink, Sir? A mutton sandwich?" while a hurried discussion between clerk and trusty as to where Loveless was located ensued. Arthur, taking the vacated seat, declined food but accepted the offer of wine. He questioned the manager about various matters pertaining to the farm, while his impatience with the length of time it was taking to locate Loveless was indicated by the drumming of his fingers on the desk top.

The governor was a tall, imposing man. A forceful chin resting on the high, stiff collar gave him a haughty, austere look. His hair was cut short and swept forward in a Napoleonic style. He looked up as heavy footsteps finally announced George's arrival. George walked over and stood in front of the desk. For several seconds governor and prisoner fixed their eyes on the other, neither dropping their gaze.

Then Arthur rose from the desk and strode back and forth across the room, hands clasped behind his back, as he addressed George.

"I hear from Magistrate Spode that two weeks ago you turned down the government's offer. What are your objections to having your wife and family brought out?"

"Sir, I would not wish them to come to such misery."

"Misery! What do you mean?"

"We are ill fed and clothed and treated as slaves."

Governor Arthur turned sharply. "Slaves! There are no slaves under the British Dominion. Only prisoners," he snapped. In a slightly milder tone, he added, "I strongly urge you to write to your wife and encourage her to come."

"They would have no means of livelihood, and as a prisoner I would be unable to support them."

"I think it highly likely the government will grant you parole when your family arrives."

"But is there a guarantee of that, Sir? I must know what means of support they will have, should my wife agree to come."

An intelligent fellow, deep-thinking, states his point of view clearly the governor noted, pacing the length of the room again. "I understand your concern regarding your family. I can only repeat that I have it on good authority that the government is considering the matter." Pivoting on his heel, he faced George. "Personally, I'd give you your freedom immediately, but as the law stands, it is forbidden until a prisoner has served four years." He paused for a moment. "You realize there are good opportunities for ticket-of-leave men if they are willing to work hard?"

"I have no knowledge of such opportunities, being shut up as I have been since I arrived here. Would the wages paid support a man's family? What if I am not set free?"

The governor made no reply.

George pondered the matter. Governor Arthur sounded almost positive about a ticket-of-leave being granted, and George had seen ample evidence of what befell those who challenged authority. At last, reluctantly, he asked for pen and paper. Indicating a small table on which there were writing implements and instructing George to be quick, the Governor Arthur turned his attention to the office manager and returned to discussing matters pertaining to the farm.

Secreting two discarded attempts in his pocket, George stood and laid his letter on the governor's desk.

> "...It will be a difficult decision for you, wife, and one that you alone can make. Let God and your own conscience guide you. Be not influenced by any desires of mine."

Within days Magistrate Spode sent for George again.

"Loveless, I have here a ticket-of-leave for you."

"A ticket-of-leave before it is learned whether my wife will come?"

"That is so. Your penal servitude is over. However, you must remain here, in the colony, until three years are up." Spode pushed a paper across the desk to George. He jabbed the bottom of page with his finger. "Sign your name here or make your mark."

Ignoring the pen Spode held out, George slowly and deliberately read the document through.

"So, a free pardon has not been granted," he said as he took the pen from Spode's impatient hand and signed. "What must I do now?"

Spode's worsening heat-rash was causing him great discomfort. His head pounded from the previous night's drinking. "Good God, man! Find yourself employment. You're responsible for yourself now, not the government."

A ticket-of-leave man. Parole! George's mind found it difficult to grasp the concept. Free to come and go as he pleased, though not truly *free*. As he picked up the document bearing the Governor's seal, Spode and George's signatures, he fought down an urge to shout out loud, burst into a hymn. Then his euphoria was overcome by a feeling of panic. *Freedom.* He had hoped for this moment, dreamed of it, and now that it had come, the prospect left him filled with apprehension.

Chapter Twenty-Seven
Workhouse 1842

THEM AS HASN'T SEEN A DORSET SPRING HAVE MISSED A wond'rous sight. First, under the trees in small woods come snowdrops and wood anemones. In Squire's copse 'tis as if a hoar frost covers the ground it be so white, and them little flowers all a noddin' in a February breeze, softer than the winds of early March. Then the hedgerows misted green with new shoots. Celandines, shinin' yeller against leaves dark and glistenin'. Primroses, pale as butter, coverin' the banks and down by the ford kingcups blazin' gold. In the millstream, just under the water, river crowfoot shows its tiny white blooms. Spring of '36 were a fair picture. Seems as if nature were makin' up for the wet, raw winter us'd had.

That spring there were a murder of crows everywhere, but not near as many song birds as us is used to. Some says as how it were because us had so many magpies the year afore. Magpies be devils for raidin' the nests of other birds and eatin' the eggs. I recalls when Tabby were only a littl'un, her marvellin' at the broken blue of a robin's egg layin' on the ground. Her askin' if it were a bit of sky as had broken off.

Regrets niggle at me when I thinks on Tabitha. Not about havin' to put her out to work. Us had to do it to save her from the workhouse, and most young girls had been found employment long afore they'd reached Tabby's age. No, my regrets be caused by the fact that Samuel and Willie come first in my affections. Be it because she's so like her mother, not just in looks but disposition too? Could it be I only has room for one Mary in my life?

'Cos Tabby were always a little leery of me after that time with the toadstool. It were when she were still quite small. Her comes trottin' up to Mary and me, holdin' one of them red toadstools with white speckles on their caps. Pretty things but cautious where they grows, so you don't come across 'em too often.

"Look!" says she. "Fairy food. You eat some, Ma."

Mary lets out a little scream when she sees as there's a piece gone from the edge, just as if someone had bit it. Knockin' it from Tabby's hands, I asks, "You et any of this, Tab?"

My voice, rough with concern, makes her tearful. "It's for me an' Ma," her says and stoops to retrieve it. Well I just grabs her jaw with one hand forcing her mouth open, and shoves a finger down her throat until she sicks up all over my hand. It were the only thing to do. Them things be deadly. 'Course she starts sobbin', and it takes a while for Mary to calm her down. Hid behind Mary for days after, when she saw I comin', and us never could tell whether her had et any of the damn thing.

One minute I be burnin' with fever and the next shiverin' as if lyin' in a snowbank naked. Hot or cold, when awake my mind keeps whirlin' thoughts around, not settlin' on one thing for more than a minute.

I ponders at times as to whether spring or early autumn be the season I likes best. Them early spring breezes seems to carry a promise – a hope that maybe life for us all will be easier – of better things to come, while early autumn time a man can see the reward for all his labours. Leastways, the farmer can.

Mary'd be right joyed if her'd got a goodly harvest from her gardenin' and what her could gather from the hedgerows. She'd give the young'uns a pail and tell 'em not to come back till it were full of wild raspberries or blackberries. In the storage place under the stairs her'd have pots of preserves covered with a stretch of animal membrane and sealed with fat, while in the lean-to against the house a sack or two of potatoes and turnips.

When I were a lad Mistress would have I pickin' apples by the bucketful. Come cider-makin' time it'd be my job to tip the buckets of cider apples up and over the side of the apple-press while the horse hitched to the press-rod plodded round and round. 'Cor, my arms did ache by the end of the day for I had no height to me and liftin' a girt pail full of apples up and over the side of the press time and time agin were exhaustin' work, but it were a job I enjoyed. Oh, the smell of that juice as it poured down the spout into the cider cask.

Now my thoughts be back with Loveless. What would my Mary have done I wonders, should I 'ave been transported? Would her have said yes, if they'd offered to send her out to join me?

Village gossip - and it be not just me but the whole village as fed on the smallest scrap of news about Loveless, Standfield and the others - well gossip had it that a man from parliament asked to see the letter George sent Elizabeth Loveless when he were on that prison hulk afore he were shipped out. This government man, Wakely I heard his name were, read the letter out in Parliament, in an attempt to convince 'em to pardon 'em all. 'Twas said Elizabeth were feared of partin' with the letter, it being all she had left since he were took. You ent no idea how I hoped that those poor men would be pardoned. If I'd a been a prayin' man, I would've prayed for 'em. That were in the late spring of '36. I gathers though, that those parliament toffs voted against it. Then nothing more were heard on the matter.

It were the carrier-man with his horse and cart, goin' from village to village, deliverin' a crate of young chicken, a keg of nails, pickin' up a sack of onions or potatoes, eggs that any might have to spare and he'd sell 'em on to a shop in one of the towns, it were him as gleaned what news there were and passed it on while doing his trading. Soon as his cart were sighted comin' along the road, the womenfolk would turn out, for the carrier-man carried a stock of things for trade or sale. But it were the news he brung that everyone were most eager for, be it politics, who'd won the prize fight held over at Piddletrenthide, the death of some distant family member, whatever could be passed on. And many a time what was told had become so changed in the telling from one to another, by the time carrier-man passed it on it bore little likeness as to what first happened.

The landlord of the alehouse I'd taken to visitin' since I weren't welcome in Tolpuddle would pounce on copies of old news-sheets the carrier-man might have, knowin' how folks were interested in what went on beyond the village boundaries. Of an evening' he'd see that the tankard of any as had some learnin' were kept topped up for free provided that person were willin' to read the sheet aloud. Seated around the inglenook, heads noddin' in agreement at what they heard or spittin' on the floor in disapproval, there were always a group to be found thirsty for news of happenings further afield as well as a mug of ale.

But about the granting of them pardons parliament and the news-sheets were silent.

Chapter Twenty-Eight
Australia 1836

"RISK TAKIN' ON A TICKET-OF-LEAVER? THAT I WON'T!" was the farmer's response to George's request for work. Quickly running his eyes over George, he returned to the study of the thick slab of bread and cheese he held in sausage-like fingers. As the man took another bite, George found himself salivating

Masticating with a slow deliberateness, the farmer continued, "Were I needing help I'd pay the Governor for a convict. It's cheaper in the long run with no wages to pay..."

"I can assure you, Sir, I'm a hard and honest worker."

"...and I can ask to 'ave 'im punished or taken back if there's any trouble. Honest, you say! If you was honest you'd not have been convicted in the first place. Stands to reason. Now I wants you off my property quick like, or I'll set the dogs on yer."

There's nothing to be gained here: a plea for food, a further appeal in the name of Christian brotherhood will doubtless get a similar response George realized shouldering his bundled possessions once more. Holding his head erect and walking with a vigor he no longer felt, in case the farmer should still be watching, George retraced his steps to the roadway. What if he couldn't find employment? How much longer could he continue without food? The rough road stretched ahead to a range of hills on the horizon. He pounded the ground with each footstep as if he were crushing all those who had brought him to this state.

Hidden in the foliage of a gum tree a bird gave a series of triple-toned calls –"In-jus-tice, in-jus-tice." Without thought George found himself bellowing back "in-jus-tice, in-jus-tice." His words, unheard by anyone, dissipated into the empty air. Ahead the road wavered, dissolved, then reappeared. "Must be the heat, exhaustion," George told himself, giving his head a shake. His leg muscles throbbed. "Take hold of yourself, George Loveless." With gentler steps he continued onwards, reciting "I will lift up mine eyes unto the hills, from whence cometh my strength," moving from one psalm to another in an attempt to silence from his mind the question: How much further to the next spread?

~~~

Mathew Loveless stood in front of his mother as she knelt on the floor. Taking another pin from between her lips she adjusted the length of the trouser leg and with a gentle push indicated that he turn around.

"There then," she said, her mouth now empty of pins, "that should do."

Nose wrinkled at the musty smell of the dark brown fabric, Mathew looked down at his legs. "They's real men's trousers, ent they, Mother?" he asked doubtfully.

"They are that, and still a lot of wear in the fabric. Go and take 'em off and I'll soon have 'em shortened." She smiled as her son's face brightened, but felt a need to add, "Now don't 'ee get too prideful." For a brief moment her hand hovered as if it would gently caress his head, but then brushed his shoulder, directing him towards the other room. "When I've finished I'll hang 'em outside. A good blow'll soon have them smellin' fresher."

~~~

As George trudged from farm to farm he saw the other side of this *freedom* he had been granted – this *responsibility* for himself. Pray God he would find employment soon.

To take his mind off his hunger he turned his thoughts to Elizabeth and the children. He must find a means of writing to her again. Tell her to remain where she was. His mind shifted to how long would it take him

And Ordered Their Estate

to save the passage home once he'd found work. An iron determination that once his feet trod English soil again he'd find some way to fight the unjustness of his being transported spurred him on.

The sky had suddenly darkened with roiling black clouds. Thrumming rain drops bounced in the swirling dust, freshened the air. Mud splattered George's boots and trousers as the rain fell in torrents. Turning his face up to the deluge, George had opened his mouth, revelled in its coolness. Even sheltering as best he could under a stand of trees, his clothing was soon soaked. The rain continued until well into the night and, in spite of his exhaustion, sleep came only in snatches.

Hunger had woken him long before the sun had streaked the purple-grey of the pre-dawn sky. Crouching beside a stream, George drank from his cupped hands. It was two days since he had tasted food and water offered little in the way of relief. Passing a small farm, he had watched while a man had fed bruised fruit to his pigs. As the man moved away from the sty, George was tempted to see if he could salvage some of the fruit, but sensed he was being watched and so resisted the urge. He plunged his hat into the stream, relishing the feel of its cold dampness as he replaced it on his head. He picked up his bundle of possessions and continued along the rough road. Was that a farm ahead? No, it looked more like a small settlement. Would he get a better reception there?

The man paused before he grasped another sack and heaved it into the cart. "Work, you say? 'Ere, give us a hand with this while I think on the matter."

George did as he was bid while the man, leaning against the cart, pulled a crude pipe and tinderbox from his pocket. It took several strikes of the match and much dragging on the pipe stem before the tobacco ignited. George had loaded three more sacks and was hauling on a fourth before the man spoke again.

"Yer could try at Glen Ayr."

"They're hiring there?"

"That I can't say, but I've heard he's willing to take on a ticket-man. That's what you are, I take it."

"How can you tell?"

"Been one m'self. Free man these past five years, though."

"In which direction lies Glen Ayr?"

"About five miles further on. Near Richmond. You hang on a bit an' I'll give 'ee a lift part of the way." Dropping George off at a track seemingly leading to nowhere, the carter instructed: "Ask for de Gillern. 'Tis him as owns it."

Major de Gillern periodically glanced up from reading George's papers to ask a question.

"What experience have you with sheep?"

"Mostly my knowledge has been gained here, Sir, though we've sheep in Dorset, but not the Merino breed that is popular here."

"I see you're one of the Tolpuddle Unionists. I've read about your trial in the papers I receive from England. It would seem you were unjustly accused."

"I'm much surprised to hear you say that, Sir. None have expressed that opinion to me before. But 'tis true. We were under the impression that unions were legal. We knew nothing of a law against illegal oaths."

"In the past I've had my own experiences of government departments and their interpretation of the law to suit themselves." With a dismissive gesture with his hand, de Gillern added, "But enough of that. It would seem you're hard-working and of good character. I'm willing to give you a chance. There's a rough shack on the property, over by those woods. It's crude but dry. Should do you."

George couldn't believe his luck. Work *and* a place to himself after three years of being crowded into confined spaces with other convicts, so many of them brutish and foul.

The shack, little more than stone-built shelter, had two small rooms, one with a hearth and a table, the other a straw-stuffed mattress. George walked from one room to the other then back again, already planning how, in the evenings, he could fashion some shelves, a chair. Shelves shouldn't be too difficult, but a chair would require the use of tools. He'd wait a while before he broached such a matter with de Gillern. Till then a piece of the felled tree he'd notice outside would do. That night his prayers were full of thankfulness, his sleep undisturbed.

Over a period of time a friendly relationship formed between the two men. De Gillern, sleeves rolled up, worked hard alongside his employees. George found him knowledgeable, intelligent and fair, and the major was impressed with George's diligence. Sometimes of an evening de Gillern would suggest George join him on his stoop and they would discuss what work was required in the coming days, the weather, and the likelihood of a shortage of water for the stock, and, of great interest to both men, the politics of the day on Van Diemen's Island and in New South Wales. On the Government Farm George had had no opportunity to gain insight as to how the colony was governed, and de Gillern was eager to share his views on the subject with George.

"I like what Governor Bourke is trying to achieve," said de Gillern. "His attempting to bring about civil rights for all. Of course, the Exclusionists are much against this."

"The Exclusionists?"

"It's a term applied to the original settlers and accepted by the majority of them. Well, these Exclusionists are against Expirees - that's those who have served their sentence and the Pardoned Convicts - being given rights, the same judicial rights as Exclusionists."

"And will Bourke be successful do you think?"

"He has much support for the reforms he suggests," replied de Gillern. "Whether we here on Diemen's will benefit remains to be seen. Should he be successful, such reforms would effect a man such as yourself should you decide to remain here."

"Until I am truly a free man, making plans for the future is nigh impossible," was George's response.

Frantic bleating mingled with the cursing of the worker assigned to herding the animals into the shearing shed, one by one.

"What was that you said, Sir?" George shouted above the noise. "You were born in Germany?"

"Yes, Germany." Turning to one of the other workers, de Gillern yelled, "Take care, Johnson. That's a valuable beast."

"I noticed a slight foreign touch to your speech, and then of course there's your name, but I understood you served in the British forces."

"Nearly eighteen years." De Gillern released the ewe he had been shearing. "Grab the next one, now. Hold it firm. That's it."

Pinning the animal to the ground, George asked, "How came you to Van Diemens Land then?"

"Sold my commission in '27 and was given a land grant here."

They continued working together silently for a while until de Gillern ordered a break. Snorting dust from his nose into a rag, George said, "You mentioned when we first met, problems you'd experienced with the government. Was it because you were born in Germany?"

"Aye. Governor Arthur. He introduced a naturalization law, his own law, mark you. Not being a British subject, my name was struck from the jury list. It meant many of my rights were restricted. I took the matter up, time and again with Arthur's bureaucrats in Hobart, but they delayed and delayed dealing with the issue."

De Gillern, putting down the water jug from which he'd been drinking, wiped his chin with the back of his hand. "Let's get on with the job." He handed the shears to George. "I'll hold. You're getting handy with the shears. You take a turn. We'll make a shearer of you yet."

Running the shears along the sheep's flank, George asked, "Is the matter now resolved?"

"Not till out of frustration I wrote direct to the Colonial Office in London. Pointed out the years I had faithfully served in His Majesty's forces." De Gillern grasped George's wrist. "Relax your grip on the shears a little. Your arm's too rigid. That's it."

George did as he suggested and found the tool easier to manipulate. "And was the Colonial Office more receptive to your request?"

"Finally, I got a response. It's taken years, mind. Wasn't satisfactorily settled 'til just before you came to me for work." He wiped his hands, greasy from the fleece, on his britches. "Yes, those with any power over here see themselves as gods." He spat a gob of saliva onto the ground, the viscous matter mixing with scattered straw and dust.

"You say you love reading, Loveless. If you're interested, I'll pass on my newspapers after I've done with them. It'll be good to have someone to talk over what's happening beyond these boundaries."

"I'd be most grateful, Sir. 'Tis ages since I've had an opportunity to read anything."

"Right then, I'll save 'em for you. Johnson, pull your weight there. No slacking!" Turning back to George, he said, "You made a good job of that ewe. Carry on, but go at it carefully. A nicked fleece loses it's value. Better to take it slower until you've had more practice."

Eating his meal one evening early in September while at the same time reading an old edition of the *London Dispatch* loaned him by de Gillern, George came across a speech in reference to Orange Lodges. A circular mark wrinkled the article, as if someone had placed a jug or can with a wet base on it.

"*...Lord Russell gave notice that orders were forwarded that the Dorchester Unionists were not only to be set at liberty, but also to be sent back to England, free of expense, and with every necessary comfort...*"

George thrust his plate aside and lifted the paper closer. He re-read the item, turned again to the front page to check the date, March 1836. Once more he read the article, this time holding the flickering oil lamp right up to the paper. Pushing away from the table and leaving his meal unfinished, George wrenched on his boots, grabbed his coat, and in the gathering darkness hurried to de Gillern's house.

"What is it man? What can be so urgent this time of night?"

"Look you, Sir. Look! Here in this paper you loaned me."

"What, this article?"

"That's it! You see what it says. I'm a free man! Why did you not tell me?"

"Slow down, man. Come inside. Let me read what it says." Taking the paper from George, de Gillern led the way into a room that served as kitchen and sitting room. He pushed aside an assortment of papers, twine, a large pair of pliers and pulling an oil lamp closer read the article, slowly shaking his head. "I can't believe I missed it. Just can't believe it! I read each page from beginning to end when they arrive. We hear so little of what's going on in the world." Placing a hand on George's shoulder, de Gillern said, "Believe me, Loveless, I wasn't holding the news from you."

"Almost a year later, and no one, *no one*, has told me I'm a *truly* free man." George slammed his hand on the table in frustration, setting a bottle and tankard jiggling.

"Steady, steady there. Firstly, let's celebrate your freedom? Will you take a drink with me?" De Gillern bent to a low cupboard. "I've something stronger here than ale."

"Ale is fine, Sir. We Methodists don't believe in strong drink."

"As you will." Taking another tankard from a cupboard, de Gillern filled it and handed it to George saying, "To freedom!" Indicating that George take the other chair, de Gillern sat down and re-read the article out loud, periodically taking swallows of ale.

"What action should I take, think you?"

"Now, let's go about this calmly." Tapping a finger against the side of his tankard and stroking his chin with his other hand, de Gillern thought hard. George, his eyes fixed intently on de Gillern's face, waited. Silence, broken only by an animal's cry far off in the bush, filled the room.

At last de Gillern spoke. "Strategy is called for, a plan of campaign. A good soldier always plans his attack. You've heard nothing from the Governor, you say?"

George nodded in assent. "Never a word. I wonder if Standfield and the others have heard anything."

"That being the case, we'll fire the first shot. You must write to the editor of the *Tasmanian*."

"A letter to the *Tasmanian*? I don't follow you, Sir."

"The *Tasmanian*, that's the best approach. The editor is sure to publish it." De Gillern pointed his finger at George in emphasis. "He's taken an active interest in your cause."

"But what will that gain me?"

"The *Tasmanian* is read widely. Lord Arthur will be forced to take action. Make some response, don't you see?"

~~~

Bent over a washtub full of laundry. Elizabeth asked, "You think we should write to Mr. Brown to find out what's happening? Together we could word a letter well enough to send. Get Mathew to make a copy, him being more skilled at lettering."

Easing the basket of wet washing resting on her hip, Dinniah replied, "It can't do no harm, though he did say as he'd let us know immediately he had news."

"You'd think *someone* from government would have written us, if they've really been pardoned."

"They's the last ones as would let us know anything! Mr. Brown be the only one us can rely on. You can feel he's to be trusted. Takes his responsibilities in deliverin' the money so serious. A real gentleman."

"You never spoke a truer word. He and Thomas would get along fine, them being much alike."

"Let's wait another week. Then, if us've heard nothing, we'll write. He left a paper with you, where us could get in touch with him if need be, didn't he?"

"I have it safe," said Elizabeth wiping her hands on her apron and reaching up to a cupboard and retrieving a folded sheet of paper. "Aye, it's here. We'll wait one more week then." Returning to her washing, Elizabeth, with forceful movements, lifted a garment from the tub and began to wring the water from it. Watching her, Dinniah gave a snort. "You'm wringing that shirt like you were wringing the neck of some government man."

Dourly, Elizabeth replied, "That be how I'm feeling at this moment, God forgive me." She eased her bent back . "You hang out that lot, Dinny, and then these'll be ready. Just don't look at 'em too close. With no soap they's still as grey as when they went in the tub."

"The sun'll help bleach 'em, don't 'ee fret."

~~~

Under George's letter, "*...I do not know whether Governor Arthur has received orders from home; I should like to know. If His Excellency has received intelligence to that effect, I hope he will have the goodness to communicate that knowledge to me...*" the newspaper stated, "We repeat our former statement, that Lord John Russell, the British Home Secretary, stated *explicitly in the House of Commons that free pardons had been sent out to the Dorchester Unionists..."*

George lay down the paper. De Gillern's strategy had worked to some extent. But how long would he have to wait until his hands actually held that elusive pardon?

Carefully, with a knife, he cut out the copy of his letter and the editor's comments, laid them in a box that contained the cutting of the original newspaper article together with sheets of notes. These notes in minute calligraphy filled every piece of paper that came his way, he'd even turned the paper sideways so that lines of neat script crossed in the other direction. One day he'd write about all that had happened to him since he'd been arrested.

Chapter Twenty-Nine
Workhouse 1842

DYING'. SEEMS I'VE SEEN A TERR'BLE LOT OF DEATH WHILST I've drawn breath. A terr'ble lot. I tries to force my mind to think on other things. Mary and me in the apple loft that time. When us were first married. Our Samuel takin' his first steps.

My father went while I were still a young lad and my mother afore that. Died givin' birth to my infant brother. Our first born, then the twins afore they'd scarce breathed. Our Samuel. It do still hurt thinkin' on Samuel. Squire's son bein' thrown from his horse, dyin' right at my feet. Our Will. Mister Kenton's new wife. There 'ave been more tears than laughter these latter years, that I surely knows.

Now that were a strange and fearful happenin'. Kenton's wife. Her were from away. 'Tis a term us uses for folks as come from places further afield. She come from a village way past Dorchester. Kenton must've met 'er when he were deliverin' flour or collectin' grain. Us did all ponder on him marryin' someone so much younger than him. She were his second wife. My Mary said as how it were good to have new blood brought in, that there were too much intermarryin'. And she were right in that respect. No stockman worth his salt keeps puttin' his cow or ewe to the same sire, and here be us all rarely travelin' further afield than the next village or two, so us tended to marry them as we grew up with.

There was nothin' to her, just a slip of a lass, though Mary said as how she were older than she looked. And that unhappy, havin' no relatives nearby. Mary said as how, many a time, she come across her cryin' her eyes out, and Mary would put her arms around her and try to comfort and befriend her.

Mid-November it were. Squire's agent had sent for I to do some hedging and ditchin' on Squire's estate. The dark was just loosin' its hold of the sky when I started out, for it be a fair old walk and I knew he could be right nasty if a man be late for work. So I were steppin' along briskly when ahead of me I sees Mistress Kenton. Did seem silly callin' her 'Mistress', she looked so young.

Just a bonnet on and a shawl around her shoulders, though it were a raw mornin'. The only thing of size to her were her belly. It were obvious she'd be calvin' soon. Leanin' back as if to balance the weight of her stomach, with her hands to the small of her back. Like my Mary'd stand and walk when near her time.

Well, as I come alongside her, she stopped. I sees tears tricklin' down her cheeks, and then she gives a loud groan.

"Mistress," says I, "you'm far from home. Where be 'ee goin' in your condition? You'd best head back."

At my mentionin' the word 'home', she says through her tears, "Mother'll be frettin'. I must hurry." But she's speakin' with a little girl's voice, like she were a child again. 'Tis obvious things be not right with her, so I takes her hand and tries to turn her back towards Tolpuddle.

"Mister Kenton'll be worryin' too, m'dear," says I. "Get you back to the mill now."

But she pulls away and carries on the way she were headin'. I knew not what to do. She were unwillin' for me to lead her back and I daresn't be late for work. We were where our paths parted anyways as I were goin' to cut across the fields. As I climbed the stile she let out another groan. I were so torn about what to do that I yells at her. Not out of temper mind, but hopin' to get her understandin'. "Go back now," I shouts, "afore 'tis too late."

Midday I stops what I be doin' and climbs through the hedge to sit by the roadside in what little bit of sun there be to eat my cold tater and cheese. It were the plaid print of her skirt that first caught my eye. "No!" I says out loud, "No!" and runs up to her.

And Ordered Their Estate

Her skirt be up round her thighs. Skirt and thighs covered in blood, big blackenin' clots of blood. More blood than ever come out of a stuck pig. Terr'ble it were. And the babe lying between her legs, the cord around its neck. I bends down, my face close to hers, to see if I could feel her breathin', but she were dead. Then, suddenly, the babe moves. Feeble like, and makes a sound so weak, it could scarce be called a cry. I pulls off my jacket, rough and dirty though it be, and wraps it round the child. What to do? There be no help around. No cottages. Then there's the sound of wheels and horses' hooves. I runs into the road and waves and shouts.

The coachman pulls on the reins, all the time shoutin' at I to get out the road. 'Tis Squire and his lady. When the coach comes to a halt, Squire leans out of the window to see what's wrong.

"Fielding? What is it? What's the trouble?"

"Tis terr'ble," I says, "Miller's wife needs help."

"For God's sake, say what's wrong, man," he says, all impatient.

By this time Squire's lady be lookin' out too. "Tis not a sight for your wife, Sir."

He gets down from the coach and stands beside me. I be shiverin' – more from shock than cold, though it be a raw day as I've said.

"Have you no jacket, Fielding?" he asks as I lead him to where Mistress Kenton be layin'. "Dear God!" says he and turns away. The baby makes another sound. "The child's alive then. The woman?"

"Dead, Sir." I be really shakin' now.

He walks quickly to the coach, tells the coachman to give me his greatcoat. Says he'll see I return it the next day. The coachman looks none too pleased but does as he is ordered. "No, my dear," he says to his wife as she makes to step from the coach. "It's a nasty business." He turns around to where I stands. "We must take the child with us. You go back to Tolpuddle and advise Mister Kenton."

"The cord be still attached to the child, Sir. I'll have to cut it with my hedgin' knife."

Squire, lookin' real green, climbs into the coach. He hands me the rug he'd had over his knees, saying, "Do what's necessary, Fielding, but be quick. Wrap this round the infant. We must get help for it as soon as possible if it's to be saved."

It 'ave stuck in my mind ever since that Squire didn't flinch at the blood and birthin' muck as were messin' up his rug. That coachman though. When I removes his greatcoat, pulls on my jacket agin and hands him back his coat, he made a great show of disgust, as if it too were fouled.

When I hands the babe into the coach, Squire looks I right in the eye and says, "Well done, Fielding," and then adds, "You're a *good* man." And he said it with feelin', as if it were truly meant. As if it were summat he'd not thought on afore.

The child survived, but it were never right. A stook of corn short the fourth sheaf, if you understands my meanin'. I think Mister Kenton would rather it had died, though he did seem greatly attached to it.

A good man. I ent never forgot that. But be I a *good* man? If I had taken that poor lass back home 'tis probable she wouldn't 'ave died, though she did resist when I tried. But had I not reported for work the agent is like to have hired another and my children would 'ave gone hungry.

Then there's them as I betrayed. But doin' so were forced upon me.

My Mary thinks I be a good man. Squire says I be. I wouldst like to think that be what I am.

Chapter Thirty
Australia 1837

RISING FROM HIS KNEES, HIS PRAYERS FINISHED, THOMAS eased his tired body onto the rough, wooden pallet. The straw mattress rustled as he lay back, hands behind his head. This was the time, just before he gave himself up to sleep, that images of Dinniah and the children were sharpest. He could see her, workbasket at her side, needle in hand, darning the heel of a sock. His sock. Greyish-oatmeal coloured. One of dozens she'd knitted over the years, four needles click-clicking, glinting in the firelight. The nights would be closing in now it was October. It was October, wasn't it? It was difficult keeping track of time, the seasons opposite to those in England. But, yes, October surely, or early November. The young'uns in bed. Peter at the table reading a passage from the Scriptures to his mother as she plied the thread back and forth, closing the sock-hole with skillful stitches.

But ... Were they still in Tolpuddle even? How could she possibly find money for the rent? What if they'd been evicted from the cottage? Pray God, Dorcas had managed to find employment, at fifteen someone would surely hire her, so that at least there'd be a little money coming in. Wearily he ordered such thoughts from his mind, tried to conjure up once again a picture of Dinniah knitting ...

Now he saw himself, Bible in hand, striding along the road with his friends to Piddlehinton where villagers would be gathering to hear George preach. How easily he moved, free of the rheumatics that now plagued his joints. A gentle sun, not one that seared, warmed his back. Queen Anne's lace blooming in delicate clumps along the roadside.

Dinniah filled his dreams. No longer knitting, but curled against him in their bed.

~~~

October. The heat of summer would soon be upon them. Sir Richard Bourke, Governor of New South Wales, leaned back in his chair. He fingered his waistcoat buttons that strained against the force of his rotund belly, unfastened a couple to give his bulk more ease. Wasn't it always the same, just when he thought he'd dealt with all urgent matters? Everything packed and ready for tomorrow's move, both he and his wife eager for the cooler temperatures of Wakalki, and now this.

He pondered on the letters from London that lay on the desk in front of him. Here was a pretty kettle of fish. How could he implement conditional pardons for the five men when he'd not yet heard if King William had been persuaded to put his signature to the documents? His legal training made him consider all the ramifications. He picked up the letter and read it through again. Aha, one of the conditions for the men's release depended on their behavior.

It was all very well for London to urge him to expedite the immediate release of the prisoners, but who knew how long it would take for the king to give his approval? It might be years. No, it was a responsibility he felt he should not rush into undertaking. Caution in all things, he told himself, as his fingers teased at the profusion of side whiskers that flowed down past his ears and across his cheeks.

Pushing the papers aside, he picked up a small, brass bell and shook it vigorously. Damn the man. Why didn't he respond? As he reached for the bell again, his secretary appeared, one hand steadying the pince-nez on his nose, the other clutching a pad of paper.

"Browning, at last! I want you to write to the Colonial Secretary. Instruct him to obtain information from the Superintendent of Convicts on the conduct of five prisoners. I have their names here, somewhere." Rummaging amongst the papers on his desk, Bourke extracted a list and read, "Thomas and John Standfield, James Brine, James Hammett and James Loveless."

Browning, his tall frame stooped over his pad, hastily jotted down the information.

"The men are widely scattered, I understand. It will be impossible for me to interview their employers myself," said Bourke. "However, be sure to stress there is some urgency about this matter."

Well, that would hold a decision in abeyance for now. A reply should be awaiting him on his return from Wakalki. "Yes, yes. That's the way to deal with the problem."

Oh dear, he was talking to himself again. At least there was no one around now to have overheard him. How his wife chided him when he had such lapses in her presence. "With none but convict servants around me, I am starved for conversation and you talk to yourself!" Bourke shook his head as if to clear it of her shrill, complaining tones. She had accompanied him unwillingly to Australia and her complaints were justified – a lack of company of her own social standing; the heat and rawness of the place; convict servants who had to be trained in the meanest of accomplishments. No, it was no place for a woman of her standing.

Taking his fob watch from his waistcoat pocket, Bourke released the catch. Eleven o'clock. Time to see how preparations for tomorrow were proceeding.

~~~

The Colonial Secretary wrote again to the Principal Superintendent of Convicts: *It is now the 29th November and I have heard nothing from you regarding the matter of the five prisoners mentioned in my earlier letter. I would stress again, this is a matter of great importance and urgency…* " He had done what he could, but what attention would officials miles away give to his request? It was to be hoped this second letter would produce results. Sir Richard Bourke would not take kindly to this delay for he was a man cautious in his actions but who expected his wishes to be carried out promptly once he had come to a decision.

179

~~~

Sitting under the shade of a jacaranda tree, John Standfield hummed as he whittled away at a piece of pine wood. Now and again he paused to study his handiwork, running a finger along the flank of the horse he was carving, pleased at the proportions he had achieved. A horse and cart for David. A small babe when he'd left, now he would be toddling. No, long past the toddling stage. Carefully laying down his knife, John tried to visualize his son as a young boy, but saw only a tiny mouth searching for Kathrine's milk.

Thoughts of David always seemed to lead to thoughts of Kathrine, and thoughts of Kathrine led to ... John's mind filled with the image of the young girl he'd seen that morning. On a rising mound on the other side of the fencing, a small group of Aboriginal males crouched in a circle conferring, their guttural tones unintelligible to his ears. The girl stood to one side, naked except for an elaborate necklace of feathers and small bones, tracing a pattern in the dust with her foot. He had stared at the lithe, glistening body, her firm breasts not yet sucked shapeless. He'd felt his penis stiffen, raise its head. He pried his feet from the ground where they seemed fastened as if by roots, moved closer. Gagging at the smell of the rancid fish oil which coated her blue-black skin, John had retreated, ashamed, back to his work ...

Standing up, John kicked at the roots of the jacaranda and cursed himself for thinking of that wild savage and Kathrine in the same way. Placing his hands on the tree trunk, he banged his head against the rough bark, the one pain disguising the other.

~~~

"Is there still no reply from the Colonial Secretary? What's delaying the man? It's mid- January!" Bourke looked angrily at his secretary as if the matter was somehow Browning's fault. "You'd best write further. No, write directly to the Superintendent of Convicts. Say, I order the five men – you have their names – to be delivered immediately to Hyde Park

Barracks to await further orders. I wish to be informed immediately they have all arrived."

~~~

James Brine crouched silently in the long grass, scarcely daring to breath. Slowly the opossum hanging from a tree branch extended a grey arm towards the fruit Brine had scattered on the ground. It picked up a wild grape and lifted it to its mouth, but suddenly, changing its mind, the opossum dropped the fruit and scrambled back into the foliage. Must have smelled me, thought Brine. He'd been trying for several evenings to entice the animal down from the tree, wanting to see if he could overcome its timidity.

Standing upright, hands to the small of his back to ease his muscles, he shook his head in disappointment. Brine was a quiet, introspective man. *You silly bugger*, he mentally chided himself. *No need to feel hurt because it's taken off.* But he knew why he had such strong hopes of getting the possum to accept his presence, recognizing his need for someone or something to care about. Since his widowed mother's death, several years before he'd been transported, he had no relatives to show concern on his behalf.

He was sure it was by God's intervention rather than chance that he'd come across Standfield and Loveless preaching. Moved by Standfield's intensity he had gone the following Sunday to hear him, had begun to follow them both on their preaching circuit, had started attending the school they held on Sunday afternoons. Thomas had become his mentor.

Plucking a piece of grass Brine chewed on the end as he walked slowly back in the gathering dusk to the hut he shared with three other prisoners. Where were Standfield and the others now, he wondered once again? Thomas was getting on in years. It was to be hoped he had a decent employer. Life was better here at Mansfield compared to his original placement. Master worked all his hands hard, real hard, be they convict or ticket-of-leavers, but they were not kept short of food. Nor was this master given to sending them before the magistrate's bench on a mere whim, asking that they be flogged, like that swine, Scott, his first master.

But he was lonely, no doubt about it. Those had been good times, walking along the Dorset lanes with Standfield and Loveless, discussing religion, politics. At first he'd mostly listened, conscious of his lack of knowledge. Loveless talked convincingly of Friendly Societies and how it was the only chance they had of getting a decent wage. Gaining more confidence, he'd questioned, even put forward an idea on occasion. He'd seen the logic in Loveless' arguments, had soon been convinced to join. No, he held no grudges on that score.

Picking up his tin plate and mug from a shelf just inside the hut, Brine headed for the cookhouse. He'd try again tomorrow with the possum.

Chapter Thirty-One

Workhouse 1842

THIS DYING DO TAKE A TIME. I KNOWS MY MARY BE BY MY side, but I can'st give her no sign of it. It were the doctor from Bere, who were standin' in for the one as usually attends the workhouse, as gave orders that Mary were to be allowed to visit. Normally men and women be kept separate. 'Tis long since three weeks that I were put here to die, and none 'ave stopped her comin'. I know she's near for I can hear her skirt as she moves. 'Tis coarse cloth they uses for clothing for us, and the women's dresses rasp rather than rustle. Not like that petticoat of Mary's, the new 'un she were wearin' at the Harvest Supper, now that had a wonnerful rustle.

Rustle! Now why have that word set my mind leapin' to thoughts of government? O'course, Lord Russell! All that summer of '35 pressure were brought to bear on the government, and Lord Russell – I ent sure who he be but his name be mentioned a lot by them as could read, and 'tis a name as sticks to my mind – well, finally he's writ to them in charge in Bot'ny Bay and whatever be the name of that place where George Loveless were sent, sayin' as how Loveless, Standfield and the rest were to be granted a pardon. I'm only goin' on what I heard, mind, but I un'erstands His Majesty were provin' difficult in signin' the pardons. So their wives knew not what to expect. It weren't till the November that the king were talked into signin' his name to the paper.

Then I hears there were problems with the pardon even though the king'd finally signed. There was letters being writ to them in charge in Bot'ny Bay, but it do take a goodly time – four months I've heard – for letters to get there and then, o'course, they've to wait for an answer. So it were all a mix-up and none seemed to know what be happenin', certainly not Elizabeth Loveless and Dinniah Standfield. They was still livin' in their cottages. There be such an outcry when their landlords tried to evict 'em soon after the trial that they daren't do it, and the money raised in London were sent regular to pay the rent and keep their families fed.

I didst so hope those poor women's problems would soon be over. 'Cos, it weren't summat I couldst say to 'em seein' as since Elizabeth Loveless spat in my face not one of them women 'ave given a sign that I exists on the rare occasion our paths've crossed.

You can be certain sure that they don't agree with Squire that I be a good man.

A good man. Since Squire said that to I, it 'ave been in my mind day and night. Naggin' away like an itch that won't be eased by scratchin'. Till they forced I to betray Loveless and the rest of 'em I likes to think I lived a goodly life. Maybe not *godly* but I harmed none, bore none a grudge, were willin' to help a neighbour. And there be no doubtin' I loved my Mary and our children.

Funny as how when Squire comes to mind, then Parson's image ent far behind. Now there's a man who 'tis certain sure don't think much of I, and he be one as makes my blood seethe whenever our paths cross. I remembers at Mistress Kenton's funeral, he were walkin' with great difficulty. Mary said later as how he had gout. "Gout!" says I. "I hears he were thrown from his horse into a ditch when huntin' and don't like to admit it. Him fancies himself to be such a good horseman. I only wish I could 'a seen it."

"You'm sure got a dislike for the man that almost amounts to hate," says Mary. "It ent good to hate so. It can fester inside a person." Then she adds with a smile creepin' into her voice, "If it be like you say, I hope it were a ditch full of water and mud."

Then in almost the same breath her asks, "You mind that time them chased that fox into the garden and you were emptyin' …?" and afore she can get any further she breaks into laughter, and my laughter joins with hers. Oh, it were good to have *summat* to laugh about.

Durin' the autumn of '35, and right through to '36 for that matter, the news sheets were still on about members of the Orange Lodges should be charged the same as the Tolpuddle Martyrs were charged. Said as how the Orange Lodges havin' hundreds of thousands of members were much more of a threat to the country. The argufying were beyond my un'erstandin' but them news sheets were stirrin' up a terr'ble amount of trouble in Parliament.

When 'twas known for certain sure that the king had signed pardons for Loveless and the others, their wives wrote a letter to Lord Russel thankin' him. But it were a long time afore them pardons were acted on. Seemed them in Parliament and them out in them foreign places were havin' difficulty un'erstandin' each other.

Chapter Thirty-Two

Australia 1836

FINALLY, A REPLY FROM THE SUPERINTENDENT. IT WOULD appear to have crossed with the instructions he had just sent. Sir Richard Bourke, one hand playing with a letter-opener of carved ivory, studied the letter. *"...have been awaiting a reply from Hammett's master. As so much time has elapsed, and hearing nothing from him, I feel I should communicate that which I know..."*

All the masters reported excellent conduct. Now what to do? Tapping his teeth with the letter-opener, Bourke leaned against his desk. No doubt the prisoners were already on their way. Once they arrived at Hyde Park he'd hold them … where? He laid down the letter-opener, drummed his fingers on the desk top. Port Macquarie? Macquarie's notorious reputation was a thing of the past, or would be once his efforts in that respect were recognized. "I've worked hard to improve conditions there," he announced loudly to the otherwise empty room. "Damn hard!" Port Macquarie would be the ideal place.

~~~

The pigs snuffled and grunted around the trough as John Standfield reached over the wall of the sty to empty a bucket of feed. A kookaburra hidden in the bushes over by Hunter River gave a shrill, discordant cry.

And Ordered Their Estate

Yesterday's heavy rain had settled the dust and polished the wattle tree leaves. A light breeze rippled the grass.

Balwarra Farm was well run and Richard Jones, his master, a fair man who didn't demand more than a man could give in the way of hard work. John was content with his placement. He had come to appreciate the rich green of the forest, was fascinated with the range of colours of foliage and soil.

Twelve shillings, he'd heard, would purchase an acre of land. Maybe when he'd served his time, he could get work in the coal fields being opened up just outside Hunter, save some money, bring Kathrine and the child out. There were possibilities here for an ordinary labourer, unlike England. The idea of ever owning land in Tolpuddle, why, it was laughable. With Kathrine and David with him, hard work, there was an opportunity for him to achieve his dream.

A shout made John look up. From across the yard his master was calling, "Standfield! Here!" John set down the bucket and crossed the yard to where Jones stood, two men at his side.

"These soldiers here. They're askin' for you."

"For me?"

"You John Standfield?" questioned one of the red-coats, stepping in front of Jones. The soldier, jacket unbuttoned exposing a hairy chest, looked hot and uncomfortable in his crumpled uniform.

"Aye. What d'you want of me?"

"Orders to take you to Newcastle."

"Hold hard," said Jones. "You can't do that. He's my employee. One of my hardest workers. I've made no complaint."

"Newcastle? What for?" questioned John, his voice rising in disbelief.

"All I know is, we're instructed to take him with us."

"Let's see your papers," demanded Jones.

"Show him, Williamson," the first solider ordered the second. "Now come on. Let's have no fuss. We've to pick up a Thomas Standfield on our way too."

"My father! What madness is this?"

Ignoring John's protests, Jones' angry insistence that he'd take the matter up with the magistrate, the two soldiers fastened a chain round John's wrists and led him away.

~~~

Hunkered down in the shade, Brine smoothed a patch of sandy soil with his hand, picked up a pointed stick. Tongue protruding slightly from his mouth, he scratched out the opening words of the twenty-third psalm, "The Lord is my shepherd." It was an exercise to ease his longing to see written words once again as much as a test of memory. Although he recited, often out loud, passages from the Bible, he longed to hold a book in his hands again. To smooth flat a page after it had been turned. To *read*. How he had admired George and Thomas for their literacy and command of language. He felt he was losing what skills he had acquired from them in reading and writing.

Leaning back on his heels he threw down the stick in disgust. He should have chosen a larger area of bare soil, he'd already run out of space. He bent forward again to scrub out the words he'd written. His hand hovered a moment. No. It would be wrong to obliterate God's word. "Best I rely on memory and recitation," he told himself.

~~~

"Why do we have to be chained?" Standing on the dock at Hunter River, John Standfield questioned a guard as he was ordered to hitch up his trousers so that irons could be riveted around his ankles.

"Following orders, is all," said the guard. "You're for Newcastle prison until you're sent on further."

"But there's no need to chain us."

"Regulations. All prisoners being transported must be chained. 'It's set down in the rules." The guard thrust John to one side while he bent to perform the same task on Thomas.

Thomas, his face creased with worry, placed a hand on John's shoulder. "There is little we can do. Let it be, Son." Wearily he added, "All we can do is pray."

"Pray! Prayer has done little for us these past years."

"Don't speak so, Son. Should we lose our trust in the Lord, we have lost all."

Turning to his father as they were led on board the packet-steamer, John asked in urgent tones, "You're sure Nowlan promised to make enquiries on your behalf?"

"Yes, John. I've told you so, and Nowlan, though not of our faith, is a good Christian."

~~~

Brine felt helpless anger surging up. Why would no one answer his questions: Why he'd been brought to Maitland? Put in a cell? Chained? If a magistrate, a guard, were alone in the cell with him now, he was sure he'd rip him apart. He could see his hands around a guard's throat, the Maitland magistrate bloodied and beaten by his, Brine's, fists. Rarely did such bouts of rage overtake him, but their suddenness, their intensity, frightened him.

He recalled an incident at Glindon, his first placement. Johnson, a fellow prisoner, had broken a ploughshare. What did the poor sod know of ploughing? Of farming? He'd been a printer's apprentice in London before being convicted of theft. But Scott, their master, drunk as usual, insisted Johnson had broken it deliberately. Said the overseer was to take Johnson before the magistrate at Maitland and demand that he be flogged. And flogged he was. Returned with his back a bloodied, oozing mess.

It was only a couple of weeks later, his back still not fully healed, Johnson was caught by Scott exchanging a few words with the black girl Scott kept up at the house. Flying into a rage, he beat Johnson about the head, shouting he'd have him before the magistrate the next day. Brine could see himself, standing just behind Scott, raising the shovel he held, lifting it over his head. Poised, ready to slam it down on Scott's skull. He'd never forget the ferocity of the anger that filled him. How it took every ounce of control he could muster to lower the shovel, turn and walk away.

Johnson had run off that night. He'd whispered to Brine that he hoped to join up with other escaped convicts.

"Don't do it, man. You'll not survive in the bush on your own," Brine counselled. "Only the blacks know how to live off this wretched land."

"I'll take my chances," Johnson replied. "Can't be no worse than here."

Time and again he'd wondered if heat, thirst, lack of food, snakes or Aboriginals got the poor devil before a patrol of soldiers did. Two hundred lashes, bolters got, before being sent to work in double irons on a chain gang. And just as rage at his helplessness had overpowered him then, so it did now. Why would none give him an explanation as to where he was heading.

~~~

"At least we're together, son. I don't think I could have borne such treatment again were I on my own." Thomas ceased rubbing his aching joints and sat down beside John on the hard cell floor. "You'd think if they can't give us bedding, they'd at least feed us." The bread, thin soup, and water that had been pushed through the door once a day was not enough to sustain them. Now the sun striped the floor with shadows of the window bars a third time.

"If only they'd tell us *why* we've been brought to Newcastle."

At the sound of a key in the lock both men looked up.

"On yer feet!" the guard commanded. "Come on, now."

"Where are you taking us?" asked John, assisting his father as Thomas struggled to rise from the ground.

"Sydney," was the laconic response.

~~~

The boat, of no great size, pitched and tossed in the storm. Huge waves pounded the decks. Thomas, racked with sickness, lay in his own vomit, his eyes closed. Occasionally he murmured a prayer. The stench in the hold affected even those not sick. John's mouth felt like a dried up stream bed in summer, but he found breathing normally through his nose made him retch. A prisoner groaned. Another cursed. One begged that the boat sink and put them out of their misery. John, frustrated and angry, struggled to find a reason for what was happening. He knew of no convicts being removed unless their employers had requested it. Both Jones and Nowlan had attested to their good behaviour, had protested their removal. Why then? Why? He tried to find ease for his leg, rubbed raw by too tight irons. 'If only they'd unchain us," John muttered to himself, "it would be a little more bearable."

Sydney dock bustled with activity. Shouted commands accompanied the loading and unloading of vessels. Still the prisoners lay chained. When, oh when will they get us out of this foul place, thought John?

"How're things with you, Father?"

"A drink of water is what I need most," Thomas replied, "and firm ground beneath my feet."

"Aye, to be out of this stench and breathing fresh air again. Listen! They're opening the hatch. But what news'll be awaiting us, I wonder"

Thomas groaned as a guard roughly grabbed at the chain holding him to the fastening ring.

"Easy now, easy!" John snapped at the guard, whose only response was to yank Thomas' chain harder.

Bellowed orders followed them as they struggled up the stairs from the dark hold. Other guards shouted from above, urged them to make haste as they staggered down the gangway, blinded by sunlight.

As they marched once again along the streets to Hyde Park Barracks, Thomas leaned heavily on John for support. The bustle, people, a cacophony of noise overwhelmed him after the quietness of Nowlan's farm. The air, heat-dried of every drop of moisture, pressed down on him. They walked in silence, John looking all about him, Thomas intent only on reaching the barracks and being able to rest

"It looks as if building has been going on apace," commented John, nodding in the direction of the spire of a new church. "And the taverns. Did you ever see so many in one place?" He immediately regretted his remark for fear it would set his father denouncing the evil of drink. But finding strength to keep moving had taken all Thomas' attention.

Chapter Thirty-Three

Workhouse 1842

WHITE. WHY BE THAT WORD *WHITE* IN MY THOUGHTS? Summat must've brought it to mind, but what I knows not. White? Be my brain shuttin' down as well as my body? Since that last fit of coughin' and blood pourin' out my mouth I ent been aware of anything around me, and now this word 'white' plagues my thoughts. Have it summit to do with them shroud things Loveless wore when I joined their union? They was white. No, that weren't what was in my thoughts.

Aah … 'tis comin' to I. Blood. White. When I has that last coughin' fit. All that blood spewin' out, and the old woman as takes care of us – there be two of 'em, but this 'un be gentler than the other – she be wipin' my face with a cloth. And she grumbles to herself: "I shouldn't be using this cloth. 'Tis new. The blood'll never wash out. We're meant to use the old uns. Hold hard, man. Hold! I wonders you've got any blood left in yer." Her turnin' to grab another piece of rag, then mutterin' to herself again: "You'd never guess it were once white!"

White. Sheets flappin' in the breeze. White.

My Mary would be up at the farm of a Monday and Tuesday, gettin' there a little after four in the mornin' to start the fire under the copper to heat the water to do Mistress Wainwright's big wash. And Tabby would walk over to her Aunt Martha's cottage to leave Will in the care of Martha's mother afore joinin' Mary at the farm to help. Tab be a big help to her mother

One mornin' as I comes past where the clothes lines be strung out I sees Tabby peggin' out the sheets, them all dazzlin' white in the sunlight. I were just goin' to give her a wave when I sees Wainwright's son watchin' Tab with a look on his face that give me a jolt.

Wainwright's son were a puny lad when he were younger, with a hang-dog air about him. Mind you, his father always yellin' at him, not givin' him any encouragement, didn't help him none. Him with his long, narrow face and needle-like teeth. Made I think of a ferret every time I saw 'im. Robert he were called. But, when he growed on more, put on a year or two and a bit more flesh, he looked better. But still mindin' me of a ferret.

It weren't right, the way he were lookin' at her.

I yells at 'im, "Your father be shoutin' for 'ee. He's still waitin' for that cuttin' tool he sent you for."

Well, he jumps at my voice, he be so lost in his thoughts, thoughts that weren't good uns, that I could tell. That look of his played on my mind all day. It weren't like a young lad that's sweet on a young lass that's for sure. I ent good with words and I can't find the one I needs to describe it … raw? … animal-like? … I'm certain sure it weren't kindly.

In bed that night, I says to Mary, "You'm must keep an eye on Tab when you're up at Wainwrights. Make sure as you keeps her away from that Robert."

"You noticed it too?" says Mary. "He be always hangin' round when it be wash day. I've warned Tabby to keep near to me if he be around. To have nought to do with him."

"That's right, you watch her close," says I. "Should he lay a finger on Tab, I knows I'd kill 'im."

If I'm honest with myself, Samuel and Will might come first in my affections, but that don't mean my love for Tabby weren't somethin' fierce.

Now my mind be picturin' them sheets again … white, so white against the blue of the sky.

Chapter Thirty-Four

Australia 1836

WALKING ROUND AND ROUND THE EXERCISE YARD, JOHN struggled still to understand why he and his father had been brought here. Two weeks now since they'd passed through the prison gates. It just didn't make sense. No charges had been laid against them, why had they been sent back to Sydney? It consumed his thoughts. Talking to other prisoners, John learned the newly appointed Barracks Superintendent was more approachable than the last. More liberal in his treatment of prisoners.

Three times he'd made application to speak with the Barracks Superintendent. Three times he'd been denied. "Tis no use you preaching patience at me, Father. I *will* see him. Someone *must* know why we're here."

Thomas studied his son. The determination of John's stance, the scarcely hidden anger in his eyes. This son who had always followed, was now leading. Placing a hand on John's shoulder, Thomas said, "Aye, Son. We have a right to know, but I caution you to speak with care when you ask again."

~~~

White-capped waves slapped the sides of the two vessels anchored some distance from each other. A strong wind caught at the half-furled sails, whined in the rigging. The sky was a menacing roil of dark clouds.

A group of dejected prisoners stood herded together. The clanking of their irons mingled with the creaking of pulleys, the screech of gulls, shouted orders. Red-coated soldiers pushed and shoved the prisoners into two groups as an officer tallied their numbers against two lists of names. Prisoners who had jackets, clutched them close against the wind. One in only a torn shirt, his arms wrapped tightly to his chest for warmth, lost his battered hat to a gust that sent it bowling along the quay and into the water. They cursed under their breath, held muttered conversations.

"You know where we're headed?" asked the prisoner chained on Brine's left, scratching at his armpit.

"No idea where we're going, or why I be here," replied Brine. "Why are they sendin' some to one group, others to another?"

"Silence. Shut your gobs or they'll be shut for yer," yelled one of the guards.

A prisoner on Brine's right expectorated a brown wad into the loose gravel near Brine's feet. "You don't know! For a chew of t'bacca I can tell 'ee, for sure." He squinted his eyes at Brine's shake of his head. "What yer got to trade then? Nothin'? Anyways, probably best you remains ignorant."

The first convict, nodding in the direction of the officer, said, "That lobster over there. Him with the list. He'd know." Scratching at his body again, he added, "Looks as if this 'un be goin' some distance judgin' by the supplies bein' loaded."

"Sydney, maybe?" suggested Brine.

"Nah! Must be further 'n that." This time he clawed at his coarse beard. "Damn cooties," he said, squashing a louse between his fingers.

At that moment there was a shouted command to embark. Each convict bent to scoop up the length of chain connecting him to the next, and slowly shuffled their way on board.

~~~

"You're John Standfield? I hear you have repeatedly insisted on seeing me." The Barrack Superintendent stood looking at John. "What is it you want? Speak up! I've other matters needing my attention."

"To know why my father and I have been brought here, Sir. There seem to be no charges brought against us."

"Charge? There's no charge. 'Governor Bourke ordered you be returned here."

"But why, Sir?"

"Why? That I can't tell you," he said, his face reflecting his lack of knowledge." I know nothing more."

"Is there anyone as can tell me?"

"Governor Bourke." The Superintendent gave a bark of laughter. "And you'll not get to speak with him, that's for sure."

Lost in thought as he returned to their hut, John did not notice who stood with his father, until Thomas' cries of, "John, John! Do you not see who's just arrived?" made him look up. His father stood with his arm round the shoulders of James Loveless while Brine stretched out his hand to John, his face alight with pleasure.

"This is unbelievable. Brine! Oh, it's good to see you." John placed his hands on Brine's shoulders and drew him close. "You must tell us how you've fared. But first, have *you* any idea why we've been brought here?'

"The barrack superintendent gave you no answer then, son?" asked Thomas.

"Said he could not. My instincts tell me he was speaking true. He could only say that Governor Bourke ordered us returned here."

"I asked the same question," said James Loveless. "My master said he'd heard something about a pardon, but knew no details."

Thomas, John and Brine turned to him as one.

"Pardoned! We're to be pardoned?" Astonishment, disbelief, hope, all mingled in John's voice, and Brine's voice echoed John's. For several seconds each man stood silent, overcome by what James' voicing of the word *pardon* would mean if it were true.

Then Thomas, hands raised heavenward, cried "The Lord be thanked. Oh, praise the Lord."

"Don't set your hopes too high, Thomas, but yes, pray God my master be right."

"But Hammett. What of Hammett? If he joins us that would certainly give credence to what you say, James," said Thomas.

197

There was a nodding of heads to Thomas' statement.

It was James Loveless voiced the question first. "Have any of you news of home?"

The others could only shake their heads and utter, "None."

~~~

Crouching in the shade of a gum tree tangled with vines, Thomas, John and James listened as Brine told his tale.

"My first master. He were a swine, that Scott. Would crack his whip across a man's shoulders for no reason as any of us could see. Spent most of his time drinkin' and wenchin'. Left the runnin' of the farm mainly to the overseer. And the overseer cut costs by keepin' us short on rations."

"Sounds as if you suffered much hardship," James Loveless said.

"You know, once, for two whole weeks, I were stood chest-deep in the river washin' sheep. The cold ate into my bones. I were ill for some time after. Couldn't stop coughin'."

John observing Thomas massaging his knees asked, "Your limbs bothering you again, Father?"

"They're troublesome, but I've known them worse." Thomas turned to Brine. "This Scott. He's a settler?"

"I heard he'd been a trouble to his family in England. They'd put up money for him to settle here. One day, I hears this shoutin' and looks up. There Scott be, up on his horse, chasin' a young Abo girl. He'd had her on the place some time, and her were big with child. Real big. Her were runnin' with hands holding her belly, and he were lashin' at her with his crop. And laughin! That were the truly terr'ble part. His laughter. After that he got himself a convict woman to cook. And keep his bed warm o'course. But the farm were run down. He went broke and I were moved to a place about another twenty mile on. Life were much better there."

Brine, replacing the twig on which he'd been periodically chewing, sat silent for a while. Spitting out a fragment of bark, he continued his story: "Like you, I were just whisked away and sent down to Newcastle. None would give a reason. Then, wouldst you believe, chained to all them other convicts, I were put on a boat for Norfolk Island."

"Norfolk Island!" the others responded in horror.

"Aye, Norfolk Island." Brine nodded his head for emphasis. "That hellish place. A thousand miles from nowhere."

"How come you're here then?"

"Storm blew up, a terr'ble storm. Boat near capsized. Us had to put back to Newcastle."

"Thank the Lord for his mercies," said Thomas.

"Aye, thank the Lord for savin' us. But I knows not whether my bein' here now, amongst you all, 'twas the Lord's doing or my protestin', for I made such a ruckus, went bloody mad, they put me on a vessel to Sydney."

"Why did you not protest in the first place?" asked Loveless.

"Well, 'twasn't till us set sail that I found out where we be headin'."

"They listened to a convict!" Thomas shook his head. "The Lord surely had a hand in saving you from such a fate as Norfolk."

"Maybe they checked their records and saw they'd made a mistake. I'll tell 'ee this, though. They beat I black and blue first. But that be why I'm here with you all now." As evidence to support his story, Brine opened his rough jacket exposing flesh still tinged fading purple, yellow, and brown. "I reckon they must've cracked one of my ribs for breathing were terr'ble painful for some while."

Thomas struggled to his feet. "Let us bow our heads and give thanks that Brine is returned to us." The three stood up, offering "amens" and "God be thanked" as an accompaniment to Thomas' prayers.

The end of February and still no sign of Hammett.

"You think 'tis possible he's dead?" questioned John of the others.

"He were very low in spirits when we were all sent our different ways," said Brine. "You knows he talked very little, except to question how his wife would fare without him. Her with a young babe an' all."

"But he's young and strong, unlike myself," said Thomas.

"Ah, but much would depend on the kind of master he were placed with," said Brine, "and I knows only too well, some be evil bastards."

~~~

A message was relayed from the barrack superintendent. They were to ready themselves for dispatch to Port Macquarie.

Huddled in a corner of the prison yard, despair marked their faces, weighed down their shoulders.

"Port Macquarie! I've heard terrible tales. Heard it likened to Norfolk," said Loveless. "Just when us dared hope that things were to get better for us."

"The vileness of the place be much spoken of," agreed Brine. "Same as you, I've heard it compared to Norfolk Island and I still shudders to think that's where I could'st be instead of here."

John, who had been hunkered down, his back to a wall, rose resolutely to his feet. "Well, I'm for trying to do something about it."

"Do! What canst us do?" asked Brine.

"Write a petition to Governor Bourke."

"A petition! To Governor Bourke! Your mind be addled."

"I've thought all night on the matter. I intend requesting Father be returned to work for Mr. Nolan and I allowed to accompany him."

Reaching into his pocket, John withdrew a crumpled piece of paper, a pencil. "You've more scholarship than I've mastered, Father, what with your preaching and reading. You'll turn a better phrase than ever I can."

"You think there's a chance?"

"What have we to lose?"

~~~

Bourke laid down the Standfield petition. If only this damned matter could soon be resolved. "*...petition that Your Excellency will be pleased to remit Thomas Standfield to the service of his former master Mr. Nowlan to whose kindness he is indebted for the restoration of his health, which had been much impaired, and being still very feeble he humbly entreats that his son may be allowed to accompany him to the same service...*"

Tugging at his whiskers, as if a solution could be pulled from their grey bushiness, Bourke debated the matter with himself. The men's pardon would be granted eventually, it was only a matter of time. But surely it would be more prudent to keep the men together in one place? Yet it seemed a fair enough request. And there was that other one, what was his name? Hammett. There was still no word on Hammett. What to do?

Releasing the tortured clump of facial hair, Bourke, picked up the bell and summoned his secretary. He would agree to the Standfields' petition and hold the others here in Sydney.

~~~

Thomas paused from sawing wood to wave to his son, who was talking to Nowlan. Now it was mid-March and the intense heat had eased. Thomas found the sun's gentler warmth eased the pain in his joints, and his son's presence had done much to lift his spirits.

Walking over to his father, John said, "Nowlan was just telling me he's heard Loveless and Brine have been sent to a government farm outside Sydney."

"Not Port Macquarie? Thank the Lord for that. But how much longer must we wait for our pardon?"

Chapter Thirty-Five

Workhouse 1842

MARY ... APPLES ... MARY APPLES...

I still be floating in this void of silence, where 'twould seem there be only me and my thoughts. One minute my mind be filled with one image and then, afore I realizes it, like a flea I has flit to another. I sees things so sharp. A thought ago I were with Mary in the apple loft. I could taste again the juice runnin' down Mary's chin. And as I lie back against the wall, Mary kneels at my side. Crumplin' up a spray of dried apple leaves she'd picked up from the floor, she sprinkles the leaf dust on my chest. Smilin' that great smile of hers. Bare shoulders and breasts the colour of unskimmed milk. How beautiful, my Mary be.

Now 'tis the perfume of blackberries that teases. Young Will did love blackberries so. I can see him clear as day, bare feet covered in dust, and hands and mouth purple with juice, laughin' as he looks up at I. Yellow-gold curls bobbin' as he laughs.

Pretty fruit, blackberries. Aah, the sun-warmed scent of 'em. Sprays purple and black archin' against the blueness of the sky. Come autumn, the leaves marked crimson round the edges, and yellow 'uns touched with pink. Even in November a few leaves still cling, the rough, crimsoned edges outlined with hoar-frost.

Laughin' Willie ... Cram his mouth with berries, Will would. 'Tis a wonder he didn't make hisself sick.

Watchin' him, little arms tryin' to circle an oak tree, tiny fingers runnin' over the rough ridges in the bark, feeling in the cracks, intent on catchin' a scurryin' ant, it come to me how dear I hold him. Give he one cough an' I be torn with worry: two and I has him laid alongside Samuel in the churchyard.

"Don't 'ee fret so," says Mary. "He be full of life." I darest not reply *and so were Samuel when he were little,* for fear the words bein' spoke would leave their mark on Will. I spends more than us can spare on milk, take note should one of Mistress Wainwright's hens nest off in the hedgerow, slippin' the eggs into my pocket on my way home. 'Tis what the doctor said to give Samuel, but it were too late then. Will an' Tabitha will have 'em, even if stealin' be the only way.

Oftimes breathin' were troublesome, as if a band of iron bound my chest, and now and then the coughin' come back, though not as fierce as in the past. But it were there. Lurkin' inside of me. Smoulderin'. The fear of sowin' more seed, be past. My cock hung limp however much Mary give it encouragement. And I would turn from her in shame. Shame, yes, for I would rather fight the urge than have no urge to fight.

When the weather were good, and dependin' where I be workin', I'd take the short-cut home. In early summer the banks along the stream were lined with flag iris and purple loosestrife and later the meadowsweet and burr-reed. The water a slow ripple, peaceful and soothin'. Crossin' the ford by the stepping-stones, up the slope, through the wall backin' the churchyard, saved I a good half mile.

Pausin' by Samuel's grave one day in the late afternoon's sunshine, I hears shoutin' and a cry I knows is Will's. Runnin', leapin' over grassy mounds, I comes on Parson shoutin' at Will. One second Will be standin' on a large, moss-speckled tomb, the next he's on the grass, cryin'. I grabs hold of Parson's raised arm.

"Don't 'ee ever strike one of my young 'uns again, Parson, or I'll kill 'ee *as sure as I killed your horse."*

My voice rings in the quietness. Iron-hard. Cold. A voice I ent never used afore, surprisin' Will. He stops cryin', looks at me bewildered. Not havin' heard my comin', Parson, startled at my presence, whips around.

Fear followed by amazement at my darin' to lay my hand on him, speak to him like that, shows on his face.

Will pushes hisself up from the ground and clutches onto my leg. I lets go Parson's arm. He brushes at it as if it had come up against some filth.

My mind be ragin'. Did I say them words: *"as I killed your horse"*? Didst I? Or were them words spoke only in my head?

Parson, realizing now that 'tis only I, Seth Fielding, challenging him, be furious. Splutterin' in his anger, he points at Will. "Desecrating graves, your offspring, Fielding. It's a disgrace. Needs a good beating."

"He be little more than a babe, Parson. What would he know of desecratin' graves, whatever that be?"

With an arm round Will's shoulders, I asks, "What be 'ee doin', Willie?"

"I standed on that big stone so as to see better when you be comin', Farver. I were watchin' for 'ee."

"There! See. The child admits it," says Parson, voice triumphantly harsh.

No *"what do you mean about my horse."* Just anger at Will and at me for darin' to lay a finger on him. No, 'twas in my head I said those words. He would be demandin' to know more about what I meant. To have I arrested.

"Get that child out of my churchyard. Out!" Parson points to the gate. "Bear in mind, Fielding, the Bible's instruction. Spare the rod and spoil the child."

He stands watchin' as I bends down, takes Will up on my shoulder. I gently tells Will there ent nothin' to be afraid of, that everything be all right.

As I walks through the gate and home, all the time I questions myself. Did I speak them words out loud or not? One thing I knows, there'll be no more work for I helpin' sexton with the grave diggin'. Sexton be getting' on in years, and his fingers be so twisted and bend inwards with the rheumatics 'tis as if they be wrapped around a cow's tit. Oftimes he'd slip me sixpence to help with the diggin', specially in winter when the soil be sogged with rain, for it were nigh impossible then for him to grip the spade.

Maryapple....willberry....horseyew....How my thoughts do dart about. Parson's poor horse. I only meant for him to run off. It weren't the poor

And Ordered Their Estate

beast's fault, his master denyin' what he owed. But in my mind 'tis as if I killed 'un.

Now why be my mind fixing on straw? I were thinkin' on Will. Now all is gone but thoughts of straw.

Straw....rain....roof. Now 'tis comin' together. The roof of our cottage be leakin' again. Stands on the furthest corner of Wainwright's acres, far from Master's sight and carin'. 'Twere built as a shepherd's shelter, then added onto a bit, a room built over. Be just one room up and one down, with the upper 'un made into two. Master offered it us soon after Mary and I were first wed. Us thought we were blessed, it bein' rent free, but many a time we wishes we'd rented in the village and not so beholden to Master.

Told Master about it leakin' but he did nothin'. With winter comin on, I brings up the matter again, sayin' as how rain runs down the wall where Little Mary and Will sleep, and 'tis so damp.

"For God's sake, Fielding, I have other things to worry on. Aren't you capable of mending a bit of thatch?"

"But 'tis more than patchin' the roof requires, Master. I ent got a proper thatcher's skills, and no ladder."

"Take the ladder from the barn home with you. Some straw. Don't bother me with such trifles."

"Trifles," I wants to yell at him. "The place be near fallin' apart. Your pigs be housed better." But, o'course, the thought of us bein' homeless, hungry, keeps my tongue still.

Havin' no one near to hand that I canst borrow one from, Mary come and helps I carry the ladder to the cottage. Then there be bags of straw to lug home on my back.

Sunday afternoon, the rain havin' given over for a while, I sets about patchin' up as best I could, though all the thatch be in a sorry state.

Everywhere be slippery and the ground a mess of mud. Will, wearin' an old coat of Samuel's, the sleeves bent back, the hem near reachin' to the floor, darts about like a dragonfly. Grabbin' handfuls of straw and tryin' to reach up and hand 'em to I.

"Stand back!" I keeps tellin' 'im, but child-like he soon forgets.

205

Flingin' handfuls of straw into the air, he backs into the ladder. Little though he be, it were enough to make the ladder slide from the wet house timbers.

It were a blessin' Willie were not crushed under the weight of the ladder. But my arm be broke.

Chapter Thirty-Six
Australia 1836

THE MOUNTAIN RANGES IN THE DISTANCE WERE NOW A series of dark purple humps fading to grey against the evening sky. It had been a long, hard day. Digging holes, lifting heavy posts, heaving on wire to pull it taut. Foot poised to thrust the spade's blade back into soil, a rustling sound caught his attention. The briefest flicker of a tail. Whatever animal it was had already hidden itself again in the leaves of the tree. "Get this last post in and then I'll finish for the day,' George told himself.

At Major de Gillern's shout he turned reluctantly. The scent of tobacco smoke hung in the air as George joined de Gillern who stood in his doorway a pipe clenched between his teeth.

"Is there something you want done, Sir?"

"No, but I thought you'd wish to know I've had a letter from the authorities enquiring if you are still in my employ?" he said, removing his pipe and tapping with it at a letter he held in his hand.

"But they *must* know where I am. My name is registered with the police-office as is required," replied George. Irritated that the enquiry had not been addressed to him personally, he added, 'Tis a poor excuse for doing nothing."

"I would suggest you write immediately and confirm that you are here. Not only that, but seeing that after all these months there is still no news about your pardon, a letter to Governor Arthur is needed." The Major paused, drew on his pipe. "I'm only giving advice, mind. I've no wish to intrude in your affairs."

"You have more knowledge of these matters than I do, Sir. Your concern on my behalf is much appreciated."

"You know, many are agitating for Arthur's recall to England. No doubt he has much on his mind. You need to bring your case to his attention again."

"That I will, Sir. I'll attend to it this evening."

George walked homeward, mulling over de Gillern's counsel. As he strode along oblivious to the scent of mimosa, rustlings in the undergrowth, the rasping croak of tree frogs, in his mind he composed the letter he would write, selecting this word, rejecting another, even speaking a phrase out loud to test its resonance.

The darkness of the cottage seemed thick, almost palpable. A small lizard scurried into the roofing of stringy-bark. He fumbled for the tinder box, pushing a low stool aside with his foot. The candle flame flickered, brightened, sending out shadows that caught against the rough walls. Opening a cupboard door, George reached in, hesitated. Too warm a night to light a fire and heat the panful of stew. He'd make do with bread and jerky.

He stooped to wash his hands thoroughly in a bucket of water and dried them on an old cloth. With slow, careful movements, using the curve of his hand he wiped a corner of the rough wooden table he'd constructed months back. Then he laid down an old newspaper to cover the pitted surface before taking from a tin box paper, ink, and a pen and placed them on the newspaper. Only two sheets of paper left. They were too valuable to be wasted. Again he went over the wording in his mind before dipping his pen in the ink and with deliberation addressed Governor Arthur.

~~~

Edward Hammett lay on his stomach in front of the fire teasing the kitten with a piece of yarn. His mother and grandmother sat at the table sewing, an oil lamp between them shedding a soft glow. They talked quietly as they worked.

"Such a nice man, that Mister Brown, so kindly," said Harriet.

"He is that," responded her mother. "How we'd manage without the money he brings, I don't know."

" I do sometimes wonder whether us gets the same as the other families. Whether those with larger families get more."

"Don't matter surely, as long as we gets by."

"Oh I were just musing. There! That's the hem done. That'll be enough for tonight."

The kitten gave a plaintive cry and struggled to get free of Edward's hands. Harriet turned to her son. "You be gentle with that kitten now, Teddy. Leave him be, you hear me?"

Relying on her mother and any others willing to ease her load, Harriet had put on a little flesh over the past three years. When she thought of her husband it was with sadness and concern for his welfare, but deep down, scarcely daring to admit it to herself, she was content with her life.

With the money from the London Dorchester Committee that Mr. Brown delivered periodically and what she and her mother managed to earn by taking in sewing, they managed fairly well. It would have been a different story were it not for the thirty pounds a year her mother received. Any questions Harriet had raised over the years about her father had been brushed aside by her mother. The yearly remittance was simply explained as a small inheritance, not to be talked about.

Edward now slept in the small bed that had been Harriet's before marriage. With her mother's body warm and comforting beside her at night, her husband's presence was barely missed.

~~~

"Loveless, Master says call at the house before you goes to your cottage." The young lad, whose facial features showed him to him to be of mixed parentage, having delivered de Gillern's message, hurried away to his supper. It was said that de Gillern had found the boy as a small child and raised him. Aboriginal women impregnated by white men often abandoned their infant after giving birth, some were even said to drown them.

Thinking on de Gillern's many kindnesses and wondering why de Gillern had summoned him, George returned his tools to the shed. He rubbed his hands against his trousers, smoothed his hair. The crudely timbered veranda that hugged the wood-framed house, creaked under his footsteps. On hearing George's knock, de Gillern opened the door.

"Ah, Loveless. You got my message. I rode into Hobart yesterday and stayed overnight with friends. Picked up the mail. There's a letter for you, official looking stamp on it, too. Here."

Stepping away from the shadows thrown by the house, so that he could see better in the fading light, George carefully broke the seal.

"Come through to the kitchen," said de Gillern. "You can't see in that light." He stepped back inside, indicating with a gesture that George follow him.

"Have a seat," said de Gillern pointing to a chair, and lowered himself into one on the opposite side of the table. In the warm glow of the oil lamp, George smoothed the letter flat on the surface. He read quietly to himself while the major sat watching him.

"Magistrate Spode tells me of my pardon. Dated 6th October, would you believe! It's taken all this time." George read further, looked up at de Gillern. "A passage has been booked for me on the *Elphinstone* if I wish to return to England."

"A free passage. That's unusual. It's why most settle here after they've completed their sentence. Can't find the funds to make their own way back home."

Rising to his feet, George held the letter to his lips and kissed it. He waved it in the air crying, "I *am* a free man." There was a catch in his voice as he repeated, "Free."

Smiling at George's unusual display of jubilance, de Gillern responded warmly. "Wonderful news, Loveless. Wonderful. My heartiest congratulations."

" I know it said in the paper back in March we'd been granted a free pardon, but though my mind took it in, my heart didn't seem to grasp the fact.

Holding the letter against his chest, he seated himself again, letting images of Elizabeth, the children – Daniel would be walking, talking by now – fill his mind while his fingertips slowly caressed the embossed seal.

Abruptly he put aside the reverie, let out a little cry. "But at Governor Arthur's insistence, I wrote Elizabeth asking if she and the children wished to join me here. Must be nine month ago."

"That's right. I remember you telling me."

"But it can only be three months at most that I wrote her again, telling her not to come, seeing the papers wrote more of our pardon. What if she has not received my second letter yet? She could already be aboard a ship." George's voice became agitated. "Tis possible we could pass each other on the ocean and not knowing of it, she to end up here and me in England."

Packing his pipe with fresh tobacco, de Gillern carefully swept dropped strands from the table top and placed them back in an open tin before replying. "Best write, making that point. Ask Spode that you be allowed to remain here until you've heard whether she intends coming or not before you claim your free passage."

"Yes, it must be done immediately. May I beg writing paper from you, Sir?" asked George. "I've used up the few sheets I had."

Taking a sheet of paper from a drawer de Gillern laid it on the table together with pen and ink. "You ride now, Loveless?"

"Aye. Not like gentry, but..."

"Set off at daybreak tomorrow. Take the old mare. You can make it to Hobart and back by late afternoon. Your letter'll be on its way more swiftly and you can pick up the bag of nails I forgot while you're there."

Accepting the offer of a lantern, George set off for his cottage, calling out his thanks once again, the sky now folds of dark purple velvet lit with stars.

~~~

Dinniah and Elizabeth, sat either side of the fireplace, punching strips of coloured rag through a piece of sacking spread between them across their knees. Dinniah's shoulder blades poked against her dress with each arm movement. It seemed the only substance to her were the thick, grey tresses of hair pulled back and firmly anchored in a bun at the base of her neck. Her hands worked rhythmically – push, hook, knot, push, hook, knot. Raising her head, she asked, "You've decided then? To stay?"

"I've prayed and thought on the matter ever since his letter arrived," Elizabeth said, pausing from her hooking for a moment. "As George says, it will be a difficult decision and one only I can make."

"But he also said you were not to be influenced by any desires of his."

"You knows his letter as well as I do, we've read it so often." Elizabeth sighed deeply, and returned to working on the rug. "But now they're pardoned. Mr. Brown, when he last brought us money, talked strongly of the government's pardon."

"He certainly gave the impression that it was all settled."

"But what if it be only that in the end? Just talk. Where do we stand then? 'Tis unlikely the government will offer us a free passage out again."

Bending to pick another strip from the pile of rags at her side, Dinniah said, "My decision were made way back, when them London gentlemen put the matter to us. You knows I said no, told 'em they couldn't talk me round."

"But you've not had a letter from Thomas tellin' you to come. 'Tis different."

"True. But had he writ, I think my mind would have still been set on staying."

Wearily Elizabeth said, "If only I could sleep at nights." Her tone caused Dinniah to look carefully at her sister-in-law. She took in the lines etched across Elizabeth's forehead, saw the pouches under her eyes, the threads of grey in her hair as if for the first time. What marks has all this left on me then thought Dinniah, and I be twelve years older than Lizzie? Maybe it's as well we have no mirror, for I fear we'd not like what we'd see. Laying down her side of the rug, she rose and, standing behind Elizabeth, placed her arm around Elizabeth's shoulders, rested her cheek on the top of her head. "Tis hard, with no man to turn to for guidance." Tears began to trace the contours of Dinniah's cheeks. "I couldn't bear it on my own if you should go."

"I have no more tears," replied Elizabeth, patting at Dinniah's comforting arm. "All my fear when they were first took, all the worry as to how things were for George, for all of 'em, whether they were even still alive. 'Tis as if it has set firm, like mortar. It sits in my belly like a rock." Elizabeth gently pulled herself from Dinniah's arms. Her voice betraying the emotion her words tried to deny, she said, "Come now. Enough. We've hoed this row over and over. Dear heavens, have the pair of us not wept enough?"

~~~

As the days passed George ceased asking de Gillern if there was a letter for him. Should he catch sight of him, George would raise his eyes questioningly and de Gillern would shake his head in response, until finally, one afternoon, the major crossed the yard and placed a letter in George's hand. Every instinct urged George to rip open the letter, but he kept them in check and with careful movements, broke the seal.

"Is it from Spode?" asked de Gillern impatiently.

"Aye," responded George, not lifting his head.

"Is the news not good?"

"I'll have to ask leave of you, Sir, to go to Hobart. The matter cannot be left like this."

"What does he say, man? Is it bad news?"

'He wastes no words, Sir: *"I have to inform you that unless you go by the present opportunity, the government will not be able to give you a free passage."*

"Damn them! Damn all bureaucrats, unthinking fools! If you think seeing them will help, then of course you must go." De Gillern rubbed at the bridge of his nose with a crooked finger. "The horses will all be in use. We'll be away rounding up stock for a few days. You think you can let the matter wait until we're done?"

"I fear time is getting short. I'd best walk, Sir, with your leave. I'll snatch a few hours' sleep before setting off."

"You realize the distance?" Seeing the set of George's jaw, his determined stance, the Major added, "Try to see the Colonial Secretary. He may see things more reasonably."

~~~

Vivid bands of orange and pink lit the sky. George paused a moment to take in the beauty of the early morning. Silhouetted against the green stalks of a clump of tree fern, the uncoiling crosiers of the newer shoots caught his eye. The brown hairs that covered the stems stood out like fur bringing to mind an organ-grinder's monkey he'd once seen in Dorchester. The hair on the monkey's arms extending from the little jacket it wore had been of a similar colour.

Another hour and he should be in Hobart. When he had started out from Glen Ayr several hours ago, the purple blackness of the sky was lavishly sprinkled with stars, so brilliant and seemingly so close that George was sure, should he extend his hand and reach up to touch them, his fingers would be scorched. An isolated farm huddled against an outcropping of rock, a small settlement, each window dark as the night. Occasionally a dog would bark or, on some distant hilltop, dingos howled.

In the town centre George put down the jacket he'd being carrying over his shoulder. He stooped and rubbed at the dust that coated his boots with a fistful of grass, rinsed his face in the horse trough, combed his hair with his fingers. As he inserted his arms in his jacket and fastened the buttons, he looked around. A large, imposing building with stone pillars and an elaborately carved door dominated a square formed by smaller, less ornate buildings. Just as de Gillern had described it. That must be the Colonial Office.

"You can't just walk in here and demand to see the Colonial Secretary. Mr. Mason's an extremely busy man." The clerk, black-suited, hands holding folders bound with red tape, looked disdainful, taking in George's rough clothing, clumsy boots.

"I've made no demands, only *requested* that I may wait to see him. I've walked all the way from Glen Ayr, out Richmond way, and am prepared to wait as long as it takes."

Stepping back out of the way, George stood with others who, in spite of the early hour, also waited to be seen by some government official: a uniformed officer, a well-dressed gentleman insisting he be allowed to see someone in authority immediately, two or three men who, by their

And Ordered Their Estate

less fashionable clothing and ruddy complexions, George judged to be settlers. Clerks clutching papers, leather-bound ledgers, entered office doors, exited with more papers.

George paced back and forth, periodically making a point of catching the eyes of the clerk to whom he'd made his request. Slowly the waiting numbers diminished. His stomach growled a need for food, his bladder also made its needs felt. Dare he step outside and risk being overlooked?

He could hold on no longer; he must find a quiet corner outside where he could relieve himself. He hurried through the huge doors and round the side of the building. His fingers fumbled with his buttons. An arcing spray of urine hissed against white brick. His trousers refastened, George hurried back inside to resume his wait. Positioned near a window, he was conscious of the elongated shadow of a nearby wattle tree.

"You *still* here?" asked the clerk.

"I told you I 'd wait until I've seen him, and wait I will."

"Go home man, there's little chance he'll be free today."

"No, Sir, I'll wait. I *must* see him. Does he at least know I'm here?"

The clerk, surprised and impressed at such determination, muttered, "I'll see what I can do, but your chances are slim," and disappeared through a door. Reappearing a short while later, he beckoned to George. "The Colonial Secretary will give you a few minutes only."

In response to the clerk's restrained knock, a deep voice called out "Enter." Opening the door, the clerk said, "George Loveless, Sir," stepping back to allow George to pass in front of him.

George was surprised at the smallness of the seated figure. The Colonial Secretary's shock of white hair was dominated by the heavily carved chair-back against which it rested. With a motion of his hand he indicated that George approach his desk.

"We can't grant everyone's slightest wish, Loveless. You've been told your passage is booked on the *Elphinstone*," said Mason on hearing George's plea.

"But my letter explains the reason for my request. I must wait to hear from my wife, lest she already be on the journey out."

"These matters take time to arrange and can't be changed on a mere whim. You treat the authorities with great disrespect."

215

"Begging your pardon, Sir, but that would be difficult to do seeing those in authority have made no contact with me regarding my free pardon until now." George fought to curb his anger.

"We had no knowledge where you were."

"My name and placement are registered with the police-office, as required by law, Sir." George's frustration was evident. In a more conciliatory voice, he added, "Imagine yourself in a similar situation, Sir. You being forced to make that long journey back not knowing whether your wife has already left England."

"I don't care for your tone, Loveless." Mason, his chin resting on his hands, his gaze fixed firmly on George's face, added "However, I understand your concern. What is it exactly that you are requesting?"

"What I laid out in my letter, Sir. That I be allowed to remain until I have heard from my wife. Should she *not* be coming out, that I then be allowed to claim my free passage."

"I see." Mason, running his tongue over his teeth, sat silent for a moment. "I'll make enquiries on the matter." He removed a fob watch from his pocket, flipped up the lid, made a tutting noise. "I must go. You will hear shortly, on that you have my word."

The letter, from the Principal Superintendent of Convicts, was prompt in arriving. '*...The Colonial Secretary has written me in consequence of your having expressed your disinclination to embark for England, by the 'Elphinstone', from having written some months ago to your wife, that you are anxious to await the result of that communication, in a matter of three or four months. His Excellency has been pleased to direct that a free passage is to be then offered you by the government that you may return to England...*'

Chapter Thirty-Seven
Workhouse 1842

BUGGER ME, MY ARM HURT SUMMAT WICKED. MARY TRIES to talk I into seein' old Granny Cairns. There's many in the village goes to her for physicin' when they're feelin' poorly. But I says wait till mornin' and I'll see someone then. Mary weren't happy but she let me have my way. Didn't sleep hardly, it painin' so.

Come daybreak, Mary said as how she'd go tell Wainwright as what happened and see if he'd agree to her doin' my milkin'. I tells Tabby to break a piece each from the remaining knob of bread gone rock hard and pour a little milk into a bowl to dip the bread in. A reliable lass is Tabby, I knows she'll keep a good eye on Will. Then I sets off.

Terr'ble swollen, my left arm. Weren't no way I could put my jacket on proper, so cradlin' the one arm with the other, I sets off for Affpuddle, it bein' closer than Bere. The barber there sets bones, pulls teeth as well as cuts hair and don't charge as much as a surgeon do. Scream, I did, when he pulls my arm straight. Then he braces it with a couple of thin boards and straps it around with a linen bandage. After he be finished I had to sit awhile until the throbbin' had settled somewhat.

By the time I gets home Mary be back from the farm. Says as how Wainwright agreed as she could do the daily milkin' and muckin' out the shed and he'd pay her one shillin' and sixpence a week, but as I couldn't work, he wouldn't pay me. If he'd a got a proper thatcher in to do the job,

I wouldn't be in this sorry state. How be us to manage on one shillin' and sixpence?

Stood hanging' around the cottage and watchin' after Will while Tabby took over her mother's tasks for a few days, then I could stand it no longer. You'd a' thought I'd 'ave been glad of the rest, but I aint never not worked since I were eight. Real work, men's work, I means. Afore that I done my share of scarin' crows, stone pickin' from the fields. But don't 'ee think them sort of jobs ent tirin', 'specially when you be only a young scrap. Besides, I were worried as to how us were going to manage with little or no money comin' in. Churned it over and over in my mind, what I couldst do to earn a penny or two. My right arm were fine, but most work requires two.

That mornin', the sun tryin' hard to bring warmth to the day, I walks down to the village. Everywhere be sogged with water, it've rained such torrents for nigh on two weeks, far more'n us usually gets this time of year. Old Dick Poldice who says he be eighty-three, though there be times when he reckons he be eighty-nine and another eighty-four, but anyways he's a fair old age and he says it ent never rained this much as long as he can remember.

Two women with black-shawled shoulders stand on the green near the naked sycamore tree, its roots buried in a carpet of rottin' leaves. Bent into each other, natterin', each determined to get in her say, they puts me in mind of a couple of cawing crows.

"Mornin' to 'ee," says I, though the both of 'em ent spoke to me since Loveless and the others were took. One woman, pickin' up her basket from the ground, says as how she ent got time to chat all day, gives me a curt nod and goes her way. But Mistress Greenaway be so burstin' with news her can't keep it to herself and I be the only one around as she can share it with.

Hands on her hips, she says, "Well, Seth Fielding, it be no thanks to you, but Elizabeth Loveless've heard from her man."

"That must be a load off her mind. 'Tis to be hoped he had good news for her," says I, tryin' to make it look as if I'm hurryin' to get somewhere. Ent no way her was goin' to let I go until she'd shared her news though.

She fixes a person with that gimlet eye of hers, and sort of holds 'em to the spot till her have emptied herself out of all she have to tell.

"I hears he's told her not to think of goin' out to that foreign place where he be sent, but to wait for his return."

"That be wonnerful news, Mistress."

"Aye, it is. But how you'll look 'im in the eye when he do return, I …" Her voice trails off for she's caught sight of Molly Trimble comin' from her cottage. She hurries off to talk with her, hopin', I'm sure, that Molly ent seen how she'd weakened and actually talked to I, Seth Fielding.

And suddenly, in spite of her havin' cut her tongue on I, the sun seemed to have more warmth, the sparrers' twitterin' merrier. It truly were wonnerful news. I were that thankful for Elizabeth Loveless, and hoped with all my heart the other wives' men would be comin' back eventually.

Reachin' the mill, I stood watchin' how fast the girt wheel were turnin' after all the rain us've had. Instead of the water bein' clear enough to see every stone and leaf frond, it be a racin', muddy swirl. Bright green clumps of weed on the river bed pulled flat by the rushin' current withered like tethered green eels, while flecks of white froth eddied around them.

I hears a shout, and lookin' up sees Kenton's young 'un runnin' my way, the one as was born in the hedgerow and ent never been right in the head. A big child for his age. The miller be a big man, but Mary've heard that Kenton be always urgin' the child to eat, eat, eat, as if food'll put right what be wrong with the lad.

Chasin' after him be the woman as looks after him, and close behind her lumbers Kenton. The lad has a staggerin' sort of run like his legs don't know what they's meant to be doin'. Kenton were shoutin' at 'im. "Come here, you imp o' Satan. God's strife, you'll be in that water."

I steps into the young 'un's path, catches him by the arm. He gives a cacklin' sort of laugh, like a chicken that've just struggled to lay an egg.

"Come on now," says I. "Yer father be callin' you."

An' the little devil bites at my hand! I yells and lets go, and he lollops off towards the white railings alongside the river, legs swingin' this way and that. I tries to catch a'hold of him again. My fingers grab at his coat just as one of his feet slips on some wet leaves. His balance bein' none too good, he slides under the railings and into the racin' water, givin' a wordless cry of fright.

Well, there be I down on the ground too. I bangs up against a post, but still manages to hang on to 'im. Though he's no age, he be a solid weight. The current tugs at him and I feels myself being dragged along the wet grass. I canst let go of the boy or be pulled in too. 'Tis as simple as that, 'cos with my bad arm pinned against the ground by my body I ent able to grasp a'hold of even a tuft of grass. And the pain! Right up to my shoulder. 'Tis unbelievable!

Right at that moment, when my brain be tellin' my fingers to release their hold, someone grabs at my leg and be pullin' I back away from the water. And I still has a grasp on the boy. Hands roll me onto my back and I finds myself lookin' up into Squire's face.

"The boy?" I manages to gasp as Squire helps I up.

"Safe, Fielding. His father has him. I saw it all, and luckily was able to get to you in time."

Still mazed by the suddenness of it all, I lets out a shakey laugh. Unsure of what to say, I takes in Squire's clothing and blurts out, "Squire, you'm all muddied."

Squire looks at I, returns my laugh, and says, "You've fared the worse." I see he speaks true; wet soil and grass covers the front of me.

"It do seem I be determined to help that boy hang onto life," I says, thinking back to his birth.

I sees then that Kenton is handing his lad over to the woman, givin' her angry instructions. That being done he comes back to where Squire and I be standin'.

"You all right, Fielding?" Kenton asks. "I thought you'd be pulled in too." Kenton's jaw be rigid, his eyes welling with tears he can scarce keep in check. "Thank 'ee, Squire, Fielding, for saving my lad. Had you lost your life, Fielding, trying to save his, it would've been a sad affair. I do what I can for him, but you can't get him to mind. He has no sense of danger." He pauses for a moment, not wantin' us to witness his emotion. "Had his life been lost it might've been a blessing for him and me, both." Then, defiant of what us may be thinkin' adds, "That don't mean I care nothing for him." Almost in a whisper, to himself he adds, "I care too much."

And Ordered Their Estate

And I know just what he means. 'Tis like I care for Will: a carin' so overpowerin' it can't be forgot for a moment.

Squire pats Kenton's shoulder, says as how us understands.

Slowly Kenton walks back towards his mill, his shoulders bent as if a mighty weight be pressin' down on 'em.

By this time Squire've taken in my injured arm. "Looks like you've been in the wars," says he.

So I tells him about how Master had I fixin' the roof of our cottage and how the ladder slipped. Hopin' he'll slip a coin into my hand, I adds, "I don't know how us'll manage. Master says he'll not pay me whilst I can't work."

"It's hard luck about your arm, Fielding. It's to be hoped it will heal rapidly and you're soon back at work." He seems uncomfortable, as if there's more he'd like to say. He bends to pick up his dropped riding crop, says, "Well, I must be on my way. The farrier'll have fixed my beast's shoe by now."

Squire starts to cross the road. Pauses. "Fielding," he calls. "You think with your good arm you could manage to exercise some of my hounds?"

"You mean, walk 'em an' such?"

"Four young pups. They need more exercise than they get in their pen. Come over tomorrow about ten. Ask to see my kennel-man. I'll have a word with him."

"Thank 'ee, Sir, thank 'ee."

Two pieces of news as will cheer Mary I thinks to myself as I walks home. Squire, offerin' me the chance to earn a few shillin', and Loveless and the others be likely comin' home.

Chapter Thirty-Eight
Tolpuddle 1837

THE CART GEORGE HAD MADE AS A PLAYTHING FOR Mathew and Sarah when they were small rattled and bumped over the stones in the lane. A sack of flour sat precariously in the confines of the small vehicle. With steps firm and deliberate, Elizabeth pulled it behind her, carefully avoiding the deeper ruts that could tip the cart and its contents over. Daniel trotted beside her, now and then lingering to examine a pebble, grasp at a tall spear of yellowed grass or point out to his mother a rabbit racing for the cover of the hedgerow.

Elizabeth's thoughts were on the miller. Wainwright and the other farmers around had turned down Mathew's request for work. Some with just a gruff refusal or saying he was too young to give a good day's effort. Others were more blunt. "I'll have no rabble-rouser's son in my employ." Kenton, however, had taken him on, set him at tasks not too strenuous for a young lad. "A true man of the faith," George had often commented. "He is that. A goodly man," Elizabeth whispered to herself.

Waiting at the mill, Elizabeth had watched Kenton's child stagger across the yard, a woman following close behind to keep an eye on him. Seeing Elizabeth, the child stopped, sidled closer to her. His mouth, contorted as he tried to form words, issued only slurred sounds. He took her hand, placed a pebble in her palm and gently folded her fingers around it.

Standing sideways, motionless, he's a pleasant enough looking child Elizabeth decided. It was face on, his eyes never working in tangent with

And Ordered Their Estate

each other, the left one sometimes disappearing entirely from sight, his lurching gait, the inability to speak; all a combination that made it impossible to forget he was a *natural*.

Mathew had questioned her about the boy. "But what do it *mean*, that word, Mother?"

A smile had flickered across her face. "You're so like your father. Always questioning, wanting to know the meaning of things. Why 'natural' means someone who's ... Someone who is *formed* by nature and will always be thus, no matter how one tries to make him different, better."

"You mean like Old Preston's son? I ent seen him around in a while."

An image of Preston's blind son, his lumpen figure sagging in a wooden chair outside Preston's cottage for hours at a time waiting on his father's return from work, his chin chaffed sore from a perpetual drool of saliva, caused Elizabeth to mentally give thanks as she looked on her perfectly formed son. "Like Preston's son is right, poor fellow. Could do little for hisself, but there was no harm in him. No, you'll not see him again. Taken to Dorchester Lunatic Asylum when Preston died, he was. There was no one else to take care of him, and the workhouse wouldn't take him in."

Daniel's excited cry was missed by his mother as she quietly voiced a prayer of gratitude that at least her three children were healthy, alert, obedient. It wasn't until he tugged at her skirt that she took in his shout. "Sarah, Mother! Sarah be callin' you."

"Come quick, Mother! There's a letter come for you."

Leaving Sarah and Daniel to pull the cart, Elizabeth quickened her pace towards Dinniah who stood in her cottage doorway waving an envelope.

"Tis from George. I recognize his hand. Quick, Lizzie, open it."

Taking the letter, Elizabeth studied the writing, turned it over and over, before breaking the seal. She sank onto the step, the envelope cradled in her lap as she read, the others gathered around her. "From the date it seems his letter's crossed with mine. He says he's in good health. Says to disregard his other letter. Not to come out to join him. To stay in Tolpuddle."

"He's well? Oh, thank the Lord. What else? Why has he changed his mind on you going out there?"

"A minute, Dinniah, a minute. Let me finish reading." Dinniah, Sarah and Daniel stood impatiently holding back questions as Elizabeth's eyes slowly scanned the page, occasionally forming a word with her lips to get its meaning.

"Says he's working for a good man who pays a decent wage. To be patient while he serves his ticket-of leave time and has enough saved for his passage home."

Dinniah's trembling lips formed a 'God be praised' before her shoulder shook with weeping. Rising from the step, Elizabeth guided her into the cottage, soothing her with words. "Tis Thomas, ent it? There'll be a letter from him soon, never you fear. And think, the children and I are *stayin'*. You'll not be left alone."

~~~

Insects scorched their wings in the candle's flame as George sat at the table reading and re-reading Elizabeth's letter. The only letter he'd had from her since his arrival in Van Diemen's Land. '… *Husband, Friends have kept me aware of the agitation for the release of you all, and since you wrote me last, parliament has granted a free pardon to you all, of which you will no doubt have heard…. I will, therefore, follow your advice to remain here and await your return. May God, grant that it will not be long before we are reunited…* '

~~~

George led the mare to the water trough and let her drink her fill before heading for the police-office. Once again de Gillern had loaned him a horse so that he could ride to Hobart to see if there was a reply to his letter requesting a passage home.

"You wants to know if there's been a letter for Loveless?" The police officer ran his finger down the page of a ledger, pausing to stab his finger at an entry. "Here. Knew I recognized the name. Letter was sent out to Glen Ayr only this morning. He turned the register round in order that George could see. January 22nd, 1837 – Loveless, Glen Ayr. "That satisfy yer?"

All the way home George asked himself how soon the letter would reach Glen Ayr. It depended, he supposed on how many calls the rider had to make. It was unlikely they'd send a rider out with just the one letter to deliver. Maybe tomorrow? That would be most likely. Tomorrow.

~~~

"Aunt Elizabeth, Aunt Elizabeth! Come quick! Mr. Brown has come with news." Abigail hovered around her aunt like a dog nipping at the legs of a sheep.

Pulling off her apron, Elizabeth carefully folded it and placed it on the chair-back, then turned to move a pot away from the fire's heat. "Abby, you keep an eye on Daniel here for me, so I can give my full attention to what Mr. Brown has to say."

Mr. Brown, his voluminous coat hiding hands placed on his hips, stood with his back to the window. He turned on hearing Elizabeth enter. "Good day to you, Mistress Loveless."

Hastily bobbing a curtsey, Elizabeth acknowledged his greeting.

"My niece says you have news, Mr. Brown."

"I thought it best to ride out and tell you, make sure you knew. News travels so slowly."

"That it does, Sir."

"It's a beautiful day. Riding along the Dorchester road ... invigorating, truly invigorating."

"It is, Sir. This news you speak of?"

"Why, your husband's and the other men's pardons have been granted. The king has signed."

"You kindly gave us that news on your last visit." You've been wonderfully kind to us, thought Elizabeth, but oh, so long-winded in your talk. Can you not see how anxious we are to hear what you have to tell? "But you have further news, Sir?"

"So I do. So I do. Yes, yes, of course."

"Where be my manners? You'll have a seat, Sir," flustered Dinniah.

"Thank you kindly, M'am. I will." Mr. Brown settled himself on the chair brought over by Dinniah, tugged at his breeches. "Yes, yes. New news. 'Tis this way. Details of their pardon – your husband's, M'am, both your husbands', and the other men. Sent to the Governors of New South Wales and Van Diemen's Island, you understand. They have been instructed, the Governors that is, that passages be booked immediately for their return to England." He turned to Dinniah. "These things take time, of course. Yes, time.

"The name of the vessel, M'am? 'Tis too early to say. But should I hear, then I will let you know. It will be only a matter of months before you and your loved ones are re-united."

Dinniah held tightly to Elizabeth: Dinniah's joy erupting in laughter; Elizabeth, able at last to release the emotions that for so long had solidified inside her, wept. Engrossed in sharing joy and comfort, neither of them noticed Mr. Brown place an envelope of money on the table and quietly withdraw without asking for the usual signature.

~~~

George's mind was not on his work. Every hour he found a reason for some task to take him near de Gillern's house. At last, a swirl of dust indicated a rider was approaching. Dropping the hammer he had been holding, George ran to meet him as he trotted up to the house.

"You've a letter for me?" George asked breathlessly.

"Depends on whether you're George Loveless."

"Loveless, that's me," said George, as the man slowly withdrew a letter from a leather pouch. George reached eagerly for it.

"Hold hard! You must sign for it first."

Hastily signing his name, George took the letter and read: *'...A passage is being held for you on the 'Eveline' sailing January 30th, 1837...'.*

George Loveless was finally going home.

Chapter Thirty-Nine
Workhouse 1842

THEY'VE TOLD MY MARY I BE DEAD. BUT MARY'LL HAVE none of it. "Look you," says she. "There! He breathed. See. His chest moved." She takes my wrist in her hand, says "Feel. He ent dead, so don't you be sayin' that he is." My pulse be so shallow 'tis a wonder she can sense it. She bends over I, strokes my forehead. "You'm still with us, ent you Sethy!"

I shouts at her, "Don't let 'em put I in a box afore I'm dead." But o'course, none of them can hear what my thoughts be screamin'.

All *they* sees is a blanket-covered bag of bones whose lungs gave their death-rattle days back. A body so frail it can scarce tent the covers. *They* sees a biddy whose hair's lost its gloss, body thickened with child-bearing, stooped over my bed, claspin' my hand. Them buggers see only what they wants to see.

But to I Mary be just as she was that Harvest Supper. Dark chestnut-coloured hair tied back with a ribbon hangin' down her back. The finest spray of freckles outlining her cheek-bones. Teeth gleamin' white. From her bodice a glimpse of flesh the colour of cream rising on a pail of milk. Blind they be. Blind.

It were some time afore my arm were fully healed, and when us took the splint off there were a raised bump where the break had mended. It felt odd and oft times when I were doin' nowt, which ent often I can tell 'ee, I'd find myself strokin' at it gently with my fingers. Not that it were real painful, mind – just a dull ache that never left. Still I could use it again and that were all that mattered.

And every day, while it were strapped across my chest, I'd go to Squire's to walk his dogs. The kennel-man were none too happy at my bein' there. As soon as he sets eyes on me he starts. "Don't know what Squire be thinkin' of. 'Taint necessary havin' you exercise 'em," says he. "I tells Squire, I can cope fine without your help. Don't 'ee think there be a proper job here for 'ee when your arm've healed." Mutterin' to hisself he walks away, leavin' me to fix a leash to the dogs' collars. No easy task, mind you, with only one hand, and them still being pups, pouncin' and playin' with each other while I struggles.

After the four of 'em nearly pulled me over the first day, I realizes it be best if I takes only two at a time. Walked miles when you takes under consideration it were a goodly distance just getting' to the kennels. And bugger me, by the end of the first week I feels fitter than I 'ave for months. Years! I could breathe easier and my cough weren't so bothersome.

And filled with well-bein', I takes my Mary again. Buries myself in her and gives but a passin' thought to the consequences.

Folks in the village could talk of nothin' else but that Loveless, Standfield and the rest be comin' home. And I holds my tongue, tries to avoid any as might ask how I feels about their return. For I were racked with fear. No, fear ent the right word. Guilt? Dread? It weren't that I feared they'd set about me, but the thought of comin' face to face with George, those eyes of his borin' into me. I imagines it, so clear. Him just lookin' at me, askin', "*Why?*"

I begins to dream at night – George and I meetin'. Would wake up all of a sweat, and Mary'd hold I tight, speak words of comfort. "You know you had no choice. They be bound to un'erstand that." But, you see, I knows, deep inside, knows as sure as sure, that were George Loveless put in a like position, he'd 'ave said no. Him and his God would've stood firm against Squire and Ponsonby, Parson and Wainwright.

Then there was rumours that landowners all around were against employment bein' offered 'em when they gets back. They was worried that they'd try and form another union, stir up unrest again. "See," I tells

Mary, "the monied folk be joinin' forces against the poor same as usual, Squire and the rest of 'em."

"Don't 'ee talk aginst Squire. He's bin right good to you since things went wrong for 'ee, Seth Fielding."

"I ent denyin' that, but it stands to reason, he'll be with 'em on this."

"Us is all right, that be all that matters."

"But 'twill matter greatly to Loveless and the others. Where be 'em to go? And what'll 'em live on? I doubts they'll get money from them London folks once they be back in Tolpuddle."

I puzzles on this business with Squire a lot. It do seem as if he's changed, though how 'tis difficult to put into words. First it were his speakin' when us would meet. Before all this union thing come about he'd scarce have thrown a nod of acknowledgement my way. Then, gradual, it were a 'good day,' till it got to him even askin' after Mary and the little 'uns.

Although he ent never spoke about all that happened, I gets a strong feelin' that he be havin' second thoughts about the part he forced I to play. Be it just me he feels regret about? Do 'ee think about the terr'ble times it 'ave brought on the men and their families? Can't be so. Men of his class don't fret on the likes of us. All they be concerned about is protectin' what be theirs.

But why then do he speak more to I? This job, walkin' his dogs. Truth be, like Brownlee the kennel man said, there were no need for my help. 'Tis a job Squire conjured up 'cos my arm be broke. And I be mighty grateful to 'un. He don't pay as much as I'd earn at Wainwright's, o'course, but he do give I far more 'en the job be worth. So Will and Tabitha still gets a drop o' milk and an egg on occasion, and us can live on 'taters. The crop were good this year and us has plenty stored so long as the mould don't get to 'em.

Though 'tis a matter I cogitates on many a time. Me an' Squire. Squire an' me. *Be* his thoughts on the matter the same now as afore all this business?

And if I were ever asked again to betray friends, fellow workers, how wouldst I answer 'em? I hopes I'd be stronger and stand up to them if asked. I tries to push such thoughts away for there be no point dwellin' on such matters for it ent likely ever to happen a second time. But it do destroy a man's spirit when he sees hisself for what he be – *weak*.

Chapter Forty
Australia 1837

HAMMETT, ON FIRE WATCH, SAT UNDER THE STARS WITH his blanket draped over his shoulders. Eyre, his master, and the other three men slept wrapped in their bedrolls, rifles at their sides, while the two black trackers lay further away, huddled together for warmth. The night was chilly, but the fire was for protection as well as warmth. Hammett listened to the wild dogs baying and shivered. Even though this was not the first trek he'd made with Eyre – they'd been away from Woodlands for months – it was a sound he'd never got used to. Rustlings in the undergrowth he no longer noticed. He'd managed to control his fear of snakes. But dingoes, their primeval chorusing still aroused a fear in him. Hammet had heard tell they could rip a man's throat as he slept.

When first arrested, sentenced, transported, his mind was fixed on how Harriet and the little one were faring. Harriet was so frail, never seemed to have got a proper hold on life.

"You'm not makin' a wise choice," his father had advised. "Pick a woman with a bit of flesh on her, one as'll be a helpmate, a good breeder. Her be nothin' but sickly looking."

"And that mother of hers. Sets herself up as better'n ordinary folks," his mother had added. "Widder woman! Folks say there never was no husband in Dorchester. Now, Abe Garrick's daughter, there's ..."

But Hammett refused to listen, had turned away with a, "Leave it be, Mother."

It was the delicateness of her that drew him in the first place. The paleness of her skin. Her hair so fine, the yellow fading to almost white come summer. She reminded him of the white porcelain figurine that his mother prized so highly, a wedding gift from the lady of the house when his mother left her position as cook to get married.

"A half sovereign would 'a been a damn sight more useful," his father would comment when riled with his wife. The figurine had pride of place on a shelf, and "Don't 'ee lay a finger on it," Hammett was instructed as a child.

His father had been right. Nature never intended Harriet to be a farm labourer's wife. Should the fire go out, she'd cry. Carry a bucket of water from the pump and she had to sit and rest awhile. With her head bent to the candlelight sewing, should her work-roughened hands catch on the fine fabric, it would set her weeping again. And Hammett could only leap to fill the buckets for her, wordlessly take her hands and stroke them, consumed with guilt. He should have kept his mouth shut, should never have talked her into marrying him.

After the first couple of months of marriage, her repugnance of the sexual act had dampened his desire. Sick from the moment she became pregnant, she birthed a large, lusty son, who, in his haste to enter the world, tore her body so badly they feared she would die from loss of blood. Where once she had reminded him of a harebell, its blue cups hanging from a stalk so fine that it wilted immediately it was picked, now she resembled his mother's figurine, white and useless.

But now she and the babe seemed a life-time away. Totally separate.

The James Hammett that married her no longer existed. Five year ago, he'd never heard of Botany Bay. A god-forsaken country was how he thought of it on arrival. He'd contemplated the matter at length, questioned whether it was the land or himself that God had forsaken. Seated by the fire, again he was lost in the unbelievableness of it all. Shipped halfway round the world, and it now seemed he'd walked the other half in the service of an explorer.

Hammett rose to tend to the fire. He liked to see the sparks flying skywards when he threw more wood on. It seems to him the sparks and stars joined. The dingoes howled again and he pulled his blanket closer.

"I was sold like a slave for a pound," Hammett was to say later, "but I were one of the lucky ones."

"Woodlands is where you're assigned" said the agent who'd drawn the slip with Hammett's name on it, indicating the direction with an outstretched arm. "Mr. Eyre'll be your master."

"Who be goin' with me?" asked Hammett.

"No one," replied the agent.

"How'll I find the right road?" Hammett questioned, fearfully. And all the agent said, finger still pointing, was: "Go to Brickfield Hill, then ask for Liverpool."

Said it was a distance of about four hundred miles. Handed Hammett rations. Sufficient for twenty-two days, the agent reckoned.

And Hammett filled with apprehension, was overwhelmed at the vastness of it all. Not one familiar sight, not a plant nor a tree he recognized. It wasn't the walking; he was well used to that. Back home in Dorset, for poor folk it was the only means of getting from one place to another. But the months on the journey out, chained most of the time, and only brief periods in the exercise yard at the barracks, had taken a toll. For the first few days, after fifteen or sixteen miles he had to rest before continuing on. And at night, scared of the noises from trees and bushes, his sleep was broken. For extra warmth, he stripped great lengths of stringy-bark from the trees to lay over his thin blanket. His food was gone before he got to Woodlands, and the coarse fabric of the trousers he'd been issued had rubbed his scrotum and thighs raw.

Hammett was set to ring-barking box trees. "Cut deep,"the overseer instructed. "Like this, see. Take off a good wide band."

"What do strippin' the bark off 'em do?"

"Kills 'em off mighty fast. Saves cuttin' 'em down and draggin' the roots out. The bloody things suck all the moisture from the soil. Grass don't grow."

It was back-breaking work, cutting through the thick bark, bending to make a lower slash, tearing the outer skin from the trunk. He spent days working on his own, but having none to talk to suited Hammett.

His once stocky frame, whittled down to muscles and sinew, skin leathered by the sun, was wiry but strong. The transformation was not from lack of food, for the food was good and not stinted, but heat and hard work.

The overseer was not a brutal man. The only time Hammett had seen him set about someone with a whip was when he caught one of the other men trying to force sex on a young black girl. Hammett learned from one of the other convicts that Eyre, his master, would not have any aborigines mistreated.

It was almost six months before Hammett set eyes on Edward John Eyre for Eyre had been away on one of his trips. Why, he be younger 'en I, thought Hammett, and I be only twenty and three. Tall and lean, Eyre had made a name for himself exploring and mapping the interior.

It was horses that brought Hammett to Eyre's attention. Early on his return he had stood watching Hammett calm a horse startled by a snake. Soothing it with gentle words, Hammett had then attended to the gash on the horse's haunch where it had rushed at the barbed fencing in its panic.

"Seems good with animals, that Hammett," remarked Eyre to the overseer. "What d'you know of him?"

"Ay, he is that. A good worker. No trouble. Sees a job through. You don't have to check on him all the time," replied the overseer.

"Trustworthy?"

"I've had no problems with him. Quiet fellow. Keeps to himself. Says very little."

"Keep your eye on him. He could be just the man to take with me on my next trip."

Eyre took careful note of Hammett. On several occasions he tried to draw him into conversation. "Where did you learn your skill with horses?"

"My father, Sir."

"Were you employed as a groomsman or stable hand?"

"When I was a young'un, I worked alongside my father."

"And later?"

"Farm labourer."

Eyre pushed his hat back, rested his foot on a tree stump. "Which part of England are you from?"

"Dorset, Sir," replied Hammett, his head bent over the rein he was repairing.

Well, the overseer's right, thought Eyre. The man's certainly not given to running off at the mouth!

Several weeks later Eyre was taken by the way Hammett looked after his tools. He watched as Hammett, with meticulous care, cleaned off his spade before putting it away in the shed, retrieved one another man had put away encrusted with soil and scraped off the blade. This man was methodical, careful, reliable. Traits needed when in the outback where a man's life depended on the trustworthiness of his companion. Eyre nodded his head in approval.

And as Eyre studied Hammett, so Hammett studied his new employer. A restless man, Hammett decided, a man who found boundaries oppressive. A farm such as this couldn't contain him for long.

Eyre spoke to Hammett of his first attempt to find more grazing land.

"There's a desperate need for good land, well-watered. The number of settlers must have doubled, tripled, since I first came."

"You've been here some time then."

"Came out not long after my seventeenth birthday." Eyre stooped to retrieve a small knife he'd placed on a stump. "First we combined small expeditions with droving sheep, followed the rivers but they led nowhere. Dwindled away into water-holes. Seems there's nothing for it but to find a way through those mountains." He pointed north to a range of mountains that seemed to take colour from the sky. "Blue Mountain Range it's been named," continued Eyre. "There has to be a way through, I'm sure of it. But no man's found it yet."

Much higher than the hills of Dorset certainly, but from such a vast distance the bluey-green mountains didn't look terribly formidable to Hammet. They seemed to roll up towards the skyline. "No way through," repeated Hammet to himself, shaking his head at the surprises this country held. Just how deceiving to the eye were such mountain ranges, Hammet was to discover.

On that first trip Hammett made with Eyre, trekking the hinterland, he had tried to guess at the height of the cliffs towering in front of them, was sure they'd never get across. It had taken endless days of climbing, back-tracking, climbing again in search of good sheep country. It seemed to Hammett it was the love of exploration, Eyre's restlessness, that drove Eyre on rather than the need for more pasture.

Hammett had felt his mind expanding until he doubted whether his skull could contain all that he'd encountered. They'd covered miles of scrub land, had crossed plains cracked with heat. He'd scaled towering cliffs gouged with huge crevices, navigated swamps where leeches would fasten themselves to a man's exposed flesh, hacked his way through forests hung with vines and creepers, been smothered with bites from horseflies of a size he'd never seen before.

He had gazed with his head tipped back at honeysuckle trees reaching to a hundred feet in height.

"Honeysuckle," Eyre had remarked. "You must've seen it growing in England."

"Never so high," replied Hammett taking a deep breath. "But the smell be the same." Hammett recalled the lane behind Harriet's mother's cottage, a July evening, the air heavy with the scent of honeysuckle, leaning against a gate stroking Harriet's hair. Abruptly he turned and gave his attention to tightening a strap under the belly of the pack-horse he was leading. It did no good thinking on such things.

Quietly, to himself, Hammett marvelled at all he saw. Dry river beds and vast stretches of nothing but sand which, a few days after the occasional rainfall, became a flare of colour as flowering plants burst through the arid soil. He was fascinated by the variety and hues of the birds, watched in wonder at a grey goshawk gliding on a current of air. He'd hesitantly tasted exotic fruits. And at night, lying under the stars thinking, he compared this new land with Dorset's subtler shades of green, trees arching over winding lanes, the gentler climate of his homeland.

Some days back, when he nearly stumbled into one of the deep ravines, he'd feared for his life. It was the quick action of one of the men, grabbing at his wrist while Hammett frantically clutched at a prickly shrub, that saved him. That night, as he'd dug out yet another thorn from his palm with the tip of his knife, he'd debated with himself whether God had had a hand in his deliverance. Why and for what purpose had he been saved? A feeling of hopelessness so heavy and black pressed on him as if it would crush him under its weight. He'd stepped away from the other men and sat on a boulder with his back turned and his head in his hands. Had his companions questioned him, he couldn't have put into words the overwhelming feeling of loss. Loss of his home, his family, his companions.

As Hammett once again stood to feed the fire, one of the horses snorted and Hammett listened as it chomped on a mouthful of coarse grass. Since their supplies ran out three days ago, they'd had to live off berries and roots. Hungry as he was, Hammett had refused the fat, grey grubs one of the trackers had pried from under the bark of a tree. The black man crunched the delicacy between his teeth with obvious enjoyment. Empty stomach roiling, Hammett turned to watch the other tracker scoop up mud from an almost dried up stream bed and wrap it in a piece of cloth. Placing his lips against the material he sucked out what moisture was hidden there. Hammett copied him. Folding a handful of mud in his shirt tail, sucking tentatively, he was surprised at the amount of brackish liquid it contained.

And then, Eyre's lucky shot. Whipping his gun to his shoulder, Eyre shot the roo before Hammett even saw it loping across the scrub grass in the fading light. The rest of the party gathered wood for a fire, fashioned a crude spit on which to cook it. The heat of the fire had scarcely got the juices bubbling before they were tearing hunks of meat from the carcass with their knives. The two trackers favoured the liver and the steaming entrails.

Hammett extended a hand from the fold of his blanket, picked up the bone on which he'd been gnawing, cracked it open with his teeth. Sucking on marrow, his thoughts turned to Loveless and Standfield. He wondered yet again what had become of them, doubted that their experiences could possibly equal his own.

Back at Woodlands a letter addressed to Eyre from Sir Richard Bourke lay unopened gathering dust.

Chapter Forty-One

Workhouse 1842

"THERE'S SOMETHIN' WRONG WITH YOUNG WILL," I SAYS to Mary. "You notice he ent so lively?"

"He be tired, is all. You'm always worryin.'"

Mary sounds weary. Her tone makes I look closer at her. She be always so active, always has some task on hand. I studies her, leanin' back in her chair, eyes closed, shoulders limp. Milkin' Wainwright's herd, muckin' out the barn. It'd been too much for her along with all her has to do here, and shovellin' cow muck be exhaustin' work.

I gets up, lays a hand on her shoulder. "You go to bed, wife, says I. "Tabby'll help I see to Will.

Mary sits upright. Gives a muted laugh. "You see to the children! I'll feed 'em in a minute. The 'taters must be nigh on ready." And she leans back in the chair, closes her eyes again.

I walks to the cupboard bed. Undoes the latch and lowers the bed down. "You'm full wearied," I says. "You ready yourself for bed."

"But I ent filled the buckets yet," Mary says, but 'tis a mild protest.

"Will!" I calls. "You sit at the table, and Tabby, fetch him a 'tater an' one for yourself. Careful now, they be hot."

Pickin' up a bucket with my good hand, the one I broke still needs restin' after a day's work, I goes outside to the pump.

And Ordered Their Estate

'Tis a drear, December evening. Wet grass brushes against my boots as I cross the lane. Why hadn't Mary said how stiff the pump handle were? I must fix that, I says to myself.

Turning at the tap-tappin' of a stick, I sees Dick Poldice watchin', leaning on a stout walking-cane.

"Now there's a sorry sight," he says with a grin. "You'll not get me on women's work."

"Ent got nothin' to do with whose work it be. If it helps Mary's load, what matters."

Poldice swings at a clump of grass with his stick. "I sees it be mended now," says he, noddin' at my arm.

"Splint come off last week," says I lettin' go of the pump handle. "Mist's rising. It'll be a murky night."

"Ay, and I must be getting' home. G'night to 'ee." He takes a couple of steps, pauses. "You'm heard that Standfield and the others be on their way back?"

Cautious like, I replies, "I heard tell as how they've been pardoned."

"They be on board ship now. Dinniah Standfield have heard from her man. On board the *John Barry*. 'Tis only a matter of weeks now afore they're back on British soil."

I be thankful for the gatherin' darkness so as he can't see my face, hopin' he won't be another 'un wonderin' on how things will be should Standfield or the others' paths cross with mine.

I grabs the bucket so quick some of the water slops over my boot. "Mary's waitin' on this," I mutters. Shoulderin' the door open, I hurries inside.

Mary be bent over a bowl at one end of the table, washin' herself. Tabitha and Will sit at the other end. Sleeves pulled down over their hands so the heat from the baked 'tater they each hold don't burn 'em, they munches away. At least, Tabby be eatin', but Will seems to be just cradlin' his for the warmth.

"Ent you hungry, Will?" I asks.

"Not very, Farver."

"Can I have his 'tater then?" asks Tabitha.

"No. Him'll eat it in a minute, won't yer, Will. Come on, lad. Get summat in your stomach afore you goes to sleep."

Mary puts down the cloth she's been dryin' herself on, leans over the table, places a hand on Will's forehead.

"He do feel a bit hot," says Mary.

"Don't 'ee feel good, Will?" I asks. "You'm got a stomach ache? Be 'ee cold? Sit over by the fire."

"Drink your milk at least, Will, then I'll tuck 'ee into bed. Good night's sleep'll make all the difference." Mary takes him on her lap, gets him to take a sip from his mug.

"Cuddle him into bed alongside you," I says to Mary. "Ent you goin' to eat somethin'?"

"Maybe later. I'll nap with Will a bit first."

Plaintively Tabitha asks, "Be it all right for me to eat Will's 'tater then?" and more to quiet her than givin' thought she may still be hungry, I nods agreement.

I stands by the bed feelin' helpless. "You think as I should go to Mistress Wainwright for some goose-grease for his chest? He sounds real wheezy."

"Leave him be, Seth. Don't fuss so." But I catches the concern in Mary's tone.

Chapter Forty-Two

Tolpuddle 1837

IT HAD TAKEN LONGER THAN HE'D ANTICIPATED, THE DIScussion with Parson Warren. "What a windbag the fellow is," muttered Henry Finchbury to himself. Over an hour to discuss repairs to the church tower! He'd spent the morning seeking a way to avoid the meeting, and Agnes had chided him, sent him off with a smile and a plea. "Henry dear, much as you dislike the man, do try to make your feelings less obvious. Remember, you appointed him."

However the matter was settled, if not to Parson's satisfaction. When Henry had pointed out that the tithes Parson received from his tenant farmer for Glebe Farm were meant to be used for the upkeep of the church, Warren had become indignant and went on at length about how hard it was to collect the tithes due to him. Henry refrained from commenting that if Warren was less confrontational towards his tenant and parishioners they would likely be more cooperative, agreeing only to paying for the re-pointing of the tower structure and a new bell rope. New bell, indeed! Putting the matter from his mind, he rode homeward.

Ahead of him trudged a figure, head bent. The ill-fitting lid on the small metal churn he carried clinked as he walked. As Henry drew along side the walker, he recognized who it was.

"Fielding. Good day to you."

Seth's only response was to touch his hand to his hat, without raising his head.

Surprised, Henry spoke again. "Milk for the family I see," he said pointing with his crop to the container Seth carried. "All well I hope?"

As Seth looked up at him, Henry was dismayed at the sorrow etched on Seth's face, the eyes sunk back so far into the sockets they might have been fastened to the back of his skull. It seemed to Henry that for a fleeting moment Seth was not fully aware who was addressing him. On finally registering Henry's presence, Seth's look of misery changed to one of anger.

"It be all your fault,' Seth shouted. "Tis all your doin'."

Henry felt himself flinching from the hate that emanated from Seth. "What is it, Fielding? What's wrong?"

"You forced I into it. Six men I betrayed a'cause of you. Six friends." Pointing at Henry with the hand holding the churn, he continued. "And I be paying a fearful price for that wrong."

"What is it you're saying, Fielding? You're being threatened? Blackmailed?"

"My young 'uns, that's what I be sayin'. Five of my children've been took, and now Will be terr'ble sick." Seth's voice cracked with emotion.

"Fielding, I'm sorry to hear your little boy's so sick. Truly sorry. But your other children? Surely they died some years back?"

"It meks no difference when they were took. 'They all be part of the price that I be payin'."

"You're overwrought, man," said Henry. "Understandably. I, too, know how it feels to lose a child. My eldest son. You were there when it happened."

"And who were it died when your'un were suckin' *his* milk? My first 'un."

Henry bent down to place a hand on Seth's shoulder in comfort, but Seth jerked away, drawing back his arm as if to throw the churn at Henry. Some milk slopped over his hand. Henry's horse skittishly jerked her head.

"Get home, Fielding. You're not yourself." Perturbed at Seth's unusual hostility and struggling with resentment at his manner, he fought down a retort. "Have you had a doctor examine your son? "

Seth made no reply. Cradling the small churn to his chest as if protecting the precious white liquid that might perform a miracle, that might save his son, he slowly continued homewards, each foot lifted as if it required great effort.

Henry signaled with the reins for the horse to move on. Passing Seth, he threw a glance over his shoulder. What could he do for the poor fellow? It was ridiculous of Fielding to hold him responsible for the death of his children, downright insolence. No, the man was distraught, wasn't accountable for his words, poor devil.

~~~

Shrieking seagulls swooped around the dock. The crew of the *Eveline* eased huge nets loaded with bales and packages over the side of the vessel. Passengers streamed down the gangway to be greeted by friends and relatives. Waiting with the other steerage passengers, the last to disembark, George stood gripping the railings of the ship, watching the many anchored vessels riding the swell. Water slapping at the sea wall was covered with a slick of oil and floating refuse.

He drew in great gulps of air. It had none of the aroma of Dorset, but it was *English* air. He searched the crowds, hoping for a glimpse of Elizabeth and the children, then rebuked himself for such expectations. Where would she get the money from to make the journey to London to meet him?

Tucked in the bundle at his feet were the few shillings the captain had presented him with that morning. "I was instructed to put this money aside from the five pounds the government allocated for your food and necessities," he said. "Orders were to give it you when we docked. Can you make your mark or sign your name? Just so as there's a record I did as instructed."

Taken by surprise, for once George struggled to find words. Gruffly he expressed his thanks. He'd wondered how he'd get from London to Tolpuddle. Did he dare spend the money de Gillern had pressed into his hand the day he left Glen Ayre on coach fare, or should he make the journey on foot? What if he couldn't find employment straight away?

At last the rope fencing off the steerage travellers' area of the deck was unfastened. Throwing his bundle over his shoulder and stepping slowly and carefully, George made his way down to the dockside.

George noted a group of three dark-suited men approaching male passengers as they stepped onto the dock. They seemed to be searching for someone. One of them came towards him. Raising his curled-brim hat, the man extended his hand and enquired, "George Loveless?"

"That's me."

"At last! This is a great day, a great day, Loveless." The man gripped George's hand in his, pumping it vigorously. "Albert Tanner's the name. We're members of the London Dorchester Committee, here to welcome you and offer assistance."

George shook hands with each of them, thanked them for coming to meet him, while at the same time glancing at any woman that approached.

"My wife? Would you have heard anything from her?" questioned George anxiously.

"We made the offer to pay for her journey up from Tolpuddle, but she was fearful of journeying all this way and of the crowds that were expected. Said to tell you, she'd await your arrival in Tolpuddle."

"Crowds?

"It was thought that a great many of those who have worked so hard to have you pardoned would turn out."

One of the other men interjected. "But with the king's dying, people's attention is focused elsewhere."

"King William's dead?"

"On his deathbed, God rest his soul."

Albert Tanner took George's elbow. "But come. If it has your agreement, you may bed at my house tonight, and a seat is booked on the Dorchester coach leaving early tomorrow." He steered George through the streets saying, "We've much to ask, but first food. You're hungry, I've no doubt."

"Aye," added one of the other men, hurrying to keep pace with Tanner. "We're all anxious to hear of your experiences."

~~~

Even the air seemed to bustle with activity, carrying the smells and sounds of Dorchester market day. Henry Finchbury carefully navigated his horse through the throng of people. He called out "make way" to a group of men bartering over a horse and paused as a smock-clad shepherd herded his sheep into a pen. Avoiding splashes from a cow defecating in the roadway, Henry moved slowly forward, alive to the mingled cries of street traders shouting their wares, the cackle of hens, the grunting of pigs, the bleating of sheep.

Halting at the hostelry, Henry dismounted as a young lad ran forward and took hold of the horse's head. "Watch yer horse, Sir? I'll stay with 'im until 'ee comes out agin."

"Take him round to the stabling and tell them to water him and rub him down." Handing the boy a penny, Henry turned towards *The Lion and the Unicorn* entrance.

Ivy and the branches of a trailing rose already showing healthy shoots climbed up the white-washed walls and crowded the mullioned windows. Perfumed gillyflowers nodded in accompaniment to the twittering of martins nesting under the thatched roof.

As he approached, a woman in a ragged dress, her dark hair straggling across her face, stumbled against him, grabbed at a bench for support. Wrapped in a voluminous white apron, a manservant pushed at the woman again. "Get yer gin-soaked carcass away from 'ere. Go on, move!" The servant, stepping aside to let Henry pass, laughed as she unsteadily set off towards the market area. "Tha's right. Do yer whoring amongst the pigs."

A babble of voices and clink of glasses met Henry Finchbury's ears as he entered the inn. A waiter gathering empty tankards looked up at Henry's approach. Taking in the cut of Henry's riding coat, his crisp white stock and the shine of his leather boots, he put down his tray and signalled the landlord. Thumbs tucked into the chest pockets of his waistcoat, the landlord greeted Henry with a snag-toothed smile.

"Good day to 'ee, Sir. Would you be one of Mr. Ponsonby's party?"

"'Morning, landlord. That's right. He's arrived?" asked Henry.

"Mr. Ponsonby. Yes, Sir. This way, Sir. I've set aside the parlour room at the back, it being quieter and more private. Mr. Ponsonby and the other gentlemen are gathered there, Sir."

Several of those seated at tables and benches looked up from their conversations and bid Henry a good day or raised a hand to a hat in recognition as he followed the landlord down a passage towards a heavy oak door. Knocking on the door and then opening it with a flourish, the landlord stood aside to allow Henry to enter.

"Can I send yer somethin' in, Sir? Mulled wine per'aps?"

"Aye, that'll do for now. Oh, and a plate of your roast beef. The ride has made me hungry."

"Yes, Sir. I'll 'ave it to yer directly."

A group of four men sat at a table, another two stood conversing by a window. Ponsonby, who had been standing in front of the fire, stepped forward to greet him.

"Finchbury, m' dear man, welcome. We'd begun to question what might have delayed you. Come warm yourself. You rode over?" His voice, as if forced from the toes of his boots up through his long frame, sounded stretched.

"Morning, Ponsonby. Fine day." Henry removed his long coat and placed it over the back of a chair. By way of an apology for his tardiness, he added, "Market place's swarming, and two acquaintances wished to speak with me."

Hands extended, the two men at the window turned to greet Henry. Removing a long-stemmed pipe from his mouth, one of the men at the table rose to welcome him and introduced his three companions.

Pleasantries were exchanged, enquiries made regarding wives and families, further refreshments brought in. Henry, a plate of beef and crusty bread in front of him, placed his tankard on the table. "Well, Ponsonby," he asked, "what's this important business your note said you wished to discuss?"

Massaging his warmed buttocks with one hand while raising the tankard-holding other hand high to gain the attention of those present, Ponsonby announced, "Right, Gentlemen! Business!" His voice scraped against his vocal cords. His pronounced Adam's apple bobbed as he cleared his throat and tried again. "As you all well know, the government has seen fit to pardon those traitors, those unionists. They'll soon be on their way back, in fact I understand George Loveless lands shortly. It's a disgrace!" He made a sweeping gesture. "Gentlemen, we must also unite."

"Unite?" questioned one.

"What's it you're talking of, Ponsonby?" asked another.

"We're all landowners here. Some of us had these men in our employ. We must make sure they are not employed anywhere in this county on their return."

"What's your reasoning on this?" asked Henry.

"My reasoning! It's obvious, surely? If they return here, we'll have them stirring up dissent all over again. Trying to unionize more farm workers."

"Like Ponsonby, I understand George Loveless will be in England soon. His ship could be docking as we speak," said one of the men at the table as he fumbled in his pockets for his snuff box. "He's the one that needs watching." He placed a pinch of snuff on the back of his hand, noisily drew it into his nostrils and extended the box to the others.

"Is that so?" responded his companion, declining the offered snuff.

"Aye, and passage has been booked on a vessel for the others, so I've heard."

"So, Gentlemen, what are your thoughts on the matter?" asked Ponsonby. Without waiting for a reply he continued, "We cannot have them back here, and if none offer them employment they'll be forced to go elsewhere. What say the rest of you? Finchbury?"

Henry chewed carefully, swallowed, before replying. "Seems to me they'll have learnt their lesson, and are unlikely to cause any more trouble."

"Dammit, Finchbury! You were all for having them charged."

"The others may have become more tractable, but that George Loveless is a firebrand," said the man at the table, pointing with his pipe at Henry. "No, I think Ponsonby's right. We must refuse to hire them and then they'll be forced to move elsewhere."

"You talk sense, Ponsonby. I'm with you on this," said another.

The others all spoke out in agreement, some reiterating that a pardon should never have been granted. Henry, digging with his finger at a thread of beef caught in his teeth, remained silent.

"Right then! We're agreed. Now it's up to us to spread the word to other landowners and acquaintances. Make sure they'll see the sense in what we say. You'll talk to Wainwright, Finchbury, seeing as your properties are neighbouring on each other?" Ponsonby asked, striding to the door to shout, "Landlord, service! We need more to drink."

Henry rose and crossed to Ponsonby's side. Lowering his voice slightly he said, "None of those men were ever in my employ so there's no question of me re-hiring them. That's as far as I'm prepared to go on this matter."

"You… But…" Ponsonby spluttered. A look of amazement followed by anger crossed his face. His nose, already red, turned redder. "You're a turncoat, Finchbury. I've said as much to Maria, and I'll say it to your face. A turncoat."

"It's not a question of changing sides, Ponsonby. I'm neither for or against what you've said. Until I've thought the matter through, I'm staying neutral." Picking up his coat and riding crop, Henry turned to the other men. "I must bid you all good day for I have a pressing matter to attend to."

A chorus of protest followed him as he exited the room.

Why hadn't he agreed with Ponsonby, gone along with the others? Riding home, oblivious to the new green in the hedgerow, the smells of spring, the late afternoon sunshine on his back, Henry's mind sought for a reason for his refusal. Of course they didn't need the workers stirred up again and Ponsonby's proposal made sense. And Ponsonby was right. He had been against labourers in the area forming a union just as much as Ponsonby. So why was he resisting Ponsonby's suggestion?

Ralph Tremain! What was it Ralph Tremain had asked at the dinner party he and Agnes had given. They were sitting round the table discussing the issue, and Tremain had said…? Dammit, it was all so long ago. Henry could visualize the scene, remembered they'd eaten pheasant. He struggled to recall what was Tremain's question. *But are their demands so unreasonable?* Yes, that was it. And they'd turned on Tremain. Told Tremain he didn't know what he was taking about.

At the trial he'd known it was likely the six men would be found guilty, but from the moment of Judge Williams' voicing, "Transportation for seven years," a sense of disquiet had plagued him. Yes, the more he thought on the matter, that's when his peace of mind had left him. To a degree, *he* was responsible for the fate of those men.

Ruminating on all that had transpired, Henry recognized that it was since the mens' sentencing that he'd become more conscious of the lives of farm labourers and the working class in general. His observations had led him to thinking more about how hard their lives were, the long hours they laboured in all weathers to feed their families. Even with the passing of time the sense of unease persisted. He'd followed the newspaper debates about whether the corn laws should be repealed, but it was a matter that impinged little on his personal world. There would always be bread on his table.

Watching several women gleaning a harvested field one day had nudged at his growing awareness of the poor around him. Accompanied by small children or with an infant shawled to her back, each woman worked bent over ready to snatch up a stalk of corn and place it in the folds of her scooped up apron or into a sack before one of the others could grab it. A girl of about seventeen, a baby on her back, her bare feet scratched by the rough stubble, tore at a spray of blackberries from the hedgerow, thrusting them in her mouth as if she'd not eaten for days. For some time Henry viewed the tableau from the back of his horse, noting how meagre were their pickings. How many fields did they have to scour, he mused, before they had gathered enough to take to the mill?

It was the Piddlehinton incident that defined his focus. A scrawny, ill-looking man, aided by a young boy, was piling household articles onto a small handcart outside a cottage, while a girl tried to sooth the tears of two little children. In the cottage doorway a man stood shouting roughly at a woman tugging on a dirty feather mattress. "…no more. I gave 'ee till noon to be out." Caught against the door jamb, the mattress split open. Feathers were blown by the wind, swirled into the angry man's face which made him rage all the more. The boy, leaving his father's side rushed to help his sobbing mother and together they struggled to haul the leaking bedding onto the cart. As boy and man began to pull the cart away followed by the weeping woman and children, the agent, still brushing feathers from his trousers, addressed the watching Henry. "Show a bit of compassion and that's what happens. Gave 'em a whole extra day to get out, and they're still not gone by noon as they were instructed."

"You've evicted them, then?"

"Got behind in their rent. Couldn't let it continue. There's plenty'll be glad to move in."

"Where will they go, do you know?"

"It's not likely he'll find work around here with so many unemployed. Only work to be found nowadays is up north in the factories or workin' on canal diggin', though 'tis mainly the Irish they take on as navies. Still, it's none of my concern."

But Treman was right. Whose concern is it then Henry asked himself as he continued on his ride?

He'd started taking an interest, albeit secretly, in his employees, something till now he'd left to Doyle, his overseer. He'd always kept the cottages in good repair, but now he improved the sleeping quarters of the groom and stable boy. He instructed Doyle to notify him of any problems with tenants or workers; he'd even asked Agnes to see the little scullery maid was not kept working after ten at night.

Once again that question, whose responsibility was it, came to mind. Unable to clarify his thoughts on the issue, he urged his horse into a gallop, striking the animal with his crop to force him to go faster. Horse and master had covered some distance before Henry took note of the beast's heaving flanks. Patting the animal's neck in way of an apology, he eased the animal to a walk.

~~~

Late into the night George talked with Albert Tanner and other committee members. Talked until his voice gave out. When they had told of the amount of money raised to help support the families of the transported men, emotion made it difficult for him to express his gratitude. He'd raised a hand to his forehead to hide tears that threatened to overflow. They urged him to write of his experiences: said they would see he had funds until the others returned and a decision could be made on the best way to assist them all.

He was up before the sun had fingered the sky awake, anxious not to miss the coach. Seated beside the coachman, struggling against sleep, George studied the bustle of the streets, the changing scenery, and now and again exchanged comments with the driver. Occasionally he drifted into a doze but was brought back to awareness when stops were made at hostelries for food and a change of horses.

Now he strode along the road from Dorchester, his feet unprotesting at the miles they covered. Gazing about him as he walked, he resisted an urge to leap into the air and shout his pleasure at all he saw. Never before had he experienced such a feeling of sheer joy. As he drew nearer to Tolpuddle his pace slackened, not from tiredness but a sudden hesitancy. Nearly four years. A long time for a man and wife to be separated. What would he find when he reached home?

~~~

For the hundredth time over the past few days Elizabeth Loveless stood in the doorway of her cottage. The letter from the London-Dorchester Committee representative had said they would meet George's vessel and send him on to Dorchester by coach, but with no news as to whether his ship had docked on the appointed day Elizabeth and the children kept up a constant watch. With a hand shielding her eyes against the sun's glare, she strained for that first glimpse of her husband. Was that…? Was it her imagination? No, no. In the distance a figure hastened his stride, waved his hat in great sweeping motions.

"Children! It's yer father. He's here," she called, suddenly finding it necessary to put out a hand to the door frame to steady herself, the other hand pressed against her chest as if to calm the rapid beating of her heart. She drew a deep breath. Stepping back into the room she removed her apron, placing it carefully over the back of a chair before starting down the steps and walking towards him. Drawing closer, her steps became brisker, then, letting go of all her usual restraint, she gathered up her skirts and broke into a run. Neighbours heads erupted from windows at the sound of her voice. Dinniah, hearing Elizabeth's shout, rushed from her doorway. Hands outstretched to greet her brother, she hesitated, stood back watching wife and children welcome him home.

Oblivious of others emerging from their houses, George held Elizabeth close. As if sealed by the heat of an Australian sun, his throat would allow no words to escape. He could only bury his face in her hair. Her face pressed into George's shoulder, Elizabeth's "God be thanked," was muffled. While Sarah clutched her father round his waist, Matthew took hold of his hand. Only Daniel, finger in his mouth, stood uncertain, staring.

Chapter Forty-Three
Workhouse 1842

DOCTOR BE STANDING BY MY BED THOUGH I CANST GIVE no indication that I knows he's there. When he speaks, 'tis as if his voice be filtered through a November fog.

"Why hasn't this body been..." he starts demanding, layin' a hand on my chest. Feelin' me draw the faintest of breaths, he says, "Well, I'm damned!" and takes up my wrist. "Did I not leave a certificate for this man with you, three, four days ago?" he asks the overseer.

"You did, Sir. Told me to fill in the date when he died." There's a hint of mockery in the overseer's voice. "But, as you sees, he ent dead yet."

As he moves to the next bed I hears Doctor mutterin', "Impertinence!"

Well it come about, just as I feared. George Loveless an' I meetin'. I were sittin' with Samuel and Will. Picked some late kingcups down by the ford and laid 'em on their graves. Tears at me, goin' in there. The churchyard. Yet there's scarce a day as I canst pass by and not visit 'em. The grass on Will's small mound be takin' hold now, and the daisy roots I planted. Will would get that excited on spyin' an early daisy openin' up afore it were really spring. Clutch 'em in his fist and run with 'em to his mother. Even though they'd already be droopin' from the heat of his little hand, Mary'd find a little pot to put 'em in and set 'em on the table. The stalks always too short so the heads would float atop the water.

The cottage seemed awful quiet with Will gone. Mary an' me locked in our grief, and Tabby circling around us, flutterin' like a wounded bird.

Since I heard Loveless were back I've not strayed far from the cottage. Exceptin', o'course, to go to work. An' wonderin' each day whether Master will've taken him on again.

Then it were bein' told around the village that Loveless be sittin' in his cottage, hour after hour, writin'. 'Twas said as how he were settin' down his experiences, sort of writin' a book.

And it happens, just as I seen it in them dreams as would come on me at nights. George just fixin' me with them gimlet eyes of his, and me fastened to the ground as if my feet be mired in deep mud.

Finally I croaks, "I swear to 'ee, I had no choice."

And he says nothin'. Could've been one minute. Could've been sixty. Him just standin' there, hands thrust deep in his pockets, feet spread apart. And me wishin' I were lying there with Samuel and Will.

Finally he speaks. "You *had* a choice. You chose to betray us." His voice were quiet but clear, and it seemed as if it rang out across the churchyard to be carried on the breeze to the whole village. Again silence lies between us like an invisible wall. Then he says, softer in tone, "But it was obvious at the trial that you were coerced into giving evidence. I seek no revenge. God on the Day of Judgement … ."

Not lettin' him finish, rememberin' hearin' him preach once, goin' on about 'Vengence is mine, saith the Lord', I cries, "Your God've had revenge. Six of you was transported. And six of my young 'uns He's taken in punishment." My voice be scratchy with choked-back tears. A fit of coughin' overtakes me, and I has to lean against the low wall of the churchyard until it's passed.

"I was told you'd lost another child. A terrible thing."

He says nothin' more. Just turns from me. Following the lane that runs around the church, avoiding the shorter way through the graveyard, he leaves. His boots crunchin' on gravel the only sound.

'Tis some time afore I can find the energy to let go the support of the wall and continue home. It's over, is all I can think. What I've dreaded these last months is over.

I keeps askin' myself why I still be here? It ent stubbornness now. I longs for these bloodied lungs of mine to give up. My heart to stop pumpin'. All I wants is to lie alongside Samuel an' Will.

I hears tell Loveless' pamphlet 'ave been published by the London-Dorchester Committee, them as raised the money for the families. September, as I recalls. He called it *The Victims of Whiggery* or some such name. Whigs is a name they gives to them parliamentary folks as I un'erstands it. Four pence a copy and selling well by all accounts. I'd like to know what it says, but four pence be money I darest not spend on summat I ent even able to read.

Then it buzzed around the village that Parson had been overheard talking to that landowner in Affpuddle. What's his name? Ponsonby, that's him. They were goin' on about what Loveless had writ, and Parson called it rabble-rousing rubbish. And Ponsonby, says as how Magistrate Frampton were wonderin' if charges could be laid on grounds of sedition! 'Tis said some in the village take care not to be seen with Loveless a feared them in authority might find grounds to charge 'em too.

And still I strains again for air... Maybe 'tis because I knows as how there be only a pauper's grave waitin'. That there'll be no hawthorn bush and singin' yellerhammer for Seth Fielding.

Comin' up the path one evenin', home from work, I hears a voice that I knows ent Mary's. More sharp and cuttin'. Sod that, I thinks to myself, realizin' it be Mary's sister. Spendin' more time than were really necessary on scrapin' my boots, I listens in on 'em. Martha does rough work on occasion at the parsonage, and she's sayin' as how Parson's wife be pressin' Parson for a girl to do the skivvying again. "It might be a chance for Tabby to be took on," suggests Martha.

Well, one boot on, one boot off, I storms inside. "Ent no daughter of mine workin' for Parson! Bugger that idea." Martha jerks back in her chair as if I'd struck her.

"I'm only telling 'ee what I've heard," she says, all indignant." Thought if Tabitha were workin' it would help. You'm strugglin' for money and all. And you know a place must be found for her before it's too..." Martha catches herself. Mary and me, be only too well aware of what it is she's not said. *Afore you be too sick to work anymore and has to go to the workhouse."*

"But it were you as told us how badly they treated the little lass they used to have," I says, real angry.

And Martha, who means well in spite of her bossiness, agrees that it were so.

"Ent worth argufyin' about," says my Mary, the peace-maker. "After what you said to Parson in the churchyard that time, there's no way they'd take on our Tabby."

"Anyways, she be too young to leave home," says I, strugglin' to get my other boot off.

"She's nigh eleven. Littl'uns of five be workin' in those factories up north, so I hears. I know she's all you have left, but you'm not thinkin' practical," says Martha and gets to her feet. "Well, I must away home." She gives Mary a hug; glares at me and says as how I needs to learn a little gratitude.

Tabitha comes and stands by my chair. Puttin' my arm around her, I says, "Don't 'ee fret, my pet. As long as you helps your mother all you can, you'm stayin' home."

Only the once since I said those things to Squire have I seen him. He gives a stiff nod. I touches my hat. And that be it. No words exchanged between us. And I likes it that way. There be them as has money, and there be us. Seems more natural, the two stayin' separate.

My chest were tight again and I were coughin' more come autumn, each bout of coughin' draining more strength from me. With many around with no work, our wages be lowered yet again. Mary works at Wainwrights of a Monday and Tuesday, helpin' with the heavy wash. As I've said afore, she's up at the farm by four of a mornin' to light the fire under the copper for the water must be heated. Tabby've learnt much from her mother and goes with her to help. Not paid, mind, but it eases Mary's load.

Most of us be strugglin' just to keep food on the table, and throughout the village everything seemed quieted as if us all were waitin' for something, though what I don't think none could have said if asked. Loveless kept to hisself. Went to London a couple of times, accordin' to village gossip.

And so the year passed. Christmas come and went, and a winter that had been mild turned bitin' cold bringin' heavy snow. Then us went from cold to spring with no thawin' spell between. The coppice were carpeted

And Ordered Their Estate

with snowdrops and wood anemones, hazel trees hung with lambs tails, and rabbits caught themselves in my snares again.

Villagers' whisperin' grew to smilin' chatter.

The ship bringing the Standfields, James Loveless and Brine docked in Plymouth and they was all welcomed there by local trade unionists. There were a public meeting held with many givin' speeches. Then on to Exeter with more speechifyin' and money collected for 'em.

A few weeks later, mid-April time, they held what were called an Official Welcome for 'em in London. The papers was full of all the goings on. A fellow in the village as had some letterin', stood on the green and reads it out to us: me standin' off to the side of the group that had collected, strainin' to hear what he read. Paper said as how the crowds started gatherin' early in the mornin'. All kinds of workers, hundreds of 'em, turnin' out dolled up in their Sunday finery and carryin' big banners. And the Lovelesses, for George were up there too, the Standfields and Brine rode in an open carriage led by a band! Paraded right through London!

Then the paper says as how there were this big banquet for 'em with six hundred people, and tents set up outside for all the rest. Paper said as how there were a lot more speechifyin'. And George Loveless got up in front of all them people and he made a speech thankin' everyone. It must 'ave been a fair old sight. Who'd 'a thought they'd be treated thus? I've pondered on it all many a time.

Imagine, ridin' in an open carriage!

Chapter Forty-Four

Tolpuddle 1838

WIPING HER FOREHEAD WITH HER APRON, ELIZABETH stooped to put more wood on the fire.

Only May but warm enough for July. She slipped some turnips into the bubbling pot careful not to splash herself.

"Letter for 'ee, Mistress Loveless," called a voice from the doorway, making her turn sharply. "From London by the looks of it," the carrier added. "There's tuppence to pay."

Placing the letter on the table, Elizabeth reached for a tin on the mantle and carefully counted out some coins and dropped them in the carrier's extended hand. George hadn't told her much when he set off for London this time, only that the London Dorchester Committee wished to discuss some matters with him. She stood by the window turning the letter over and over before breaking the seal.

"*Dearest Wife, Much is afoot here in London and it will be a further few days before I return. Members of the Friendly Society have offered to take up the leases on two farms in Essex and to put up a sum of money to purchase stock ... .* "

Essex! Dear Heavens, where was Essex? There was obviously too much information in this letter to be ingested by one mind; she needed Dinniah's thoughts on the matter. Her bonnet? There on the hook! Bonnet strings tied with care, the letter in her apron pocket, she stepped briskly to the Standfield cottage.

"Dinniah, Dinniah,' she called, seating herself on the bench just inside the door.

"Comin', Elizabeth," a voice called from the back room. "Saw Postie from the window calling on 'ee. Was readyin' myself to see what news you had. Couldn't find my shoes."

"Where's Essex?"

"Can't say as I knows exac'ly. What you want to know for?"

"George says the Committee be takin' up leases on two farms in Essex for us."

"On two farms? Us move, you mean?" queried Dinniah, her voice full of concern. "Leave Tolpuddle?"

"That's what the letter says. Here, you read it," she said passing it to Dinniah. "Us knew, and as George and Thomas've come to realize, there's little chance of employment here for 'em. But leavin' Tolpuddle! It'll take some gettin' used to the idea."

"It will that. But a farm. Our *own* farm!" Overcome with the enormousness of the concept, Dinniah sank down next to Elizabeth, shaking her head in disbelief. While Elizabeth fanned herself with her bonnet, Dinniah slowly read each line, sounding out some of the words to herself, going back over a sentence. "George do go on a bit, don't 'ee."

"He does that, but 'tis mainly about what's happenin' there. He don't say where this Essex be."

Putting her arm around Elizabeth's shoulder, a catch of laughter in her voice indicating her excitement, Dinniah said, "Us'll just have to be patient a little longer 'til he returns. And the Lord knows, we've had plenty of practice at being patient."

Crammed into the Standfield's cottage, all fixed their eyes on George standing at the head of the table. The smaller children squatted on the floor while the women nursed the young ones on their knees. An early afternoon sun danced patterns on the wall through the open door and windows. Humming bees could be heard busying themselves in the hollyhock cups growing against the walls. Dinniah poured some water for her daughter-in-law, Kathrine. Alice, James' wife, fanned herself with a fluted piece of paper.

"Before Thomas and I tell you our news, it is only fitting that we first give thanks to the good Lord for all those who have contributed funds on our behalf and for the support and help we have received from the London Dorchester Committee." The fervent 'Amens' at the end of his prayer were a mixture of gratitude to God and pent up excitement. Daniel poked at his cousin with his foot but George quelled his son's exuberance with a swift frown. Elizabeth leaned over and pulled Daniel to her side, a finger held to her lips.

Hands pressed firmly on the table, George continued. "Thomas and I have been to inspect the two farms and the leases are signed. They're on good, rich soil and the houses should well please you womenfolk.

"Now we've talked the matter over," he inclined his head to indicate the other men, Thomas, James, John and Brine, "and have agreed thus. Thomas, Dinniah and children and John and his family will take over Fenner's Farm. Forty-three acres, isn't that so, Thomas?" Thomas nodded his head in agreement. Holding up his hand to the barrage of questions bursting from everyone, George continued. "Let me finish. New House Farm's about five miles over. Village called Greensted. Brother James and our good friend Brine and I will work New House, with all us men helping each other out when the need arises."

While Dinniah and Elizabeth plied George and Thomas with questions about the accommodation, with Kathrine and Alice adding their queries whenever the opportunity arose, James, John and Brine immersed themselves in the logistics of moving everyone to their new homes.

The children, their requests for information unheeded, headed outside, all except Mathew who considered himself old enough now to be aligned with the men.

It was plaintive appeals for food from the children that drew the adults attention to the lateness of the hour. As each family set off for home still talking, Dinniah, standing in her doorway, caught sight of Brine talking quietly to her daughter Beth. So that's the way the wind's blowing, she thought to herself. I wonder if Thomas has noticed.

~~~

Five year old Edward Hammett liked to hear the peas' pinging noise as they hit the bottom of the pot. He reached for another pod, pressed its side and listened for the gentle 'pop'.

"Don't drop 'em on the ground," his mother cautioned. "Watch what you're doing now." Edward looked up at his mother. He sensed from the tightness of her mouth that it was best to be careful.

Shaded from the sun by ropes of honeysuckle, his grandmother dozed propped up in an easy chair with cushions. The left side of her face drooped. Her left hand hung down the side of the chair, twisted and useless. It was six months now since the stroke had left her helpless and drooling.

"I've some good news to tell 'ee, Teddy. Your father's on his way home."

If it's good news why doesn't Mother look happier about it wondered Edward. She was looking at him as if she expected some response, so Edward asked, "How long will it take 'im? You said as how he were gone across the sea."

"In a few more weeks. About August time."

"Will he live with us when he gets back?"

"Course he will. He's your father."

Edward gave his mother's reply some thought. He'd always had difficulty with the concept of having a father. "But where be 'ee to sleep?"

Instead of answering, his mother got up and crossed to her mother. Raising the dangling arm, she laid it on her mother's lap, brushed a strand of hair away from her face.

"Are *you* glad he's comin', Mother?"

"What a question to ask. Now your Granny's helpless, it'll be good to have someone to lean on. Now you finish off them peas while I fetches my sewing."

Selecting another pod, Edward tried to picture this father of his. His name was James Hammett his mother had told him. Said he looked like his father. He thought back to the time just after his grandmother was taken ill. His mother had been talking to the man that brought the money. "But where be my man, Mr. Brown?' she'd asked. "Why ent there news of my man comin' home?" her voice etched with bitterness. "You can see how things be for us with my mother took sick. I scarce has the strength to lift her from bed to chair."

"We've written many letters, to the government, to the authorities over there, but still none have been able to locate him. It's not from want of trying I can assure you."

"Loveless and the others be all nicely settled. Been back more'en a year. And all you can say is there's still no news."

But now this man, his father, was coming home. Edward wasn't sure how he felt about it.

~~~

The sun was playing hide-and-seek with the clouds as the two carts passed through the village of Greensted. Creaking harness, iron-bound wheels rumbling over loose gravel, drivers' voices eager to have the journey over urging the animals on, the sounds all mingled with the excited shouts of the children. The loaded carts jounced over the rough ground as George and James Loveless directed the horses down a sloping lane that flattened out as a stone farmhouse surrounded by fields came into view. A light breeze stirred the leaves of the huge August-green oak trees that interspersed the hedges of hawthorne and briar.

"Oh husband, look at the size of it! Why, it must be five, ten times bigger than the cottage," Elizabeth exclaimed, her hand going up to her mouth. She turned round to the second cart following them. "Alice! Look at it," she called to her sister-in-law.

Alice, her arm round her small daughter, laughingly agreed to the young boys' request that they be allowed to walk the rest of the way. James Loveless slowed the horse's pace while the two boys leapt down and ran ahead.

At the sound of their voices, Brine came from behind a barn and hurried to greet them, smiling broadly. His words of welcome were cut off by George's enquiries about the new stock and the shrieks of excitement from the children.

"All's well, George. Couldn't be better. You need me to help unload? If not I'll get back to what I were doin'." As he started back towards the barn he called over his shoulder, "Thomas 'ave bought a sow. I walked over yesterday evenin' to have a look at it. Her's a fine lookin' animal."

Elizabeth whispered to Alice, "And I'll warrant it weren't just the sow he went to see. Dinniah says she thinks Brine've taken a fancy to her Beth."

Struggling with a large bundle, Alice laughed. "I'm surprised you ent noticed afore. I've caught 'em holdin' hands more 'en once." Dropping the bundle at her feet, she added, "Can you get a'hold of this? It'll need the both of us to get it inside."

For the family Bible-reading that night, George selected the text, "And God delivered them from the wilderness."

BOOK TWO

Chapter Forty-Five

Workhouse 1842

WITH HANDS RED AND RAW FROM THE LYE, I WERE SCRUBbing the workhouse kitchen floor. A huge pot simmered on top the stove sending up steam that hung as if stuck to the air with its greasy stench. Bones stewing, watery soup. 'Tis what be given us for supper most nights. Thumpin' her great stirrin' stick onto the wooden table, Mistress Ashthorne, her in charge of cooking, turns to get summat from the pantry and the stick rolls from the table onto the filthy floor just missin' my pail of water. Cursin' at me as if 'twere my fault, she bends her bulk to retrieve it, and thrusts it back in the pot, mutterin' under her breath.

The two other women as helps cook were busy at tasks in the scullery so I were alone when the overseer's assistant come with news of Seth's death. Though I've been expecting it for days, it still catches me like a blow. There be I, down on all fours with dirty grey water puddled around me, strugglin' to catch my breath.

"You'm sure this time?" I forces out, remembering once afore they'd missed his thready breathin'.

"There's no doubt. Doctor's pronounced 'im dead and signed the certificate."

"I wants to see 'im. One last time to say goodbye. To be certain sure."

I thought he were going to refuse, his face were full of denial. But he'd a kinder side to him than the overseer. He thinks a minute, glances around and says, "Come on then. Overseer's busy elsewhere. Quick now!"

Jingling his bunch of keys he adds, "Ten minutes, is all. Then get this floor finished or cook'll be cursin."

I stands and looks at my Seth laying there. Eyes closed. Skin yellowed so his hair seems even whiter. Lovely head of hair had Seth. First thing I noticed about him. His hair and his smile, sort of lopsided. I knelt by the cot and took his cold hand in mine.

Hundreds of nights I've lain with my head on his chest, the beat of his heart lulling me to sleep. Now, when I places my head there, I hears nothing. No wheezing lungs giving the faintest of movement to his rib cage, his ribs standing out like staves of a broken barrel. I puts my arms around him and lifts his head and shoulders. Holds him close. As light as Will he seems. I can weep no tears, but low moans well up from inside of me as I rocks the both of us.

The assistant leaves us alone for some while afore he taps me on the shoulder, says, "Enough, Missus, enough. Come on now, 'tis time to go."

Gently lowering Seth back down on the thin pallet, I runs the back of my hand against his cheek.

In the next cot a man cries out for help. Vomit splashes on the wall, pools on the floor. A sickening odour fills the chilly room.

"Come on now, Missus, or there'll be trouble for the both of us."

"What'll happen to him now?" I struggles to get the words out.

"Undertaker's cart has already picked up the woman that died last night, so they won't be out again until t'morrow for this 'un." He takes my arm and steers me from Seth's side, adding, "They usually holds paupers' burials of a Thursday. Buries 'em together if there be more'n one."

I pulls away from him. "My Seth were a good man," I cries at him. "A good man. He deserves better'n that."

He clicks his tongue against his teeth with a tsh-tshing sound, and I allows him to guide me out.

Back in the kitchen, I leans against the wall staring at the pail of dirty water, the brush and cloth alongside. Sees it, but don't see it, if you un'erstands my meaning.

Through the open door to the courtyard a man comes in, a sack of flour on his back. 'Tis Arthur Polsey, my sister's husband's cousin. As my brain takes in who it be, I knows without thinking about it, what to do. 'Twas as if a voice be whispering in my ear, a hand be pushing me forward.

Making like I were going for fresh water, I picks up the bucket and walks past the women choppin' turnips. Goes through the door into the walled yard. Setting down the pail, I darts a look around; there be none but me and Kenton's dray. In one movement, scraping my hip against the edge, I were up on that cart. Seemed that hand as steered me from the kitchen were behind me boosting me up. I crawls under the canvas covering they uses to keep the sacks dry should it rain, lays catchin' my breath.

I peers out to check none've seen, blinking as the feeble noon sun catches on the shards of glass topping the girt wall - a wall to keep us inmates from getting out, for there be none as would wish willingly to try and get in. I draws my head in as Polsey comes out and heaves another sack onto his back. Back he comes again, climbs into the driver's seat. Gathering up the reins and clucking at the horse to move forward, he 'ave no idea that I be there. As soon as we're through the gateway, the gateman drags the heavy doors shut and locks 'em.

Never will I go back I tells myself. I'll sleep in a ditch, die there if that be the way things turn out.

Which way be Arthur turning? There's still a few sacks on the dray so 'tis to be hoped he's not going far afield. Two he leaves in Bere, then he takes the left fork towards Affpuddle.

Laying curled up on the wooden floor there's nothing to soften the jolting of the cart. I reasons Arthur be unlikely to turn around and take me back seeing the distance we've covered, so pushing back the canvas I makes my presence known.

"Where be 'ee goin' next, Arthur?" I asks.

Well, he nigh falls off his seat, he be so startled. "Struth, where did 'ee spring from? Who be 'ee?"

"Why, 'tis me, Mary Fieldin'. You knows me. Martha's sister."

"But ent you and Seth in ..."

"Seth's dead. Died this mornin.'" And with the voicing of the fact, that Seth be truly gone, I can no longer hold back my tears. Sitting there, legs drawn up, head resting on my knees I weeps a river. For Seth. For Will. For Samuel. For us all.

Arthur calls "Whoa" to the horse. He turns around, climbs down into the cart, and awkwardly puts an arm around my shoulder. "I be right sorry to hear that," says he, not knowing what to do. Removing his arm, he asks "Where be 'ee plannin' to go? You knows they'll not take yer back if you runs off, and it'll be a vagrancy charge if they finds yer wanderin'. Prison."

"Tis of no matter now," I forces out between sobs.

Arthur sighs a deep sigh, removes his hat and runs his hand over his head in bewilderment. "Master Kenton will be at me if I don't get back sharpish."

Raising my head, for the first time I takes in the handsome entrance pillars to my right. And the hand that pushed me from the workhouse, that helped me onto the dray, now urges me to get down, to go through those posts.

"I knows what I has to do. Where I's headin.'" I stands up and steps to the edge of the dray. Seeing I intends to get off, Arthur holds out his hand and helps me down, all the time asking, "Where be 'ee goin'?" What be your plans?" though mingled with his concern I detects a hint of relief that I be leaving him.

As I starts to trudge the length of that long, curved driveway, that unseen hand be at my elbow encouraging me on. I looks up at the bare chestnut trees that line the drive, their brown, fat-fingered leaves sogged with last night's rain form a carpet on either side. I shivers, folds my arms across my chest against the chill. I realizes for the first time all I have on be the thin, grey workhouse gown and a sacking apron tied around my waist. I takes the apron off and drapes it over my shoulders.

I walks faster, fixing my mind on what I has to do. Breathes in air free of the stench of poverty, of clothing rank with body smells. Air that carries the twittering of sparrers in the tree branches instead of shouting voices, wails of misery. I knows where I be heading. To shut my mind to the nagging notion that 'tis likely I'll not be listened to, I speeds up my steps while tryin' to keep count of the markers along the driveway.

They worked us hard back in the workhouse, miserable, tedious work, but my legs have become unused to walking any distance for 'twas rare for us to get outside. I has to take a rest now and then. But no sooner do I stop for a moment than I hears Sethy's voice tellin' I not to linger.

The parkland and driveway don't seem to have changed much from that time I walked up here years back. Just after the birth of our first 'un. Squire's wife's wet nurse had been sent packing. For stealing, it were whispered round the village. I was told as how it wouldn't be for long, just until their young 'un were weaned, three months at most for hers were eleven months older than mine.

I had walked slow then, too, delaying the time I'd be separated from my babe and Seth. I was that reluctant to go, but us had nothing to start a home with apart from the odd bits, a quilt and table my mother had given us. What little money us had been able to save, Seth, soft touch that he were, had loaned to his brother, he being sick and laid off work. Died of the lung-rot, with the debt unpaid. Not that us would've thought of pressing for payment. And afore I walked back down again, our babe were dead too. Cow's milk didn't suit his stomach so I were told. Why didn't they sent for I? 'Tis the one grudge I've held against Seth in all these years.

'Tis as if Seth be at my side, urgin' me to hurry, that's tellin' me there ent much time. At last I sees the house.

"Round the back," says Seth. *"The likes of us don't go up them steps to the big door."*

Tired, I snaps at him. "I weren't born yesterday, Seth Fieldin'. 'Course I knows to go to the back." Finds myself apologizing out loud to him.

Chapter Forty-Six
Tolpuddle 1842

HENRY FINCHBURY SAT SLUMPED AT HIS DESK, HIS HEAD cupped in his hands. He had been sitting there for some time, oblivious of everything around him. Somehow he had to break the news to Agnes, tell her the enormity of the situation. Up until now, he'd managed to keep the details of his losses in that newly floated canal construction company venture to himself. It had seemed a sound investment, a sure way to recoup what he'd lost the year before last in a shipping investment. Not only recoup but show a profit. But now, on top of everything, to find out he had been swindled, cheated, and for such a long period of time, by Doyle. The perfidiousness of the man, his own agent! And to think he'd trusted him to such an extent.

He pushed his chair back and rose to his feet, the abruptness of his movements sending a stack of bills and dunning notices he'd found in Doyle's office sliding to the floor. Shoving them aside with his foot, he walked towards the door. Best find Agnes, get it over with, tell her all was lost, gone. Gone like the cutter the *Hamilton Flyer* to the floor of the ocean. Gone like Doyle, who'd fled in the night. Gone, all gone!

"Doyle a swindler? Gone? I can hardly take it in." Agnes, hands clasped to her chest as if their pressure would calm the rapid pounding in her chest, paced back and forth. "I never felt at ease with the man but he always seemed efficient in his work. No, I'd never have questioned his loyalty, his honesty." She turned to face her husband. "This scheme you invested in. You're saying it has proved to be like that South Sea Bubble swindle of Walpole's government, the one my grandfather lost a fortune in?"

Henry crumpled on the settle, surprised his wife knew anything of such matters, lifted his eyes to look at her. "No, no. Nothing like that. This was ... should have been a sound investment, but it appears reports of the vessel's seaworthiness were falsified." Henry's raised hands dropped to his lap. "It's a loss I could have covered, even the canal company failure, but Doyle's trickery ... Almost everything's gone." His dejection overwhelmed him again.

"What do you propose to do, Henry?" Agnes Finchbury struggled to keep her voice low and non-accusatory.

"Well, I've reported Doyle's disappearance, of course, but even if they catch him I doubt they'll be able to recover much." He thumped at the armrest of his chair with his fist. "Damn it, I trusted the fellow!"

Henry fell silent again. Agnes sank into a seat opposite him. A door being opened somewhere in the house, voices, the ticking of the marble clock on the mantelpiece all seemed magnified. Leaning towards Agnes, his head dropped in his hands, his words slow and low, Henry spoke. "I don't know what to do... Agnes. I ... I didn't mean to bring such ignominy on you. I ..."

"Don't say you're sorry again." Agnes' voice had risen several octaves. Hands gripped tightly together, she made a deliberate effort to soften her tone. "Undoubtedly news of Doyle's disappearance is now common knowledge amongst the servants, but we must try and keep the true picture from them for as long as possible. You agree on this point, Henry?" The clock ticked steadily. There was a hissing from the fire as flames licked at sap oozing from a log. Henry stirred in his seat. The muttered, "...trusted him," escaping from his lips was more to himself than in response to his wife's question.

"You have always been too trusting," Agnes said quietly. "You're a dear, sweet man, Henry, but not very astute." Both sat absorbed in their thoughts: Henry's thoughts moving back and forth through shame, anger, and anguish; Agnes's searching for solutions.

Finally Agnes spoke, her voice firm and authoritative. "As I see the situation, first, you must arrange to sell whatever can be sold. Home Farm.

Timber from the park. Find a tenant for this place if necessary." Agnes' gentle face had taken on a determined look. "Henry! Are you listening to what I'm saying?"

"My dear, you don't grasp the enormity of the situation. It could mean …" Again Henry left his sentence unfinished.

"I think I do, husband. Listen and be guided by me, please."

Chapter Forty-Seven

Tolpuddle 1842

I PULLS ON THE BELL ROPE THREE TIMES AFORE ANYONE comes.

"Yes?" the manservant says, the questioning look on his face changing to one of annoyance. "How dare you come begging here? Be off now!"

" You think I'd walk the length of that carriageway just to beg a scrap of food, Joe Grayling? You be Tom Grayling's son, I knows."

If his face be anything to go by, he's even more offended that I knows his name. "Who are you, woman?" he demands. "What do you want?"

"I must see Squire. 'Tis terr'ble important."

"*You* see Squire Finchbury? You think the squire speaks with any that come to the servant's entrance. Begging!"

"I ent beggin', I told you. I *must* speak with Squire."

"The Master'll not see you. Now be off." He goes to close the door but I be too quick for him. Sets down right in the doorway. That has him flummoxed. His face flushes red. I can see he don't know whether to push me out or call for someone to help. "Go! Now, before there's trouble, woman."

"Not till 'ee takes my message to Squire. 'Tis a matter he must know of right now. Tell him, I begs you. 'Tis about Seth Fielding."

I hears footsteps and a voice callin' out: "What's keeping you, Grayling?" and there's another man starin' at me. "What's going on here? What's this ... this woman ... doing in the doorway?"

"She won't leave, Mr. Cutter, Sir. Says she must speak with the master."

"See the master!"

I reaches up and catches hold of his leg. "I ent beggin', Sir. I have a message for Squire. 'Tis important. I *must* see Squire."

This Mr. Cutter looks at me and then signals to Grayling. They both reach down to take hold of me, but I ducks down and crawls between Grayling's legs into the passageway, leaving Grayling clutching the piece of sacking from my shoulders.

"Get out! Get out!" Cutter hisses fiercely. "Get rid of her, Grayling."

"You'll not get me out till you takes my message to Squire." I be crying and shouting now. "When he hears 'tis about Seth Fielding, Squire'll come, you'll see."

"What's your name, woman? Who's this Seth Fielding." He pauses a moment, mutters, "Fielding " to himself, turns to Grayling. "Wasn't Fielding the fellow who had something to do with those six that were convicted and that child born in the hedgerow? Master loaned him Coachman's coat?"

"Aye. Jones thought he'd never see his coat again." Another thought comes to him. "And Master had him working with the kennel-man for a while too."

Cutter stands thinkin' a second. Shakin' his finger at me he says, "There's no chance Master'll speak with you. Give me your message and I'll relay it when the opportunity arises." When I keeps on insisting on seeing Squire, he throws up his hands in disgust. Instructing Grayling to watch me closely, and ordering me not to touch anything though there be scarce anything to touch, he goes through a door, closing it behind him.

I looks around me to take my mind from the worry that Squire'll not see me. We seems to be in a small room not much bigger than a passageway, and on the other side of the closed door I'd caught sight of the kitchen as Cutter went through. On a small table lies an open book with ruled columns, the page edges patterned with swirls of red and blue. Above the table, on a ledge, a small clock. Coats hang from some pegs.

Grayling stands to the side of me, makes a show of turning his head away as if I smells. 'Tis likely I do - too many of us round them buckets of water of a morning to get a proper wash.

And Ordered Their Estate

Ent nothing to be heard except the tickin' of the clock, and Grayling's heavy breathin'. Then footsteps. Cutter open the door and steps back to let Squire through. Squire looks terr'ble, his face all drawn.

I bobs a curtsy. I wants to kneel in front of him, clutch at him, beg, plead. But I just stands there, hands clasped tight at my waist.

"I'm told you insist on seeing me, something to do with Seth Fielding. Who are you?"

"Mary Fielding, Sir, Seth's wife." I dips another curtsy.

"What of Fielding? Why did he not come himself?"

"He be dead, Sir." Tears which won't be checked start spilling down my cheeks. "My Seth died this mornin'. I be here for your help, Sir."

"I'm sorry to hear your news." Squire just stands there, then as if his voice be comin' from his boots, he says, " but what is it you want of me?"

" I begs you, Sir. Have him buried proper."

Squire looks uncomfortable. Shoves his hands into the pockets of his coat, takes 'em out again. He turns to Grayling. Tells him to fetch a chair for me. Dismisses Cutter with a nod. While Grayling be after the chair there's a long silence between us. Then, just as I"m openin' my mouth to say more, Squire asks, "Buried properly? What do you mean?"

I wipes at my tears with my sleeve. My words have difficulty leaving my throat.

"They'll 'ave him in a pauper's grave. Word must be sent quick. They collects the bodies early mornin'. "

As Squire says, "I'm not getting your meaning, Mistress Fielding. Collect the bodies from where?" Grayling returns with a chair.

Catching Squire's nod, I seats myself as I replies, "The workhouse. Us were sent to the workhouse when Seth were took so sick."

"Dear God!"

"His mind were fixed on layin' alongside his boys. That's what I be askin', Sir. That he be buried in the churchyard next to Sam and Will."

Squire seems to have difficulty in takin' in what I be sayin'. There's another long silence afore he asks, "Have you no family, relatives, you can turn to?" I shakes my head. From some great distance he responds, "No, of course not or you'd not have been sent to the workhouse. I'd no idea."

The word *workhouse* seems to stick in his mouth. Rubbing the back of his neck with his hand, he paces back and forth muttering, "Dreadful business. Dreadful." He pauses by my side. "You want me to stop them taking the bo ... Fielding, elsewhere and arrange for him to be buried next to his sons? Is that correct?" He stands, finger tips against his lips, palm pressed against palm. Paces some more.

"I know 'tis a lot to ask of you, Sir, but you'm the only one as seemed to have concern for my Seth."

He gives no indication that he's heard. Stands with back turned. And I sits there on the chair. Sits there, scarce able to breath, waitin' on his answer. Then, placing a hand on the chair back, he looks up the clock, takes out a watch from his pocket and compares the two. "There's time still. I'll send the stable boy now with a message. Have a word with Parson Warren tomorrow."

I slips to my knees, pouring out thanks. Embarrassed he takes my elbow, lifts me up. "Enough, Mistress Fielding."

Oh, him addressin' me like that, as if I were someone of worth, someone as didn't smell of workhouse poverty, it did catch at my heart.

"I give my word a note will be sent to the workhouse. Fielding shall be buried next to his sons."

Grayling, who have been standing back against the wall, goes to open the door, when Squire pauses. "Dear God, what am I thinking of. You said you were both in the workhouse. How did you manage to get here?"

"I slipped away afore any noticed. I knew of no one else as could help, Sir."

"The groom shall take you back and deliver my message at the same time."

"I ent goin' back to *that* place. *Ever.* I have a sister'll give me a bed on the floor overnight. She'd take me in but she 'ave five of her own to feed as well as our mother livin' with 'em."

"Grayling," Squire orders, "Tell the groom to bring the trap round. I'll write a note now and he can deliver it to the workhouse after he's taken Mistress Fielding to her sister's home."

Chapter Forty-Eight

Tolpuddle 1842

AGNES, WHO HAD BEEN SORTING THROUGH THE BILLS ON Henry's desk trying to get some idea of how much they were in debt, dropped the letter she was holding and let out a deep sigh. Looking up at Henry's approach, she asked, "What did she want, Henry? Who was the woman?"

"Seth Fieldings' wife."

"But what was so important that she must see you?"

"She had news of her husband's death. Wants him buried alongside their sons."

"But that's nothing to do with you. It's Parson Warren she needs to see." Hand extended towards the pile of papers, Agnes paused, turned to Henry now standing beside her. "But why come to you? Did you give her money, Henry? No, you can't have, not when..." She gestured at the desk, the bills. "Oh, how could you?"

"No, not money. A promise." At Agnes' look, both questioning and imploring, Henry added defensively, "It will involve money, but a paltry sum compared to all this." With a voice cracking with emotion, he tried again. "Bad as things are for us, my dear, people of our standing are spared the indignity, the fear of the workhouse."

"Workhouse! Of course not." Appalled, Agnes reached for his hand and clasped it tightly in her own. "Is that what you've been fearing?"

Gently pulling away from his wife, Henry replied, "I was just making a comparison. No, we have no fear of the Workhouse or Debtors' Prison." He placed a hand on his wife's shoulder. "Things may be bad, But not as bad as that, m'dear."

Agnes gave a shudder. "Of course not. But looking through these bills. Some have demanded payment many times." Agnes picked up a handful of letters. "But others like these!" she pulled out several, "they're not for the running of the house. The property. They're acknowledging donations you've made. Large donations. This one here. To the Lunatic Asylum!"

"It was for Preston's idiot son. When they took him there. To get him treated decently, poor devil."

Agnes sighed. Her tone softened. "But Henry you can no longer accept responsibility for such people. Fielding's wife. You *must* tell her you've reconsidered."

Henry crossed to the window and stood staring out. It seemed to Agnes that minutes passed before he responded. "Fielding … Mistress Fielding … I can't explain it to you, m'dear." He drew a deep breath and slowly exhaled. "Can't even explain it to myself." Again there was a long pause before he continued. "It just seems…" He struggled for words that would express how deeply he felt about the matter. "... terribly important …no, essentially right. It just seems essentially right that Fielding rests alongside his sons. By granting his wish I will have done something to right a terrible wrong."

Agnes, studying her husband's back, sensing the deep conviction of his words, decided to say no more on the matter. She picked up a bronze paper-weight in the shape of a fox and placed it on top of one of the larger piles of paper that tilted precariously on the edge of the desk.

Chapter Forty-Nine
Tolpuddle 1847

THAT DAY, THAT AFTERNOON THAT SETH WERE BURIED, the sun come out briefly though with little strength to it. The bell tower's shadow stretched across the grass, pointin' at the piled earth round Seth's grave. A strong breeze were blowin', whiskin' at the dead leaves from the hawthorn tree. Sent some floating down atop Seth's coffin as it were lowered into the hole 'twixt Samuel and Will.

Squire were as good as his word. He saw to it Seth were coffined decent, that Parson read the burial service. Weren't that many of us gathered. Me and Tabby o'course, Martha and her family. I were surprised to see Master Kenton from the mill there. Three or four from the village as had forgiven Seth for what he done come, and Squire. Yes, Squire were there. He come just as Seth's coffin were carried through the churchyard. Stood right alongside me and Tabby. Sunk in misery as I were, it still filtered through my sadness as how terr'ble he looked. Dark ring under his eyes; stooped shoulders. Be he ill I wondered? Later, even Martha spoke on how aged he seemed.

The wind catches at the pages of Parson's prayer book as he starts readin' the service at a gabble as if he feared the wind'll snatch the book from his hand if he didn't finish fast enough. Squire looks hard at Parson, gives a deep "aahem", and Parson slows his reading to a pace more respectful for a buryin'.

Earlier Martha had caught me searchin' the wet grass round the tree near her cottage. "What you lookin' for? You're feet'll be soaked."

"An apple."

"An apple? Why us've eaten what few there were long since. Tree's old, there weren't much of a crop this year."

"Just hoping I'd find a dropper hidden in the grass." Martha looks at me odd like. "To put in with Seth, he were that fond of apples." And Martha gives a shake of her head as if she ent heard aright, then puts her arm around my shoulder.

Parson finishes his readin' and closes his book. Squire withdraws as soon as Seth's coffin be lowered into the grave, pressing a half-crown into my hand as he left. Soon as Squire's gone Parson leaves, not speaking to I, not offerin' a word of comfort.

Crouchin' by the graveside I whispers, "See, you'm buried proper my sweet, alongside your boys." The sun had disappeared and the sky were now full of roilin' clouds, and I struggles to rise to my feet but 'tis impossible to get my knees to work. To stand upright.

At last Tabbie takes my hand. "Tis time to go, Mother. Sexton's waitin' on finishin' his work and Aunt Martha'll be expectin' us back at her place." I glances up and sees Sexton leanin' on his spade wantin' to get on with fillin' in the grave, a job Seth had oft-times done for 'un when Sexton weren't up to it.

As she leads me away a sparrar starts chirpin' from a branch of the hawthorn tree. "Listen to that," say I. "Your father'll be right pleased to hear 'un, though it were the yellerhammer he were particular fond of."

And so Seth were laid to rest next to his boys.

It were terr'ble hard at first. Trampin' from place to place, sleepin' rough, grievin' for Seth. Scared all the time I might get charged with vagrancy. Found work at last in Dorchester in a laundry. Should I hear mention of hell, 'tis a picture of that laundry as comes to mind. I doubt there's any can imagine the like of it. Huge, deep vats steamin', and yer arms feelin' they're bein' tore off as yer struggles to lift wet sheets out over the sides. Then forcin' 'em through rollers and heavin' 'em over the dryin' racks. Hands always raw from the lye. Clothin' and feet always soaked. Working hours at a stretch with never a moment's rest. But it were work. Didn't pay much. Enough to rent a small room with three others. Sharing a bed. And fleas. Even so, to my mind, it were better than the workhouse. I had my pride back, and that means a lot to a body. 'Tis lost pride as turns so many to the gin bottle.

Worked there nigh on three years afore I heard of a position lookin' after an old man. His son, who'd risen a bit in the world, wouldn't have his father live with him. It were the son hired me with few questions asked, just wanting someone as cheap as possible.

The old fellow can't get around on his own any more, spends the day sittin' in a chair or in his bed. No teeth, so he feeds mostly on slops. Only thing that seemed to give him any pleasure were uncoverin' hisself, but I put an end to his tricks. Took delight in it, he did, thinkin' I'd be shocked. First time he tried it, I turned my back, pretended I ent seen nothin'. Third time, I told him it weren't the first cock I'd seen, and my Seth's manhood were a sight better to look on than were his. Stood there leanin' over his bed with a jug of steamin' water in my hands and threatened to tip it into his lap. Watched those cunnin', red-rimmed eyes of his tryin' to figure whether I meant what I'd said. Must 'ave decided I did, for he were better behaved after that. Later he even proposed marriage. Marriage, to the likes of him!

Not that I didn't turn the matter around in my head for a bit, tryin' to think practical about the future. I knew it weren't likely he'd live more 'en a couple of years and the cottage weren't to be sniffed at. Little more'n three rooms and in need of repair, but liveable. But images of Seth kep' muddlin' my reasonin', and when I thought on Seth, I cringed at the idea of me and that old man. Talked on it with Tabby once. She give me a searchin' sort a look, and then said as how it were certain sure the son would've seen to it that the cottage would go to him when his father died.

"Don't 'ee worry on such things. You'll be alright," she says placin' an arm around me, a little smile playin' at the corners of her mouth.

I cocks an eye at her, but her won't say more. So I puts all such thoughts of the old man aside and feel happier for it. Lookin' after him be a sight easier than the laundry. The pay be a pittance, but I has a room of my own, food. I can live clean, and 'tis but a short distance to Tolpuddle.

Chapter Fifty

Essex 1844

IT WAS DANIEL WHO WAS SENT OVER TO FENNERS FARM to deliver the message. "Father says can you, Uncle Thomas, and Uncle John come over and join us for a meal Thursday evening? He says as how he has something very important to discuss with you both."

"Must be worried about how we're all going to manage, with little harvest to speak of again. That's sure to be what he has on his mind," responded Thomas, his face taking on a look of concern.

Fearful of forgetting any of his father's message, Daniel rushed on. "Father says he don't mean to give offence and he'd be right glad for Aunt Dinniah and Aunt Kathrine to come seein' as what he wants to talk about concerns them as well, but we'll be pressed for room if the young 'uns come too, us bein' so many ourselves. He says it'll be difficult to have a serious talk under such circumstances."

"That's true enough. The older girls can see to the little ones. I wonder if there's more on his mind that can't wait other than another poor harvest." Thomas bent to pick up a coil of wire. "We'll be there, tell him. Now, I should be in Second Meadow, giving your Uncle John a hand. Go up to the house and your Aunt Dinniah'll give you something to fill that frame of yours before you set off home. In another year you'll be as tall as me, young Daniel." Patting Daniel's shoulder, Thomas added, "Give my regards to your mother."

Thursday evening there was little elbow room, crowded as they were round the table in the kitchen of New House Farm. The clucking of hens waiting to be enticed into their coop with a handful of grain could be heard through the open window. Steam from a pot of water simmering on the grate mingled with the smell of cooking. George and James Loveless, Brine, Thomas and John Standfield sat together while the wives made final preparation to the meal.

At first all had concentrated on the business of eating but, now replete, the men's conversation centred on the worsening economic situation. The only sound from the children, taught not to talk during meals, was the scraping of spoons, the mastication of food, the occasional wail or gurgle from an infant. Now Elizabeth with a nod of her head indicated to her daughter Sarah to take the babies away so that the adults could talk without interruption. Gathering an infant cousin up into her arms, Sarah took the hand of a toddler and steered two more little ones from the room.

John Standfield raised his tankard and drank deeply. He replaced the tankard on the table and wiped his mouth with his sleeve. "Money's going to have to be found from somewhere to see us through. It was hardly worth the journey to market, we got so little for our produce. Besides we'll need what little we have left for our own use. And our hay crop won't see us through the winter." His voice was filled with frustration and disappointment.

Swallowing a last mouthful of food, James Loveless produced from the pocket of his waistcoat some pieces of paper. "I've been doin' some figurin'. It's certain sure we'll not manage much longer here with six families to feed between us. We've worked our guts out, but four bad harvests in a row! Things are as bad as '33, and that's a year none of us are likely to forget."

Polishing his plate clean with a crust of bread, George looked at Thomas. "Which brings me to the reason for asking you, Thomas, and John over. What would be your response to the idea of emigrating? Selling up and moving to Canada?" His eyes still fixed questioningly on his brother-in-law, he raised the gravy-sodden crust to his mouth. He nodded in his brother's direction and continued, "It was James first raised the idea, and it's an idea worthy of consideration. The papers are full of advertisements of land for sale there. What's your reaction?"

Not totally surprised by the question, Thomas was silent. James and Brine, who had talked many times previously on the matter, hastened to express their views.

George indicated with a gesture that the others help themselves to more food, an invitation rejected with a staying hand, a shake of the head, a "That were a fine meal, but I've room for no more." Rising to his feet, George offered up a short prayer of thanks as the others bowed their heads. To an accompaniment of the scrape of benches and chairs being pushed back, he said, "Let's move to the parlour while the women see to the dishes." He turned his attention to his younger family members. "Daniel, you know your job. See to the horse and fill the water buckets. The rest of you children be about your tasks and then play outside for a while." Catching the look Mathew gave him, he added, "Yes, come with us, Mathew. You do a man's work like the rest of us." Still talking on the idea of emigrating, the men moved to the other room.

Alice, hands immersed in a bowl of water, glanced up from the low sink under the window and stood for a moment watching Sarah outside holding Brine and Beth's infant daughter in her arms.

"Friday tomorrer, another week gone by," she commented almost to herself as she lifted another plate from the water and placed it on the draining board. "How the days be drawin' in. It'll soon be dark afore supper." Her sister-in-law, never one for a lot of chatter, seemed even quieter than usual. Alice's hands sought a spoon at the bottom of the bowl. Turning her head to Elizabeth working beside her, she said slowly as if her tongue sort to express thoughts as elusive as the spoon, "The idea of moving again, and to foreign parts .... I don't know how I feels about it."

"That the last of 'em?" was Elizabeth Loveless' response as, with swift efficiency she wiped the plates and set them on the shelves of the oak dresser. Through an open doorway to the parlour the men's voices could be heard.

Continuing her monologue, Alice passed the final dish to Elizabeth. "Canada! It'll take some thinking about." Stepping away from the sink, she gently massaged her swollen stomach. Scouring at the plate with her cloth as if she would remove what was left of the faded pattern, Elizabeth made no reply.

"You'm very quiet. You feelin' under the weather?"

Elizabeth still did not answer Alice's question immediately, but removed her apron and then, raising a hand to her head, patted at hair drawn back in a bun at the nape of her neck. Alice looked at Elizabeth curiously. Catching her glance, Elizabeth spoke. In almost pleading tones she asked, "You've been happy here too, Alice?"

"You know I have. We all have. Why, haven't you?"

"I've been very content. Blessed, is how I see it." Elizabeth fell silent again. Lifting eyes brimming with tears, she looked at Alice imploringly. "I understands George's reasonin', but surely things will improve come spring."

Alice, surprised at such a show of emotion from Elizabeth, felt an urge to put her arms around her, but knew Elizabeth usually shied away from any show of demonstrativeness. In that briefest moment of indecision, Elizabeth, with a shake of her head, a bracing of shoulders, had turned from Alice and headed towards the parlour.

Chapter Fifty-One

Dorset 1846

I WALKS OVER TO TOLPUDDLE WHENEVER I GETS THE chance to see Tabby when she's free of work. Other times I goes to the churchyard and spends time with Seth, Samuel, and Will. 'Tis a peaceful, pleasant place. My Sethy would tell of how, on his way home from work, he'd pause a while on a spring evening' to listen to the bleating lambs in the neighbourin' fields or the twitterin' of nestin' birds. I'd found a small apple tree as had managed to take root near where his old granny had her cottage. I were that careful diggin' it up, tryin' not to disturb the roots too much, so as to plant it nearby the three of 'em. I be hopin' someday it may bear fruit, though it be a weak, spindly thing at present and likely not to survive the transplantin'.

On occasion I meets up with some of the folks from the village. They be friendlier again now, time havin' softened people's feelings. I comes across old Kate Greenaway one afternoon leanin' over her gate. Us calls her old for her've lived longer than most folks do around these parts. Seems to spend much of her day at her gate, always wearin' that straw bonnet of hers as shows the puffed frill of her head-cap, though the bonnet brim be bent and cracked in places and the head-cap 'as taken on a grey tinge. Her never wants to miss a soul as might have a morsel of gossip for her. I recalls as how Seth once wondered as to whether Kate held the gate up, or the gate supported Kate. He had a dry sense of humour, my Sethy, and could oft-times make I laugh. Then his laughter would join with mine and afore you know it us'd be clutchin' at each other shakin' with mirth. 'Tis how I likes to remember him.

Well, while Kate and me be talkin' I sees a woman as I don't recognize turnin' into Mill Lane holdin' onto the hands of two small children. Kate dips her head to the woman and waves her hand, but the woman acknowledges Kate with the briefest of nods and passes on, not speakin'.

"Newcomers to Tolpuddle? Who be 'em?" I queries.

"Why, 'tis Harriet Hammett and her young 'uns."

"Harriet Hammet! Never! You be mistook! Harriet were always such a thin thread of a woman, a right frail creature. No, that ent Harriet," says I, for the woman were well covered with flesh.

"I'm tellin' 'ee, that be her," says Kate, all affronted that I should doubt her word.

"I never heard tell as they was back in Tolpuddle."

Well, that got Kate Greenaway goin' in full flood. "Hammett were the last one to return home, as I thinks you know" says she.

"I always wondered on that. You'd a thought they'd all've been brought back together."

"I heard as he were put on a charge out there and that were why he weren't shipped home with the others."

"On a charge?" I questions. "That don't sound like the James Hammett as lived here afore. Quiet fellow, you could scarce get a 'good-day' out of him."

"Well, I ent sure of the truth of it, but 'tis what I've heard. There's some as say that out there in that foreign place they couldst be put on a charge for nought."

"Put on a charge when they ent done nothin' wrong?"

"As I says, I don't know if 'tis true. Them as told I, *said* it was God's truth."

I thinks to myself that whether a thing be true or not ent never stopped Kate from passin' on whatever she's gleaned, and who's to say she ent right? 'Tis what happened to Loveless and the rest, and that were right here in our own country!

"Didn't them folks from London do anythin' for 'im, like they did for the rest of 'em?" I asks.

So then Kate tells as how he and his wife joined Loveless and the Standfields at that place they moved to. Essex, I think she said it were. But Mistress Hammett, as Kate says her likes to be called, weren't happy. So after a time she presses her husband to move back to Tolpuddle. Kate says as how he were taken on by a builder and is doin' right well. Says as how his young lad Edward already be workin' alongside his father. I remembers the boy was just a babe when the men were took.

Afore I takes leave of Kate I asks if her've any news of Squire as I'd heard he'd been took ill again.

"He ent aged well," says Kate. "That business a few years back when his agent took off with his money. He ent never really recovered from it all. Had to sell Home Farm and the timber from his parkland. But you'll have heard all about that. Took a real toll on his health, that did. Us don't see him out ridin' often now like us used to."

"But he still be alive then?"

"Oh yes, he still be alive."

Us are both quiet for a minute or two thinkin' on Squire. "He be a goodly man," says I. "Done a lot for different folks around here, without makin' a show of it."

"You be speakin' true there," responds Kate, her head bobbin' up and down in such vigorous agreement it sets the brim of her bonnet crackin' a bit more, the straw be so brittle.

"His daughter got married a while back. A grand affair. Church were packed. Scores of carriages. 'Tis that other son of his that sees to the estate now."

Takin' leave of Kate I walks on up the lane ponderin' on the news about Hammett. A builder's labourer! And doin' well for hisself. I wonder what Sethy would've made of that?

Chapter Fifty-Two

Essex 1844

THE PARLOUR, SMALL IN SIZE, SEEMED FILLED WITH bodies. Brine, leaning against the deep window sill, blocked what little light there was left to the day. Thomas was speaking as Elizabeth and Alice entered the parlour. "... looks no better for the coming year, I agree with you, George. But the thought of setting foot on a vessel again at my age needs some serious consideration."

"It's not something to be rushed into lightly, I agree," said George to his brother-in-law." But with our leases on the farms expiring next year, a decision has to be made whether to renew them and continue struggling here, or make a completely new start elsewhere. Things are much the same the length of England due to poor weather and low prices. And there's the question of whether our leases *will* be renewed"

"Yes, the renewal of the leases. That could be a problem, there's so much unrest throughout the countryside again," said Thomas. "It's our names that are raised each time there's trouble."

"If we decide on emigrating we had best plan carefully and make sure we arrive before planting time," added James, standing to offer his chair to his heavily pregnant wife and taking a seat on the floor at Alice's feet.

"What if some of us younger ones went first?" suggested Brine.

"I know you and I have talked on the idea," said Elizabeth looking at George, "but the more I think of leaving here ..." She paused a moment.

"Who's to say next year things won't improve? I feel sure Dinniah will be as reluctant to the idea of moving again as I be."

"Any decision we make must have *everyone's* agreement, "George stressed, "but facts must be faced. Year after year of bad weather, low prices for what we do manage to harvest and so many to feed."

"But as long as we can keep food in our bellies, surely we can wait things out?"

"I agrees with Brine, Aunt Elizabeth," said John. "Did you see the papers be using the term 'Hungry Forties'? They're right on that. There's hundreds leaving, especially from Ireland, on every boat that sails."

Thomas, still overwhelmed at the idea of uprooting his family and starting afresh in a new country, sat listening to the others, occasionally asking a question or expressing a view. Eventually John stood up. "The more I thinks on the idea, the more it has appeal. There was a period in Australia when I thought on the possibility of settling there after my time were served. The papers are full of the opportunities to be had in Canada. But 'tis gettin' late. I'll go put the horse in the cart or it'll be dark afore us is home. Thank 'ee for your hospitality Elizabeth, Alice."

Thomas, following his son's example, also rose to leave. "Yes, morning'll be on us soon enough. Now, where's my coat?"

As George helped Thomas up into the cart, he said, " I say we should start making serious enquires, for a decision must be made soon. Our leases, Thomas. I'm of the opinion they'll not be renewed."

"You're referring to the letters against us again in the papers. Seems every time there's unrest anywhere in the county, more Chartist protests, we're deemed responsible."

"That's what I'm thinking, right enough. The *Morning Post* is particularly bitter against us."

Already up in the cart and ready to urge the horse homewards, John said, "No disrespect, Uncle George, but I have to say that you've not tempered the wordin' in your letters and articles you've written to the papers. They've antagonized many people. I agree with the views you express, but your ..."

George looked up at his nephew, taken by surprise at the accusing tone of John's remark. "I'll not apologize for what I've written. I determined once my foot was on the deck of that vessel taking me to Van Dieman's Land that I'd never be silent again about any injustices. That I'd speak out on any cause I felt strongly about."

"I'm not sayin' that your views be wrong. Just as how your writin' so vehemently on certain matters has aggravated feelings against us even more."

"Let matters be, son," said Thomas. "The night's drawing in."

"Goodnight to you both," said George, hand raised in a farewell wave. "We'll talk more on the matter soon, when you've had a chance to mull over the idea with Dinniah and Kathrine."

George stood in the lane watching the cart become lost in the late September dusk, his mind already working on where he could get reliable information on emigration to Canada.

Chapter Fifty-Three

Dorset 1847

TABBY MENTIONED THAT NEXT TIME I COME OVER SHE wanted me to meet the fellow that's been courtin' her. "So that's the way the wind blows," I says, lookin' at the happiness on her. It seemed as if her *glowed*.

Kenton's son be a big, lumberin' lad now and there ent been need for Tabby to look after 'im for some time. But Kenton kep her on workin' in the house. Has her workin' alongside an older woman, doin' the cleanin' and washin'. And helpin' with cookin', puttin' up preserves to see 'em through the winter months, makin' the meals for him and his son as well as the apprentice. Tabby've been right happy there.

Kenton never took another wife after that poor young thing died such a dreadful a death in the hedgerow. Tabby says as how the son struggles to talk but he can't somehow make his tongue and lips work proper and all that comes out be just garbled sounds. She've told me many a time that she be sure he can understand things. It be just that he ent got no control over his limbs nor his tongue. It must be a terr'ble burden for poor Miller Kenton.

So, o'course, when next Tabby be free of a Sunday afternoon, I sets off to Tolpuddle. The day has a nip in it and I'm mighty glad of my cloak. Sewed it myself afore the winter set in, sittin' of an evening by the fire while the old man slumbered and snored in his bed. Made it from a piece of fabric I picked up cheap – a lovely rich, dark green. Ent never owned such a good quality garment afore. My Seth were always on about how one day he'd get I a warm cloak, fretting over the fact the old un I'd had for years were worn so thin. I knows as how he'd be right glad to see me so set up. But a little sad also 'cos he'd never been able to give me such things. I can still see him now, so wonnerful proud and happy when he give me that red vase. That vase meant more to me than if he'd give me all the gold and jewels in the world. Took it off me they did when us went to the workhouse, God rot their souls. Refused to let I keep it. I wished I'd passed it on to Tab when us had to leave our home.

Passin' through the village, who be leanin' over her gate as always, but Kate Greenaway. Much as I enjoys a good chat I has no wish to stop long as I knows Tab'll be waitin', but Kate weren't goin' to let me go afore she'd passed on her latest bit of gossip. She goes into a long tale as how she come by the news - the peddler-man come into it somehow - but it were too twisty a story for me to follow, bein' in a hurry as I was.

Seems the Lovelesses and Standfields and Brine have left England. Sailed in two groups accordin' to Kate. But not Hammett and his family. His wife had no wish to leave Tolpuddle and he be doin' well for hisself it would seem. But the others, all gone to Canada! I knows not where it be, but I'm told 'tis far, far away. I can't imagine livin' anywhere but Dorset. 'Tis all I knows. Leavin' all you knows behind. Crossin' all that water. No, it would take more courage than I'll ever have. Anyways, I hopes with all my heart things be goin' well with 'em. That they be prosperin' and happy.

Soon as I meets Tab and her man, I knows Seth would've taken to him right quickly, like I done. Dick Wilton, one of Kenton's men. Not much taller than Tabby. Fuzz of fair hair for side whiskers, and a shy grin on his face. I could tell as how he'd dressed up to meet me: clean neckchief, good jacket.

"We plans to marry come spring, Mistress Fielding, if we has your blessing," says Dick with an arm around Tabby's shoulders, and Tabby claspin' his other hand in hers and smilin' up at him.

"As long as you're good to my girl, like her father were to me," I says, "then 'ee surely has my blessin'. Treat her well. Should things get hard for 'ee, keep showin' her you loves her." And then I gives him a kiss on his cheek which makes him blush bright red.

Dick says as how Kenton's just put him in charge of lookin' after the machinery, so it would seem he be doin' well at the mill. Tabbie and him be full of news about a place they've heard of as is likely to be for rent about the time they wants to marry. It were Dick as says to me, "Don't 'ee worry, Mistress Fielding. When the time comes, you can be certain sure there'll be a home with us for you," his voice soft-spoken like Seth's.

Afore I sets off back home, I goes to the churchyard to visit with Seth. I does it every opportunity I gets. Puts whatever flowers I can find on their graves. The hawthorn bush've grown to a fair-sized tree and the apple tree be still alive though strugglin'. I lets the leaves lie come autumn. Makes a warm blanket for 'em, as I sees it.

Watchin' Tab and Dick together earlier, brung back powerful memories. That harvest supper, and Seth so bashful it were me as had to ask him to dance.

A gentle man, my Seth. A good man.

ACKNOWLEDGEMENTS

I AM VERY GRATEFUL TO MY FAMILY, THE BRITISH MUSEUM Library, and the many people who have given me encouragement and have taken the time and trouble to review early versions of my manuscript, especially Keith Harrison of Vancouver Island University. A very special thanks to Catherine Egan for her computer skills, assistance and patience, for without her help this book would never have come to fruition.

NOTES

IN 1833 TRADE UNIONISM WAS LEGAL, BUT THE TOLPUDDLE Martyrs were charged under an old Mutiny Act of 1797 which made it illegal for working men to organize into combinations or societies. A further Act of 1817 was 'for the more effectually preventing Seditious Meetings and Assemblies'. If a member of a society or club swore an oath not required or authorized by law he was swearing an illegal oath, and it was this Swearing of Illegal Oaths that the Tolpuddle Martyrs were charged with.

Tuberculosis, also known as consumption, lung-rot and even the graveyard cough was rampant in 19th century Britain. In the 1830s and the 1840s nearly one infant in three failed to reach the age of five. Diarrhoea, cholera, and typhus added to the toll of deaths in infants and adults. During this period food prices were high; poorer classes were underfed and had less resistant to contagion.

James Hammett is buried in Tolpuddle Churchyard and the head stone was erected by the Trades Union Congress. Every Labour Day the T.U.C. place a wreath on his grave.

George and Elizabeth Loveless are buried in Siloam Cemetery, London, Ontario.

John Stanfield became mayor of his district in Ontario.

SUGGESTED READING

The Tolpuddle Martyrs by Joyce Marlow

Tolpuddle An historical account through the eyes of George Loveless.

Pub: Trade Union Congress.

Victims of Whiggery; Being a statement of the persecutions experienced by the Dorchester Labourers by George Loveless

The Workhouse by Norman Longmate

The Fatal Shore by Robert Hughes

The Floating Brothel by Seán Rees

Lightning Source UK Ltd.
Milton Keynes UK
UKOW05f2153300617
304449UK00001B/80/P

9 781525 504471